LORDS AND TYRANTS

LORDS AND TYRANTS

Chris Wraight • Ian St. Martin • Alec Worley • Justin D Hill
Robbie MacNiven • Ben Counter • Cavan Scott
Josh Reynolds • Steve Lyons • Rob Sanders • L J Goulding
Peter Fehervari • Mike Brooks • Gav Thorpe

BLACK LIBRARY

A BLACK LIBRARY PUBLICATION

First published in 2019.
This edition published in Great Britain in 2019 by
Black Library,
Games Workshop Ltd.,
Willow Road,
Nottingham, NG7 2WS, UK.

10 9 8 7 6 5 4 3 2 1

Produced by Games Workshop in Nottingham.
Cover illustration by Vladimir Krisetskiy.

A CIP record for this book is available from the British Library.

ISBN 13: 978 1 78193 975 8

See Black Library on the internet at

blacklibrary.com

Find out more about Games Workshop
and the world of Warhammer 40,000 at

games-workshop.com

Printed and bound by CPI Group (UK) Ltd, Croydon, CR0 4YY

It is the 41st millennium. For more than a hundred
centuries the Emperor has sat immobile on the Golden
Throne of Earth. He is the Master of Mankind by the
will of the gods, and master of a million worlds by
the might of His inexhaustible armies. He is a rotting
carcass writhing invisibly with power from the Dark Age
of Technology. He is the Carrion Lord of the Imperium
for whom a thousand souls are sacrificed every day,
so that He may never truly die.

Yet even in His deathless state, the Emperor continues
His eternal vigilance. Mighty battlefleets cross the
daemon-infested miasma of the warp, the only route
between distant stars, their way lit by the Astronomican,
the psychic manifestation of the Emperor's will. Vast
armies give battle in His name on uncounted worlds.
Greatest amongst His soldiers are the Adeptus
Astartes, the Space Marines, bioengineered super-
warriors. Their comrades in arms are legion: the Astra
Militarum and countless planetary defence forces, the
ever-vigilant Inquisition and the tech-priests of the
Adeptus Mechanicus to name only a few. But for all their
multitudes, they are barely enough to hold off the ever-
present threat from aliens, heretics, mutants — and worse.

To be a man in such times is to be one amongst untold
billions. It is to live in the cruellest and most bloody
regime imaginable. These are the tales of those times.
Forget the power of technology and science, for so much
has been forgotten, never to be re-learned. Forget the
promise of progress and understanding, for in the grim
dark future there is only war. There is no peace amongst
the stars, only an eternity of carnage and slaughter, and
the laughter of thirsting gods.

CONTENTS

ARGENT

CHRIS WRAIGHT

I come round, and the pain begins again. It is severe but manageable, so I do not request control measures. I look down and see my arms stripped of their armour, and that momentarily alarms me because I have been armoured for a very long time. I flex my fingers, and the pain flares. Both my forearms are encased in flexplast netting, wound tight, and there are spots of blood on the synthetic fabric. For a moment I look at the dark fluid as it spreads in spidery, blotted lines. My wounds will take a long time to heal even with the assistance of the medicae staff, and that is frustrating.

I realise that the drugs I was given have dulled my senses, and I blink hard and flex my leg muscles and perform thought exercises to restore mental agility.

I take in my surroundings. I am in a cell made of metal floors and metal walls, perhaps five metres by six. A single lumen gives off a weak light, illuminating a narrow desk and an even narrower cot, on which I am lying. The blankets are damp with sweat and tight to my body. I guess that I am back in the ordo command post beyond the Dravaganda ridgeline. I consider whether I am strong enough to move, and place my hands on the twin edges of my cot. Pushing against the metal tells me that I am not – the bones are still broken and incapable of supporting my weight. I could perhaps swing my legs around and stand, though. I would prefer to keep moving, to get my blood flowing again. I am not a child to be protected – I am a grown woman, an interrogator of the Ordo Hereticus, a warrior.

But I do not move, for the door slides open and my master enters. I can tell it is him even before the steel panel shifts, for his armour hums at a pitch I recognise. I believe that he could have chosen to have the telltale audex volume reduced, but he sees no use for stealth and sees many uses for a recognisable signature. To know that he approaches is a cause for dread, and I have witnessed the effect often during actions on terrified subjects.

A part of me dreads his coming too, even now, after I have been a member of his retinue for over a year and served on numerous missions. Inquisitor Joffen Tur cultivates fear as another man might cultivate an appreciation of scholarship or the contents of a hydroponic chamber, and I am not yet entirely immune to his practised aura.

He enters, ducking under the door's lintel. He is in full armour – dark red lacquer, trimmed with bronze. The breastplate is an aquila, chipped with battle damage. His exposed head is clean-shaven with a bull neck and a solid chin. His eyes do not make a connection with me – as ever, he does not focus, as his thoughts are at least partly elsewhere. A man like Tur is always giving consideration to the unseen.

'Awake, then, Spinoza,' he grunts, standing before me.

I attempt to salute, and the pain makes me wince.

'Don't bother,' he says. 'You'll be useless to me for another week. Just tell me what happened.'

'On Forfoda?' I ask, and immediately regret it. My wits are still slow.

'Of course on bloody Forfoda,' Tur growls. 'You're in bed, both your arms are broken, you're a mess. Tell me how you got that way.'

I take a deep breath, and try to remember.

First, though, I must go back further. I must recall the briefing on the bridge of the *Leopax*, Tur's hunter-killer. This is only one of the vessels under his command, and not the largest. By choosing it he is sending a signal to the other Imperial forces mustering at Forfoda – this world is not the greatest of priorities for him, he has other burdens to attend to, but he deigns to participate in order to reflect the Emperor's glory more perfectly and with greater speed.

Tur does not place great store on courtesy, and I admire him for this. He knows his position in the hierarchy of Imperial servants, and it is near the top. One day I aspire to command the same level of self-belief, but know that I have some way to go before I do so.

We assemble under the shadow of his great ouslite command throne – myself, the assassin Kled, the captain of stormtroopers Brannad, the savant Yx and the hierophant Werefol. In the observation dome above us we can see Forfoda's red atmosphere looming, and it is easy to imagine it burning.

Tur himself remains seated as we bow, one by one. He does not acknowledge us, but rubs his ill-shaven chin as flickering lithocasts scroll through the air before him.

'They're torching everything,' he says in due course. 'Damned animals.'

I stiffen a little. He is not referring to the cultists who have brought this world to the brink of ruin, but to the Angels of Death who are now hauling it back to heel. I do not find it easy to hear those blessed warriors described in such terms, as used as I am to Tur's generally brusque manner. When I first heard that we would be in theatre with the Imperial Fists, I gave fervent thanks to Him on Terra, for it had long been a dear wish of mine to witness them fight.

But my master is correct in this, of course – if we do not extract the leaders of the insurrection for scrutiny then we miss the chance to learn what caused it.

'I'll take the primus complex,' Tur says, squinting at a succession of tactical overlays. 'We need to hit that in the next hour or it'll be rubble. Brannad, you'll come too, and a Purgation squad.'

I am surprised by that. Tur has been insistent for months that I develop more experience in conventional combat, and I had expected to make planetfall with him. He is concerned that my reactions are not quite where they should be, and that I am at risk of serious injury, and so I have pursued my training in this area with zeal.

He turns to me.

'You'll take the secondary spire. They're scheduled to hit the command blister in three hours. Go with them. See they do not kill the target before you can get to her.'

I do not hide my surprise well. 'By your will,' I say, but my concern must have been obvious, for Tur scowls at me.

'Yes, you'll be alone with them,' he says. 'Is that a problem? Do you wish for a chaperone?'

I am stung, and suspect that I blush. 'No problem,' I say. 'You honour me.'

'Damn right,' he says. 'So don't foul it up.'

* * *

The target is the governor's adjutant Naiao Servia, whom our intelligence places within the secondary spire complex. Her master is holed up somewhere in the central hub, defended well, and thus Tur is correct to devote the majority of his resources there. I cannot help but think that my assignment is more about testing me than utilising our expertise optimally. That is his right, of course. He wishes me to become a weapon after his own design, and in the longer run that goal honours the Emperor more than the fate of a single battlefront.

So I ought to be thankful, and I attempt to remember this as I take my lander down through Forfoda's red methane atmosphere towards my rendezvous coordinates. I do not know how Tur arranged it – he tells me only what I need to know – but he has persuaded the warriors of the Adeptus Astartes to let me accompany them, and that is testament to the heft his word carries here.

'Accompany', though, is a misleading word. I am to serve my master's will in all things, and his will is that Servia is taken alive. I do not yet know how the Imperial Fists will react to this, and on the journey over I catalogue the many factors weighing on an unfavourable outcome.

I am a mortal. Worse, I am a woman. Worse still, I am a mere interrogator. None of these things are destined to make my task with these particular subjects easy, which is no doubt what Tur intended.

We make planetfall and boost across the world's cracked plains towards the forward positions. In order to divert my mind from unhelpful speculation, I look out of the viewports. I see palls of burning promethium rising into the ruddy clouds above. I see the hulks of tanks smouldering in the rad-wastes between spires. I see the northern horizon burning, and feel the impact of shells from the Astra Militarum batteries. This front is heavily populated by both sides – there must be many hundreds of thousands of soldiers dug in. A full advance would be ruinous in both human and equipment terms, so I am sure the commanders back in the orbital station would prefer to avoid it.

My transport touches down on a makeshift rockcrete plate set out in the open, ten kilometres behind the first of our offensive lines. I check my armour-seal before disembarking. Yx told me with some relish that I would last approximately ten seconds if I were to breathe Forfoda's atmosphere unfiltered. Only in the enclosed hives can the citizens exist without rebreathers, and our artillery barrages have compromised even that fragile shell of immunity.

I give my pilot the order to return to the *Leopax* and make my way towards a low command bunker. On presentation of my rosette I am waved inside by a mortal trooper in an atmosphere suit. His armour's trim is gold, and he bears the clenched fist symbol of the Chapter on his chest. Just catching sight of it gives me a twinge of expectation.

I am shown inside by more armoured menials, and taken to a chamber deep underground. I enter a crowded room, dominated by six warriors in full Adeptus Astartes battleplate. They are as enormous as I expected them to be. Their armour is pitted and worn, betraying long periods of active service, and it growls with every movement – a low, almost sub-aural hum of tethered machine-spirits.

Intelligence has already given me their names and designations. Four are Space Marines of a Codex-standard Assault squad – battle-brothers Travix, Movren, Pelleas and Alentar. The fifth is a sergeant, Cranach. The sixth is far more senior, a Chaplain named Erastus, and I immediately sense the distinction between them. It is not just the difference in livery – the Chaplain is arrayed in black against the others' gold – but the manner between them. They are creatures of rigid hierarchy, just as you would expect, and their deference to Erastus is evident.

As I enter, they have already turned to regard me, and I look up at their weather-hammered, scarred faces. The Chaplain's is the most severe, his flesh pulled back from a hard bone structure and his bald head studded with iron service indicators.

'Luce Spinoza,' Erastus says, his voice a snarl of iron over steel. 'Be welcome, acolyte.'

'Interrogator,' I say. It is important to insist on what rank I do have.

Cranach, the sergeant, looks at me evenly. I sense little outright hostility from the others – irritation, perhaps, and some impatience to be moving.

'Your master cares little for his servants,' Erastus says, 'to place them in harm's way so lightly.'

'We are all in harm's way,' I say. 'Emperor be praised.'

Cranach looks at Erastus, and raises a black eyebrow. One of the others – Travix, perhaps – smiles.

Erastus activates a hololith column. 'This is the target,' he says. 'The summit of the upper spire thrust. Here is the command nexus – too far to hit from our forward artillery positions, and shielded from atmospheric assault, so we will destroy it at close range. Once the target is eliminated, we will move on, and the Militarum can handle the rest.'

'The adjutant Servia, present in that location, must be preserved,' I say. Best to get it out in the open as soon as possible, for I do not know how far Tur has already briefed them.

'Not a priority,' Erastus says.

'It is the highest priority.'

He does not get angry. I judge he only gets angry with obstacles of importance, and I hardly qualify as that.

'This is why we have been saddled with you, then,' Erastus says.

'Fought before, acolyte?' Cranach asks, doubtfully. He looks at my battle armour – which I am fiercely proud of – with some scepticism.

'Many times, Throne be praised,' I say, looking him in the eye. 'I will not get in your way.'

'You already are,' Erastus tells me.

'The Holy Orders of the Inquisition have placed an interdict on Servia,' I tell him. 'She will be preserved.' I turn to Cranach. 'Do not call me acolyte again, brother-sergeant. My rank is interrogator, earned by my blood and by the blood of the heretics I have ended.'

Cranach raises his eyebrow again. Perhaps that is his affectation, a curiously human gesture for something so gene-conditioned for killing.

'As you will it, interrogator,' he says, bowing.

So that is my first victory – minor, though, I judge, significant.

'Study the approach patterns,' Erastus tells me. 'If you come with us, you will have to be useful.'

'I pray I will be so, Brother-Chaplain,' I say.

'Why did you say that?' Tur asked.

'Say what?'

'*I pray I will be so.* That was weak. These are the sons of Dorn. They only respect resolve.'

'I did not consider my words.'

'No, you bloody didn't.'

Something in my master's tone strikes me as unusual then.

Is his speech a little… petulant? I have spent some time with the Adeptus Astartes now, and the contrast cannot help but be drawn.

But that is unworthy. Tur is a lord of the Ordo Hereticus, a witch-finder of galactic renown, and on a hundred worlds his name is whispered by priests with a cross between reverence and fear. He speaks as he chooses to speak, and there is no requirement of an inquisitor to be decorous, especially to the members of his own retinue.

'Did you understand the attack plan?' he asks.

'It was a simple operation, suited to their skills,' I say. 'We were to approach the spire using an atmospheric transport, breaking in three levels below the command dome where the shielding gave out. From there to the dome was only a short distance. They would seize it, kill the occupants, set charges to destroy the structure, then break out again to the same transport.'

'And you ensured they knew what I demanded?'

'A number of times. They were in no doubt.'

'Did they know the manner of corruption in the spires?'

'No. Neither did I. As I recall, at that stage none of us did.'

Tur grunts. He has a surly look about him, perhaps due to fatigue. He has been fighting for a long time, I guess, and there must be many actions still to conduct.

'Go on, then,' he says. 'What happened next?'

I strap myself into my restraint harness within the gunship's hold. Set beside the Space Marines I feel ludicrously small, even though my armour is the equal of any in the Ordo Hereticus and has performed with distinction in a hundred armed engagements on a dozen worlds.

We are transported in a mid-range assault gunship – an Imperial Fists Storm Eagle. The entire squad is assembled within its hold, and the craft is piloted by two of their battle-brothers whose names I am never given. The Space Marines do not volunteer much information, which suits me, as I am used to that.

We take off amid a cacophony of engine noise, and the entire craft shakes atop its thrusters' downdraught. The machine is heavily built, a mass of ablative plates and weapon housings, and so enormous power is required to lift it. Once moving, however, the speed is remarkable, and we are soon shooting across the battlefields. I patch in an external visual feed from the craft's auspex array, and see the war-blackened spires rush towards us. The plains below are scarred by mortar impacts, their rock plates burned and broken. Our target becomes visible – a slender outcrop of burning metal, jutting high above the rad-wastes like some sentinel monument.

I turn my attention to my companions. Erastus is silent, his skull-face helm glinting darkly under the glimmer of strip lumens. He holds his power maul two-handed, its heel on the deck. My eyes are drawn towards it. It is a magnificent piece, far too heavy for a mortal to lift, let alone use. It has a bone casing, scrimshawed with almost tribal savagery, and its disruptor unit is charred black.

Cranach is reciting some oath of the Chapter, and I do not understand the words – I assume he uses the vernacular of his own world. Movren has taken a combat blade and is turning it under the lumens, checking for any hint of a flaw. They are reverent, these warriors, and I find their sparse dedication moving. In my vocation I am frequently presented with sham piety or outright heresy, and it is good for the soul to see unfeigned devotion.

'Vector laid in,' comes a voice from the cockpit, and I know then that the assault will begin imminently. 'Prepare to disembark.'

I tense, placing my gauntlet over my laspistol's holster. It is a good weapon from a fine house of weaponsmiths, mono-grammed with the sigils of the ordo and fashioned according to the Accatran pattern, and yet it looks painfully small set against the bolt pistols and chainswords of my companions.

The Storm Eagle picks up altitude, still travelling fast, and we are rocked by incoming fire. The lumens are killed, and the hold glows a womb-like red. I begin to wonder at what point our suicidal velocity will begin to ebb, and only slowly realise that it will not be until the very point of ejection. The pilot slams on airbrakes hard, jamming me tight against my restraints.

The Space Marines are already moving. They break free and charge across the bucking deck-plates with astonishing poise, given their immense weight. I join them just as the forward doors cantilever open and the flame-torn atmos-phere howls in.

The gunship is hovering just metres away from a vast hole torn into the edge of the spire, and lasfire surrounds us in a coronet of static. Erastus is first across the gap, leaping on power armour servos and landing heavily amongst broken metal structures. The rest of the squad jumps across, until only I remain, poised on the edge of the swaying gunship's gaping innards.

I look down, and see a yawning pit beneath me, falling and falling, streaked with flame and racing gas plumes. That is a mistake, and my heart hammers hard. I curse the error, brace myself and leap, flying out over the gap and feeling the wind tug at me. I land awkwardly, dropping to all fours amid the tangle of blown rockcrete and metal bars. By the time I right myself, the Imperial Fists have already lumbered further in, their bolt pistols drawn and their chainswords revving. The gunship pulls away, strafed with lines of lasfire,

and the backwash from its engines nearly rips me clear from
the spire's edge.

I run hard, leaping over the debris. My breath echoes in my
helm, hot and rapid. I have to sprint just to keep up with the
Assault squad, who are moving far faster than I would have
guessed possible. They are smashing their way inside, breaking through the walls themselves when they have to, making
the corridors and chambers boom and echo with the industrial clamour of their discharging weapons.

By the time I get close again I can see their formation. The
four battle-brothers are firing almost continuously, punching
bloody holes through an oncoming tide of Forfodan troopers.
Cranach carries a combat shield, and uses that in conjunction
with a power fist to bludgeon aside any of them that get in
close. But it is Erastus who captivates me. He is roaring now,
and his voice is truly deafening, even with my helm's aural
protection. His movements are spectacular, almost frenzied,
and he is hurling himself at the enemy with an abandon that
shocks me. His power maul is a close-combat weapon, and it
blazes with golden energies, making the cramped spire interior seem to catch fire.

I am firing myself now, adding my las-bolts to the crashing
thunder of bolt-rounds. I do some small good, hitting enemy
troops as they attempt to form up before the onslaught, but
in truth I do not augment the assault too greatly, for its force
is entirely unstoppable, a juggernaut of power armour that
jolts and horrifies in its speed and overwhelming violence.
It is all I can do to keep up, and I struggle to do that, but
at least I do not slow them. By the time we have cut and
blasted our way to the target location, I am still with them.
It is another small victory to add to the tally, though I can
take little pleasure in it.

I see the approach to the command dome beckon, a long flight of white stone steps, over-arched with gold. I hear more gunfire, and glimpse movement from within – many bodies, racing to meet the challenge. At that stage all I think is that the defenders' bravery borders on madness, whatever foul creed they have adopted, for they are surely doomed to die quickly.

I do not know what we will meet inside, though. We have not got that far yet.

'You did not contribute much,' Tur says.

'I did my best.'

'Did they wait for you to catch up?'

'No.'

My master looks down at my broken arms, my blood-mottled bandages, and the heavy shadow of disappointment settles on his unforgiving face.

'It might have done you some good,' he says, 'just to witness them.'

'It did,' I say.

'They're crude things, the Adeptus Astartes,' Tur says. 'Don't believe the filth preached by the Ministorum – they're not angels. They're hammers. They crush things, and so we use them as such – never forget that.'

'I will not.'

And yet, I find his words lacking again. The warriors had not been crude, at least not in the way he meant. They were direct, to be sure, but there was an intelligence to their brutality that could be detected up close. They were incredibly destructive, but only as far as was required by the task. I almost tell Tur then what I thought I had gleaned from that episode – that their viewpoint may have been narrow,

targeted solely on a limited set of military objectives, but
within that ambit they were more impressive than any breed
of warrior I had ever served with.

Since entering the ordo I have willingly embraced the
diversity of our calling – its dark compromises and the
necessity of working within flawed and labyrinthine political structures. I have accepted this, and learned to use the
knowledge to my advantage and to the advantage of the
Throne, but, for all that, when I saw the Angels of Death in
action, and observed the purity of purpose they embodied,
and reflected that the Emperor Himself had created them
for this reason and no other, a faint shadow of jealousy had
imprinted itself on me.

I am not proud of this. My vow is to eradicate it, lest it
divert from the tasks I will have after Forfoda, but I cannot
deny that it is there, and that it must demonstrate some kind
of moral truth.

'You entered the command dome with them?' Tur presses.

'I did. I was with them at the end.'

He looks down at my shattered limbs, then up at my face
again.

'Go on, then,' he says.

Erastus is the first one into the command dome. He is still
roaring – in High Gothic now, so I understand fully what
he is saying.

'For the glory of the primarch-progenitor!' he cries. 'For
the glory of Him on Earth!'

In isolation, those battle-shouts may seem bereft of much
purpose, a mere expression of aggression that any thug from
an underhive gang could match, but that is to misunderstand
them. The volume generated by his augmitters is crushing,

and it makes masonry crack and the air throb. The echo-ing, overlapping wall of sound is almost enough by itself to grind the will of our enemies into dust. The effect on his battle-brothers is just as profound, though opposite – they are roused by their Chaplain's exhortations to further feats of arms, such that they fight on through an aegis of audio-shock, a rolling tide of sensory destruction. I am caught up in it myself, despite my status as an outsider. I find myself crying out along with the Chaplain, repeating the words that I recognise from the catechism where they occur.

'For the Emperor!' I shout as I fight. 'For the Throne!'

And yet I am still appalled at what I witness. We have been misled, all of us, and did not understand the degrada-tion that had been visited on Forfoda. Until then, we had been fighting human-normal troops, carrying standard weap-onry, and our intelligence had told us the insurrection was of a political nature. I now see that this is a front, and that extreme corruption has come to this world. Among the stand-ard troops there are now bloated and diseased things, their organs spilling from their flesh, their weapons fused to their limbs in webs of glistening cables.

I wish to gag, but I am surrounded by those who will not hesitate, who have made themselves impervious to horror. They tear through these new enemies, and I see their churn-ing blades bite into unnatural flesh. That fortifies me, and I fight on, taking aim at creatures with lone baleful eyes and swollen, sore-crusted stomachs.

For the first time, we are tested. The command dome is crowded with these nightmare creations, and they come at us without fear. The air tastes like suppuration, and there are so many to slay. I stay close to Erastus, whose fortitude is undimmed. My laspistol is close to overheating now, and

I reach for my combat knife, though I do not think it will serve well against these things.

The situation blinds me to the objective, and for a moment I am fighting merely to avoid annihilation, but then I see her for the first time – Naiao Servia, recognisable from Tur's vid-picts, cowering among the capering fiends she has unleashed. She is obese, her lips cracked, her cheeks flabby with sickness, so I see that she has reaped the rewards of her betrayal. Lines of black blood trace a pattern down her neck, and I do not wish to speculate where it has come from.

Cranach is fighting hard, using his shield and power fist to great effect. His squad members work for one another, covering any momentary weakness of their brothers, carving into the horde of decay as a seamless unit. I see Pelleas go down, dragged into a morass of fluids by three pus-green mutants, and the others respond instantly, hacking their way to his side. They are selfless, a band of soul-brothers, trained from boyhood to keep one another on their feet and fighting.

It is then that I know they will prevail, for the enemy has none of this. These opponents are perversions, individually formidable but without cohesion. I keep firing, giving my laspistol a few more shots before it overloads, aiding the progress of Erastus towards Servia's unnatural bulk.

The adjutant has become huge, far beyond mortal bounds, a slobbering mountain of rotting flesh. Her tongue, slick as oil, lashes from a slash-mouth filled with hooked teeth. Her body spills from the ruins of her old uniform, and tentacles lash out at the Chaplain.

He leaps up at her, swinging with his crozius, and drives a gouge through her swelling stomach. She screams at him, vomiting steaming bile, and he fights through it, his injunctions never ceasing.

I move closer, aiming at the creature's head, trying to blind her, narrowly missing. Then one of her tentacles connects, wrapping around the haft of the Chaplain's power maul, grabbing it and wrenching it from his grip. The weapon flies free, burning through the corrupted blubber and making the fat boil.

Without it, the Chaplain is diminished. He fights on, tearing at the monster with his clenched fists. His brothers are fully occupied and do not see his peril. Only I witness the maul land, skidding across the fluid-slick floor and coming to rest amid a slough of fizzing plasma.

Servia can overwhelm her prey then, pushing him back. Bereft of his weapon, Erastus will be overcome. I feel my laspistol reach its limit. I look over at the maul, crackling still in a corona of energy, and know what I must do.

I race towards it, discarding my laspistol, and reach for the crackling weapon. Lifting it nearly breaks my ribs – it is as heavy as a man, and my power armour strains to compensate. Disruptor charge snakes and lashes about me, and the thing shudders in my grip as if alive. I can barely hold on to it, let alone use it, but Erastus is now in mortal danger.

'For the Emperor!' I cry, mimicking his strident roars, and throw myself at the creature.

I swing the maul at its spine, two-handed, putting all my weight into the blow. This betrays my ignorance – the weight and power of it is far too much, and as it connects I realise my error. My arms are smashed even through my armour, and the wave of pain makes me scream out loud. The released disruptor charge explodes, throwing me clear of the impact and cracking open ceramite plate. I cannot release the maul – it remains in my grip, locked by ruined gauntlets amid gouts of flame.

But the blow is enough. The creature reels, its back broken, and Erastus surges towards it, ripping the tentacles free of its twisted body. His battle-brothers fight through the remains of the throng, subduing the attendant horrors to bring their fire to bear on the leader.

I am in agony. I can feel my bones jutting through my flesh, my blood sloshing inside my armour, and I am light-headed and nauseous. It takes all my strength merely to lift my head and stay conscious.

I see Erastus punching out, driving Servia back. I see the rest of the squad level their bolt pistols, ready to destroy it.

'No!' I cry, raising a trembling, ruined arm. 'Preserve her!'

Erastus halts. He looks at me, then at the trembling mass of blubber before him. Cranach is poised to wade in closer, to rip its heart from its diseased chest. His battle-brothers make no move to comply. Soon they will kill it.

'Hold,' the Chaplain commands, and they instantly freeze. Servia shrinks back, crippled but alive.

Cranach moves to protest. 'It cannot be suffered to–' he begins.

Erastus cuts him dead. He nods in my direction.

I try to keep myself together, and know that I will fail. I see them looking at me, bristling with barely contained battle-fury. They want to kill it. They live to kill it.

'*Preserve her,*' I tell them, down on my knees in puddles of blood.

Cranach looks at the Chaplain.

'She has the crozius, sergeant,' Erastus tells him.

That is the last thing I remember.

Tur does not say anything for a while.

'When they brought you back here–' he begins.

'I remember none of it.'

He nods, thinking. 'They didn't tell me everything.'

'I do not think they speak of their battles,' I say.

'No, maybe not.' He is struggling for words now. I do not know if he is proud to learn what happened, or maybe disappointed. Tur has always found castigation easy – it is his profession – but praise comes less naturally.

'You did well, then,' he says eventually. 'The subject is on the *Leopax*, and I'll speak to her soon. She'll regret being alive. I'm not in the mood to be gentle.'

When is Tur ever in that mood? I might smile, but the pain is still prohibitive.

'And you are recovering, then?' he asks, awkwardly.

'Yes, lord,' I say.

He nods again. 'Weapons training,' he says. 'When this is over, you need more of it. Perhaps this is an aptitude I have overlooked.'

I do not say anything. I do not think it will be necessary, for reasons I will not disclose to him.

Do not misunderstand me. I remain loyal to my master. He is a great man in many ways, and I aspire to learn from him. One day, in the far future, my ambition is to be as devoted a servant of Terra as he has been, and to have a reputation half as formidable. I cannot imagine serving under another as dedicated to the Throne. Indeed, I find it hard to imagine serving under anyone else at all.

But I have learned much on Forfoda, and some lessons are still to come.

'As you will, lord,' I say, hoping he will leave soon.

It takes three weeks to subdue the remains of the insurrection. The Imperial Fists linger in theatre longer than originally intended once the scale of corruption is revealed. Many of the spires are destroyed wholesale, and many millions of survivors are deported in void-haulers, ready either for slaughter or mind-wiping. Our strategos estimate it will take months to purge the world, and that the Ministorum will be required to maintain scrutiny for decades after that, but it has been retained, and its forges and its manufactoria remain ready for use by the Holy Imperium of Man.

I take much satisfaction in that. Once my arms heal, I begin the process of regaining strength. I take up my duties as fast as I am able. Tur does not visit me again, for he is detained with many cares. Yx tells me that Servia's testimony was instrumental in the recapture of the industrial zones north of the spires, and that gladdens my soul.

Near the end, I have the visitor I have been expecting. He also does not have much time, so his presence here honours me. When Erastus walks into the training chambers in the Dravaganda command post he seems even more gigantic than before. His armour is a little more worn, his angular face carrying an extra scar, but the energy in his movements is undiminished.

'Interrogator,' he says, bowing. 'I would have come sooner, but there were many calls on us.'

I bow in return. 'It is good to see you, lord Chaplain,' I say.

I notice then that he carries his power maul, the thing he called a crozius. It looks different to me – smaller, as if cut down somehow. Perhaps I damaged it. I know how much the warriors of the Adeptus Astartes venerate their weapons, and so the thought troubles me.

'This is Argent,' Erastus says, hefting the heavy piece as if it weighs nothing. 'It has been in the Chapter for a thousand years. For an outsider to handle it, even to touch it, earns the wrath of us all.'

He is still severe. Perhaps he knows no other way to be.

'I did not know,' I say, wondering why he has come here to tell me this.

'We protect that which is precious to us,' he says. 'But we also understand what is truly significant. Take it, and observe what has changed.'

I receive the maul again, and then see truly that it has been heavily adapted. It is shorter, lighter, its power unit truncated and the bone casing modified. Even then I struggle to hold it steady, and my armour-encased arms ache.

'Why have you done this?' I ask.

'Because it is yours now,' he says.

I cannot believe it. I move to give the weapon back, unable to accept such a gift.

'If you spurn the offer,' Erastus warns me, 'it will be a second insult, one I will not overlook.'

I look down at the crozius. The detail on its shaft is incredible. It is a thing of beauty as well as power. The gesture overwhelms me, and I do not have the words for it.

'You do me too much honour,' I say at last, and it seems like a weak response.

'I have only just started,' he says, standing back and regarding me critically. 'You hold it as if it were a snake. Grip the handle loosely. I will show you how to bear it without breaking your bones.'

It is then that I know why he has come. He will instruct me in how to wield it, and I understand then that it will henceforth become my own weapon, the one I shall carry in preference to all others.

It will hurt. I will damage the healing process by doing this. Tur will be angry, for he desires me back in service within days.

None of that matters. I do as I am bid, then look to the Chaplain. I do not know if such a thing has ever been done before. My soul fills with joy, and I determine to make myself equal to the gesture. Perhaps that will be my purpose now – to live up to this deed, to ensure that Argent is used as it ought to be used, for the glory of Him on Earth.

That would be a fine ambition, I think, one worthy of my high calling.

'Show me,' I say then, hungry for the knowledge.

LUCIUS:
PRIDE AND FALL

IAN ST. MARTIN

Just a fraction of an inch, the tiniest miscalculation, and he would miss.

Concentration edged his brow, framing eyes that took in a scene that had arrived before him a thousand times before. Speed and attention to detail were paramount, and all would be for nothing were he to make a mistake here. He gripped the tools of his trade, ancient implements that had gone almost completely unchanged over the course of mankind's history, ones that had served with him for so long they felt as natural to him as the hands that held them.

A din wailed around him from all directions. The edges of his sight sparkled with glaring flashes of light, his hearing filled with the squeal and crunch of clashing metal. Once, it had been disorientating, but experience had long since pushed it all to the back of his mind, shrinking it to a dull rumble whose distraction would not rise high enough to challenge his focus.

The world shrank to his target. He had to be quick – more just like the one before him were coming in a seemingly unending procession. He drew a breath and held it, everything else vanishing as he found an opening and brought the metal in his hand to bear.

'Shift end!'

Tobias looked up from his place on the assembly line, wiping the sweat from his brow with a grimy work glove. The flat circle of machinery he had finished soldering shivered as it moved away down the thick carpet of segmented rubber, the new wiring assembly gleaming from its mechanisms after its installation. He smiled at his contribution and looked up to the ceiling. The chronograph flashed, an industrial whistle blared twice, and the crew of coverall-clad manufactorum workers rose from their stations.

A cluster of sharp pops brought a grimace to Tobias' face as he stood. He took a moment to stretch, fighting against the crooked posture earned by two decades working over that very assembly line. Age made its mark upon a man in many ways, and none were clearer to Tobias than in his back.

'Return to your domiciles,' the flat voice of the overseer droned from tinny speakers that ringed their section of the factory. 'Praise the Emperor, and thank Him for thy rest. The next work shift for assembly group 39.821-EpsilonAA23 shall commence in five hours, fifty-three minutes time.'

Tobias joined the line of exhausted workers filing off the factory floor. He pushed his goggles up onto his forehead, and brushed bits of metal from the coarse beard that hung to his chest. He surrendered his lathe and other tools to the equipment station flanked by a pair of armed guards. After passing through three separate checkpoints, where specialised servitors with scanners in place of arms panned his body to ensure he left with none of the factory's materials, he walked through the exit and stepped out into the street.

'Come on, then,' called out Solk from where he stood with a gaggle of other workers. 'Boys are getting a drink!'

Tobias grinned, like he always did, and shook his head to decline the offer, like he always did. The others laughed, tossing a few good-natured barbs his way, before heading off towards the work camp's canteen. Tobias moved down the streets as the sodium lightposts flickered to life, moving as quickly as his aching joints would allow him. The only sky above the camp was a ceiling of hewn rock, but he knew from the standardised chronograph that it was getting close to sunfall.

If he hurried, he would make it just in time to see a sight that made all his labours worth doing.

Half an hour later, Tobias pushed the thin plastek door to his hab-chamber aside, closing it softly behind him and hanging his worn cap on the hook he had screwed into the wall. The single room domicile was cramped, with a low ceiling and walls covered in stained vinyl. A threadbare kitchenette occupied one corner, a cot and a shrine to the God-Emperor another. The sole source of light came from a cracked lumen strip in the ceiling, which buzzed and sputtered intermittently as it sipped power from an aging generator.

Sitting at a low table, one that rocked from a broken leg he had patched back together more times than he could count, Tobias saw what he had been waiting all day to see.

The girl's eyes went bright. Her mother set her down, and she ran towards Tobias as he went down to one knee, arms spread wide. The child's lips parted, and she drew breath to call out her father's name.

* * *

'Lucius!'

He heard the name, but listened to the warning in the tone. He pivoted on his heel, feeling the static of an energised blade crackle over the scars covering his face. His own sword came up, moving so quickly the blade lost its shape, like mercury. The impact shot up his arm as the tip punched through layers of iron and cogwork, and then into the withered, vital flesh beneath. The sword was withdrawn before the truncated cognitive routines that had replaced his attacker's mind registered that it had been struck.

The alien steel was steady in his hand, as if forged to be there, its edge already thirsting for the next. And the next. All of this occurred in the time it took for him to blink.

Lucius spun away with fluid grace as the combat servitor came crashing down. What little that remained of the female convict wired into its core was dead before the cyborg hit the ground. A thin curtain of dust rose from the impact, rising on the wind to disperse into a cold and lightless sky.

He heard the voice again, coming from a face painted in lilac and gold leaf. 'Cutting it close,' Krysithius chuckled, hefting his sword towards the Eternal in mock salute. 'You're losing your touch.'

Lucius stared at Krysithius, his marred green eyes cold. He flung out his arm, hurling his lash at his brother. A barbed tentacle snapped a hand's breadth over the renegade Space Marine's head, decapitating another of the cyborg soldiers as it poised itself to strike at Krysithius' back.

'Am I?' said Lucius, before hauling back the lash with a whip crack.

Tobias woke with a start. He clamped a hand to his mouth, stifling a cry and breathed deeply through his nose. Once his heartbeat had steadied, he swept back the clinging locks of his hair pasted to his brow by cold sweat.

Gingerly, he sat up, careful not to wake his wife and daughter sleeping next to him. He swung his legs over the edge of the cot and stood, moving slowly through the dark to the washbasin next to the kitchenette.

Vestiges of the nightmare clung to Tobias' mind. Half-formed images of bleeding things and inhuman screeching. And laughter. They faded as he splashed water against his face.

Tobias did not know what the nightmare meant, or if it was supposed to mean anything. He sighed as he knelt before the shrine to the Emperor, lighting a votive candle that bathed him in its soft, tiny light. His eyes fell over the holy iconography in worn plastek, drifting to the frayed regimental patch set beneath it from his service in the planetary militia. Most of the manufactorum workers were veterans of the planet's conscripted defence force, but nothing he had seen out on the rim chasing pirates was a match for the monstrosity that had filled his sleep. He sighed, trying to rid his mind of it all. Sometimes a man just had bad dreams.

Tobias flinched as a hand rested upon his shoulder.

'Grace,' said Tobias, his eyes meeting hers before flicking back to the cot. 'Did I wake her?'

'She's fine,' his wife answered with a warm smile. 'Are you okay? You look pale.'

'It's nothing,' said Tobias, trying to push the last lingering images from his mind. 'Just a dream.'

Grace took his hand in hers, and Tobias smiled, his fear banished as they began to pray.

To his credit, Krysithius recovered well. He chuckled again to mask his discomfort, the sound a twisted, unwholesome noise that whistled from between his filed silver teeth. Krysithius turned and threw himself back into the fighting, hunting for something deadly enough to be worth the expenditure of effort to kill.

Lucius spent a moment to survey the battlefield, such as it was. The surface of, well, whatever the planet was called – he had not bothered to learn it – was barren rock, a coarse, worthless exterior laid over what the *Diadem*'s scanners had revealed to be an equally worthless core. The neighbouring worlds of the system, however, possessed depths laden with vast mineral wealth. Cobalt, osmium, tungsten and myriad others were apparently buried just beneath their crusts, sufficient deposits for the Adeptus Mechanicus to garrison a maniple of battle servitors in-system to ensure that it was they who would reap the benefits of their exploitation.

The economics of interstellar mining was one of a long list of subjects Lucius found severely uninteresting, but the value of such materials was hardly lost on him. There were countless cabals of the Dark Mechanicum within the Eye of Terror who would pay greatly for such raw, untainted resources.

But to Lucius, they were nothing. The prize Lucius sought was not the minerals, nor the automated mines that extracted them, but here on this desolate rock. Just beneath his feet lay a vast arcology whose factories, teeming with workers, processed and made use of the other worlds' bounties. The slave decks of the *Diadem* had gone hungry of late, both for skilled labour and those used by the warband for pleasure, and the continued existence of his Cohors Nasicae was threatened until they were filled to bursting again. And once the gaggle of lobotomised puppets that opposed him had been dispatched, Lucius would be free to go beneath this world's bleak skin and ensure they were.

A wail of jet turbines brought Lucius' attention to Vyspirtilo. The lord of the Rypax was perched atop the prone body of a combat servitor he had felled with his spear. Scraps of metal and gouts of oily machine lubricant flew around the Raptor chieftain in a bizarre swirl as his claws defiled the android, searching for flesh or the marrow within bones with all the desperation of a drowning man fighting for air. Unsatisfied, he tore his spear loose and leapt back into the air with a frustrated screech, leaving in a spray of diluted blood and hydraulic fluid.

Lucius had not witnessed the Eagle King speak in years. He wondered if he ever would again beyond animal screams, and felt a pang of regret at the thought. Vyspirtilo had the most beautiful voice.

The most beautiful eyes Tobias had ever seen watched him as he left the domicile, just as they did every morning when he departed for his shift. He put on his cap, careful not to show the sleeplessness of the past nights in front of his daughter, and slid the door closed behind him.

Tobias took a wheezing breath as he left the tenement building. The wheezing became coughing, and the coughing retching as he vomited a glob of black slime onto the street corner. Tobias' breath caught in his throat, his eyes wide as he watched the ooze hiss and bubble on the rockcrete. Vertigo weakened his knees and blurred his sight. He panted, holding a hand out to steady himself against the wall until his vision cleared.

'Tobias?' said a voice from behind the reeling factory worker. He dragged a hand down his face and turned, seeing a group of his fellows, Solk at their fore. 'You all right, brother?'

'Fine,' he lied. 'Long night, that's all.'

Solk chuckled. 'I guess you do your drinking at home.'

'Right.' Tobias forced a laugh. 'Go on ahead, I'll catch up with you.'

The workers made off down towards the factory. Tobias gasped. His skin felt burning hot to the touch. He pulled up the sleeve of his jacket, and gagged as he saw the dark lines of his veins threading through flesh that had gone deathly pale. He had to breathe, to just take a moment to collect himself.

The chronograph on the street corner chimed. Tobias sighed, groaning as he pushed off from the wall. He had to hurry. The call for the start of his shift would come in just a few minutes.

Just a few minutes had passed since they had arrived on this planet, and Lucius was already starting to notice the number of combat servitors beginning to dwindle. He had only allowed a small number of the warband to accompany him on this raid. Too many of the Cohors Nasicae in a battle of this size and things could have easily spiralled out of control. Lucius intended to leave with the prize he sought intact, or at least as intact as possible.

He was sowing a path of destruction through the fighting, using his lash to swing a servitor about like a massive flail, when an ear-splitting buzz assailed his ears. He released the ruined servitor, which collapsed in pieces as his lash uncoiled from around it, and turned in the direction of the noise.

He was confronted by a cohort of skitarii. These were different than the standard robed infantry of the Adeptus Mechanicus, spindle-limbed and clad in suits and masks of red leather. They bore sonic weapons, claws and flat-bladed swords that emitted a crackling buzz that played delightfully against Lucius' eardrums. He knew them, if not by experience then by reputation, as Sicarians. The Mechanicus' assassin caste.

'Ah!' Lucius exclaimed, his smile widening as he spun his sword with relish. 'Blessings of the Youngest God be upon you, I was beginning to think this was going to be boring!'

The Sicarians moved with flawless synchronicity as they blurred over the ground towards him. The air trembled around their weapons. They attacked as one, like fingers joined to make a fist.

Two of Lucius' warband intercepted them, one striking from above with a pair of glittering sabres while a Havoc set himself in a crouch as he brought his heavy bolter to bear. The skitarii assassins did not break stride. Two split off from the cohort, their claws and swords nearly impossible to see as they carved the airborne Chaos Space Marine apart until he crashed to the ground as a series of component parts. Another blurred around the cacophonous firing of the heavy bolter, dragging its energised blade through the links of the cannon's ammunition chain. The mass-reactive rounds detonated in a string of flaring explosions that travelled upwards to the magazine contained within the warrior's backpack. The ammunition reserves exploded, blowing the Havoc apart into a rain of gory mist and broken armour segments.

'Impressive,' said Lucius. The skitarii reformed, and he leapt into the midst of them. His mind had gone wandering thus far, hardly occupied by fighting second-rate opposition. For these mechanical killers he might actually need to stay focused.

Tobias fought to concentrate. Sweat streamed from his brow, soaking his hair and face. His fingers trembled with his tools as the machinery stopped before him on the assembly line.

The lathe slipped in his grip. It spun from his hand, bouncing against the floor with a discordant ring. The workers on either side of him looked up from their own stations. Tobias heard the plodding footsteps of the overseer nearby, and his heart sank.

The servitor clanked to a halt, turning its cold, empty gaze upon Tobias.

'Request for clarity – why is there inefficiency present at this workstation?'

'Forgive me, overseer,' said Tobias. He fought to keep from coughing again, but the pain leaked out in a wheeze that coated his words.

The servitor straightened. A red laser beamed out from its right eye, scanning over Tobias' face.

'Query – are you experiencing illness or debilitation?'

'No, overseer,' Tobias answered quickly.

'Notice – I am administering direct intravenous stimulant.' The servitor jabbed a syringe into Tobias' neck, injecting a cocktail of amphetamine chemicals into his bloodstream. *'Notice – decrease of productivity is unacceptable. Report any occurrence or worsening of symptoms and submit to mandatory medical evaluation immediately should illness or debilitation occur.'*

'Yes, overseer.' Tobias' teeth chattered from the effects of the injection.

Lucius howled in glee as he slammed another narcotic into his veins from his suit reserves. The Sicarians' weapons were good, he gave them that. His armour was covered in incidental scrapes and gouges that would have easily sundered standard-issue power armour. Lucius' attackers had no way to know that while he was many things, he was far from standard. The six faces pressing against his war-plate's surfaces wailed, and the armour cracked and shifted as the scars shrank away to nothing.

A claw sliced just shy of Lucius' face, wrapped in a shimmering skin of waspish sound. The frequency at which they resonated changed with every instant, testing and retesting to determine an intensity capable of slicing the Laeran Blade – or Lucius' spine – in half. He did not let them live long enough to find either.

Lucius bifurcated the claw-wielding skitarii with a clean strike through its midsection. Two more of the Sicarians died, slashed to ribbons by a downward slash from the bladed tails of Lucius' whip. Another flew past, clattering to the ground as the Eternal sidestepped its attack and decapitated it. A lightning series of cuts and thrusts reduced the last of them to trembling corpses with neither limbs nor heads.

A sudden sickness soaked through Lucius, as though he were standing too close to the *Diadem*'s Geller field generator. He staggered as something crashed into him from behind, scrambling across his shoulders. Slender, bird-like limbs sought purchase between the plates of his armour. Lucius snarled, throwing himself into a somersault to dislodge it. A figure in long crimson robes landed softly upon the ground before him in a crouch, looking upon Lucius with clusters of whirring blue eyes.

It was another of the Mechanicus' clade killers. This one emitted a warbling aura of interference from the antennae that sprouted from the armoured dome of its head. The destructive wavelengths crashed over Lucius, burning his flesh, causing blood to stream from his nose and ears, and filling his eyes with stinging tears.

It was glorious.

Lucius reached out, ensnaring the Infiltrator with his whip, and drew the assassin closer.

* * *

'Papa?'

Tobias could barely make out Grace as she buried the child's face into her chest and carried her away from where he lay shivering on the cot. His vision tunnelled sharply as he curled into a ball, gripping the thin sheet over him so tightly his knuckles cracked.

Death was a fact of life for those who toiled in the factory. Men falling ill, to mould or rustlung or plain exhaustion was far from uncommon. Tobias had seen more than one of his friends carried from their stations by the overseers, to be provided with 'medical treatment'. None of them had ever returned.

This was something different. It was as though Tobias' nightmares had infected him with fever. They were no longer content to remain in his dreams, hauling themselves out into his waking life. Tobias gritted his teeth against the pain, a marrow-deep agony that filled his guts with razors.

'Tobias?' said Grace, tears streaming down her face as she cradled their child.

Tobias squeezed his eyes shut. For days, people had stopped being recognisable to him. All he could see were horrible, skinless things that grinned with broken fangs.

'I don't know what to do,' sobbed Grace. 'Tell me what to do.' Tobias could just hear her voice as she pleaded to the shrine in the corner of the room. '*Deus Imperator*, please, I don't know what to do.'

'Oh,' hissed Lucius as the lash tightened around the Infiltrator's chest. 'We didn't count on that, did we?'

He squeezed the barbed coils tighter and tighter. Blood and oil began to weep from every crack and seal on the skitarii's domed head. Diodes and lenses shattered. With a sharp bark, Lucius drove the tip of the Laeran Blade through the skitarii's head. The giddiness of its interference mechanisms ceased as the mortal parts within its shell died.

More of the Infiltrators advanced, a wall of distortion rippling out before them that dulled even Lucius' preternatural perceptions. He sniffed away a nosebleed and made ready to attack, when a shadow fell over them.

Lucius leapt back as a blurred red shape hurtled down into the skitarii from the sky. He recognised the distinctive rounded shape of a Kastelan battle robot just before it made impact. Bits of rock and smoky thunder filled the air from the booming crash. Lucius stared into the aftermath of the blast, wind clawing at his face and armour, and watched as a silhouette enveloped in crackling mauve lightning appeared through the pall.

The Composer stepped forth from the veil of smoke and dust. He raised his palm, lifting the smoking battle robot over the Infiltrators. Lucius saw many of the rail-thin skitarii had survived, now twitching and clawing to drag themselves away. The Composer lowered his hand and smashed the Kastelan down into them again, leaving nothing behind but a crater filled with mounds of sparking wreckage.

'Loathsome,' said the sorcerer, the derision in his tone at odds with the beatific faceplate of his silver helm. 'To those of us who are blessed to hear the Song, theirs is a truly vacuous contribution.'

Another shadow, one much taller and broader, detached from the smoke beside the Composer. Afilai stopped a short distance behind and to the side of the sorcerer he protected, the bulky servos of his cobbled-together Terminator armour clanking as he swept his storm bolter across the area. Dirty light drooled from the bloodied talons of his lightning claw.

The Composer ignored his slave and raised his staff to Lucius in earnest salute. 'Hail, Eternal One!'

'Find your own things to kill,' spat Lucius. He regretted allowing the witch leave from his prison atop the *Diadem*. Were he not eternally shadowed by his Terminator-clad pet, more of the warband would be working to kill him than the enemy.

With no further bloodshed available to occupy their attention, the gaudy killers of the Cohors Nasicae formed up in loose ranks behind Lucius. He could feel the eagerness dripping off them, the hunger. Their prize loomed within reach.

With the skitarii butchered, the path down into the arcology was now clear. The defences had been broken, and nothing would be waiting for them but token militias cowering behind hastily erected barricades. Now the taking of flesh could begin in earnest.

'With me!' roared Lucius, waving his warriors forward as power blazed across the Laeran Blade. Then he was charging ahead, moving so effortlessly and so swiftly that he barely noticed the piece of shaped iron he brushed against with his hoof.

Lucius experienced the world in a blur.

A burst of light and sound.

Silence, and the feeling of weightless spinning.

The earth and sky alternating.

Earth. Sky. Earth. Sky. Earth.

Blackness.

Death swallowed Lucius, just as it had before. And then the screaming began.

Tobias could only hear screaming now. There was no other sound than the din of agony that howled from behind his eyes. Black ropes bulged and squirmed beneath his flesh, his veins aflame with poison. He stumbled through the streets, his mind knowing not where his body was carrying him.

Twisted, inhuman faces leered down at him at every turn. He recoiled as they jostled and shoved him away, their shouts and curses muted by the shrieking.

Tobias burst into the factory, his arms flailing as black ooze streamed from his eyes. He stumbled blindly through a corridor, moving towards the sound of machines. He collided with a doorframe and was bowled over, collapsing at the entrance to the assembly line.

The workers who witnessed Tobias fall called their fellows and ran to his aid, ignoring the shouted warnings from guards and overseers. Screams and cries of alarm sent them staggering back from their friend's stricken form.

A revolting wet tearing sound filled the air as Tobias' skin split into flayed ribbons, spraying everything around him with an oily mist of blood. The flesh beneath was discoloured, the deep red of it morphed to an unsettling shade of purple that glittered with an oily sheen like an insect's carapace. His skeleton snapped as it reformed, some bones elongating far beyond that of a normal man, others splintering and sharpening into alarming spikes.

The workers fled from what Tobias was becoming. His body writhed in bone-breaking convulsions, a lump of meat that twisted as its wet, slick noises changed to those of a cracking, squealing shell.

Limbs burst out from the mass: arms and armoured fists holding weapons that condensed into being from blood and shadows; legs ending in cloven hooves. Tobias' skull collapsed, his face never halting in its cries as it receded and was drawn tight over a rapidly forming breastplate of purplish-pink armour. In its place another skull breached the quivering knot of transformation, skinned with hairless consumptive flesh that was covered in hideous overlapping scars. A savage maw grinned as it was filled with needle teeth and a vile, reptilian tongue. Two sunken pits twitched, fighting the blood and mucus gumming them as they strove to take in the world once more.

The eyes opened, and the screaming that had filled the assembly line was overtaken by laughter.

'Yes, I know,' said Lucius, rising with a grunt to tower over the group of stunned factory workers. 'I am truly beautiful to behold. The worm giveth birth to the butterfly.'

The Eternal watched with amusement as a servitor approached, scanning him with an eye-mounted laser and raising a hypodermic needle.

'Notice – I am administering–'

Lucius put his fist through its face, not deeming the android worthy to taste the edge of his sword. It crashed to the floor in sparking pieces. Men and women cried out, sprinting away in panic.

Lucius' head was swimming. He was underground, in a large industrial space, but this was not the planet where he had died. This was somewhere new. He could be halfway across the galaxy for all he knew. Such had happened before.

Lucius laughed at the idea, wondering at the cosmic joke he had been set to play upon the galaxy. The stabbing sense of dislocation and confusion waned. He ran his mind through the inventory he had learned to perform on the previous occasions he had expired, knowing from experience that it would allow him to quickly return his mind to fine form. He flexed his limbs, spun his sword and blinked the blood from his eyes after an instant to savour its sting. His mind retraced memories, grand triumphs and duels won. These thoughts anchored him, centring him as he reasserted control and ownership over his body.

Another ritual awaited, he thought with a grin. Lucius looked down, scanning the handful of wailing faces straining against the crackling plates of his armour until he found his newest pet.

There. The seventh and newest addition to his growing menagerie. This one was gaunt and sickly, though in fairness none of the caged souls who had become bound upon Lucius' war-plate could be described as exemplars of good health. The man's lips were locked in an agonising rictus, teeth bared within a scraggly beard. It was hardly the face of a bloodthirsty champion or peerless master assassin. It was not even one of the Legions.

Lucius had never seen him before. Every other time, he had fallen before his killer at sword's length, face to face. This was new.

'Hello,' Lucius smiled at his new screaming soul. 'I'm not yet certain how we both came to this, but don't worry, we have an eternity to get to know each other.'

The man screamed inside of Lucius' head. It was an incomprehensible dirge, jostling and merging with the others. For a rare moment, there and quickly gone, Lucius believed that he could make out was he was saying. It almost sounded like names.

Lucius took stock of his surroundings, bloodshot green eyes flicking here and there. It was then that Lucius realised where he was. He was standing in the centre of a munitions factory. He thought back, retracing his memories to the last moment he could recall, before the blackness of death had engulfed him.

A landmine. By Ruin, it had been a damned landmine.

Such a revelation galled Lucius, on a great number of levels. He couldn't fathom which was worse – that he, the greatest champion of the entire galaxy, should meet such an end, or, equally infuriating, that such a creature as this would dare to derive satisfaction from its miserable existence.

'You were proud of this?' Lucius glared down at the wailing visage of Tobias. Of all the Ruinous Powers that could have bestowed their blessings upon him, Lucius had to have been chosen by the one that possessed a sense of humour. He wondered how many of the Cohors Nasicae he would have to kill before any word of this embarrassment was quashed forever.

Anger ticked out from a vein on Lucius' temple. His teeth creaked within snarling jaws. This simply would not do. Not at all.

A casual flick of Lucius' wrist sent his lash flying out, a barbed tendril snapping around the leg of a fleeing munitorum worker. The man cried out as he crashed to the ground, tearing at the deck plating as the whip hauled him back until he left crimson streaks upon the dark, indifferent metal.

Lucius lifted the man up off the ground, suspending him upside down by his leg, raising him until they were at eye level. He played the blade of his sword over the worker's body, delighting at each recoil and the pathetic, animal noises that squealed from the man as its cutting edge came just close enough to split flesh.

'Do you know who I am?' asked Lucius, grinning at the tiny arcs of electricity from the Laeran Blade singeing the man's grubby uniform and even grubbier skin, before he extinguished the power field down to bare alien steel.

'*Please.*'

Lucius chuckled. 'That's not my name! Though so many

of you mortals seem to think so.' He read the crudely stencilled patch on the man's coveralls aloud. '*Solk*,' declared the Eternal with mock triumph. 'See? I have made the effort to learn your name.'

The man moaned, squirming and struggling to look away.

Lucius tutted with disappointment. 'No, no, no, little man,' he leaned forwards. 'Look at me. *Look. At. Me!*'

The roar froze Solk, who looked at Lucius with glazed eyes. His body went limp, save for the slightest trembling that shook every inch of him.

'You don't,' Lucius sighed, appearing reflective for a moment before his face was creased once more by his lunatic grin. 'That's fine, I forgive you for your ignorance.' The worker named Solk suddenly became very aware of the bizarre sword in Lucius' hand. His entire world became that blade, pearlescent and covered in swirling, painful runes, as its shimmering edge was lifted to rest just beneath his jaw.

'I am going to teach you,' whispered Lucius. 'I will teach every last one of you who I am. I am going to carve my name into this world, and no one will ever be able to forget what I am about to do here.'

The worker gasped, the sound quickly becoming a gurgle as a casual caress of the blade opened his throat. Lucius discarded the dying man, his victim immediately forgotten as he broadened his focus outwards. He smiled as he tasted the fear upon the air of the world he was about to slaughter.

'My name is Lucius.'

WHISPERS

ALEC WORLEY

Marcus Amouris bounded up the steps of the village shrine and appealed for calm as the Thunderhawk circled overhead. The ship's sudden appearance, materialising out of the early morning mist like some mythological bird of prey, had interrupted the tribe's dawn rituals and driven them into a panic. Mothers screamed, racing from the doorways of their huts to retrieve awestruck children from the storm of leaves and dirt churning beneath the transporter's powerful turbines. The menfolk had already gathered into a mob, brandishing hunting mattocks as they beat their chests and bellowed challenges at the hovering vessel. The village shaman huddled on his knees, absorbed in frantic prayer to his obsolete deity.

Marcus tried not to smile. He always savoured this moment, when the scales finally fell from the eyes of the converted and they beheld the glorious light of the Emperor for the first time.

'People of the Sundered Claw,' he bellowed, his weathered

robes snapping in the booming downdraught. 'Your faith in me this season has been rewarded.'

He had mastered the nuances of the local dialect within weeks. His genius for languages had not dimmed in the years since he was an orphan boy, studying at one of the holy academies of the Schola Progenium.

His strident voice caught the ears of the tribe's chieftain, a brute almost the size of a greenskin and flanked as always by his two hulking champions. The chieftain raised his ceremonial mattock – the Sundered Claw itself, its head fashioned from the talon of some prehistoric beast – as he roared for silence. All who heard it ceased their clamour and stood, squinting into the wind, all eyes on the Imperial missionary as he continued.

'The curse upon your sacred forest shall soon be lifted,' cried Marcus. 'Your noble hunters shall be preyed upon no more.'

He gestured with a flourish towards the Thunderhawk, as though he had conjured it into existence. 'Did I not promise an end to your famine? Did I not promise deliverance?'

The ship continued to circle the village, surveying the scene below. Its thrusters tore the mist into curling shreds, revealing the peninsula of low hills that opened to the south, then whipping the branches of the fathomless pine forest that otherwise enclosed the village like a bulwark.

'Your honoured ancestors called the same god by many names,' said Marcus. 'The Grey Father, Cloudbearer, Ward of the Forest. But he has answered my prayers, granted me a portion of his command, because I know his true name.'

Marcus looked out over a sea of starving, enraptured faces, gazing at him like children spellbound by a campfire tale. Marcus welcomed the force of their attention. He absorbed their devotion like warmth, feeling something nourished deep within him.

'And this is my gift to you,' he said. 'Your god's true name…' He paused, relishing the moment's tension. 'The Emperor.'

They gasped on cue. Several dropped to their knees as if with the weight of their revelation. The shaman was speaking into the ear of the perplexed chieftain. Ignoring them, Marcus singled out a thin woman nearby clutching her wailing child, her cheeks gaunt from weeks of hunger. He reached towards her with a gesture of entreaty.

'And the Emperor does not stand by while the children of his disciples starve.'

He indicated the Thunderhawk once again as he addressed the rest of the tribe, directing the force of his words at the chieftain.

'The Emperor has despatched a band of mighty celestial warriors, brave men whom he has sent to purge evil from your hunting grounds.'

The Thunderhawk finally peeled away towards a low hill outside the village. Marcus beamed at the thought of introducing the wide-eyed chieftain to a platoon of Imperial Guard: strangely armoured warriors summoned out of the sky. The tribe had never seen guns before and Marcus planned on ordering the squad to shoot a volley of las-fire into the air, overawing the tribe with a demonstration of the Emperor's might.

As the dust subsided, Marcus got his first clear view of the Thunderhawk as it prepared to land on the tallest of the nearby hills. His face fell at the sight of the two crimson and black Rhino transporters the ship had clamped to its belly.

Emblazoned upon the side of both vehicles was a white fleur de lys.

Euphoria melted into panic as he leaped down the steps of the wooden shrine. His mouth was dry, his voice trembling as he hurriedly warned the tribe to remain within the village, not to venture near the ship until he had greeted the visiting warriors and assured them of the tribe's faith. He pushed past several bemused tribespeople as he ran to the hill, his heart pounding, cursing whichever fool in the orbiting watch station had relayed his orders to the Ministorum.

He had requested assistance over two weeks ago, during which time he had been left to wonder whether his summons had been forgotten or relayed at all through his barely functioning vox-caster. The village food stores had continued to run low and the shaman had been asking too many questions, muttering too often into the chieftain's ear. Skilled though he was in creative hyperbole, the missionary had found himself running out of excuses.

Marcus reached the crest of the hill. He gripped his knees, panting as the Thunderhawk's front ramp yawned before him.

A towering figure in ebon power armour descended towards him, a scarlet tabard flowing from her waist. The woman wore a pistol holstered on her right hip; the beaded chain of an Imperial rosarius swung at the other. She wore her black hair short and straight, cut in the severe fashion of the Adepta Sororitas, the Sisters of Battle.

Her squad followed close behind, their boots clattering upon the metal ramp. The Battle Sisters were smaller than the monstrous Space Marines, but no less intimidating. Some carried bolters, their faces bare, expressions pitiless, eyes eerily intense. Others were encased entirely within their black power armour, faces hidden behind white crested visors as they hefted double-barrelled storm bolters.

The hazy morning sunlight revealed their commander's

face. She was pale as marble, sculpted yet scarred, a dark Y-shaped fissure running down one side of her face. She halted at the foot of the ramp and gazed at Marcus, her face immobile, eyes vivid green and unreadable. They were heavy-lidded as if with weariness, arched black eyebrows twin peaks of disdain. If her breath had not smoked in the cold air, Marcus felt he could have mistaken her for a statue.

'Ave Imperator,' she said, her lips motionless. Her voice emanated from a vox-grille in her sculpted gorget, the device giving her words a haunting metallic resonance. She continued: 'I am Sister Adamanthea, Dominion Superior. I am told you need me to kill something.'

Marcus saw the two-handed hilt of the immense eviscerator chainsword she had clamped to her back. He felt suddenly nauseous and forced himself to speak before fear could prevent him.

'Blessed Sister,' he said, attempting a smile. 'You are a heartening sight indeed for a weary pilgrim. But I'm afraid there has been an error. I requested a detachment of Astra Militarum, and did so for a crucial reason.'

Adamanthea's expression remained glacial.

'Are you questioning the decision of the Ecclesiarchy?'

Her left cheek bore the tattoo of a single red tear, an icon of the Order of the Valorous Heart, whose Battle Sisters were infamous for the paranoid nature of their zealotry. Marcus had heard tales that these women could literally *see* sin radiating like an aura from the weak and faithless.

'I question nothing, Sister,' he stuttered. 'I only serve. I am merely suggesting that our masters may not have been made aware of the delicacy of this undertaking.'

He turned to see the tribe approaching the hill. Cold fear swam through Marcus' veins as he saw the shaman babbling and gesticulating at the Battle Sisters. The chieftain, his lumbering champions and the village hunters followed close behind. The sight of the women stopped every one of them in their tracks and their expressions curdled with outrage.

'Sister,' said Marcus hurriedly. 'You must understand, these people are simple-minded barbarians. Such are their savage traditions, their sacred forest may be entered only by men! To contravene this law is an affront tantamount to blasphemy.'

Marcus cried out as Adamanthea strode past him towards the gathering mob. The squad remained as he hurried after her, cursing.

'This tribe dominates all others in this region,' he told her, struggling to contain his rage. 'The Missionarus Galaxia has calculated that their conversion will spread the Imperial Creed across the entire continent within a generation. Your presence here risks undoing all I have achieved thus far.'

'Stay back,' she told him as they neared the tribe.

The shaman rushed forward, halting Marcus, gibbering curses in his face. The gathered tribesmen stared in both dismay and wonder as the Dominion Superior strode towards the appalled chieftain. The brute snorted with fury, folding his arms as his two champions advanced towards her, casually swinging their vicious tools. They were burly, bear-like men, hulks of scar and muscle, veterans of the countless wars of aggression waged upon neighbouring tribes. Sister Adamanthea ignored them as she continued towards their chieftain.

Marcus watched, helpless, months of work about to be demolished by capricious violence. The champions sauntered towards Adamanthea, confident their threatening presence alone would deter the woman. But still she advanced on their chieftain as though neither guardian existed.

One of the men went to grab her shoulder. The motion

seemed to animate Adamanthea; her aura of stillness suddenly vanished as she flinched away from the champion's outstretched paw. Snatching the brute's wrist, she drove her power-armoured forearm into his elbow, snapping the limb in an explosion of screams and splintered bone.

She was on the other man before he could bury his mattock in her shoulder, her hands shooting past his guard like striking snakes, closing the distance before he could land a blow. Grabbing the weapon, she wrenched it from his grip with a savage motion, then swung the pommel upwards into his teeth with force enough to hurl him senseless onto his back. She cast the weapon aside as she stepped over his body and the enraged chieftain charged at her, swinging the Sundered Claw about his head.

Adamanthea drew her bolt pistol and shot him in the foot.

The chieftain shrieked and fell to the ground, his tribesmen screaming in primal terror as the pistol's bark echoed over the hills like thunder. They cowered before Adamanthea, their chieftain still howling, staring with horrified eyes at the bloody wreck that dangled from the end of his leg. Marcus was surprised to feel a surge not of rage, but of anguished envy. What a thing it must be to inspire awe by force of arms alone.

Adamanthea turned to Marcus.

'I did not come here to play with savages,' she said, her face a mask of tranquillity, oblivious to the spray of blood that now freckled her cheek. 'I came to destroy whatever is preying upon them.'

She marched back up the hill towards the ship, adding, 'I require further instruction, Brother Marcus. Quickly, for the Emperor's time is precious.'

As a missionary, Marcus was accustomed to closed minds

and knew the futility of chiding the Battle Sister for her reck-lessness. At least she had left the tribe in no doubt of the Emperor's power. He felt another rush of envy and cursed himself at having to scurry after her like a lackey. The tribe retreated further back, carrying their wounded chieftain with them, as the two Rhinos crawled out from beneath the Thun-derhawk, their engines rumbling like beasts hungry for war.

Standing nearby, Adamanthea surveyed the immeasurable forest. Dark spires of pine gradually faded into mist until the vast mountains beyond were but ghosts. Strange birds crossed a cold, white sky.

'Sister Adamanthea,' said Marcus, joining her as he stifled his lingering annoyance and mustered his most authoritative tone. 'I studied this region extensively prior to my departure and suspect an indigenous predator to be the source of our troubles. The mountain region to the north is home to sev-eral carnivorous species affected by a diminished source of prey. I'm certain one or several such creatures have migrated to this area in search of food.'

'Bodies?'

'None. Every group of hunters sent into the forest to search for their brethren has failed to return.'

One of the Sisters approached to confirm the squad's readi-ness. Adamanthea nodded and gave the order to embark.

'The coordinates you gave us point to ancient ruins, brother,' she said, as they walked to the lead Rhino. 'The Ecclesiarchy believe they are almost certainly Imperial. Our historians say this world was civilised millennia ago during the Reign of Thor.'

'My studies brought me to precisely the same conclusion,' said Marcus. 'However, the tribe know the site as "the City of Whispers". They regard it as a fearful place, and believe their men were spirited away by ghosts. Now none of them dare enter the forest. They'd prefer to starve to death than be dragged to hell.'

'Local superstitions may harbour ruinous truths,' said Adamanthea, her disembodied voice ringing like steel as her mouth tightened into a frown. 'Did you not think to summon the Inquisition?'

'The Emperor's time is precious, as you say,' he said, offering an innocent smile. 'I wouldn't think to waste it when so much evidence points to natural causes. The site is located near a major water source drawing abundant prey, making the ruins a natural lair for any mountain-dwelling predator such as the *glacies lupus* or the common *lacundum ursus*.'

Adamanthea's impatient scowl pleased him.

'Hunting beasts is a base labour, Sister,' said Marcus, nodding sympathetically. 'Wholly unworthy of the Adepta Sororitas, but *fides ante vanitas*. "Faith before vanity," I always say.'

Adamanthea nodded towards a figure bearing baggage nearby. It was the young tribeswoman whom Marcus had chosen to school as his maidservant. He reluctantly bid her approach. She was pretty and full-figured, despite the ravages of hunger. Marcus tried to ignore Adamanthea's penetrating gaze as the girl bowed low, her eyes downcast as she handed him his flak jacket. He took his coat and stopped her as she tried to kneel and kiss his hand.

'"Faith before vanity," indeed,' said Adamanthea. She watched Marcus flush with embarrassment as he dismissed the girl, snatching his backpack and the cloth wrap containing his lasrifle. The girl retreated with an extravagant curtsy, which Marcus now sorely regretted teaching her.

'Clearly you are an asset to these people,' said Adamanthea. 'Perhaps it would be best if you stayed behind.'

'I'm afraid not,' said Marcus, irritated as he fished a painted claw from inside his vestment. 'You see this pendant? It is a totem of honour worn by every hunter. It means I have sworn an oath to these people to enter the forest, confront their enemies and return triumphant. Though it embarrasses me, I am forced to abide by their ridiculous traditions if I have any hope of guiding them into the light.'

Adamanthea had already turned to follow the last of her squad into the back of the Rhino. Taking her silence for acquiescence, Marcus went to follow her up the ramp when she turned and addressed him, her voice a tinny hiss.

'I heard that you united the warring hordes of Kordaius Quintus, brokered peace between them in the name of the Emperor. I also heard that you are now worshipped among them as a prophet of – some would say excessive – renown.' She leaned in. 'Do you believe a person of weak character might develop a taste for such adoration?'

'I believe they might, Sister,' said Marcus coolly. 'I have seen valour turn to vanity in many a warrior. But, of course, *superbia vocat corruptionem*. "Pride beckons corruption." Words spoken by Sister Lucia, the founding saint of your Order, I believe.'

'Sage words indeed,' said Adamanthea with menace, her green eyes gleaming as she studied him. Marcus failed to stifle a shudder as she unhooked the eviscerator from her back. The blade's purity seals fluttered stiffly in the breeze, dark with dried blood. She ducked inside the transport, taking the seat nearest the door.

Marcus huddled into a space near the driver's hatch, struggling to dismiss the sting of Adamanthea's words. These Battle Sisters were as brutish as Space Marines, as ignorant as the savages he had devoted his life to enlightening. What did this Sister Adamanthea know of the nuances of converting a populace? He knew that mere men were not enough to inspire the masses, to prompt unwavering devotion to the Throne. No – the people needed legends. Heroes of song and saga, vision and valour.

He allowed himself a tight smile and looked over at Adamanthea as the ramp closed, activating the photon-candles set in the recesses of the Rhino's interior. Like the rest of her squad, she was already deep in prayer, touching her forehead to the hilt of her eviscerator, oblivious to all but her own devotions. Marcus could sense her dormant vitality radiating like heat.

Prove your worth, Marcus Amouris. The notion came to him as clearly as if someone had whispered it in his ear. He nodded to himself, swaying in his seat as the Rhino thundered down the hill, towards the forest.

'With me,' barked a voice.

Marcus woke from a heavy doze to find himself addressed by a lone Battle Sister. She was young, smooth-skinned, but with a thick scar across her crumpled nose. She motioned with her bolter, urging him towards the open ramp and the brightness of the world outside. He blinked and gathered himself, embarrassed at having fallen asleep, unwrapping his lasrifle and strapping on his pack as he followed her, wincing at the cramp in his legs.

The perfume of pine and earth was a welcome change from the dank odour of sweat and sacramental oil that permeated the inside of the Rhino. The Battle Sisters had set up a perimeter around their two idling transports and were scanning the surrounding trees.

Marcus sniffed and wiped his nose. Twilight was an hour

away but the air was already freezing. White vapour wrapped itself around the trees, swallowed the towering pines, reaching up, up into the high branches where it framed beams of dying sunlight. The silence here was so intense that Marcus thought he could detect a strange hiss, like static in the air.

His bodyguard nudged him up the road and he clutched his lasrifle, making a show of looking alert to his surroundings as he approached Sister Adamanthea. The Dominion Superior was conversing with two of her squad beside the hunting trail, which terminated in a crumbling ledge that had halted their progress. Marcus gazed across the gloomy expanse beyond. Then, shivering with involuntary excitement, he scrambled to higher ground as he realised what lay before him.

The City of Whispers. A dead metropolis of ruined Imperial basilica. Domed roofs like shattered skulls, rubble impaled by the prevailing trees. The splendid wreckage lay strewn for miles, drowning in a sea of boiling mist that merged into the distant grey horizon. A landscape of once-proud pinnacles stood strangled and splintered by the cloying vegetation, interspersed by a grave community of immense statues, silently contemplating eternity as they disintegrated into the murk. Everywhere Marcus looked he saw the detritus of faith fighting a slow and hopeless war against the creeping advance of nature.

But might not someone turn the tide of this conflict... retrieve these stones from the pagan earth and re-consecrate them in the name of the Emperor?

Marcus saw before him not a city lost to ruin, but a grand opportunity. Glory for the taking. Once the Sisters had driven out whatever nuisance lurked here, Marcus himself could resurrect this holy site and welcome all those whom he enlightened to come and pay tribute. They would raise statues of him in gratitude, of course. Proof indeed of his worth. How might he be known? Amouris the Intrepid? The Beneficent? Father of the Faithful?

The young Battle Sister caught Marcus' arm, pulling him back down the steep bank of trees he had climbed to gain a better view of the ruined city. He went to protest when he saw just how close he had been standing to the edge of the steep cliffs that encircled the city; perhaps the remains of some monumental moat that had surrounded this place an aeon ago. Looking back at the crumbled ledge that had halted the Rhinos' progress, he saw it was the remains of a stone bridge, a section of which had collapsed and disappeared into the misty canyon below. The bridge appeared to have once been part of a grand pavilion leading into the upper tier of an extravagant cathedral. The building appeared relatively intact from what Marcus could see. Was that a flight of stairs leading up to an open archway, and high above it the remains of a circular lattice where an immense rose window had once stood?

He suddenly ached to see what was inside and once again felt that sense of something seething in the air, like ghostly rain. Was it some trick of the wind? Of climate or air pressure? It was easy to see why the local tribes shunned this place.

'Are you sure this is the correct trail, brother?'

Marcus jumped at the sound of Sister Adamanthea's sonorous voice. Before he could answer, two Battle Sisters trudged into view from a steep rocky slope that descended nearby into the canyon beneath the ruined bridge.

'It came down recently, Sister,' panted one of them. 'Likely within the last day.'

Adamanthea immediately snatched the lasrifle from Marcus' hands. Before he realised what she had done, she had tossed the weapon to his bodyguard and slammed him against the side of the Rhino, pinning his throat with her forearm.

'Who have you been talking to?' Her voice was cool and measured as it rang through the vox-grille at her throat.

'I don't know what–'

Adamanthea jammed her forearm deeper into Marcus' throat, her face impassive as he choked and squirmed.

'No animal did this. Someone knows we're coming,' she said. 'What do you hope to lead us into?'

She held him a moment longer, watching him with those languid green eyes as he gasped. She stepped back, releasing his frantic reply.

'I swear by the Throne,' he coughed, his words impassioned with fear and confusion. 'I have no idea.'

Several other Sisters now surrounded him, their bolters aimed at his chest.

'Sister Clarice.' Adamanthea gestured to Marcus' bodyguard. The young Battle Sister with the broken nose grabbed Marcus' arm and twisted him onto his knees, pinning his face against the Rhino's muddy flanks as she stripped him of his backpack. A knot of impotent rage tightened in his chest as she rummaged inside his flak jacket.

'The remains of the bridge show no sign of explosives.' One of the other Sisters was speaking. 'From what we can see, it looks like someone removed the keystone and demolished the supports with tools.'

Marcus' thoughts raced. How could anyone know they were coming? Was there a conspiracy afoot in the village? The shaman perhaps? Unlikely. They were half-starved simpletons terrified of this place. So who had destroyed the bridge? And if they wanted the squad dead why not loosen the stones and wait for the transports to drive across? Did someone want them – or him – alive?

'No vox-caster, Sister Superior,' said Clarice, concluding her search of Marcus' pack. 'Nothing.'

Marcus wiped the mud from his face and clambered to his feet.

'Watch him,' said Adamanthea.

Clarice nodded and Adamanthea ordered the rest of the squad to move down the slope, into the misty canyon beneath the crumbled bridge. They murmured a prayer of sanctity in eerie unison as they marched towards the top of the path down.

Sister Clarice slung Marcus' lasrifle over her shoulder as she shoved him into line.

Marcus turned to her, imploring. 'Sister, there must be other bridges, other entrances further along these cliffs. We are clearly walking into an ambush. Why?'

'Because,' Adamanthea cut in, the trace of a smile on her frozen lips. 'I am impatient to meet those who believe they can challenge the will of the Emperor.'

Marcus couldn't stop shivering. It was even colder down here on the swampy floor of the canyon, the mist even more impenetrable as evening neared. The fog seemed to swallow up every sound beyond the clink of the squad's war gear and the squelch of their boots. Several Battle Sisters probed the path ahead, searching for tracks while the Dominions trudged several feet behind them, clutching their storm bolters. Adamanthea stalked beside them, her bolt pistol drawn. Marcus plodded among the rear guard, young Sister Clarice close by his side as the squad advanced towards the distant cathedral, following the course of the shattered pavilion high above.

The ruins rose about them like colossal tombstones. Marcus felt miniaturised, like something out of an absurd dream. The air stank of mulch and stagnant water, seeming to crackle and tighten like freezing ice, writhing with whispers that seemed to hiss at him from among the flooded rubble.

Some malign intelligence was at work here. Something the Battle Sisters would have to eradicate before he could fully enlighten this world, before he could cleanse this place and secure his legacy. He felt borne up by faith: a faith, if not in the holy Emperor, then in himself, in his own ability, his own talent for survival. Although he missed his lasrifle, he felt a strange absence of fear.

Prove your worth, Marcus Amouris.

Marcus repeated the thought over and over, like a mantra. So immersed was he in his benediction that he was slow to realise a murmur of activity had taken place at the head of the column. Subtle gestures had been exchanged and the Battle Sisters' formation was now shifting. He watched curiously as one of them threw something at a line of toppled masonry ahead.

He realised she had thrown a grenade only a split-second before it detonated with a boom of sundered rock that filled the air with smoke and a rain of spinning leaves. Screaming figures bounded through the pall as though the blast had released them from the earth. The Dominions answered their appearance instantly with a deafening battery of storm bolter fire that sent Marcus' heart into a spasm of fright.

Panic electrified him as a second storm of bolter fire erupted. The Battle Sisters guarding him were blasting at howling figures leaping at them from the mist, muzzle-flare sending shadows capering about the ruins. One of the fur-clad figures dashed in as a bolter round obliterated its shoulder, flinging its right arm back into the mist. The ghastly wound failed to slow him as he and another crashed into Sister Clarice, driving her onto the ground. As the three of them fought like maddened animals, something landed nearby. Marcus' lasrifle.

He ran to retrieve the weapon as the cascade of bolter fire continued like a thunderous choir, mingled with the oaths of the Sisters and the bellows of the monstrous things they fought. Something charged into his side, winding him, smothering him with its huge arms. As Marcus struggled to free himself, he caught sight of his attacker's wild, lidless eyes. A drooling mouth bore a sneer of ruined teeth. The creature's flesh was mottled, smeared as though scarred by fire, a gaping nasal cavity puffing strings of mucus as it fought to drag him from the fray.

Around its neck, it wore the claw totem of a tribal hunter.

Sister Clarice rose before him, eyes wide in a mask of blood and filth as she slammed her bolter into the skull of Marcus' misshapen kidnapper. The hunter staggered forward, releasing him. As the missionary scrambled for his lasrifle, Sister Clarice fired a torrent of bolter rounds into the stricken creature, the blaze illuminating a look of terrible ecstasy on her mud-splattered face. The sound of joyous, sonorous prayer had now joined the surrounding clamour.

Marcus snatched the lasrifle and turned, seeking targets. He saw another of the malformed hunters thrust the butt of his pickaxe into Sister Clarice's face, breaking her nose anew. The Battle Sister staggered back, snorting through the blood bubbling over her lips as the hunter gathered himself for an overhead swing, aiming to bury the point of his weapon in Clarice's head while she was still dazed. Marcus already had the lasrifle to his shoulder, and fired a blistering red bolt through the back of the creature's skull.

Sister Clarice looked up. Spraying blood as she sang, she joined her Sisters in prayer, her eyes wide, enraptured. Their resounding hymn drowned the cries of the retreating hunters fleeing into the mist-shrouded trees. Marcus fired wildly after their routed attackers. His heart soared as he joined the Sisters in song, the air thick with reeking gunsmoke. Sister Clarice gestured for him to cease fire as the hunters disappeared back into the mist.

But Marcus could hear them howling anew. They had rallied and were charging once more, darting through the cover of the mist and trees back towards the squad. The Battle Sisters did not return fire. Another figure was already running through the mist towards the hunters; a figure wielding a snarling eviscerator with both hands.

Sister Adamanthea surged through the trees like a crashing wave, twirling the chainsword, guiding its immense weight, sweeping through trees and bodies alike and casting a crimson trail in her wake. She fought without fear, reckless as the hunters' mattocks struck sparks from her armour. She struck back like a maddened serpent, making no effort to parry, only to kill, hurling herself into the fray as if to embrace death.

Marcus was reminded of the Sisters Repentia, those of the Adepta Sororitas exiled for terrible transgressions of the Imperial Creed. These disgraced souls took up the red rags of the penitent and sought redemption on the battlefield. Armed with nothing but faith and a ceremonial eviscerator, they fought in the very teeth of every conflict, drawn to the most desperate of odd, berserk martyrs gambling their survival upon the omnipotent Emperor's infrequent willingness to see them spared.

Seeing her in combat, Marcus couldn't help but wonder whether Sister Adamanthea had once walked the path of the Repentia. Absolution – let alone survival – was so rare it was considered a miracle.

Adamanthea's squad murmured blessings and prayers of reverence, some kneeling, some thumbing the beads of their rosariuses as Adamanthea spun her chainsword from victim to victim, each body parting like curtains to reveal the next. To her fellow Sisters of Battle, the Dominion Superior was a living embodiment of the Emperor's grace. This woman enacted the holy miracles about which Marcus merely preached.

Prove your worth.

The thought came, and he felt himself bolstered once again. He would help the Sisters purge this place of evil. He would battle alongside Sister Adamanthea, comrades in faith and arms. He would return to the tribe victorious, living proof that the Emperor's will had prevailed. He would be revered by the tribe as a prophet, and, as the Imperial Creed spread, his legend would surpass Adamanthea's own. His legs shook with adrenaline. His breath tightened, making him giddy. Yes, his own legend was almost within reach.

'Casualties?' said Adamanthea, her face drenched in gore, her hair dripping. Marcus realised the hunters were all dead and she had returned to her squad.

'Nothing prayer cannot mend,' reported one of the Sisters.

Adamanthea's sense of stillness had returned. It was as though she had spent all her living energy on combat and ossified once more into a woman of stone. She was staring at one of the hunters' bodies.

'Your missing tribesmen,' she said without looking up at Marcus. 'As I expected.'

'But did you expect this?' said Marcus, pointing at the corpse's face.

The flesh looked as though it had been somehow creamed onto the skull like clay. Fish-like eyes gazed in opposite directions, the mouth impossibly crooked, the features in disarray as though clumsily assembled. No natural predator had done this. Something had corrupted these hunters, mutated them, bent them to its will.

Once again, Marcus could sense that whispering static in the air. The more he focused upon it, the more it seemed to somehow emanate from within the cathedral ahead. His mouth felt suddenly dry. His limbs trembled as if eager to carry him up those stairs and destroy whatever lurked beyond. He felt fear only as a distant thing, trivial next to the grand destiny the Emperor was offering him.

One of the Dominions called to Adamanthea, relaying a message from her vox-feed. 'It seems the Rhinos have located another bridge. It's intact, a few miles to the south. They've requested permission to join us.'

'No,' cried Marcus before Adamanthea could reply. Her eyebrows peaked in rare surprise.

'We need no such aid against these wretches,' he told her, breathless with excitement. 'Hunters from the other tribes have disappeared as well. We face a mere few dozen more. That's all. I'm sure of it!'

'Stray animals was your last hypothesis, brother,' said Adamanthea.

Marcus stemmed an angry retort. 'We must move now. Strike before they can gather.'

'I saw one of them try to capture him, Sister,' said Clarice, gesturing towards Marcus. The lower half of her face was still caked with blood from her ruined nose. 'It could have killed him. Instead it tried to carry him away, like it wanted him alive.'

Adamanthea silenced Marcus as he went to respond. 'Return to the transports, Sister Clarice,' she said. 'And take Brother Marcus with you.'

A chill shot through him. He stammered, the inside of his head hissing with static, words of protest refusing to form.

'Do not fear, brother,' said Adamanthea, her metallic voice as cold as ever. 'We shall clear the site for you, but the honour shall remain yours, for the sake of your oath to the tribe.'

Marcus touched the painted claw dangling from the cord around his throat, suddenly reminded of its presence.

'If you truly wish to ensure this world be brought into the light,' she added, 'if you truly serve the Throne above all else, then you will return with Sister Clarice and do so without argument.'

Marcus felt her words strip him of his destiny. He felt it as keenly as though he were being skinned. The zealot despised him, wanted an excuse to claim his glory for her own. She turned away, her voice amplified to a brazen roar that galvanised all who heard it.

'Sororitas! The Emperor's grace is mysterious indeed. He sent us to this world to hunt beasts. Instead we find corruption and heresy. The Sisters of the Valorous Heart shall purge these sacred walls of the mutant's presence, and that of his progenitor, whatever it may be.'

She cradled her dripping eviscerator as though it were her child, her eyes glazing as she envisioned some murderous rapture.

'For by Lucia, we shall not suffer the mutant to live!'

'Ave Imperator!' cried her squad, clutching their rosariuses, voices ecstatic. Sister Clarice took Marcus' shoulder, her touch sending a current of terror through his body, rousing him.

He jerked his elbow into her face, pulverising her wounded nose. He heard her gasp with surprise and pain as he bolted towards the cathedral, gripping his lasrifle. The squad gave chase. Power-armoured bodies pounded after him as he sprinted through mud, vaulted over broken stone, dodged every root that threatened to snare his feet. It was as though the Emperor's will was guiding him past every obstacle, ensuring nothing impeded him from grasping his destiny, a destiny that Sister Adamanthea – in her arrogance – had tried to deny him. He heard her synthesised yell ring through the fog. She was far behind him now. He felt like laughing, his limbs trembling, electrified.

His rosarius bounced at his thigh, flashing in the evening gloom. Armed with nothing but faith and lasfire, Marcus Amouris would prove his worth indeed. He would draw the mutants to him, engage them in time for the Battle Sisters to join him. Together, they would cleanse this place – but the fight would be instigated by *him*, not her. Tonight's triumph would be the cornerstone of his legend on this world.

He could no longer hear the cries of the Battle Sisters. He had left them far behind, swallowed up by the mist. He ran on, spraying hot spittle with every panting breath, as the mist cleared before him, finally revealing the towering flight of stairs that ascended into the cathedral.

Marcus thought he should probably stop and give the squad a chance to catch up. Instead he found himself bounding up the broken stairs, ignoring the agony in his legs, the fire in his lungs, his breath smoking before him.

Prove your worth. Prove your worth.

His racing heart seemed to pound out the words. The thought flowed through him, animating him, working him like a puppet. He stared at the dark archway of the cathedral above. It looked like a maw poised to devour him. Exhausted, he finally willed himself to stop, to wait for the Battle Sisters to at least draw near. But his body refused to obey.

Cold horror consumed Marcus as he realised some invisible force had taken possession of him, was driving him up the stairs, sending his lungs into convulsion, choking him as he ran.

He stumbled, fell, the respite a blessing. But his arms and legs were already forcing him upright, sending waves of fresh agony through his tortured body. As he rose, the beaded chain of his rosarius snagged on a crack in the step. He willed his hand to reach out and free it, but his limb did no such thing. Instead his wilful body strained until the chain snapped and Marcus found himself resuming his agonised ascent. He heard the rosarius chime like a bell as it bounced down the steps and found he was unable even to cry out in despair. The force that had taken hold compelled him up the last of the stairs and onwards, his every step a torment as he staggered through the darkened archway and into the ruined cathedral.

The walls loomed either side of him, tidal waves of wreckage. The immense vaulted ceiling had succumbed to gravity millennia ago, the fallen detritus creating meadows of ruin far below. Marcus stumbled around the remains of an iron chandelier the size of a drop-pod. He panted like an animal, his lungs begging for breath, but his legs gave him no mercy. He was running towards fires that burned half a mile away in the cathedral's crossing, dimly illuminating the rows of cavernous arches that gaped like some colossal choir. As he dashed past each darkened portal, Marcus thought he could see pale figures stirring within, but his head refused to turn and look.

Prove your worth, Marcus Amouris.

The words were not a thought. They were a whisper; a voice that was not his own, that had never been his own. They were uttered by the force that was drawing him towards the fires ahead. Terror seized him.

Surrender your weapon.

He felt his hands loosen around the lasrifle. Then, something stopped him from releasing it. Whatever it was, it broke the awful spell and his legs gave way instantly, dropping him at the foot of a hill of rubble. He lay there, helpless and gasping. Voices whispered from all directions, promising the glories that awaited him upon reaching his sacred destination.

But another voice had risen among the whispers, and was now drowning them in glorious song.

'*A morte perpetua, domine, libra nos.*'

A chorus of fearless female voices. Their chanting refrain rang about the halls like church bells, driving away the darkness, returning strength and agency to Marcus' exhausted limbs. He gathered himself, then froze. A pale, ape-like thing was clambering down the rubble towards him.

It was naked and genderless, lidless eyes staring, open-mouthed as its flesh oozed up its body like molten wax, like a candle dissolving in reverse. It appeared to be of the same corrupted species as the hunters, but in an even more unfinished state of evolution. It resembled a figure crudely sculpted from some living clay. Marcus fired in panic as it pounced, livid red bolts flashing past its head before two more lanced through its chest, killing it. He turned to flee and saw salvation mounting the fallen stone some distance behind him.

Black power-armoured bodies seemed to materialise out of the gloom like angels, their pale, chanting faces framed by curtains of black hair as they unleashed a booming hail of flickering bolter-fire. Marcus threw himself to the ground as more half-melted figures exploded about him, showering him in gobbets of hot, steaming flesh.

Sister Adamanthea seized the air, impassioned with faith as she sang before her Dominions. Her scarred features were tight with rage as the vox at her throat amplified her voice to a terrifying roar.

'And though they may cower and hide, naught shall save them from His righteous fury!'

She threw down her hand and the Dominions fired. A chorus of pounding thunder shook clouds of dust and debris from above. Marcus crawled away as the explosive rounds demolished boulders and bodies alike.

Adamanthea howled. 'Neither stone nor steel shall save them from faith unbreakable.'

As if in obedience to her declaration, the Dominions' gunfire dislodged a huge statue, which slowly toppled onto several of the creatures as they fled.

Marcus scurried into an archway where he lay in darkness, panting and weeping, clutching his lasrifle to his chest. He watched from behind a pillar as several more mutants loped past him towards the advancing Battle Sisters. The creatures' forearms bulged as they moved into position among the rubble, their hands swelling into monstrous club-like appendages. One of them squatted beside a chunk of masonry nearby and Marcus recoiled in horror as the skin of its swollen fist peeled back to reveal a toothed, circular maw, the throat of which already glowed with witch-fire.

Marcus felt a horror that plunged into his very bowels.

Witch-fire! These creatures were daemonic in origin, the insane heresy of the warp made fire and flesh. He groped instinctively for his rosarius when he remembered it had been lost, torn from him during his uncontrollable ascent of the stairs outside. He suddenly felt as though he were falling, shrinking, lost to despair. Even the litanies of protection he had spent his life memorising failed to reach his whimpering lips.

The Sisters of Battle marched, faltering neither in step nor in song as the mutants rose and vomited fire from their arms. The inferno brightened the walls, revealing rows of cracked aquila that crested the great arches, watchful as the Battle Sisters below were consumed.

Two of the women staggered forth, their bodies wreathed in flames, bolters still blasting, screaming in either agony or rage. The others returned fire, shredding three of the mutants where they stood. But the creatures flooded in from the depths of the cathedral, joining their obscene brethren as they dowsed the Sisters' line with streams of fire. The Sisters could only answer the blazing volley with more screams and a dwindling holler of bolter-fire.

Weak with terror and exhaustion, Marcus retreated deeper into the archway as one of the mutants approached, the flesh of its face writhing about its staring eyes as it sniffed the air.

'Suffer not the mutant to live!'

The silvery cry of Sister Adamanthea rang out as the Battle Sisters charged, bellowing prayers of strength and protection, their verses unbroken as two more fell screaming in flame. Adamanthea held her eviscerator aloft with both hands and charged at one of the flame-throwing mutants, heedless as the abomination smothered her in fire. The flames washed over her power armour as she sprang, slashing the monster in half. Its cleaved remains hissed and smoked, its fires drowned in blood.

Adamanthea hurtled on without pause. Her blade cart-wheeled through two more mutants as her Battle Sisters destroyed yet more with point-blank bolter-fire, slashed them with combat knives, tore open their flesh with power-armoured fingers.

The heat was becoming unbearable, but the screams of the dying Battle Sisters seemed only to urge their surviving com-rades to sing all the louder. Adamanthea moved to protect them as more pale fiends scampered towards them. Terror gave way to desperation and Marcus raised his lasrifle. But as he tried to steady his quaking sights against the nearest mutant, something fell upon him.

Gelatinous paws wrestled the weapon from his grip and dragged him, shrieking and kicking, from his hiding place. The whispers closed in once again, masking the indomita-ble howls of Sister Adamanthea. Marcus watched the world burn behind him as the mutants dragged him towards what-ever horror awaited at the heart of the cathedral.

The whispers intensified as they hauled him by his arms towards the fires burning at the cathedral's crossing, barely illuminating the vast derelict halls of the transepts either side. He could hear a heavy slopping sound nearby. The mutants led him to what had once been the cathedral's baptistery, laying him before the ruined shrine as though presenting an offering.

Marcus looked up at the crumbling two-storey structure. Cracked pillars surrounded a fathoms-deep baptismal well. Pilgrims from across the galaxy had once come here to be reborn in the light of the Emperor, perhaps to become mis-sionaries, spreading the faith wherever they roamed. Now, the well had become sanctum to something else: a pale, undulating thing that crooned and gurgled at Marcus as he shivered before it.

The daemon rose to get a better look at him, faceless though it was. It stood at least four times the height of a man, its long, slender body a column of molten meat, streaked with pulsing veins. The creature flexed its whip-like limbs, splattering dollops of fat across the floor. Eyeballs streamed around its body, clustering like bubbles as they stared down at the helpless missionary.

The well in which the thing had been lounging brimmed with swirling flesh, liquefied somehow by the alchemy of the warp. This pale sludge slopped and oozed over the lip of the well, creating huge polyps that bulged onto the floor. They swelled and wriggled into humanoid forms that hurried away to join the battle Marcus could hear, still raging far behind him. He gagged, sickened, not only by the majestic sacrilege before him, but also the growing sense that some part of him welcomed it.

He watched, hypnotised as the daemon's face swirled, forming a vortex at its centre, an iris of flesh that seemed to open a hole in the very fabric of reality. It created an aperture through which Marcus could hear things that made his sinews itch, eldritch words with the power to corrupt both minds and flesh, to shape the course of destiny itself.

The daemon extended a welcoming arm towards him, the flesh of its hand spiralling into a tentacle. Marcus gave a silent scream as he saw himself reach, unwittingly, for it.

The tentacle curled around his hand and slithered up his sleeve like a snake. Marcus felt his flesh burn at its touch. The thing dissolved into his arm as it swam through skin and bone towards his throat. He felt its psyche merging with his own. He blinked, and found himself staring down through countless eyes at his own choking body.

Marcus' terror-stricken mind flooded with moving images – snatches of strange memories, frantic and emotive – one streaming after another like water flooding the hull of a sinking ship. The daemon's consciousness was fusing with his own as it absorbed him body and soul. But as his perception expanded, Marcus comprehended with dizzying horror that these memories belonged not to the daemon, but to himself. The creature had infiltrated his mind months ago.

Tendrils of arcane influence had been whispering through the cracks in Marcus' faith without him even realising. The daemon knew his thoughts because it had helped shape them, goading his pride, luring him with his own desire to prove himself.

His awareness alighted upon another image, another soul ensnared by the daemon's psychic coils. Marcus found himself staring through the eyes of a man prowling the forest alongside his brothers. All of them had been hypnotised by alluring whispers in the trees that promised a hunter's bounty, but instead led them to their doom. The image vanished, replaced by that of Adamanthea's stony visage. The daemon had been eavesdropping when Marcus directed her towards the City of Whispers. The image rippled into another. Marcus saw hands before him, gnarled by mutation. The fallen hunters, their bodies smelted into liquid flesh, then clumsily remoulded to carry out the daemon's bidding. The hands were prising ancient stones from their moorings, tearing away the brittle cement of the aeons-old bridge. The image melted away. Now, they lay in wait for the unwitting missionary and his protectors. They wanted him alive, and Marcus felt the daemon gorge on his terror at the thought of it.

Fear. Marcus' heightened senses could feel it radiating from these ruined walls, from the entire city. The outlying tribes had projected their terrors upon this place for generations, drenched it in dread, softening reality like sodden parchment until it tore. The daemon had whispered through this opening for centuries, luring the weak, the proud, the arrogant, rendering their living flesh into a perfect mercurial state, gathering clay enough to form a legion of horrors. But the daemon wanted more.

Marcus gasped as the tentacle fused around his throat. He suddenly comprehended a great web cast across the galaxy. A nexus of threads moored to every world; strands of influence tugging and tensing, teasing fate towards some unfathomable goal. The whispers coalesced into a single word that gurgled up from his throat like vomit: the name of his new master, the dread being that dwelt like a venomous spider at the centre of a cosmic web.

'Tzeentch! Tzeentch! Tzeentch!'

His lord craved an envoy, a missionary, one skilled in the use of subtlety and words, who could whisper the ruinous creed to the outlying tribes, gather worshippers whom the Changer of Ways could warp to his purpose to raise a cathedral of corruption that would radiate his influence around this world and make it his own. Marcus would indeed become a prophet of legend, a chosen of the Architect of Fate. His burning ambition would soon become flesh.

The world went black.

Marcus thought he was dead, only to realise he was lying on the floor, gasping in pain. Beside him lay a severed tentacle, thrashing as it dissolved into ash. A suffocating wave of heat washed over him, brightening the surrounding ruins like dawning sunshine. The daemon was breathing a jet of fire from the vortex in its face, chasing an armoured figure from pillar to pillar. Above the chugging growl of the woman's eviscerator, Marcus could hear a sinister chime, like a blade repeatedly drawn from its sheath. Sister Adamanthea was laughing.

She charged, bounding over broken masonry, lashing out at the liquescent daemon as it heaved itself backwards, gathering itself to unleash another hail of fire. The blade whooshed several times through empty air as Adamanthea slashed the great weapon about her with the grace of a dancer. The creature rolled about the well, avoiding each furious swipe.

It exhaled another column of fire, but Adamanthea had already dodged aside and was hurdling over the gaps in a broken flight of stairs. They led onto a balcony overlooking the well. She dashed around the circumference of the terrace above the daemon, barely outrunning the jet of flame scorching her heels, her eviscerator carried low, trailing behind her like a saw-toothed tail.

She scooped up a rock the size of a cannonball and flung it at the daemon's head. The missile shattered on impact and the creature reeled, flames guttering in its strange maw. Seizing her chance, Adamanthea sprang from the balcony with a shriek like tearing metal as she spun through the air, gathering momentum. She swung her eviscerator around and down and hacked the churning blade into the daemon's exposed neck.

The creature lurched like a tide as its arms whipped up, wrapping around the Battle Sister's wrists, halting her lethal stroke. She snarled in frustration as it prised her hands from the hilt, releasing the trigger. The eviscerator's teeth stilled, quenching the spray of blood and meat. The huge weapon stood silent, lodged deep in the centre of the creature's neck as streams of flesh swirled up its body to seal the grievous wound and remount its half-severed head.

The daemon turned a livid red as it swung Adamanthea through a pillar. A section of the balcony collapsed in an avalanche of dust and tumbling stone as the creature flung her limp body into the floor, the weight of her power armour punching a crater into the slabs. Pinning her with its arms, her eviscerator still embedded in the centre of its neck, the daemon poured a weight of molten flesh down through its limbs on top of Adamanthea, streaming through the cracks in her shattered armour. Her torso enveloped in streaming flesh, the daemon hoisted her into the air, as if it wished to get a better view of her agony as it bent her to its will.

Marcus heard cries and bursts of bolter fire. Whatever was left of Adamanthea's squad was approaching, but the clamour sounded too distant for them to arrive in time to save their commander. Adamanthea struggled weakly beneath the cocoon of rippling flesh and Marcus clapped his hands over his ears, moaning as the whispers intensified once more. The daemon turned crimson as it squeezed her. Marcus could feel it straining to make her speak. Its rage boiled as it tried to force its name from her lips as it had done to him. Through the daemon's eyes, Marcus could see the Battle Sister staring back at him – not with anger, not with hate, but a cold serenity.

She was praying. Her faith was immaculate, impervious to doubt. A single immovable truth existed at the core of her being: though her body may be broken, no force in the galaxy could break her faith. She was the Emperor's will incarnate, His righteous fire was her own. The Adepta Sororitas had no need of augments or gene-engineering, not when their strength flowed fierce and pure from the Emperor himself. Should their bodies be rent asunder it would be because He willed it.

Faith was Sister Adamanthea's true armour. It was also her greatest weapon, the force with which she performed such fearsome miracles upon the battlefield. This was the certainty that burned at the heart of every Battle Sister, a spirit that would endure, ferocious and unyielding, until the very last of their sinews had perished and the Emperor summoned them to dwell in His eternal light. Martyrdom was their immortality. Death only spurred the living to achieve even greater heights of valour. As such, Adamanthea and her Sisters were immortal, their faith a fire unquenchable.

Marcus felt tears streaming down his face in helpless awe of Adamanthea's faith. The daemon fought to break her, but it may as well have been trying to wring words from a stone. It hurled her to the floor with a howl, fragments of broken power armour scattering as the creature smashed her down.

The daemon loomed over the wounded woman, swelling as it guzzled the last of the melted flesh from the reservoir in which it stood. A buckled pauldron slid from Adamanthea's shoulder with a clang. She was clawing steadily up a chunk of a wrecked pillar as she hauled herself upright, blood pooling at her feet. Marcus could feel waves of hate crashing inside the daemon as it glared at the wretched mortal beneath it, an inferno of thwarted rage preparing to erupt.

Adamanthea was still clambering up the broken pillar when the creature abruptly drowned her in fire. The conflagration rose and boiled until it filled the chamber with clouds of flame.

Marcus cowered nearby. He whimpered beneath the scorching heat, his eyes closed, but still seeing what the daemon saw: a churning chaos of flames that would reduce the woman to a smear of ash for her insolence.

A figure burst through the flames like a tiger, clawed hands outstretched. Shielded by faith alone, Sister Adamanthea's body was miraculously intact, as if the firestorm were but a breeze.

She caught the protruding hilt of her eviscerator as she pounced on the daemon's chest. As she clutched the trigger with both hands, the weapon roared into life in a flurry of churning ichor. The daemon staggered back. Adamanthea let herself drop, dragging the blade downwards, unzipping a deluge of gore in her wake.

She landed on the lip of the well as the daemon emptied itself above her. She slashed the creature into chunks as it fell, its severed limbs dissolving in mid-air as she whirled the eviscerator about her. When the daemon's head finally dropped within range, she delivered her final stroke.

Marcus' vision turned black once more. His head spun as he fell into a faint.

Marcus awoke to find three bloodied Battle Sisters kneeling nearby. They were chanting prayers of sanctification, restoring the Emperor's presence to their polluted surroundings. They continued their litanies as Marcus cried out, agony suddenly flooding his body. He stared in horror at his hands, the flesh of which stirred on the bones, winding about his fingers like smoke. He touched his face and the flesh came away on his fingers, like strands of hot tar. The realisation of what the daemon's touch had done to him hit like a blow. He curled up and retched in pain.

'Sister Adamanthea?' His once powerful voice had withered to a croak.

The Dominion Superior knelt beside what remained of her squad. She was drenched in blood and filth. Her brooding green eyes were piercing in her blackened face. Her gorget had been shattered, her vox-grille destroyed, revealing a small cybernetic port in her throat, surrounded by welters of scar tissue.

'Will you hear my confession?' said Marcus, feeling for the corded claw that hung from his neck. He tugged the pendant free and offered it to Adamanthea.

'Return to the village wearing this,' he said. 'Fulfil the hunter's oath in my stead and you will bring this world into the light.'

Adamanthea received the talisman grimly. Her face twitched with a pang of frustration as she absently touched the great scar at her throat, unable to speak.

'*Superbia vocat corruptionem,*' he said, faltering. 'Pride indeed beckons corruption. My love for myself, for my own ambition, exceeded my love for the Throne. Forgive me, Sister.' He raised his hands towards her, as he heard a familiar whisper in his head, the name of the kingly terror that had possessed him.

He gasped before the voice could overwhelm him. 'Suffer not the mutant to live!'

Adamanthea's face seemed to soften at his words, as though he had spoken a spell that brought life to cold stone. She pressed something into his ruined hands.

His rosarius.

'Ave Imperator,' he sobbed, kissing the icon. Adamanthea rose. That terrible rigidity returned to her face. Her surviving Sisters murmured a blessing over her eviscerator as Marcus bowed his head, exposing the back of his neck. He shuddered with grateful tears as the weapon roared into life.

A heartbeat passed before darkness snatched the whispers away.

THE BATTLE FOR MARKGRAAF HIVE

JUSTIN D HILL

'What the hell is happening?' Madzen shouted across to Minka as auto-rounds ricocheted off the rocks about them.

Minka threw the straps of the vox-box off her shoulder and threw herself forwards into cover. She had one eye closed. The other lined her sights up with the head of a heretic. 'They're trying to kill us,' she said between gritted teeth as she moved on to the next target and fired again. A double shot, just in case.

'I guessed that,' he snarled, his cheek pressed against the stock of his own lasrifle. 'I meant…'

She didn't bother to hear what he meant. And when Grogar's heavy bolter opened up, it filled the subterranean chamber with muzzle flashes, fist-sized bolts and a thunder that drowned Madzen's explanation.

A few moments earlier they'd stumbled out of an old sewer pipe into this vaulting space, lit throughout by the luminous green mould that covered ceiling and walls. The catacomb had been broken and reshaped by millennia of hive-quakes. The cracked ceiling sagged, the floor slanted steeply to the left, and a filthy pool filled the sunken end, where vast stalactites stabbed down from the ceiling like the fangs of some prehistoric monster. They'd had a brief moment to get their bearings, and then the ambush had been sprung. And now they were fighting desperately for their lives.

Minka fired a quick salvo into the darkness, lasrifle ready at her shoulder.

The heavy bolter roared once more, strobe-lighting dirty, bestial faces swarming forwards through the gloom.

The Cadians did not panic. They knelt and fired, and fired once again. They were tight, disciplined, experienced. Like Minka, they'd all learned how to strip and fire a lasrifle before they could read. Fighting was more normal than civilian life.

If their attackers had been half-trained, the Cadians would all have been dead now. But they were not. They were hive scum. And worse than that, they were *heretic* hive scum who'd turned their face from the light of the Emperor and deserved nothing more than a las-round to the face. It was like a wild force of nature coming up against the indomitable brickwork discipline of Cadia. And the Cadians cut the heretics down in droves.

At last the roar of the heavy bolter subsided and, for a moment, it seemed the attack was over. All Minka could see was twitching piles of dead and wounded. She scanned the chamber then lowered her lasrifle.

'Over there!' Sergeant Gaskar shouted from the middle of the line. In the darkness and confusion she couldn't see where he was pointing to, but at that moment more heretics erupted from the pool water only yards behind her. Spray hit her face and hands as she spun about.

Too late.

The blow hit her in the middle of her back and punched the air from her lungs. It slammed her face against the rockcrete slab and cut her lip as well. There was blood in her mouth as she whirled round and fired wildly.

The heretic was on her, and she knew in an instant that he was bigger and stronger than her. He bundled her face first into the dirt, his filthy and emaciated arms and legs enveloping her like a spider on her back. His black nails were in her mouth, grabbing at her throat, scratching for her eyes. But she was Cadian. She broke his fingers, dislocated his arm, and then dragged herself up to one knee and gutted him with her bayonet.

She put a pair of las-bolts into his belly, as well. Frekker.

The second wave came up out of the water and through a crack in the ground that allowed them to sneak right up to the line of rubble the Cadians were holding. It got tense, then. And close quarters.

Minka could never tell how long a battle lasted. It could be seconds or hours. The bark of the heavy bolter, the brief flashes of las-bolts, the scrape of knife on bone and steel, the shouts and screams of orders and of pain. She killed and killed and killed, and the intensity of the moment seemed to fill time. But at last Sergeant Gaskar put up a hand and shouted, 'Hold!' and Minka rested a shoulder against the fallen roof-beam before her and realised how much her ribs hurt.

The vox-unit lay on the floor, and two yards from that Madzen lay on his back. His throat had been cut from ear-to-ear. His head was pillowed in a pool of his own gore. She felt sick in her gut. Markgraaf underhive wasn't worth the loss of Cadian lives, especially not Madzen's. Any dead Cadian was a waste. She cursed the braid-wearing frekker who'd dreamed up this mission.

The heretic who'd jumped her was lying a stone's throw away, face down, his back twisted at an unnatural angle. She couldn't see what he'd hit her with, but Throne it hurt. For a moment she relived his attack, felt his fingers on her face, scrabbling for her eyes, in her nostrils, in her mouth. She wanted to kick him again as she pulled her flak-armour plates forwards to see how bad his blow had been. There was no blood. Her fingers felt along the line of her ribs. Nothing broken, she thought, and then let out a long breath.

Sergeant Gaskar started the roll call. Grogar. Matrey. Rellan. Leonov. Aleksei. Isran. Artem too, unfortunately. She shouted her own name.

'Anyone else?' Gaskar shouted.

'Madzen's dead,' Minka shouted, and one by one the fallen were named. They'd lost six troopers. Three in the first seconds to auto-rounds and the others in hand-to-hand combat. Minka watched as the medic, Leonov, knelt by the wounded. There'd been ninety-six troopers in Fifth Platoon when they'd entered the underhive five days earlier.

They had stood on the pollution-grey ashen earthworks and looked up at Markgraaf Hive: a teeming termite mound of humanity that rose precipitously into the sky, burning and trailing a banner of smoke.

'They're under siege up there,' her sergeant said, meaning the patrician hive lords of the Richstar family. The sergeant's name was Fronsak. His regiment, the Cadian 2050th, had been amalgamated with Minka's the year before. He was a solid commander, with the professional manner typical of the Cadian officer class, and made it his duty to obey orders, take objectives and to keep them all alive, as much as possible. 'They're fighting a slow retreat up the hive.'

Minka stretched her head back to take in the mountainous bulk of the hive city. The peak of the massive conglomeration was too high to see with the naked eye. Fronsak handed Minka the magnoculars. She looked up, past the layers of smoke and burning, five miles above her head, to where the isolated white pinnacles and buttresses of the hive sparkled with ice. The hive lords couldn't have had more than thirty levels left to go before they were driven from the top of their home.

She handed the magnoculars back and looked about. Lines of Chimeras idled as the rest of the Cadian force disembarked, platoon by platoon. Further off, Hydra platforms scanned the sky for any counter-attacks, and over the mounds and heaps of slag, she could see lines of local Calibineer troops filing towards them. They looked weary and stoic, quite unlike the Cadians, who stood about with a business-like readiness.

And over the slag heaps a procession of skitarii accompanied three huge, tracked transporters that made the files of armour seem as small as beetles upon the plain.

Upon the back of each carriage, tended by servitors and fussing tech-priests, lay a vast tube hastily painted in the colours of the Richstars, the family whose various branches seemed to run this whole sector of Imperial space.

'What are those?'

'Hellbores,' Fronsak said.

Minka said nothing. They looked like armoured tubes set with drill-teeth at one end. Each of the monstrous forgings was large enough to fit a platoon inside. A tunnelling transport that ground its way through earth and bedrock, under fortifications and behind the enemy lines. Which meant they would be sent deep into the heretic territory. A suicide mission if ever she'd seen one.

An hour later her platoon had filed up the ramp into the cramped troop compartments inside the Hellbore. They were rammed in. Face-to-face. Shoulder-to-shoulder. No room to drop a grenade, no way to pull a knife. The doors slammed and locked. A grating whine started as the tunnelling mechanism began to turn, and they were all thrown violently forwards as the Hellbore slid from its mountings and started to drill through the topsoil as easily as ploughing through snow.

The difficulty began when its ceramite teeth came up against bedrock and rockcrete foundations. The grinding mechanism screamed. The tube juddered, and they could hear the rumble of hive-quakes set off by the burrowing. From there on the journey stretched for hours, a gut-wrenching ordeal almost as unpleasant as warp transit. There had been sickening lurches, the constant noise and the habitual terror that their transport might break down or fail, or that a hive-quake might crush them all.

The heat and motion made her feel sick. What if we meet rock too tough to grind through? she thought. A cold sweat covered her hands, her forehead, the small of her back. Her stomach lurched. Her mouth was full of saliva. There was no room for her to vomit, though others did. She swallowed her bile back. It went up her nose. She could not keep it down. She shut her eyes as the stink began to fill the stifling chamber. She prayed to the Throne, to the Omnissiah, to Saint Hallows, the patron saint of Cadia.

Hellbore indeed, she thought, finally realising how apt the name was.

It was almost a relief when the thing finally jolted to a halt, throwing them all forwards into each other. Lights flashed, a klaxon rang, the assault ramps crashed down and they spilled out into the half-collapsed tunnels of the lowest strata of Markgraaf.

There had been no sign of the enemy, just dripping cata-combs that dated from the earliest days of the hive. The broken tunnels and sump-holes forced them to break into small units. It was slow-going into a world that had not seen the light of the sun for thousands of years. At first they used lumens, but everything was covered in a thick, wet mould that gave off a faint green luminescence, and once their eyes grew accustomed to its illumination, they saved their power packs for moments of need such as when con-sulting their maps.

Each squad had been issued with a rudimentary schematic, a rough impression of the hive, with their objective – the Great Chamber – clearly marked. They picked their way along crazed tunnels that meandered away, some collapsed, others flooded, or cut their way through vast pale slugs of congealed fat and filth from the city above, not knowing if they were drawing closer to the centre of the hive or not.

'What is this Great Chamber?' Ansen asked at one point.

'There's some kind of contraption apparently. Old mine shaft,' Fronsak told them. 'It's the only place where there's access to the upper levels.'

Or that was what they all had thought. The heretics clearly had other ways down into the underhive, because within hours it seemed that the Imperial counter-attack had been discovered and heretics were swarming into the under-hive like rats. They were a motley band of tattooed gangers and underhive scum, drawn from the deepest pits of the mountain-city, their emaciated bodies burning with the conviction of heresy.

The Cadian thrust turned into a nightmarish city-fight in the collapsed intestines of the underhive. Sergeant Fronsak died on the second day of fighting, and there'd been three more sergeants since as the sump-war became a living hell of heretics and rock falls. Life by life the strength of the Cadian 101st was being whittled away, like a cathedral full of candle flames extinguished one by one. The longer it went on, the more Minka felt that she was part of a dying breed, a lost way of life, a species on the edge of extinction.

Now she crouched in this unknown chamber, her ribs aching from the blow the heretic had dealt her. She looked to Sergeant Gaskar. 'So,' she said, 'which way now?'

Frekked if I know, Gaskar's expression said. He jumped one of the cracks in the rockcrete floor, skirted the side of the water, pulled out his lumen and used it to pick his way round the edge of the flooded end of the chamber. A fallen metal joist blocked the way between two stalactites. It was embedded in pale drip-lime. He clambered over it, brushed the luminous mould off his hand. It was an unconscious gesture that left a glowing smear across his chest. Perfect target for a sniper to aim at. Gaskar clearly thought the same thing. He cursed and rubbed at the smear with the cuff of his sleeve, scratching his chin as if thinking. 'Looks like the hivers came this way,' he said, pointing to the far end of the chamber.

He turned and looked at them. From where she sat, Minka could see what Gaskar saw. The squad needed to rest. They were exhausted. You could read it in their faces.

Gaskar spat and pushed his helmet back from his head.

'All right. Rellan and Aleksei, stand guard. Everyone else, get some rest.'

Grogar and Matrey set up the heavy bolter in the middle of the chamber while Minka found a hole next to Isran where they could watch the pool. Isran was one of those strange creatures who kept his lean body going on a combination of liquor, stimms and lho. He sat with his lasrifle between his legs, his hands folded over the top end, staring out into the darkness. Minka took a ration pack from her breast pocket. The foil seals were broken. She used her nails to pick the foil from the semi-hydrated slab within and held it out. 'Want some?'

Isran shook his head. 'Nah,' he said, still staring out into the dark.

There was a tremble in the air. She lifted her hand and felt the vibrations come again, stronger this time. Dust drifted down from a crack in the ceiling and freckled the dark water's surface. She thought for a moment of the vast, oppressive weight of the hive above her head and wished she hadn't.

The rumble came again, longer now.

'Think that's a hive-quake?' Minka said.

'Could be,' Isran said. His tone said there was nothing they could do about it.

The trembling faded. Minka ate some more. It came back a few moments later. It didn't sound like hive-quake. But there was another sound. 'What the hell is that?' she said. It sounded like wet mouths feeding, out there in the shadows.

'Rats,' Isran said. Vermin and battlefields went together. It was nothing to be surprised at.

Minka washed the dehydrated food down with a short swig from her battered tin canteen, then dropped the ration pack to the floor. She looked about. Leonov had shut his eyes, but the rest of them were sitting watching, cleaning their weapons, checking their webbing, smoking lhos. Minka shut her eyes and imagined herself anywhere but here. She found her memory taking her back to a Whiteshield camp in the highlands above Kasr Myrak. She had been only fourteen or so, a young Whiteshield with a head full of dreams of fighting for the Imperium of Man. She remembered how her hair had whipped across her face as she watched the dawn breaking over Cadia, how the rising sun had lit the jagged mountain peaks, before cresting the ridge and bathing the world with light. The sun did not give heat at dawn, but it did give hope, and she closed her eyes and remembered that moment now. Cadia. Sunrise. The promise of another day to fight against their foes.

The trembling came again. Isran smiled. 'Maybe that's our reinforcements coming.'

Minka reached back for the vox. She'd been lugging this useless box around with her ever since the operator, Hama, got himself killed. It was three days ago that they'd last heard anything from HQ, and that had only been some high-ranking idiot giving orders as if there were any order down here to impose. Almost out of boredom she lifted the receiver and flipped it on. There was nothing but static. She tapped it against the wall. The note of the static remained unchanged.

'Turn that off, will you!' Artem hissed.

Every squad had a bastard, and Artem was theirs. Minka ignored him.

'I said, switch it off.'

'Frekk you,' Minka told him.

Then Artem was looming up out of the shadows. His eyes were wide and white. They shone in the sickly light of the chamber. He grabbed the vox handset and slammed it against the broken slab of rockcrete. It was Munitorum issue, designed for rough conditions – the toughest the galaxy could throw at them – and the blow barely scratched it.

She gave him a look that said, *That's Munitorum equipment, break it at your peril*. But he slammed it against the rock again.

'Sit down!' Gaskar told him.

'Turn the frekking thing off will you!' he shouted and threw it back at her. 'It's useless,' Artem said. 'Useless. Understand?'

Minka despised weakness, and she saw how the underhive had broken him. When he came forward she shoved him back, both hands, the heels of her palms connecting with his sternum. 'Get a hold of yourself!' she said, but he kept coming, and the third time she reached for her knife. The sharp, ground steel gleamed pale green in the luminous light.

Minka wasn't letting a frekk-head like Artem screw about with her. Her hand trembled. Not with fear but with fury. She could feel that surge of strength rising through her. 'Try me,' she said as he came for her again.

Suddenly Sergeant Gaskar was between them. He shoved them both back. 'Stop this now,' he shouted. 'Throne! You're Cadians!'

'Cadia's fallen!' Artem hissed and threw his hand off. 'Didn't you hear?'

'I said sit down, trooper. That is an order.'

Artem hesitated for a moment.

'I said that's an *order*.'

Artem turned and sat down. Gaskar turned to Minka.

'You, too.'

'Yes, sir,' she said and smiled as she slumped back against the cavern wall. Isran gave her a sideways look that was hard to read. Minka realised she still had her knife in her hand. It was non-standard issue, a heavy blade that curved in on itself. Colonel Rath had given her one after Cadia. 'You cannot unsheathe it without giving it blood,' he said.

Minka had been with Rath throughout the siege of her home kasr. Now it was in her hand, unbloodied. In a casual, almost practised gesture, she ran the blade along the inside of her arm. Just enough to raise a bracelet of blood beads along her skin before slamming it back into the sheath.

She flicked the vox off. The sound of munching grew louder. She sat up and looked about. No one else seemed to have noticed it.

'Sergeant Gaskar,' she called. 'Can you hear that?'

'What?'

Something was tugging at her foot. She thought it was Isran at first, then remembered the rats. She looked down and saw what looked like a giant maggot fretting at the leather of her boot. It was as long as her forearm, a blind, translucent creature with a dark head and round, munching jaws.

She leaped up in disgust, stamped on the thing, ground her heel on its head. Even Isran stared down. 'Throne,' he said, and called out to the others. 'You should see this!'

Gaskar and Matrey stared at the maggot. Leonov found another one as big as a dog and lit it up with las-bolts. The smell of burnt flesh hung in the air. The sound of eating mouths grew louder. 'Oh, Throne,' Rellan said, his lumen stabbing out into the darkness. 'There are hundreds of them.'

The floor of the chamber seemed to be moving. 'Time to move out,' Sergeant Gaskar announced abruptly. They stood up, slinging their packs onto their backs. Minka hauled the vox up as Gaskar led them down the centre of the chamber. He jumped the crack and started along the middle of the room, keeping well away from where the maggots were feeding on the dead.

They were halfway along the chamber floor when they came across another crack, deeper and darker than the rest. It was nearly two yards wide and exhaled a cold, rancid smell. Gaskar led them across, and when it was Minka's turn, she put her thumbs through the vox-unit straps, checked her footing and jumped. Isran caught her and hauled her forwards. She turned, about to help Leonov across, when a las-round flared out from across the sump-lake. It hit Matrey in the shoulder, and he grunted with pain. More las-bolts flashed in from the right, and then the left, and in an instant it seemed they were surrounded, half on one side and half on the other.

Isran pulled Minka down to the side of the crack, where a roof-fall provided cover. Gaskar shouted bearings to each pair as they started to return fire, and Grogar set the tripod down, kicked the ammo feed to the side and started to shoot.

In a moment the sump-lake surface was wild water, with the boots of charging warriors, stitched shots of heavy bolters and the hissing steam of las-rounds all churning it up. A small figure climbed up between two stalactites. It stood for a moment, hands on the stalactites to either side, silhouetted by the luminous glow, crucified in silhouette. Minka fired and missed. She cursed herself. She had a moment to aim once more and made sure this time. She felt the hum of her lasrifle as the power pack engaged and spat a bolt of blue-white out of the barrel.

The flare filled her vision, and the bolt lit an eye-searing stripe across the pool surface. It up-lit the target's face for a moment – a shaggy mess of hair, a snarling face that might once have been human – then the las-bolt connected and kinetic energy turned to searing heat.

Minka had seen the puff of steaming flesh many times. The figure fell into the lake with a splash, but where it had stood, three more figures appeared, clambering forwards. And when they were down, there were five behind them.

'They're coming up out of the water!' Isran said.

She nodded and saw the point on the far side of the pool where they were emerging.

They worked together. She was in awe of his ferocious rate of fire. He was calm and methodical, as if he were working his way through the firing range. 'It's easy,' he always said. 'You pick out the highest priority target, kill it, then move on to the next.'

Minka felt a maggot at her boot. She kicked at it and aimed once more. Gaskar was shouting orders. It sounded like Aleksei had been hit as well. Leonov crawled over to him.

'Flesh wound,' Leonov called out. He was scrabbling through his pack for a medikit. Artem was shouting about the worms. Minka was too busy shooting to turn and look at what was behind her.

'They're coming up from the crack!' Gaskar shouted.

Minka risked a look behind her, and at that moment she saw a spinning grenade land near her elbow. Time slowed. She saw that it was Munitorum issue. Plain green drab with stencilled white serial numbers. She knew that it would kill both her and Isran if it went off, and that it would go off within seconds or even milliseconds, so instinctively she screamed a warning as she batted it back into the crack. She had no idea if Isran heard or not. She was ducking when the explosion went off. Shrapnel hit the back of her head and, to her left, a demo charge went off with its sudden distinctive *whoosh!* which brought part of the roof down. The force of the blast threw her down hard enough to knock her face into the rock before her. She couldn't tell if her flak jacket had saved her. Her shoulder ached, her lip was bleeding, there was blood on her chin and on the back of her palm.

A shape loomed over her. Her helmet clanged as metal scraped along it. It connected on her collarbone. She snarled and drove her bayonet into the figure's groin. She fired twice just to make sure, the las-bolts burning deep holes as they buried themselves into her assailant's soft, coiled guts.

She had to twist out of the way to pull the bayonet free. She staggered to her feet and slammed the lasrifle's butt down into the heretic's face, before loading a fresh power pack into the weapon.

To her left she heard Rellan go down. Isran was half-buried in rubble. Throne knew how they'd get out of this fix. Isran was moaning. She wanted to help him, but her focus was forward. So much so that when a hand rested on her shoulder she jolted and spun about, expecting a knife in the kidney or neck. But looking down at her was a Cadian. An older man. Grey stubble. Lop-sided face. His name-badge read 'Bardski.'

Bardski barely acknowledged her. He didn't stop to talk but knelt beside her and started to pump las-bolts across the chamber. Through the green glow she could see more Cadians picking their way stealthily forwards. A motley collection of about thirty survivors, pausing every so often to aim and fire. Thank the Emperor, she thought, but then she saw the figure at the back. He wore a dark leather cloak and a peaked hat. She caught Bardski's eye, and he gave her an apologetic look.

'Why the Throne did you have to bring him along?' Minka said. A commissar was all they needed.

Minka helped Isran pull himself out from under the girder that had fallen over him. His left arm was clearly broken. His face was pale. He swallowed back his pain as Minka plunged the needle into his shoulder. 'Morphia,' she said. 'Won't take long to kick in.'

Isran nodded. His eyes wandered, and she thought he might faint. 'Heh,' she said, tapping his cheek. 'You were right. It's our reinforcements.'

Commissar Haan wasted no time in introducing himself to those who were left of Minka's platoon. His face was disfigured by an old burn scar that pulled the side of his mouth back into a fierce snarl, and he seemed almost angry that Minka's squad had got to the cavern before them.

Minka could see at least five different units within his warband. Mostly Cadians; a couple of local Calibineers, their velvet jackets smeared with mud and mould; and a lone Valhallan Ice Warrior in a greatcoat and fur cap. The coat looked two sizes too big, like he'd taken it from a dead body, and his face was gaunt.

The commissar looked over his ragtag collection of troopers as a butcher would inspect his knife. 'Any sign of the Great Chamber?'

'None, sir,' Gaskar said. 'The hivers came from the water. And from up this crack here.'

The commissar looked down into the darkness and seemed not to find what he was looking for. He looked across the pool. 'I don't see where.'

'They came up out of the water. There must be a sump-hole there.'

The commissar seemed to like this. 'Right,' he said. 'That must be the way up.'

Gaskar didn't wait for the order. 'Cadians, forward!' he called out, and stepped down into the water, pushing the floating bodies aside, feeling his way as he waded knee-deep towards the other side of the chamber.

One by one the troopers followed, strung out with their lasrifles raised high through the dragon-maw of stalactites. Gaskar shone his lumen down into the water. 'I can't see anything,' he said. The spear of white light panned back and forth, looking for an opening among the sunken rocks.

Commissar Haan pushed forwards. 'It's there somewhere.' He took the lumen himself, but couldn't find anything. At last, he said, 'You, soldier. Give me your lasrifle.'

'Me, sir?' Artem said, blinking as the lumen shone in his face.

'Yes,' the commissar said, turning the light down into the water again. As he did so something flicked through the beam. It was the tail of a maggot, twitching itself through the water.

'What is that?' Commissar Haan said.

'Hive maggots,' Sergeant Gaskar said. 'This room seems to be full of them.'

Commissar Haan pulled out his bolt pistol, used the lumen to locate the maggot's body. It was a yard long and thick as a man's waist, wriggling as it tried to push itself through the water. He fired a single bolt-round into the water. The spray hit them all. No one could tell if he'd killed the maggot or not.

'I can feel one,' someone said behind Minka. 'Throne! It just bit me.'

Minka could feel unseen creatures brush past their legs. Two maggots surfaced next to her. She drew her knife and slashed at them, but even cut in half they continued to writhe. She could feel discomfort start to turn to panic as another man was bitten.

'I said into the water!' the commissar ordered.

Artem's hand started shaking. 'But the maggots...' he started.

Commissar Haan's face showed disgust. 'The God-Emperor of Mankind does not care about hive maggots!'

The leather-coated figure stepped up beside him. Minka knew what was coming. She'd seen it before. Heard the moment recounted many times around campfires and during long warp transits. Seen men lift up their fingers, pistol-style to the side of the head and say the words 'In the name of the God-Emperor!'

She felt that it could have been any of them. Anyone could be standing there now with the cold barrel of a bolt pistol resting against their skin. 'Into the water, trooper,' the commissar ordered.

Artem closed his eyes and the sight transfixed Minka for a moment. She willed him to move. Willed him not to let his life end like this. At least for Cadia, she thought. For the shock troopers.

But then the bolt pistol fired: a bright flash of light and a moment later the report. The shot floored Artem sideways like a hammer to the head. Minka felt cold dread. This was how it would end, she thought, as the commissar turned towards her.

'You!' he snapped.

Minka could not move.

'Yes, sir!' It was the man beside her who spoke. The Valhallan. She turned in astonishment as he pulled off his greatcoat and his cap and let them drop. She felt a moment's shame as the Valhallan plunged into the water and the commissar used the lumen to follow his course. But then the man exploded out of the depths and the commissar caught hold of his webbing and dragged him up. The largest maggot they had seen was hanging off his shoulder. Its body was pulsing as it tightened its grip, dark gobbets of blood moving down into its gut.

Minka slashed with her knife. The first blow ripped the maggot's belly open, the second cut it in half, but still the head clung on, and even as she dragged at it, the mouth-part would not come free. Suddenly the chamber shook. It was the dull roar she'd heard before, but now it was raging, and loud, and closing.

The whole company stopped and stared behind them. They looked back in disbelief as a lone figure entered the chamber and straightened to its full height. It seemed to fill the vaulting space. It was a giant – eight feet of power-armoured horror – with glowing red eyes that turned towards them and focused on them.

The thing was wrapped in chains; skulls hung from its loincloth, and impaled on the brass spikes that rose from its pauldrons were the decapitated heads of Imperial Guardsmen – Cadians, by the look of it – from which fresh gouts of gore still dripped. The monster stalked forwards, exuding pure evil.

Each leg was a column of plated might; each footfall was the crunch of ceramite on shattered rockcrete. It paced to where they had fought the last engagement and crossed the two-yard crack in a single stride. One great boot splashed down into the water. Only then did it engage the weapon that it held, a giant chainaxe that made the whole chamber shake. It was the roar she had heard as she'd eaten. It was the sound of doom. Of murder. Of unrelenting frenzy.

And then the axe fell silent. 'Throne help us,' Gaskar said as the figure took another giant step closer. Minka took an involuntary step backwards. She had a brief awareness of the Valhallan struggling to find his footing as it approached. It had the manner of a jungle cat coming across a wounded gazelle. It savoured the expectation of slaughter.

Commissar Haan rallied them. 'In the name of the Emperor!' And somehow Grogar spun the heavy bolter round, and shots hammered the air about the giant. The beleaguered soldiers of the Astra Militarum fired in a blinding fusillade. Las-bolts flared out and many of them hit, but nothing stopped it. Not bolt-rounds. Not las-bolts. Not hive maggots. The single warrior was like a tank rolling towards them. It did not slow or pause, nor did it accelerate. It triggered the chainaxe again just as it reached their lines.

It cut the nearest Cadian into two unequal halves, and stove in the ribcage of another with a massive armoured fist. Commissar Haan held his ground, but it didn't help him. His bolt pistol barked, the rounds pinging off the ruddy armour as he went for a weak spot. He did not find one. The gory blades of the chainaxe whined as their attacker swung, and the pitch of its engine went up a note as the ceramite teeth snagged on skull – but then it was through, and the chainaxe opened the commissar's torso up from neck to sternum, like a zipper on a camo suit. The commissar splashed down to his knees, and he paused for the briefest of moments as if praying in front of the Golden Throne, before slamming ruined face first into the bloody water.

The remaining men panicked. It made no difference. There was nowhere to flee to.

Isran shouted something about Cadia before he died to a blow of the chainaxe, which sprayed shreds of flesh and flak armour, bone and blood, webbing and human hair across those remaining.

Leonov's head tumbled before her as her blade scraped uselessly across the ceramite, and snagged in the piping of a knee joint. The vast creature pistol-whipped Bardski. The casual blow dislocated his skull from the vertebrae of his neck and showering his teeth across the chamber. Matrey went low, hoping to stab through the thing's groin-armour, but he died as its power-armoured knee connected with his face and broke his neck with a sharp snap.

Terror held Minka in its cupped palm as the denizen of hell turned towards her. It seemed to fill the chamber, four-foot broad shoulders and visored mask turning to focus on her with the eyes of a predator. She took another step back, and another, and stumbled as the ground beneath her gave way.

The liquid was shockingly cold on her scalp and neck. Something squirmed past her face. She felt the rough surface of a maggot's mouth brush past her ear and kicked furiously down. She kept expecting to hit the bottom but she fell a yard or more. She kicked up for air as the chainaxe roared down at the place where she had just been. Water erupted from its spinning teeth as she sucked in a breath and ducked down once more, pulling herself deeper. Something caught her ankle. She wanted to scream but she couldn't waste the breath. She felt for the edges of the rock. They cut and stung, but she did not care.

A maggot's smooth, bulging body pressed against her face. Her hands scrabbled forwards, searching for an opening. As she went deeper she could not tell what was a passageway and what was a contour of the rock. She found what she thought was an opening but butted up against stone. She backed up, found another and hit a wall of slime that might have been a maggot nest, and had to retreat again.

She had to exhale. The need went from insistent to a compulsion. But if she did she knew she would die. She had to go down. The heretics had done it. They must have come this way, and if they could do this, then by the Golden Throne, she could as well.

At last she found a way forward, but it was too narrow. She let the vox-unit go, but felt her shoulder pads catch on either side. She tore at her webbing. She could feel her lungs bursting within her chest. She fought so violently she cut her hand on the sharp rocks. There was something behind her. She felt her feet being grabbed and let her scream out in bubbles, and sucked in a lungful of filthy water that made her choke and gasp. She couldn't go forwards. Couldn't go back. She kicked free, but her lungs were full of filth.

She wrenched at the clips that held her armour in place. She got one arm free, then the other, and suddenly a hand was on her, dragging her up.

Minka found herself lying on a stone floor. She wheezed and coughed for what seemed like an eternity as vomit and filth came out of her nose and mouth.

At last, she opened her eyes and sucked in the sweetest breath she had ever inhaled. Wiping the water from her face, she blinked, trying to see where she was.

'Are you all right?' a voice said.

She blinked again as she pushed herself up to her knees. She couldn't make out who was talking to her. 'Who is that?' she said.

'Me.'

'Who the frekk is me?'

'Grogar,' the voice said.

She cleared her eyes and looked at the heavy bolter gunner in disbelief. She was full of questions but they could wait. None of that mattered. They were here and they were alive.

'Where are we?' Minka said.

Grogar pulled his lumen from its pouch. He wiped the casing dry, and gave her a look to say, *Let's see if this works*.

It did. The light flickered for a moment, then held true. He turned the beam upwards. In the circle of light, they could see a vaulted ceiling, mouldy plaster shapes crumbling away and, here and there, the glimmer of gold.

In niches in the wall there were statues. Somewhere nearby they could hear running water.

'Is this the Great Chamber?' Minka said, her feet squelching within her sodden boots.

'No,' he said slowly. 'It can't be. It was supposed to be a way up into the hive.'

They emptied water from their footwear, then Minka led Grogar over the fallen masonry to the nearest statue, which was about thirty feet across the tiled floor. It stood in a niche carved with interlocking aquilas. The figure stood on a bronze pedestal, thick now with verdigris, half-buried in dust and dirt and rubble.

It looked like it had once held a spear, but the spear had gone, and the other arm was broken off at the elbow. Despite the mould and the dust, it was unmistakably the figure of a female saint. Minka looked for an inscription. She could not find one, but she felt an immediate closeness with the helmed figure. She reached up and put her hand on the saint's leg and flinched for a moment.

'Do you feel that?' she said to Grogar.

He put out his hand and touched the statue as well. 'It's warm!' he said.

'I don't think any heretics have come here. They would have defaced it.' She closed her eyes and let the warmth in the statue calm her. Conviction that she would not die here filled her. This must have been a chapel once. Whatever it had been, there was a power here still that the heretics avoided.

Grogar looked about. 'This is some hole we've found ourselves in. Just the two of us. No las. No vox.'

Minka had seen tighter scrapes than this. 'You weren't on Cadia,' she said. 'I mean, at the end.'

'No,' he admitted. 'I wasn't.' The big man's cheeks coloured. The 2050th had been recalled to Cadia, but they'd been held up in the warp, and never made it. They felt guilty and resentful that they had not been there, to see Cadia fall.

'I was,' Minka said. She remembered the flight from her home and how, despite the terror and the horror and the loss, there was hardly a trooper who had not seen angels protecting them, or showing them the way.

When you were in a hole as deep and dark as this one, faith was the one thing that kept you alive.

'Do you remember Cadia?' she said urgently. 'I mean, can you picture the place still, in your mind?'

Grogar pulled a face. 'Not really. I mean, I was only fifteen when I left...' He trailed off. 'It's been twenty years. I've seen so many other planets, they all start to blur.'

Minka was intense. 'Try and remember,' she said. She reached out and touched the statue. 'Picture yourself on the Caducades. Or picture the first time you saw Kasr Tyrok.'

Grogar pulled a face but she was insistent.

'Do it!' she ordered.

He shut his eyes, and she put his hand back to the statue and held it in place. Then she shut her own eyes. 'Think of Cadia. Can you see it?'

Minka could. The recollection of her home world was so powerful it almost made her weep. She pressed her eyes together and could smell the distinct salt-air smell of the rocky beaches along the Caducades coastline. She could feel the wind on her face, could feel herself clambering up the rocks to the top of the island, to listen to the moan of wind in the honeycomb of the pylon that stood there. She could see the searchlights of Kasr Tyrok, the flights of Thunderbolts heading into the sunset, and hear the klaxon sounding as the night watch began.

She did not know how long they stood there. The sensation of warmth grew, then receded. When it had gone entirely Minka felt almost deflated. But then she noticed something had changed. 'My clothes are dry,' she said. She took his hand and put it on her sleeve.

Grogar looked at her, and then looked down at his own Cadian drab combat suit. Only his boots were still wet. His jacket, trousers, flak armour were crusted with dry salt. He started to laugh. 'I'll be damned,' he said, but he was a simple-minded warrior and this was beyond his understanding.

But Minka understood. It was a miracle or a sign. Of that she was sure. She slapped his arm. 'Defeat is not an option. We have to get out of here. Don't you understand? This is the hour of utmost darkness. But we're Cadians. We survived. And the Imperium needs us.'

He nodded slowly, only just grasping what she meant. But one thing was easy enough to comprehend: this was the hour of darkness, and the Imperium needed them more than ever.

A BROTHER'S CONFESSION

ROBBIE MACNIVEN

Once, before it had been carved from its bedrock and cast adrift among the stars, the Chapel of the Dioskuri had been a high, cold place. Mountain raptors had called it their home as readily as the lonely pilgrims who had trekked through snow drifts and along knife-backed ridges to reach it. Stories were told among the Primaris Space Marines that the fragile bones of birds and woven votive offerings left by worshippers could still be found in its darkest corners. Kastor, who frequented the chapel more than any of them, had certainly never come across such relics. They had long since crumbled to dust, for it had been ten thousand years since the Dioskuri had lain heaped beneath mountain snow, or moaned with the bitterness of a midwinter wind. Ten millennia had gone by since it had been uprooted and rebuilt, stone by stone, on board the battle-barge *Spear of Macragge*. Now its pilgrims were god-warriors of the former XIII Legion, and its attendant, Kastor, wore the skull-helm of an Adeptus Astartes Chaplain.

He donned that helm now, though there was no immediate threat of battle. The black armour and vestments of a Chaplain were as ceremonial as they were functional. They represented the wearer's grave charge: to uphold the faith and purity of his battle-brothers, and act as both judge and executioner for those who failed. In that moment, as the *Spear of Macragge* traversed the currents of the warp on its way from combat operations in the Atari system, Kastor stood in judgement.

'It is time, brother.'

The accused had surrendered himself of his own volition and now knelt before Kastor and the chapel's altar, shrouded in the black cloth of judgement. His name was Polixis, and he was the Apothecary of the Fulminata – one of the strike forces of Primaris Marines who, a century earlier, had joined the Ultramarines Chapter. Light from the tallow candles set around the chamber flickered along the strong lines of his face and gave his blond hair a deeper, golden sheen.

'Speak now, before the Emperor's sight.'

The ritual words rang through the chamber, scraping from the vox vocaliser of Kastor's helm like an executioner's blade across a whetstone.

Polixis was silent before answering, his head dipped, as though he was trying to find the words that would most succinctly convey his guilt.

'I killed my battle-brother,' he said eventually, his voice low but firm.

Kastor remained still.

Polixis raised his burning gaze to meet the Chaplain's darkened visor. 'I killed Artimaeus Tulio, of the Fulminata.'

Five Days Earlier

The de la Sario manor house shook with gunfire, screams

and the fury of the Primaris Space Marines. The Fulminata rarely tasted defeat, and yet on this day, their objective was slipping away.

Polixis launched two shots from his bolt pistol. The hard rounds punched through the charging Tchari supplicator's bare breast and burst open his chest cavity. The man, clad only in a white loincloth and a silver hook-nosed mask, dropped instantly. Two of his cult kindred threw themselves into adjacent doorways. A spray of las-fire whipped into the dark stonebark panels that lined the hallway as they attempted to keep the Primaris Apothecary at bay, forcing him to one side.

Polixis advanced, using speed to close the distance before either cultist could pin him. He slammed another shot into the doorframe that sheltered one of them. A hail of splinters ripped through the man's torso. He dropped, screaming. His comrade managed to fire two last las-bolts into Polixis' left greave and breastplate before his weapon's power pack whined, its charge empty.

Neither shot penetrated the Space Marine's white battleplate.

The Apothecary fired a double-tap at point-blank range into the man, shredding his muscled body and painting his blood up the walls. He turned to the other, who lay on the floor with several wooden stakes protruding from his abdomen. Polixis' fingers wrapped around the struggling man's throat, then twisted. There was a loud crack and the cultist became limp in his hands. He tossed him aside, then moved on down the corridor without pause, reloading as he went.

Time was running out.

The door at the far end of the corridor caved beneath his boot just as Intercessor Squad Nerva stormed the chamber beyond from the other side. The dining space resounded with the click-crash of auto bolt rifles and the shattering of glass. Polixis arrived in time to split another of the Tchari in two as he fumbled for a grenade from the bandolier strapped over his chest. The round blew half the cultist's skull away and sent his broken silver grotesque spinning across the room.

'The hall is ours,' said Sergeant Nerva.

'There's no sign of the governor in the servant's quarters,' Polixis added, striding across the room to join the squad as they spread out.

'Aerial scans show him being removed to the west of the manor house by the cult,' Nerva said, voice grim, while four Primaris Marines from his combat team – Ovido, Plinus, Priscor and Quintillius – secured the battered room, scanning the heretical Tchari corpses. 'The captain has ordered an air strike to neutralise him.'

Polixis said nothing. It took a conscious effort to bury the anger that surged through his thoughts. Nerva and the Primaris strike team had arrived at the manor as dawn broke, hoping to recover Governor de la Sario before the cult could reach him. Only the ruler of Atari could access the gene-vault that contained the codes for the planet's orbiting weapons platforms. Unless the governor was now neutralised, the heretics of the Tchari – daemon-worshippers who had risen in a coordinated revolt against Imperial rule – would have access to weaponry capable of scouring Atari bare.

'The western and northern portions of the estate are overrun,' Nerva continued. 'The captain is moving to secure the vault as we speak, but there are over four hundred cult members converging on us. We have orders to evacuate.'

'What about his daughter?' Polixis asked. 'Her gene-stamp will be as effective as his.'

'My second combat squad were searching for her, but their

flanks are overwhelmed and time is tight,' Nerva said. 'If both father and daughter are lost to the cultists, we need to extract and consolidate at the vault. The heretics can't be allowed to access it.'

Polixis was about to reply when the heads-up tactical display scrolling across his visor pinged.

'The second combat team are taking casualties,' he said. The sigils that represented the vitae-signs of the two members of the Intercessor squad – Scaevola and Tulio – had both blinked yellow. A second later, the clipped tones of Tarquin, leader of the five-man detachment, crackled over the vox-link.

'*More cultists entering from the west. At least a platoon in strength, including heavy stubbers. Still no sign of the girl. Another minute and we'll be intersected.*'

'Withdraw,' Nerva ordered. 'We are out of time.'

Even as the automatic confirmation blinked over the visor, the vox was chopped by the furious thudding noise of a heavy weapon, playing counterpoint to the beat echoing through the manor. The mark representing Tulio's life feed turned red.

'*Brother Tulio has been hit,*' Tarquin said, words barked over the crashing sounds of a close-range firefight. '*His Belisarian Furnace triggered but he has been cut off.*'

'Withdraw,' Nerva reiterated. 'I am not returning to the Fulminata having lost half of my squad.'

'His progenoids must be recovered,' Polixis interjected.

'If they attempt to retrieve his body, they will suffer more casualties. The Codex is clear on this matter. There is too much to lose for too little gain.'

'I was not suggesting your Intercessors retrieve him,' Polixis said. 'It is my duty to retain his legacy for the Chapter.'

'With all respect, Brother-Apothecary, I could not countenance losing you either. This building is too large and complex to secure, and cultists are flocking here every second we delay. The more of us that fall, the more emboldened they will become.'

'Tarquin will be drawing the main body of the Tchari after him. I can use the tactical display to outflank them and get to Tulio. The speed of the cultists' assault ensures they won't have time to mount a static defence.'

Nerva was silent for a moment before speaking again, his tone reluctant.

'You know I cannot stop you, Brother-Apothecary, but we will be gone from this accursed place in under ten minutes. If you are not on board the extraction, there will be angrier brothers among the Fulminata than just Captain Demetrius.'

'I will see you aboard the extraction, Sergeant Nerva,' Polixis promised, already moving towards the hall's main doors.

Polixis strode out of the dining hall, bolt pistol raised. Data bursts transmitted between the withdrawing Intercessors' autosenses had mapped out much of the manor on the heads-up display, but presented no information about the location of the Tchari supplicators. There were half a dozen corridors and rooms between the Apothecary and the withdrawing combat squad, but the cultists in their leering silver masks were flooding into the estate grounds from all directions. Tarquin and his brethren could already be cut off.

The Apothecary passed down a narrow, bare service corridor and into the kitchen block. Gleaming work surfaces, stoves and ovens stretched away from him. He entered through the swing doors just as armed cultists, with eye-achingly blasphemous sigils painted onto their bare breasts and arms, emerged at the opposite end.

Polixis fired first. One of the Tchari went down, his left

shoulder reduced to a bloody ruin. The other briefly hesitated, frozen between fight and flight. He chose fight.

A single las-bolt blew a cluster of hanging herbs to dust and ricocheted from a spread of cutlery laid out beside one of the kitchen drainage units. The man did not have a chance to release another shot before Polixis ended his existence. The Apothecary passed through the kitchen, bolt pistol tracking behind the counters and meat cryo blocks for targets. Yet there were none.

He stepped over the two bodies, scanning them as he passed through the doorway and into the corridor. One cultist's vitae signs still showed, but were close to flat-lining – he was unconscious and would be dead from blood loss in just over a minute.

The Apothecary didn't pause. He moved down the secondary service passageway and up a short flight of steps into a storage locker, stepping between barrels of salted meats, dried fruits and heavy sacks of flour.

Beyond, he met the remains of Tarquin's combat team.

'Apothecary,' the Intercessor said as Polixis emerged into a small annex connecting to the manor's librarius. Four members of the team were present – Sergius, Valent and Tarquin standing over the prone form of Scaevola. He'd clearly been dragged from their last contact zone. His breastplate had been split by three heavy-calibre hard round impacts, and numerous small arms shots perforated the scarred ceramite.

'We were caught in crossfire as we retreated from the foyer,' Tarquin said as Polixis knelt beside Scaevola, a hint of bitterness creeping into his clipped report. 'We tried to reach the governor, but there were too many. Well over a hundred contacts. They used their own bodies as shields so they could get him away from us.'

Polixis didn't answer as his diagnostor helmet scanned the patient, linking with the output of his armour's autosenses via the black carapace interface. The rune representing Scaevola on the vitae display blinked red. Still, he ran a diagnostic over the body anyway, plugging his prognosticator into Scaevola's tasset node. The secondary readout confirmed the first – he was beyond the Apothecary's skill.

'He is slain,' Polixis said simply, indicating his narthecium. 'I must remove his progenoids immediately.'

While Tarquin checked the tactical updates, Polixis blink-triggered his reductor. The tool, built into the gauntlet of his narthecium, came in two parts – a fine-toothed carbon alloy chainblade extractor, and an adamantium drill bit. It was the latter that he activated first, placing it firmly against the centre of Scaevola's breastplate. There was a familiar shriek of cracking plasteel, and Polixis gritted his teeth as the drill bored its way through first blue-painted ceramite, then the plasteel beneath. After an exact depth of penetration read-out on the Apothecary's modified helm display, he removed and deactivated the bit, placing the reductor's extractor tube in the perfectly circular hole in Scaevola's armour.

Polixis pressed down. The sharpened edges of the reductor pierced the toughened flesh, penetrating the durametallic sinew coil-cables all Primaris Marines were blessed with. He grunted as he carried on through bone, the full weight of the modified gauntlet required to pierce the fused abdomen.

There was a hideous crunching sound. Polixis twisted his fist and activated the reductor's flesh-clamps to keep the wound open as he burrowed into the split chest cavity.

His visor display had linked with the thumbnail-sized pict responder fixed to the top of the tube's end. With it, he was able to see the reductor as it penetrated Scaevola once more.

Before him was a grey glob of fleshy tissue – the very life force of the Chapter made manifest. He pressed the tube's end over the progenoid and activated the suction valve. There was a whirring noise as it ripped the precious gland from the flesh, shunting it into one of the cryo-receptacle vials fixed to the narthecium's rear.

As he removed the tube, there was a screech of las-bolt against ceramite behind him, followed by rapid return fire. Polixis looked over his shoulder and saw Sergius and Valent loose shots into the horde of cultists that swelled from between the librarius' bookshelves.

Polixis knew he needed to hurry. He triggered the reductor's small chainblade. Normally what he was about to do would be considered sacrilege, but under the pressures of a field operation it was necessary. He tilted Scaevola's helmet back, exposing the gorget's neck seal. With a precise, sharp slashing motion, he cut open the Space Marine's throat. As blood flooded the gorget, he inserted the reductor's flesh clamps to keep the wound from automatically sealing, then buried his fingers in the incision. A few seconds of probing located the fallen warrior's second progenoid, secreted in the neck. He cupped it and applied a slow but firm pressure, ripping away the connective tissue and dragging the gland, undamaged, from its spot nestled against the trachea. With the bloody grey matter in one gauntlet, he slipped it into the reductor's tube and triggered the suction valve once more. The second extracted gene-seed joined the first.

The chrono display that had triggered on his diagnostor's visor froze as the secondary progenoid thumped into the small cryo-receptacle. The entire operation had taken just fifty-six seconds.

'He is recovered,' Polixis said, intoning the rite of the fallen. 'His legacy endures.'

'We will take his body and battleplate with us,' Tarquin said, motioning for Valent to heft Scaevola's remains. 'Come, Brother-Apothecary. Sergius and Valent will provide cover.'

'No,' Polixis replied. 'I must extract brother Tulio's progenoids.'

'He cannot be reached.'

'Perhaps from the route you have taken.'

'Trying to locate Tulio in these conditions is unwise,' Tarquin countered.

'It is unorthodox,' Polixis corrected. 'But war is rarely an orthodox matter, Brother Tarquin.'

A colossal explosion rocked the manor house, shattering its glass windows and doors. The brothers fell silent, and the unmistakable stench of burning flesh filled the air. Static crackled across the vox-channel.

'Aerial strike successful. The Governor has been terminated.'

Polixis' mouth set in a grim line. 'Link up with Sergeant Nerva. I will see you during the extraction.'

As the second combat team fell back towards the dining hall, Polixis took the third door out of the annex corridor, avoiding the Tchari cultists that had flooded the librarius. Following the tactical map, he broke down a door leading to a small study room then turned north once more, into the stately entrance corridor leading from the manor's western entrance foyer into the building. It was there that he found Brother Tulio.

Neither the artificial miracle of Mark X power armour nor the organic miracle of a fused ribcage and Primaris sinew coils had been enough to save him from the fist-sized wounds caused by the point-blank discharge of a heavy stubber. He was slumped against one of the walls halfway down the corridor, the bloody remains of supplicator corpses scattered around him. The Ultramarine's Belisarian Furnace, the so-called Revitaliser, had allowed him to endure far longer than was normal for a Space Marine. He had continued crushing skulls and snapping necks in a frenzied close-quarter melee that had bought enough time for the rest of his brothers to withdraw deeper into the sprawling manor.

Polixis took it all in with a split-second assessment. He also noted the masked cult members advancing cautiously down the far end of the corridor. A burst of bolt rounds sent them scrambling back to where they had set up their heavy stubber. Polixis stepped back around the corridor's corner as las-bolts snapped past, reviewing what his memory had recorded from the several seconds of unobstructed sight.

For a moment, beyond trying to delay the cultist rush, he couldn't see why Tulio had chosen this particular corridor to make his stand, but then he noticed a twitch of frightened movement in one of the alcoves dispersed intermittently down the walls. There was someone between the Tchari at the far end and Polixis' position – a small girl, pressed into one of the corridor's bust niches, cowering behind a likeness of one of her ancestors. It was Governor de la Sario's missing daughter.

Polixis assessed the situation. To attempt to reach Tulio, who had fallen so close to the cultist's hastily assembled weapon emplacement, would be difficult. There were also Scaevola's remains to consider. If Polixis fell invading the Tchari's position, not only would the Chapter lose Scaevola's genetic inheritance, but his own and Tulio's too. Yet Polixis could not simply abandon his fallen brother. In his mind's eye, he saw once again the Intercessor he had shared over a decade of combat operations with, in the heat of battle, at prayer, servicing his arms and armour. That he had fallen was not what tore at the Apothecary, for they would all fall some day in the Emperor's service. It was the possibility of losing his legacy, forever cutting off his inheritance by failing to retrieve his gene-seed, that made Polixis hesitate.

Then there was the girl. It would be impossible to reach Tulio while keeping her from the crossfire. He could neutralise her to ensure she did not fall into the hands of the cult, and instead retrieve Tulio's gene-seed, but doing so would mean sacrificing access to the vault.

'Brother Tarquin has re-joined us and the Thunderhawk is circling,' clicked Nerva's voice over the vox. 'Hurry, Apothecary.'

In that instant, the decision was made. He swung out from his cover, bolt pistol thundering. Blood blossomed and las-fire returned as the clutch of separatists responded. Breaking down the corridor, Polixis was exposed for barely three seconds, but to his heightened senses, it felt like long minutes. He saw each las-bolt as it arced down the narrow space, glittering crimson lances that flared and burned as they punched holes through wallpaper and wooden panels. He felt the impact of three hits against his power armour, warning runes winking across his visor as the bolts seared black holes into white ceramite. He felt the sudden jolt of pain as a fourth, set to its maximum megathule range, drew blood from his thigh. The sensation was gone in an instant, smothered by the potent mix of combat stimms pumping through his body.

The Tchari supplicators were still struggling to reload the stubber's belt feed as he slammed into the alcove the girl was sheltering in. He knocked the bust aside to make space in the niche, the pale marble thumping across the carpeted floor. The child stared up at him and screamed.

'Be still,' Polixis said, trying not to snap.

The child pressed herself against the wall, tears streaming down her face. Polixis stifled a curse and leant back into the corridor, loosing off a shot to keep the supplicator's heads down. Another flurry of las cracked back at him, searing holes in the woodwork.

He knelt before the girl, reached up to his gorget and unclamped his diagnostor helm.

'My name is Polixis,' he said, hoping that speaking to her face to face would calm her long enough to convince her not to try and flee out into the shot-lashed corridor. 'We must leave. *Now.*'

She stared at him with wide eyes, apparently stunned to find the great, battleplated automaton was actually flesh and blood, albeit with the broad, solid features of a giant. Finally, she nodded.

'Hold onto my arm,' he said, offering his left gauntlet. She looked at the wicked, bloody blades of his reductor and the pulsing, fleshy gene-seed locked in the narthecium's cryo-receptacle. Another flurry of las-bolts cracked past their hiding place. She took his arm, wrapping her skinny limbs around the ceramite.

Polixis lifted her easily and cradled her against his broad breastplate. He keyed his vox.

'Sergeant Nerva, I have the governor's daughter.'

Without waiting for a response, he stepped out into the corridor, back facing the supplicators, and began to run.

Almost immediately, his body registered penetrating shots to the rear joint of his left knee, thigh and the lower-right side of his back. The injuries didn't slow him – thankfully, none had found vital organs or struck bone. He kept going, as more crimson bolts arced over and past him, keeping his unarmoured head bowed and the girl cradled in front of him.

He was nearly at the corner when the heavy stubber opened fire. Its battering discharge filled the narrow space and the air swarmed with splinters and glass shards as a storm of high-calibre rounds ripped up the woodwork and wallpaper around the Apothecary. A trio of shots clanged and scored from his backpack before one punched a hole into the small of his back. He grunted but kept going, servos whirring, boots pounding the carpet underfoot.

A side door ahead of him swung open and two more cultists with guns began to emerge, eyes wide in their masks. Polixis hit the door shoulder-first without pause, the pauldron banging the wood back into the men's faces and throwing them into the room they had emerged from.

Another stubber round slammed into the back of his right thigh. He stumbled, his right hand hitting the wall as his armour's stabilisers kicked in and he found his balance. A few steps more. Another injury to his right leg, the calf this time. The wounds ached and blood stained his armour red in half a dozen places as the damaged tissue clotted with ugly black scabs. But he was close, so close.

A further round hit his right pauldron, ricocheting up into the ceiling and raining plaster down on them. The girl's eyes were screwed tight shut, her whole body tense. A bust to their left disintegrated in a hail of shattered marble as it was hit.

Polixis rounded the corner as the storm of gunfire riddled the wall ahead. He paused for the briefest second, letting out a slow, shuddering breath as he scanned the girl and his own injuries. She was unharmed, though her vitae signs – heightened blood pressure and heart rate – showed extreme stress. At least three of his own wounds would require immediate treatment upon extraction, but they weren't yet debilitating. The pain was turning to a familiar, dull throb. He mag-locked his bolt pistol, twisted the primer on a frag grenade to ten seconds and dropped it on the floor next to the corridor's corner.

'Nearly there,' he said. The girl whimpered. With a grunt of pained exertion, he began to run again, dodging into a study just as the grenade's blast thumped through the building, followed by the screams of their pursuers.

The sound of bolt rifle fire filled Polixis with relief as he raced back into the dining hall. Squad Nerva were still in position. The Intercessors were firing out of the windows, pinning the Tchari trying to rush in on them from outside, while keeping the rolling lawn clear as the vast, armoured bulk of the Thunderhawk gunship *Dromidas* came in to land, ground-plates extended. Shots sparked from the Space Marine flier, and its bolters answered, thundering as they swung back and forth on their pintles, shredding the carefully arranged shrubbery and hedgerows that bordered the lawn.

'Not a moment too soon, brother,' Nerva said over the cacophony.

Behind the sergeant, the Thunderhawk's prow ramp had started to lower, revealing the hold interior. The fire from the circling Tchari was intensifying.

'Squad, embark,' Nerva barked. Valent and Plinus laid down covering fire as the Ultramarines broke out across the short, grassy space towards the flier, using their heavily armoured bulk to shield the human carried by Polixis from the hard rounds and las-bolts that whipped and cracked from all sides. A rocket-propelled grenade corkscrewed up from the ruined remains of a nearby garden pagoda, barely missing the gunship's flank.

'Quintillius, Priscor,' Nerva shouted to the last of his Intercessors covering the hall. While the two Primaris Marines stood and dropped back towards the flier, Polixis reached the Thunderhawk's hold, carrying the girl to one of the transport benches. As the Intercessors came in after him, Nerva glanced down at his narthecium, and saw that only one of the gene-seed vials was full.

'Tulio?' he asked.

Polixis looked up from the restraint harness he was securing around the wide-eyed girl's shoulders. He shook his head.

'I could not reach him. If I had tried, I would not be here now with Scaevola's legacy intact.'

Nerva said nothing, expression inscrutable behind his red-and-white helm. He placed one gauntlet on Polixis' pauldron.

'I know that you will have done everything in your power to bring him back, Brother-Apothecary,' he said, as the deck of the *Dromidas* lurched with lifter thrust. 'That you went back for him shows your dedication to the Chapter, and to my squad. We thank you for your efforts.'

Polixis inclined his head, not trusting himself to speak. Possessing the governor's daughter would grant them access to the vault, and through it, victory. That was enough, he told himself. It would have to be enough. As he locked himself into his own harness, the gunship shuddered with a powerful discharge. Its spine-mounted battle cannon had sent a fire-primed infurnace shell hammering into the manor house, through the hall's broken windows.

Amidst the sudden, violent fury of flames and smoke, the *Dromidas* pulled away.

The Chapel of the Dioskuri was silent. Polixis' head had been bowed as he related his confession, but he raised it now to meet the red visor lenses of Kastor's skull helm.

The Chaplain reached up and disengaged the sealant lock, removing the grim piece of armour and setting it on the altar with a thud. The face revealed was the same as Polixis' – firmly set, dark-eyed, with hair the colour of a golden harvest. The similarities went beyond the changes wrought by a primarch's shared genetics.

'Do you remember when I saved the pup from the waters of the Icaldon?' the Chaplain asked. Polixis remained looking up at him, processing the question. The fact that Kastor had removed his helmet broke with the protocol of the confessional.

'I do not,' the Apothecary admitted eventually. 'You know my memories of those days are less complete than yours.'

'Morik the agri-master's flock-hound had plunged into the river and its pup had followed,' Kastor said. 'Both were swept away. I pursued them, and you would have followed had father not dragged you back. I managed to reach the pup, but its mother was gone. I could not save them both.'

'A pup is a different matter to a brother of the Fulminata–' Polixis began to say, but Kastor raised his hand for silence.

'I have only one question for you,' he said. 'Have you come here to confess your guilt to the Chaplain of the Fulminata, or have you come to confess it to your blood-brother?'

Polixis said nothing.

'Your silence is an answer in and of itself,' Kastor said. 'You have committed no crime worthy of a confession. The tactical situation was clear and the Codex supports your actions. Tulio was lost, and the fact that you recovered the daughter of the de la Sarios was an achievement that you should look back on with pride. With her gene-lock we were able to access the weapons vault and turn the orbital defences on the heretics. Had it been the other way round, this entire strike force would have been decimated, and the world of Atari lost.'

'But could I not have recovered both her and Tulio?' Polixis said. 'The Imperium needs warriors, now more than ever. The loss of even a single battle-brother's legacy is a grievous failing. I alone am accountable for that.'

'The Imperium needs humanity,' Kastor corrected. 'That is the very reason that we exist – to preserve mankind and all of its great works. You are right to speak of legacy. You preserved a legacy when you saved that girl. She will never forget that her life was paid for by one of the Emperor's warriors. In all likelihood, she will grow up to be a firm and righteous leader, one ever-mindful of the dangers that threaten the Imperium and the warriors that stand ready should she have need.'

Polixis said nothing as he considered his brother's words. Kastor went on.

'You are right – a pup cannot be compared to the memory of Brother Tulio. But Agri-master Morik rejoiced when I emerged from the swell with the dog in my arms. He knew that the future of his flock was secure. And the Imperium's future will be secure too, so long as we make the sacrifices required for victory. Atari still stands because you completed the mission. If some of our number are lost – even you or I – in doing so, that is not something to mourn. It is both our duty and our privilege. You should not hold it against yourself either. That we must suffer on occasion is inevitable. We are warriors.'

'It is a difficult lesson,' Polixis admitted. 'One that I fear I must relearn every time. It still hurts.'

'And that is to your credit,' Kastor said, extending one gleaming, black-armoured hand. Polixis grasped it, the white gauntlet meeting the black, thumb-to-thumb, the brother's grip rather than the warrior's. He stood.

'We are a torch, set aside for mankind's darkest hour,' Kastor said. 'That hour is upon us now. May we burn brightly, you and I, and never waver. We owe that to Tulio's memory, and the future lives of those we save.'

RISE

BEN COUNTER

It was a rising and seductive pain; a delicious, serpentine thing that wound around his bones and seethed through his muscles. He felt it galloping up and down his spine, accompanied by the slow suffusing of his brain until his senses were bathed in red agony.

It would devour him, if he let it. It would become a part of him from which he could not separate, and he would never wake up.

Skanis demanded his body fight it. He felt his wrists and ankles straining at the straps that held him down. Another restraint around his neck choked him as his body arched against the slab. He forced his eyes open and his sight, sharpened by hours in darkness, picked out the glimmer of metal.

The face of the haemonculus grinned down at him. Its name surfaced from Skanis' memory. Urviel. The haemonculus' face was a mask made from the skin of another creature, fastened to the front of its skull by metal staples. Its emaciated ribcage was skinless and organs slithered between the white bones. Four many-jointed arms sprouted from his shoulders, each ending in medical implements and powered saws instead of fingers. A filthy length of hide was wrapped around its waist, with pockets and loops holding blades and drills of every dimension.

'It wakes,' said Urviel. One of its extra arms ran bladed fingers down Skanis' chest.

'Is it done?' gasped Skanis. The tide of pain was receding, slowly relinquishing each joint and organ.

'Oh, little bird,' said Urviel. 'It will never be done.'

Skanis thrashed against the restraints. A panic welled in him and he wondered if he would ever leave the haemonculus' lab. He realised the creature's promise to transform him could have been a trick to lure him upon the slab in order to experiment on him forever, to turn him over and over again into new shapes of malleable flesh until his life finally gave out.

Urviel held up a hand. A mockery of contriteness passed over its mutilated features. 'I jest,' it said. It released the buckle holding the strap around Skanis' neck, then freed one of his hands. Skanis pulled at the strap around his remaining wrist as the haemonculus backed away.

The laboratory was almost pitch black and infernally hot. Body parts from a dozen species hung on the walls, arms and legs racked together, heads hanging by lengths of chain from the ceiling. Cages held heaps of spoil and rags that might once have been alive. The floor was swamped with noxious fluid. Every workbench and operating slab was covered in the detritus of Urviel's work. Scalpels and forceps. Vials of corrosive. Rib spreaders, circular saws, industrial shears, bottled organs and a bowl of eyes.

Skanis released his ankles and slid off the slab. He stumbled, his legs unsteady beneath him. His body felt different – tauter, quicker and more sensitive. He still wore the battlegear of his warrior clan, now opened up in several places, recut and cinched in around his new, slenderer frame. The pain was pooling now in the areas the haemonculus had worked on – his knees, hips and shoulders, two hot red strips down his back, a deep throbbing ache in his bones. His whole body felt tuned up and tightened. He moved an arm experimentally, and the limb reacted with an insect-like quickness.

'What have you done?' he asked, his throat so raw that the words came out in a croaking hiss.

'All that you asked,' said Urviel. 'I hollowed your bones. Your pelvis is new – something of my own design. Do you like vertebrae? You have many more. My speciality.' Urviel's fingers folded in on themselves like the fronds of an anemone. 'I like spines.'

Skanis craned his neck, trying to get a glimpse behind him.

'Indeed, it is as you wished,' said Urviel. 'They are there. Freshly harvested. I am so glad I found a home for them before they decayed.'

'I have to use them.'

Urviel shook his head. 'Not here. You will never leave the ground. You need thermal currents for the first time. I have seen it. Commorragh will not let you go with ease. You must rise above it first.'

'Then I will.' Skanis reached a hand behind him. He felt delicate frills of flesh there, and the nerve endings he found fired back sensations from skin and muscle he had never possessed before. 'I will leave this city of filth behind.'

'You will return,' said Urviel. 'It is addictive. You will never find another drug quite as intoxicating as the changing of the flesh, little bird. But before you go...'

'What?' said Skanis impatiently.

'You must know how few of you find what you seek,' said the haemonculus. 'Always they say they will be the one to prevail. If one in a hundred, one in a thousand survives, every one believes it will be him. I have done fine work. None better in fact. But even so, the fates say you will die.'

'What do you care?' retorted Skanis. 'You have your payment.'

'Six corpses,' agreed Urviel. 'Young and fresh.'

'I can never go back to my kabal because of what I did to get them.' Skanis looked up through a gap in the ceiling of the ruin that served as the haemonculus' lab. The spires of the city rose in every direction, dark spears thrusting up into the cloud layer, their pinnacles lost in the smog that blanketed the city. He felt the new talons of his toes digging into the flagstones, and the grit of the floor beneath him made his stomach cramp in disgust. 'And I will never return here, either. My feet will never touch the ground of Commorragh again.'

Kaledari Spire was the tallest structure in this region of Commorragh. Skanis had heard of it, but never entered, for his kabal had been obsessed only with holding onto the wretched patch of the city they considered theirs. To them, that tangle of streets and slaughterhouses was the entire galaxy. As Skanis looked up at the dozens of levels of the spire, he caught a glimpse of how vast reality was, of how endless a single soul's experience could be if he only left the filth of the streets behind.

The spire entrance yawned, unguarded. The lower floors were in disarray. Fallen rubble choked the surrounding alleyways, and the archways were dark and blinded. Skanis' sharp eyes caught movement, focusing in like a bird of prey seizing on its quarry.

A tiny winged shape struggled down in the murk. Skanis crouched down and saw it was a young razorwing chick. Half-lizard, half-bird, the razorwings were raptors uniquely adapted for the toxic atmosphere and cruel ecosystems of Commorragh. They were survivors. This one, however, was mewling and writhing on the ground. On the lintel of the archway above was a nest of metallic fibres and bones from which the chick had fallen.

'You tried to fly too soon,' said Skanis. He picked up the chick, and the ruffling of its knife-like feathers was a strange cascade of pain against the inflamed nerve endings of his palm. Its plumage was dark red and gunmetal, its beak bright silver and its eyes tiny flecks of flint.

'Come with me. We will fly together.' He placed the razor-wing chick carefully on his shoulder. It dug its talons into the flesh and perched there, the pinpricks of pain a reminder that Skanis wasn't quite alone in his quest.

He walked through the shadowy archway into the spire's ground floor, aware that his talons had left the soil of Commorragh for the last time.

The lower levels of the spire were barely lit by age-clouded lanterns that shed pools of painful green light. Old, gnawed bones clogged crusted drains cut into the floors. Skanis realised this place had once been an abattoir where the fruits of drukhari raids had been dismembered for a purpose Kaledari Spire had long forgotten. Sculptures of kabalite warriors, with their features hidden behind the smooth faceplates of their armoured helms, stood sentinel along the walls. Chains and manacles were rusted away to brown stains. Acts of savagery had played out in dark splendour here. Now, it was worse.

Skanis felt eyes on him the moment he had walked through

a second archway. It was not long before he heard the sound of skin against stone and glimpsed the flicker of a moving shadow.

Everywhere in Commorragh had its predators. Here, they were slithering things without faces that lurked and waited, shivering with anticipation of the first glimmers of body heat. Skanis knew the tales. Their own unnatural flesh was no good. They needed outsiders. They needed something warm.

Skanis backed up against the wall as he heard something slapping on the wet floor. His hand went to the splinter pistol in its holster at his waist. It was a custom model, one he had crafted himself, fully loaded with a core of fragmenting crystal. In his other hand, he had the curved dagger that he had possessed for as long as he could remember and honed against the bones of other kabalites.

The creature emerged into the light. Skanis had never seen one so close up before. Its flesh was not just dark; it glowed like black crystal, and the interior sparkled as if it were a portal onto a view of the void. Green light played along the rises and falls in its almost featureless face. It carried a pair of serrated blades and wore the remains of a set of dark burgundy robes, now barely clinging to it.

'Come with us,' said the mandrake, its voice a dry slither. 'We will show you the way.'

'You lie,' replied Skanis. He was aware of more movement behind him. They were trying to surround him and cut him off, like a feral pack closing off the prey's escape routes.

'Grant us payment,' said the mandrake. 'A finger. Just a finger. It's all we want.'

'I remember your kind,' said Skanis. 'The archons hired you to spy on our enemies. You took gold and living slaves for your services. Everyone spoke of you with dread. But what are you now?' Skanis indicated the chewed bones on the floor. 'This is what they feed you? Scraps from their table? They have turned the mandrakes of Commorragh into animals, and you let them do it.'

The lead mandrake took a few steps closer. 'We are suffered to live. One day we will rise again. We will eat our fill and take our desires. One day, outsider. For now, just allow us a taste. A few red drops and we will take you to them.'

'You will devour me alive.'

The mandrake's head tipped slightly to the side. With no features on its face to read, it was impossible to guess whether it was smiling or not. 'Maybe. Would you like us to?'

As a second mandrake lurched screaming out of the darkness, Skanis' reflexes surprised even him. The splinter pistol was out of its holster and levelled at the creature instantly. He pulled the trigger and a stream of crystalline shards punched through the face and upper chest of the mandrake. Liquid blackness poured out of its torn body.

The razorwing chick squawked and leapt off his shoulder, flittering off into the darkness.

Skanis reeled with the unfamiliarity of his new body. He staggered and the wounded mandrake leapt at him. Its full weight barged Skanis into the wall behind him and his head rang off the stonework. Serrated blades stabbed towards his abdomen and he squirmed out from under the mandrake, falling back to the floor as the mandrake's knives drew sparks from the wall.

Skanis' mind whirled. He commanded his uncoordinated limbs to obey him. They jerked and spasmed as if they were wound too tight to be controlled. He scrabbled away from his attacker, and its vestigial features contorted in what might have passed for a smile.

Its hunger was its weakness.

The mandrake pounced on Skanis, eager to rend and devour. Skanis rolled out from under it and drove a hand into the back of its head, slamming it face-first into the floor. He raised his knife hand and drove it down, aiming for the place where spine met skull. Resistance gave way and the mandrake flopped down to the ground.

Skanis was back onto his feet and running without seeming to will it. The other mandrakes had smelt blood and were following him, led by the one who had spoken. Skanis wheeled around a corner and backed against one of the kabalite statues.

Their hunger was their weakness. In their desperation to feast on him, the mandrakes were no more than animals. They could not think. That was how he would beat them. While he was still learning how to use his new body, Skanis had to rely on his mind.

The lead mandrake rushed around the corner headlong, heedless of Skanis lying in wait. Skanis fired once, the shard flying wide, before he ran at the mandrake and let it stab its knife towards his chest. Within his guard, it was off-balance and Skanis parried its second blade, catching its arm in the crook of his elbow, wrenching it back and down.

He had learned to fight and kill while claiming his place among the warriors of his kabal. Skanis had been destined to be a future dracon or even archon, to assassinate his way into a position of power and lead an army of Commorragh. He cared for none of that now, but knew the murderous ways he had learned to get him there would serve him here too.

The mandrake's shoulder separated. Skanis slammed his other elbow into its back, forcing his weight down onto it. A third creature screeched as it leaped and kicked off the walls towards him, but Skanis shot it out of the air with a shard through the throat. It tumbled as it hit the ground in a flurry of obsidian limbs.

'You were once nightmares,' spat Skanis. The thing beneath him howled and hissed. 'Fear itself! Now you are vermin.' He drove his knife into the side of the mandrake's head. It spasmed under him, just once, then was still.

Skanis' heart was hammering faster than it ever had before. Finally, the pain caught up with him. He looked down and realised one of the mandrake's knives had sliced his forearm and opened up a long gash. Warm blood ran down his arm and dripped off his elbow.

He had been too slow. He was still getting used to his new form, and as heightened as his senses and reflexes were, he was not immortal. The first mandrake had nearly killed him. Had they been in possession of their senses, the next two would certainly have finished him. His hollow bones were fragile now, and if he was caught unawares, he would die.

Skanis tensed as he spotted movement again, but realised it was the flickering of tiny wings. The razorwing chick hopped between the scattered bones and onto the corpse at his feet. Skanis held up his hand, slick with the Mandrake's blood. The chick landed upon it and nipped at his fingers to lap up drops of cooling blood.

Slithering footsteps sounded in the darkness. 'There will be more,' Skanis told the chick. 'I can't kill them all. Not yet.'

Ahead of him was an area of collapse and disrepair. A section of the floor above had fallen in, the debris forming a crude staircase. Lights glimmered in the levels above, and from somewhere Skanis could hear the strains of music.

'Upwards,' said Skanis to the chick. It let out a purring trill in response. 'Let us find who throws the scraps to these vermin.'

* * *

Music was coming from an orchestra of skinned and articulated corpses. Each body was from a different species. The huge shoulder muscles of an ork bunched and contracted as it worked the bow of a stringed instrument as tall as itself. The delicate rise and fall of its tones made a mockery of the creature's brutal frame. A human body bent over a drum made of another creature's ribcage and stretched skin, its finger bones tapping out the rhythm that underpinned the music. A four-armed, snake-bodied sslyth played a complex reed instrument with compressed air piped through its glistening jaws.

The music played for the benefit of a grand court inhabiting the lavish, perfumed mansion that took up this floor of the spire. Skanis' jaw clenched as he looked across the scenes of the court. He had hoped he could move through here unnoticed, reach the entrance halls past the main audience chamber and continue upwards. But that would be impossible.

The lord of this court watched over the grand hall. His bulk was considerable, though most of it seemed taken up by the machinery mounted on his back that hooked dozens of cylinders of narcotic fluids up to his spine. The skin of his face sagged like melting wax beneath the half-mask of idealised features. Surrounded by a pungent haze of opiates, the lord sat on a throne of near-naked drukhari, whose athletic bodies were twined into the shape of a high-backed chair big enough to support the lord's mass.

A trio of dancers moved in time to the corpse-orchestra's music. They had the lean, dangerous athleticism of the wych-cultists who fought in the arenas of Commorragh. A beautiful lady with an elaborate ivory-coloured dress and a silver half-mask watched them, as did other, lesser ladies-in-waiting gathered around her like a flock of attentive birds. A gaggle of sycophants and fawners surrounded the lord's throne. Many of them were all but insensible from the narcotics pumped into them through lines hooked up to the lord's own apparatus, while others stood patiently to wait on his every need.

Knots of courtiers lingered everywhere, all in the impractically flamboyant fashions of Commorragh's nobility. Some admired the dancers or whispered advice to those more grandly dressed than themselves. Others simply observed, sending pages to carry messages back and forth through the court of Kaledari Spire.

The noble lady in white approached Skanis, accompanied by two handmaidens who carried the train of her long dress. Her silver half-mask had red-rimmed eyespots, giving her a ravenous, daemonic look.

The razorwing chick trilled in alarm and discomfort, as if it smelled something on the lady it did not like.

'You are a newcomer,' she said with a smile. Her voice was as clear and brittle as glass. 'Few come to Kaledari Spire. Certainly not one as exotic as yourself.' She ran a hand through the fleshy fronds protruding from Skanis' back, and he shuddered with the input from the new nerve endings the haemonculus had implanted there.

'I'm not surprised you are alone,' said Skanis. 'Your pets below are less than welcoming.'

'A passing fancy,' said the lady with a dismissive wave of the hand. 'The lord once doted on them. Now they are left to their own devices. They keep out the low-blooded and weak. You, then, are neither.'

Skanis looked her up and down. Her limbs and neck were overlong and her torso had a serpentine curve to it. He guessed her body had been elongated and altered, perhaps

to give her greater height and presence, perhaps to fulfil some
base desire of her lord. Beneath the silver mask, he could see
the sutures around her jaw and hairline where her face had
been removed and replaced.

'I do not intend to stay,' he said.

'Lord Fithrichol would wish to speak with you,' she said.
'It is not wise to deny him such a simple courtesy.'

Though the tone of her voice did not change, one of the
wych dancers pirouetted close enough for Skanis to see the
array of blades concealed in his close-fitting body harness.
By the standards of the courtly machinations of Commorragh, it was not a subtle threat.

Skanis followed the lady across the grand hall towards the
throne. Every courtier watched him, some with a smirk of
mockery, some with open curiosity or even desire. Skanis
tasted bile as he felt their eyes on him. This was the world
of lies he hated even more than the brutal politics of the
kabals. At least there was an honesty to the stabbed backs
and slit throats that were a kabalite's world.

A narcotic fug surrounded Lord Fithrichol's throne. The
pupil of the lord's one visible eye dilated as pistons in his
back forced another massive dose into his system. 'Who is
this you have brought us, Lady Chagrine?' he said in a voice
well-oiled by courtly manners.

'Just a traveller,' said Skanis. 'I am passing through your
realm.'

'To the spire pinnacle, I take it?' said Fithrichol. 'Those new
appendages of yours will do you little good down here. You
need to get above the smog of the city. But why the hurry? In
our desire to reach our goals, we so often forget to wait and
while and experience what this wondrous city has to offer.'

Skanis looked from one face to the next. The courtiers

near the throne were a mixture of wyches, nobles and lesser servants, their features slack with sedate oblivion. The ones still in possession of their senses were either there to wait on Fithrichol's needs, or had been selected for their beauty to act as living ornaments for the court. The drukhari who made up Fithrichol's throne sweated and creaked as he shifted his abnormal bulk.

'I must refuse you,' said Skanis. 'I cannot wait here. The sky calls to me.'

'Perhaps you have made an error,' said Fithrichol. 'Perfectly understandable. You are an outsider. You are new to the ways of my court. Let those errors be dispelled. I am Lord Fithrichol of Kaledari Spire. This is my kingdom. Everything in it is mine. When you walked over the threshold, you voluntarily entered my service unto death. This is the way it has always been. So you see the wondrous new life the fates have granted you. Service to me, in return for the deepest wonders of the mind, the sacred oblivion where the only freedom lies. You are a keen and deadly warrior, that much is clear to me. I value such individuals greatly. There will be much pleasure in return for your service.'

Skanis recoiled inwardly and hoped his new body was under enough control to hide it. If he stayed here too long, someone in the court would find his guard down. A needle would prick his skin and he would fall into the stupor with which Fithrichol controlled the lackeys of his court. With so many eyes on him, there was no immediate way to escape without every able-bodied soul in the court giving chase.

'I see you doubt my hospitality,' said Fithrichol. 'Again, understandable. You have not yet learned. Take a token of my good will.' He waved a sagging-fleshed hand at the handmaidens attending Lady Chagrine. 'Choose one. Choose two or three. Do with them what you will. Ravegar here is a flesh-crafter, purely as a hobby, but he has some skill.' Fithrichol indicated a slender, sharp-faced attendant wearing simple black. 'Purely an amateur, but he can make of your prizes whatever you desire.'

'It would be my greatest honour to serve the lord of Kale-dari Spire,' said Skanis.

There was a truth about this place, concealed beneath the surface by a web of lies so thick only an outsider could see it. It was in the fawning curtsey Lady Chagrine gave to her lord as she beckoned Skanis to join her and her handmaid-ens. It was in the way the wyches gyrated and pranced to the rise and fall of the corpse-orchestra's rhythm. Skanis could just glimpse it beneath the veneer, something buried deep, something dangerous.

Something Lord Fithrichol was terrified of.

'Choose,' said Lady Chagrine. Skanis looked from one handmaiden to the next. They were all dressed in less lavish versions of their mistress' ivory-white garb, all with the same slender, brittle beauty. Skanis chose one at random. She had pure black hair and eyes.

'Her,' he said.

'Varithrya,' said Lady Chagrine. 'Honour your master.'

Varithrya gave Skanis a coquettish smile and curtseyed before him. Skanis leaned in close to her. His senses were full of her perfume.

'Give me the chance and I'll kill him,' he whispered to her.

Though her face did not change, he could sense her body go rigid with anticipation. The tiny talons of the razorwing chick pricked the skin of his shoulder, feeling the tension alongside him.

'I just need a moment. It'll be me doing the killing. No

one need suspect you. Just give me the opportunity and I shall end him.'

Varithyra paused just a moment too long before she beamed at Skanis. 'Will my master not present me to his lord?' she said.

'Of course,' replied Skanis. 'I must show off my prize.'

He led her by the hand back to the throne. He could feel her pulse quickening.

This was the truth, Skanis realised. The buried horror. The dread that occupied Fithrichol's every thought. It wasn't even a secret, not in the truest sense, because everyone in the court knew it. They just didn't know that everyone else knew it too.

They hated Fithrichol. Every single one of them. They despised the way he manipulated them into slavery and kept them balanced against one another in a constant game of allegiance and servitude, reward and threat, patronage and abandonment. The whole court despised everything Lord Fithrichol was, but none of them dared act upon that hatred because each one thought they were alone.

'A fine choice,' said Fithrichol as Skanis presented Varithrya before the throne. 'I had an eye on her myself.'

Varithrya bowed low with an expansive sweep of the arm. Her hand brushed against one of the many valves and switches controlling the narcotic-dosing apparatus mounted on the lord's back.

Fithrichol sat back on his living throne. His one visible pupil dilated and he sighed out a long breath as a sudden spike of narcotics flooded his system.

In the half-second that gave him, Skanis' dagger was in his hand. As Fithrichol's focus returned, Skanis was aiming the dagger at his throat. By the time the tip of the blade touched his skin, Fithrichol was fully aware once more.

But it was too late.

Skanis felt bloated, sagging flesh parting under the blade, then gristle and bone. He rammed the blade all the way through Fithrichol's throat and gave it a twist, opening up a ruby-red void in the lord's neck. Hot, dark blood spurted down the front of Fithrichol's clothing. Skanis angled the blade upwards and thrust it home again, punching it through Fithrichol's palate and into the base of his brain.

The razorwing chick squawked as Fithrichol gurgled out a mouthful of gore.

The court merely watched. The music continued, for the corpse-orchestra had no understanding of what had just happened. But the wych-dancers were still and the courtiers had stopped their scheming and fawning.

No one moved.

Skanis gripped Fithrichol's body by the collar and threw it to the floor in front of the throne. The remaining air rattled out of the lord's lungs.

'Who wants it?' demanded Skanis to the court, indicating the empty throne of twisted bodies. 'Take it! Take it!'

It was Varithrya who reacted first. She grabbed a knife from Fithrichol's body, an ornamental weapon with an ornate hilt and gilded blade. She leapt up onto the throne, brandishing the knife in all directions.

'You treacherous whelp,' screeched Lady Chagrine. 'Tear her down!' she shouted to her handmaidens. 'Remove her from my throne!'

But the handmaidens did not obey. They surrounded their mistress, and the hate in their eyes was finally given form.

The wyches drew their knives. Those courtiers who were not lolling insensible grabbed whatever weapons they could find. In a few moments, the court was transformed from a place of fawning hierarchy to a melee where each individual turned against whoever was closest, and blood spattered onto the tiled floor as a scrum erupted in front of the throne.

No one noticed as Skanis took his leave of the scene of bedlam the audience chamber had become. He skulked away as raised voices and screaming echoed around the place. Varithrya was fighting off Ravegar, the amateur fleshcrafter. As the handmaiden rammed her gilded dagger into the courtier's eye, Skanis ducked through a side passageway.

Past the audience chamber was a grand staircase. It wound around a statue of a much younger and less artificial Lady Chagrine, sculpted frolicking in a fountain. Skanis ran past it and up the steps.

The screams of the dead and dying took a long time to fade as Skanis forged upwards. And even when they had fallen silent, the music of the corpse-orchestra remained.

It was after a long and punishing climb, through ruined floors and abandoned finery, that Skanis came to a realm of chains and cages.

The air was thrumming with the rumble of bestial breaths and heartbeats. In the near-total darkness, beasts paced or slept in their cages. Other gibbets and cells were suspended from the high ceiling that had once been part of a grand cathedral to a past lord or lady of the spire. The altar, where the lord had once accepted prayers and sacrifices, was surrounded by smaller cages with jewelled lizards and vicious rat-like predators kept captive.

The air was thick with the smell of dung and blood.

Skanis backed against a wall, keeping it between him and an enormous shaggy creature that slept chained to a pillar. He recognised the massive, powerful limbs and many-eyed crimson face of a Clawed Fiend, and knew it was a fine specimen worth a fortune in the city's fighting pits and execution arenas. Other cages nearby held khymerae, skinless quadrupeds with exposed skulls for faces, or fungus-based predators that accompanied orkoid war fleets and were little more than odious round bodies and teeth.

The razorwing clung more tightly to his shoulder. Everything here was new and uncertain to the creature, and truth be told, it was to Skanis as well. He had never been this close to the beasts of the arena and battlefield before. His old archon had kept a gorewyrm, a vicious tube of muscle with teeth at one end that sprayed acidic bile. It had been a child's pet compared to some of the creatures here.

Skanis crept through the menagerie, trying not to wake or disturb any of its thousands of inmates. Above him, a thing like a massive lizard crossed with a bat roosted in chains. A sslyth, with its fangs pulled out and fresh drill wounds in the side of its cranium, sat and drooled. A hive of insects mauled one another silently with their pincer-like mouthparts, encased in a glass maze.

'It is not often I have a guest who walks on two feet,' came a voice from the shadows.

Skanis tensed and cursed himself. The low susurration of sleeping animals had masked the sound of the other's footsteps, and the clutter of cages and cells had cut off his vision. Even before he had been given new senses by the haemonculus, he had never been surprised like that. If he had, he would be dead.

From between two cages walked a muscular female figure in a close-fitting armoured bodysuit. On a loop at her waist hung the coiled whip of a beastmaster. Strapped to her back was a staff that ended in a two-pronged globe, and her armour was covered in vials of poisons and sedatives. Her face was broad and sharp, and her shaven head was disfigured by three scars across her scalp deep enough to expose the bone. 'Are you, by any chance, responsible for the delightful commotion from below?' she asked.

'What does it matter to you if I am?'

The beastmaster shrugged. 'I prefer their screaming to their music,' she said. 'Fithrichol was a bad customer anyway. He always butchered my beasts and served them up to his followers.'

'Fithrichol is dead, and half his court with him.'

The beastmaster smiled. 'And none shall mourn them,' she said. 'But you're different. I haven't come across one of your kind before.'

'I am just passing through.'

'Did Urviel make you? Another customer I would not be sorry to lose.' The beastmaster took a few more steps closer to Skanis, who felt his muscles tense automatically. The beastmaster's eyes ran up and down him, as if she were assessing the pedigree of a valuable pit-beast. 'Good haunches,' she said. 'I wonder where he got them from. Talons from a ripperspine, grafted in with khymera skin. Did he give you the nerve-bundles from a barbed scuttler? Very good for the reactions. It's a signature of his. Tell me, do you have any idea where half of you is even from?'

'It doesn't matter,' said Skanis. 'I will soar above Commorragh. I will ride the winds over its spiretops. I don't care what beasts had to die to make it possible.'

'But you're so close to a beast yourself,' said the beastmaster, with a smile that made something recoil inside Skanis. 'You have shed what makes you drukhari and replaced it with something else. You are as enamoured with these creatures as I am.' She turned and indicated her caged menagerie with a sweep of her hand. 'I put them in cages. I train them. I buy and sell them. They exist at my pleasure. But you want to be one of them.'

The kabalite pride, the hot fury, wouldn't let Skanis walk away. 'If you are so far superior, beastmaster, then why do you lurk here in this filthy place? You are a slave to the lords and archons like every other vermin of Commorragh. What is it about this existence we find so alluring? This misery. This desperation. This servitude. Why does every single drukhari not strive to leave it behind?'

'Because one day,' said the beastmaster, face to face with Skanis now, 'I will loose my beasts on the courts of the great and cruel, and I will become a lord of Commorragh. Then I will have everything I ever desire.' She ran a hand along Skanis' arm. The nerve endings flared up at her touch. 'And I desire a lot.'

Skanis pulled his arm away. 'Everything I desire,' he said, 'lies far above here.'

'Wait,' said the beastmaster as Skanis turned to walk away. 'That plumage. Steel and the rust of old blood. I have sold thousands of razorwings but never one in those colours.'

Skanis glanced at the razorwing chick out of the corner of his eye. It still clung to his shoulder, shivering in discomfort with the presence of so many strange creatures. 'It is not for sale.'

'Everything is for sale. What is your price?'

'To leave here,' said Skanis.

'Oh, my dear,' said the beastmaster, leaning close against Skanis. He could smell the spice and leather on her. 'That is the only thing I can't give you.'

Skanis spun out of her grip. In response, she drew the whip

from her waist. He threw himself backwards as she lashed it at him and felt it draw a line of pain down one shin with a tremendous crack.

The noise woke the sleeping beasts. A rising cacophony erupted from everywhere at once as Skanis rolled past a cage of squawking, flightless birds and into the cover of a pillar.

'Give me the razorwing and you live,' called the beastmaster over the din. 'The best deal you will ever make!'

Skanis drew his pistol and fired in the direction of her voice. He heard the shards bursting harmlessly against stone.

The beastmaster struck again, the whip extending into a barbed length that wrapped around the pillar and scored a dozen deep furrows against Skanis' ribs. He roared in frustration as the weapon was withdrawn. He fired again, glimpsing the beastmaster with her lash in one hand and the pronged spear in the other.

Skanis swapped a new shard cylinder into the pistol. He lost sight of her and knew he was outclassed. The beastmaster had the range on him and this was her territory. Only a lucky hit from the pistol would win this for him. That wasn't a good enough chance. If she caught him well with the barbs, if she approached from an unexpected direction and pinned him in place with her spear, he would be dead before he could pull the trigger again.

He broke from the cover of the pillar. The crack of the whip and the swish of air past his ear told him the beastmaster had almost caught him around the neck. He skidded into the cover of a bank of khymerae cages, and flinched as the feline horrors snapped and snarled on the other side of the bars.

'I have a cage just for you,' snarled the beastmaster.

Skanis saw what he sought through the gloom – not the beastmaster, but the Clawed Fiend. It had woken up with the commotion and was growling and pacing, stretching the chain that tied it to the pillar.

He might only get one shot. He sighted down the pistol, expecting the barbed whip to take his hand clean off. He squeezed the trigger slowly but firmly, as he had learned in the bleeding halls of his kabal a lifetime ago.

The shards sheared through the chain holding the Clawed Fiend. The creature flicked its head and the chain thrashed around it, clattering off the stone of the pillar.

Skanis broke and ran as the Clawed Fiend burst into the menagerie. Its huge, shaggy bulk threw cages to the floor, and where they broke open, other creatures were set free. Shin-high predatory lizards hopped and shrieked. A muscular worm-like creature bunched and sprang, leaving a spray of purplish mucus in its wake. One of the khymerae was loose and it pounced on the smaller creatures suddenly scurrying around its feet. Its jaws closed in a flash of red and it threw a writhing furry body aside.

'You maniac!' cried the beastmaster as the bloody tumult spread like a fire.

Skanis could see the scars on the Clawed Fiend's back and the burned patches where the beastmaster's prod had been used like a branding iron. She cracked her whip as it loped towards her, but it had suffered so much it didn't seem to notice the new red line opening up among the old scars.

'You are mine!' the beastmaster shouted at the Clawed Fiend. She cracked the whip again, but the creature didn't flinch. 'Obey me! Obey!'

Skanis didn't stay around to watch what followed. He ran for the far end of the menagerie, darting around the beasts until he reached a twisted mass of rusted steel that granted access to the floors above.

He felt the razorwing chick shoot past his ear and grabbed it out of the air as he ran. Behind him, the Clawed Fiend bellowed and the beastmaster's voice reached him from the tumult. He couldn't tell if she was still cursing him, or screaming.

It didn't matter. He would never be down here again.

To the ignorant, it might have seemed beautiful.

This high up, the layer of smoke and cloud was a hazy, translucent layer of grey laid over the city. Commorragh looked like the spiny hide of a flayed beast beneath the fug. The uppermost spires pierced the clouds, each trying to outdo its neighbour. Some were shattered and dark, long abandoned save by the few creatures able to survive at this altitude. Others blazed with light where the archons and nobles tried to banish the desperation of their lives with the pursuit of power or pleasure.

The outside of the spire's pinnacle was covered in vanes and spikes, the remains of a communications system that had gone dark centuries ago. Skanis clung to one of the vanes against the shriek of the cold wind. His chest burned with each freezing breath but he exulted in the feeling. The lungs Urviel had given him were efficient enough to function up here. Any normal drukhari would have wilted and fallen asleep, never to wake up. Skanis was not normal.

Commorragh was beneath him now. Above him was just the sky, the veined purple of festering meat. Tiny winged specks wheeled in the upper cloud layer, forming loops and spirals as they swarmed. A flock of razorwings out hunting.

Skanis took the razorwing chick from his shoulder. It ruffled its red and steel plumage. He held the chick up into the wind and it spread its wings, and hopped out of his palm.

The tiny razorwing caught an updraught and soared high

above the spire pinnacle. Then it looped down again, newly assured in its flight, and arrowed down towards the flock below. Skanis watched it merge with the pattern.

Now, it was his turn.

Skanis gripped the vane with both hands. He felt the flickers of pain down his back and the wrenching in the places where his ribs met his spine. He gasped out loud as, even through the high scream of the wind, he could hear the sound of bone cracking and skin tearing.

Finally, with a wonderful wash of agony, his wings were fully spread.

They were beautiful. Skin – his own and donated from dozens of specimens in Urviel's lab – was spread across a framework of carved and hollowed bone. Scalloped lengths of flesh formed feather-like trailing edges. Urviel had carefully spliced new veins and arteries into the muscle, and they ran in a pulsing spider's web across Skanis' whole wingspan.

Skanis could have hung there forever, letting the knifing wind ignite the pain receptors of his new wings. But he had not come this far just for the sensation. That kind of quest was for the vermin of Commorragh, who destroyed themselves looking for a new experience to cloud over their misery. He opened his eyes, bunched up the grafted muscles in his legs, and launched himself off the spiretop.

The wind caught his wings and he flew straight across the top of the cloud layer. Protective membranes slid across his eyes to protect them from the wind. He hurtled, gathering speed, and angled his wings to soar up in a loop so fast and wide he thought he would breach Commorragh's atmosphere entirely. But then he reached the apex and dived again, pulled up to skim the smog layer, and left a rippling wake of disturbed smoke as he went.

Another spiretop rushed past beneath him. He glimpsed an eyrie built into its architecture – a nest-like structure where others like him survived far above the darkness of the city. He saw their wings, some feathered and some bat-like, and their masks that resembled narrow raptor beaks. They watched him as he soared overhead, and raised their daggers and swords in salute.

There were more spires too, stretching off further than Skanis' altered eyes could see. They had their own eyries, their own new angels, whose place was so far above the streets that they lived in another world.

The Scourges were the drukhari who had escaped Commorragh. They roosted in its abandoned spiretops and flew the air currents above the clouds. They were his people now, his species, apart from the rest of this miserable society. Skanis would find them and join them in abandoning the desperate cruelty of the drukhari. He would finally find what he had never had in the kabal – his own kind. He would be new. He would be complete.

The sensations of the flight were so overwhelming he didn't notice the wound on his forearm opening up again. The slashes in his leg and ribs were pulled apart too, and fresh blood flowed from them, dissipating in droplets into the wind. He left a trail of red as he circled and dived.

The blood fell through the cloud layer and into the swirling flock of razorwings. The creatures caught the scent and formed into a great dark wave of bodies, swelling upwards to hunt down the source.

Skanis did not notice them until the first of them broke his line of sight and soared above him. He banked and flew with his new companion in the sky. Another joined it, then a dozen more, and as one they hurtled down at him head-on.

Where they passed him in mid-air, their knife-sharp feathers sliced deep into his skin. He cried out and tumbled, having to fight to stay aloft. More of the flock darted at him, slashing at him with every pass. His blood showered down and drove their feeding frenzy higher.

Skanis twisted and dropped to get out of the heart of the flock, but the lure of his blood kept them on him as if they were each tied to Skanis' body by an invisible thread.

One tiny shape detached itself from the swooping mass of razorwings. Its uncertain wings took it on a wide, halting loop until it fell back down towards Skanis, folding its wings back as it gained speed.

Skanis just saw it as it shot towards him. The razorwing chick he had rescued from the gutters outside Kaledari Spire.

The chick arrowed straight into Skanis' left eye.

Skanis cried out as the razorwing thrashed in his eye socket. He lost control of his flight and he fell, spinning end over end, into the cloud layer. His wings were tatters now. A hundred wounds sprayed blood into a fine red mist around him. The razorwings followed him, slashing and devouring as he fell.

The pet grotesque loped eagerly down the alleyway at the scent of putrefaction. Urviel followed it through the gloom, tossing bones and body parts into the hide bag carried by a second grotesque beside him. Each grotesque had been made of the same scraps he found here in the lowest levels of Commorragh, where the trash of the spires eventually found a way into Urviel's domain.

It was a good day. Something had happened up on Kaledari Spire and the bodies were still falling. Fresh corpses, still wearing the garb of a great lord's courtiers, were littering the gutter-levels. Urviel had almost filled the bag with severed limbs and caved-in heads.

'What have you found?' the haemonculus hissed as the lead grotesque snuffled and growled at a heap on the ground. Urviel approached to see a pale, thin-limbed shape, broken against the stone where it had landed.

Urviel recognised the tattered wings that still clung to the corpse's back, and the unnaturally elongated bone structure.

'Hmm, yes, one of mine,' said Urviel. Patients and experiments came and went and Urviel no longer recalled names or faces, but he knew the pattern of feathered skin along the edge of the wing. Urviel lifted the draping tatters of membrane for a closer look. 'Did I know your name?' He paused. 'Yes. You thought you would be the one in a thousand who finds the eyries of the Scourges. But now you have come back to me. They always do.'

The grotesque gathered up the shattered body and threw it into the hide bag. Urviel's harvest for the day was complete, and it had been good. No matter how many drukhari came to be altered on his slab, no matter what dreams they had of moving beyond Commorragh, they always came back to him in the end. Another would come tomorrow, with the same dream, and the city would drag him back down, too. His flesh would become part of Urviel's next creation. Commorragh was a living thing. This was its life cycle.

Commorragh would hunger again. And there would always be another to feed it.

FLAYED

CAVAN SCOTT

Alundra was running, feet pounding on the dirt-covered road. She'd run everywhere all her life, always in a hurry. This way and that. Always being told to calm down – to stop and take a breath. She couldn't stop today. No one could, not if they wanted to live.

She turned a corner, tearing into a paved side alley, the soles of her sandals slipping on the slick flagstones. Something wet. She didn't look down to see what it was, didn't want to know.

Seventeen years she'd lived in the township. Her entire life. She knew every corner, recognised every sound: the chirp of the birds, the braying of the grox in the fields to the south, the clamour of market day. Not today. Today there were no birds and no bustle – only screams and explosions and the incessant rattle of shots being fired.

There had been raids before. Of course there had. Perversely, the attacks had become just as much a part of life as the daily grind of washing and cleaning. They had learned how to deal with them, the people of Sandran. At first sight of the invaders, a bell would sound, the streets clearing immediately. The rich would make for their bunkers, the poor to whichever crumbling hab they called home. Raid shutters nailed against windows, families huddling together in the dark, praying that they wouldn't be found.

Alundra could still remember her first time. A strange brew of absolute terror and the comforting smell of her mother, drawing her in tight and whispering gently in her ear. *It will be over soon, my darling, just you see.*

So many memories. Cautiously emerging onto the streets when the danger had passed, assessing the damage.

Clearing away the bodies.

So many bodies.

She'd seen her first corpse at the age of six, running into her aunt's hab after a raid and discovering that one of the monsters had materialised *behind* the shutters, within the imagined safety of the four walls.

Alundra had lost count of how many raids there had been since then. How many sleepless nights cringing in the darkness, listening to the screams.

But this time was different. This time, everyone was going to die.

There had been no peal, no warning. Just the roar of engines in the sky.

The Flayers were close behind, drawn to bloodshed like dust moths to a flame.

Her grandfather had warned them when she was just a kid. The old man had found Alundra fighting her brother one blazing summer afternoon, the two of them trying to claw each other's eyes out. There hadn't been a raid in two years, maybe three. Grandfather's calloused hands had pulled her from Husim, still kicking and screaming. It wasn't anything unusual. Husim and Alundra were always scrapping, too similar in temperament. Headstrong. Stubborn.

It had been the first time she'd ever heard Grandfather raise his voice.

'Don't you realise what you're doing? The Flayers can sense violence from two systems away. Do you want to bring them back, risk another raid?'

'That's rubbish,' Husim had sneered, full of childish arrogance. 'They don't exist. Galeb says. It's all lies.'

That night the bell sounded. All four generations of the family next door were slain. Husim and Alundra promised never to fight again.

As if that was ever going to happen.

Where was he? Alundra had already tried two of her brother's usual hangouts. One had been abandoned; the other had already been raided. She couldn't identify the remains, but the clothes didn't look like Husim's, even under all that gore.

Behind her, Alundra could hear the heavy tramp of booted feet, the all-too-familiar bark of handguns. They were close. Too close. She took a corner fast, belting down the narrow gap between two shops. There was an alley behind the buildings. She could avoid the main roads, make her way to Torin's place. If he couldn't come home, Husim would have gone there, probably dragging hapless Galeb with him.

'Frag, no.'

Alundra skidded to a halt, kicking up a plume of dust. A dead-end; tall redbrick buildings boxing her in. How could she have gone the wrong way? She ran over to the far wall, trying the solitary door's handle. Locked. Of course it was. There were a couple of windows on the upper levels, but was it worth chancing the old pipes that snaked down to a heap of barrels in the corner? No, she should head back to the main streets, get her bearings. Time was running out.

Alundra spun on her heels and felt the blood freeze in her veins. A ghoul stood in the entrance to the alleyway, swaying back and forth, hungry red eyes fixed on her. It seemed to be waiting for her to make the next move, the noonday sun reflecting off what little of its metal frame was exposed. Its grimacing skull was still visible, as was a blood-smeared chest-plate and long, knife-like fingers. The rest of its body was bound tightly in gory strips of human skin. Some of the bands looked old, like brittle leather baked in the sun, while others looked disturbingly fresh, edges caked in rapidly drying blood.

A Flayer.

Alundra had heard the name during her first raid. Grandfather had gathered her near, gently explaining what they were hiding from.

'They are daemons, my child, mechanical devils forged from steel and fury. They come to Sandran for one reason and one reason alone – to gorge on any living soul they encounter. They exist only to feed a hunger that can never be sated.'

Even as a child the very idea had seemed illogical.

'But they are machines, Grandfather,' Alundra had pointed out. 'They don't need to eat, do they?' The old man had merely shaken his head sadly. He didn't answer all of her questions that day. She'd asked where they came from, but he said he didn't know, no one did. She asked what happened to the bodies of their victims. He'd just sent her to help her mother, but not before warning her that they would strike again. The inevitability in his voice was more chilling than the stories of the ghouls themselves.

It was only later she discovered how the Flayers earned

their name – how the lifeless raiders wore the skins of their victims on their metal backs, a trophy for every kill. Some went even further, carrying exuviated torsos as grisly standards, testament to their madness.

Perhaps he had been trying to protect what little of her innocence was left. Maybe he had been right to. Three years later she glimpsed a Flayer through a gap in the raid shutters, watching in horror as it shaved the skin from the medicae as easily as someone might peel an apple. From that day on, her nightmares were filled with tarnished skeletons appearing from nowhere. That was the thing that actually scared her the most. Not the butchery itself, but the fact that the Flayers simply shimmered into being. No spaceships descending from on high or smouldering drop pods crashing to earth. These mechanical devils just materialised from thin air, flensing talons scraping together in fevered anticipation.

Just like the abomination standing before her.

The Flayer cocked its head one way and then the other, as if trying to ease out a crick in its neck, the fractured skulls it wore as a belt clattering as it swayed.

Who's going to make the first move? Alundra asked herself, amazed she was even capable of rational thought in such a situation. Who's going to run?

Time seemed to slow down, seconds stretching into minutes, hours, before she realised what she was going to do. She had always been fast, but could she outrun a Flayer? Only one way to find out.

Alundra feinted to the left as if she was going to attempt to run past it. The ghoul responded how she had hoped, racing forward to intercept, claws outstretched.

The gambit paid off, a move perfected over years of playing ball games with her brother and his friends, having to match their strength with fast feet and cunning. She immediately doubled back, racing for the barrels. She leapt on top of the containers, grabbing for the perilous drainpipe.

Realising its mistake, the Flayer dived towards her, talons closing around Alundra's ankle. She screamed as the Flayer yanked, the rusty metal of the pipe stripping the skin from her palms as she slipped back down.

Kicking back with her free leg, Alundra somehow managed to find the Flayer's head, although her thin leather sole was little use against a living metal skull. The raider grabbed at her, one of its claws piercing the back of her calf, not deep, but enough to remind her that this was a battle she could never win.

She would die here, in a litter-strewn alley, a crazed raider carving her up like a cheap grox steak. Worst of all, she would never see her brother again.

The alleyway erupted with the thunder of gunfire. Alundra felt the robot's claws whip away, looking down to see the Flayer flatten against the wall, shells punching into its body in quick succession. She followed the line of fire to its source, a giant stomping into the alleyway, an excessively large bolter held steady in a gloved hand. Her saviour was clad head-to-toe in heavy monochrome power armour, a winged skull emblazoned across a monumental chest. A similar death's head was displayed on its bone-white pauldron, this skull painted over a pair of crossed ebony scythes.

The Death Spectres, another name whispered by Grandfather all those years ago: a Chapter of Space Marines dedicated to protecting humanity from the terrors of the Ghoul Stars. No, that wasn't right. Dedicated to protecting the Imperium. There was a difference.

Whatever its mission, Alundra offered a prayer of thanks to the Angel of Death's God-Emperor. Just because she didn't believe in Him didn't mean He wouldn't listen. He might even deliver her from this madness, transport her far away from the vengeful Space Marine and the Flayer that was dancing like a deranged marionette under the Death Spectre's onslaught.

'Alundra. This way!'

She looked up, amazed not just to hear her name but also to recognise the voice that said it.

'Husim?'

Her brother was leaning out of the window above her, a toned arm reaching down. 'Keep climbing.'

Alundra didn't need telling twice. As the Space Marine emptied its weapon into the stricken Flayer Alundra climbed, ignoring the pain from her palms and calf. The pipe creaked under her weight and with a sickening ping started to pull away from the brickwork. As it arched back, she threw up her hand, finding her brother, and let herself be hauled up.

Her fingernails scraped against the stone sill as she scrambled for a hold. Husim leant further out of the window, grabbed the thin material at the back of her tunic and pulled her through. They tumbled to the floor on the other side. She was inside. She was safe.

The bolter fire had ceased.

'I need to see,' she exclaimed, scrabbling back up to the window.

'Alundra, wait!' Husim made a grab for her, but she shook him off, almost throwing herself back over the sill in her haste. The Flayer lay on the ground, twitching where it had fallen. As if the punishment hadn't been severe enough, the Death Spectre raised its grinding chainsword and severed the raider's head in one practised move. The metal skull rolled away from the decapitated torso, coming to rest face up, staring straight at Alundra. Their eyes locked for a second, before the lights beneath the Flayer's heavy brow flared and extinguished forever.

She became aware of another set of eyes upon her. The Death Spectre pointed its chainsword up at the window, uttering a single, solemn command.

'Stay where you are.'

Husim pulled her away from the window. 'What are you waiting for?' he shouted. 'Come on. We're upstairs.'

Dazed, Alundra dragged her eyes away from the Space Marine and limped after her brother.

'This way. Quickly.'

Husim grabbed her hand, guiding her down a corridor and through a storeroom. The place was crammed with sacks of grain and empty wooden trays. They were above the bakery.

'What are you doing here?' she asked, as her brother ushered her up a stairwell.

'Hiding, what do you think?'

She took the stairs two at a time, coming up into a sawdust-covered room stacked with boxes from wall to wall.

'Are you alone?'

'No. Galeb's here too,' Husim said, following her.

'What about Torin?'

Husim simply barged past, ignoring the question.

'Galeb needs your help.'

'He's hurt?'

'See for yourself.'

Husim pushed back the tattered curtain that was covering a doorway at the back of the room.

'What happened?' Alundra asked, rushing over to the boy lying on the floor. Yes, she knew that she should think of Galeb as a man now, but he'd always be her little brother's playmate, getting into scrapes and always coming out the worst.

But never as bad as this

'One of them got Torin,' Galeb wheezed, breaking into a wet, hacking cough.

'The idiot tried to stop it,' Husim said, his voice wavering despite the tough talk. 'Got slashed across the belly for his trouble.'

'It was killing him,' Galeb argued, wincing as he tried to push himself up.

'He was already dead,' replied Husim, flatly.

Alundra examined the blood-soaked shirts wrapped around Galeb's stomach.

'You did this?' she asked her brother.

'It was all we had,' Husim snapped back. 'I had to think quick.'

'You did well,' Alundra said, trying to still her brother's defensiveness. 'But we're going to need to find more supplies if we're going to get him out of here. Proper bandages.' She glanced around the room. There was a small pile of food in the corner, a couple of loaves, some migan fruits and a few nuts. It wouldn't last them long.

'We can't go back out there.'

Alundra fixed Husim with a look that told him he was being stupid. 'We have to.'

'No way,' Husim insisted, pacing back to the curtain and checking the room outside. 'We're safe here. We'll wait until the raid is over and then we'll get him home. Mother will know what to do.'

Alundra felt tears prick her eyes. She knew she should tell him why that wasn't possible, that Mother was no longer waiting at home, but it wouldn't have helped. He'd stick his heels in even further.

'He's right, Alundra,' Galeb wheezed, grabbing her arm with a trembling hand. 'If we head outside, we'll be taken.'

Alundra looked up into the rafters, feeling a fresh breeze across her face, cool against the stifling heat of the small room. She could just make out a hole in the ceiling. There must be an attic above them, maybe a way out onto the roof. Not that Galeb was in any fit state to clamber up and out of the building.

She closed her eyes for a second, letting the draught wash over her. She wished Grandfather were here. He'd know what to say, how to persuade the boys.

She squeezed Galeb's hand, forcing a smile. 'Listen to me, both of you. We've got to keep moving. Everyone is gathering in the town hall. They're going to find a way of getting us out of this.'

Husim snorted. 'What are they going to do? Reason with them?'

'They're going to try,' she snapped back. 'Better that than hiding in darkened rooms.'

'That's what we always do,' Galeb pointed out, his voice catching with the pain.

'This time is different,'

'Yeah,' snorted Husim. 'This time the ghouls aren't the problem.'

Alundra sighed, stood and walked back to her brother, placing her hand on his shoulder, giving it a squeeze in the same way Mother always had when she tried to get through to him.

It was amazing how soon you started thinking of someone in the past tense.

'We've got to move Galeb.'

'And how do we do that, genius?' he asked, shrugging her off.

'We'll carry him. If we're careful–'

A noise from below cut her off.

'What's that?' Galeb whimpered, only to be told to shut up by Husim who peeked around the curtain.

'There's nothing there.'

'It's coming from downstairs,' Galeb insisted, fixing Alundra with a panicked stare.

Footsteps.

They weren't alone in the building. It could have been the baker, of course – if the baker had started wearing exceptionally heavy boots.

'Husim...' Alundra hissed, willing her brother to make the right decision.

'Okay, okay,' he finally agreed, throwing his hands up in surrender. 'There's a hole in the wall in the far room. We can crawl through to the next building.'

'I won't be able to,' Galeb sobbed.

'You'll have to,' Husim insisted, moving over to his friend. 'Put your arm around me and keep quiet, will you?'

Alundra crept over to the little food Husim had scavenged, trying not to make too much noise as she shoved it into her brother's leather satchel.

The stairs creaked.

'It's coming up,' Galeb snivelled, drawing a glare from Husim. The three of them froze, staring at the thin curtain as they listened to the hydraulic pumps hissing with every step.

I should have got them to move straight away, Alundra scolded herself. Stupid. They could have been out of the building by now, heading to the town hall.

Whoever was on the other side of the curtain stopped. Alundra glanced at her brother, Galeb's arm around his shoulder, his own hand looped around his friend's waist, holding him close. Galeb's eyes were so wide they looked like he was no longer blinking.

Then, above them, something moved. Wood creaked. Metallic limbs glinted over their heads.

Alundra yelled a warning, forgetting about keeping quiet. Husim looked up to the ceiling and tried to pull his friend to the side, but it was too late. The Flayer dropped down from the rafters, landing on top of Galeb. Husim was shoved back, cracking his head on the far brickwork before slumping to the floor.

Galeb screamed as the monster's tapered claws pushed deep into his belly. The cry was replaced by the sound of someone choking on their own blood as the raider yanked free a handful of intestines and attempted to cram the fresh meat into metal jaws that couldn't even open. The entrails spilled through its fingers, slopping back down onto Galeb's convulsing body.

Trapped behind the Flayer, Husim threw himself forward, slamming against the metal body, trying to shove the ghoul from Galeb. The Flayer merely thrust out a hand, claws puncturing Husim's chest, pinning him against the wall.

Alundra looked around, frantically searching for something to use as a weapon. A water pipe ran around the foot of the wall. She gripped it hard, the rusted surface cutting into already punished hands, and yanked. It shifted, but not enough. She dropped down, pressing a foot against the wall and heaved again. Once, twice, until finally it came away from the wall.

Screeching like a banshee she rushed forward, bringing her makeshift quarterstaff down on the skin-covered back. It connected sharply with the ghoul's exo-skeleton, sending vibrations shooting back up her arms, almost forcing her to drop the pipe. But she carried on battering the living robot, screaming in fury with every strike.

The attack was short-lived. With a hiss of annoyance, the

Flayer turned, slashing out with bloodied claws, and swatted her aside. Gashes opened cleanly across her side and she was propelled headfirst into the wall, the pipe clattering across the floor. Alundra threw up her hands to protect herself, the skin tearing from her arms as she skidded down the bricks.

She landed in a crumpled heap, reeling from shock and pain, her head spinning. Husim's screams seemed to be coming from all directions at once.

'Leave him, abomination, and feel the Emperor's teeth.'

A shadow fell over Alundra, a giant figure pushing its way into the tiny room, ripping the curtain from its pole, chainsword held aloft and growling like a mechanical hound. Her saviour from the alley. The Death Spectre.

The Flayer whirled around, flinging Husim aside, but it was already too late. The chainsword bit into the Flayer's shoulder plate, cleaving the monstrosity in two in a blaze of coruscating sparks.

Alundra scrabbled behind the Space Marine, gathering Husim into her arms, trying to gauge how badly he was hurt. Her brother's chest was a spider's web of lacerations, each ebbing dark, treacle-like blood. His eyes were rolling in their sockets, his body going into shock. She shouted his name, trying to get him to stay with her.

'You must come with me,' a reverberant voice growled above her. The Space Marine was looming over her, its power armour splattered with gore and oil. 'Leave the boy.'

Alundra all but snarled at her rescuer. 'He's my brother.'

The Death Spectre reached out a gauntleted hand and pushed her aside to examine Husim, the Angel of Death's touch gentler than Alundra had expected.

'The injuries are severe,' the hulking figure concluded categorically. 'He will not survive.'

'He won't if we leave him here,' she snapped back, her fury giving her courage she never knew she possessed. The Space Marine could snap her neck in an instant, but she didn't care anymore. There was no hope of rescuing Galeb, trampled beneath the Flayer's bisected corpse, but she wasn't going to abandon her brother.

A shower of sawdust rained down from above. The fight had attracted more ghouls, hoping to scavenge carrion. Three of the creatures were attempting to claw their way through the hole in the ceiling, stuck halfway in their haste. It wouldn't take long for them to burst through. The ceiling was already bulging, cracks spreading as they struggled, consumed with blood lust.

'Get out,' the Death Spectre barked, snatching his mag-locked bolter from his leg and firing into the Flayers, the report of the gun like thunder in the enclosed space. 'Get out now!'

Alundra grabbed Husim, ignoring his screamed protestations, and bundled him out of the room even as the ceiling gave way. Behind her, flensing claws squealed against cer-amite armour.

She didn't look back.

'We're nearly there,' Alundra coaxed, half carrying her brother down the back stairs to the ground floor. She'd slipped twice, Husim landing painfully on her own injuries. There was no time to rest. It sounded as if the building were about to come down around them.

'Hurts,' Husim whined, sounding like the child she had known growing up. 'Really bad.'

'I know, Hu, but you've got to help me. We can do this together.'

'Okay, Ma,' Husim replied weakly, at least attempting to put one foot in front of the other. Alundra didn't correct his mistake.

The stairs ended in another storage area, crammed with mops and buckets. She struggled over to the door, praying that it wouldn't be locked, that they wouldn't be trapped here. She could hear talons skittering on floorboards above. Perhaps even an Angel of Death hadn't been strong enough to hold back a flood of ravenous Flayers. A renewed volley of bolter fire told her differently. If the Space Marine could keep the Flayer busy she might still be able to get Husim to a semblance of safety.

She twisted the handle, cursing when the door wouldn't budge. Hefting her brother, she put her shoulder to it, offering thanks to a Throne she still didn't believe in when it shifted in the frame. Just stiff. They could get out of this. She tried again and it sprang open, nearly sending them sprawling across the bakery's tiled kitchen.

Outside she could hear concussive blasts and the deafening howl of transports thundering through the air. The evacuation had already started.

'This way,' she said, guiding Husim around a large wooden preparation table and into the passageway. There was a heavy thud from above, knocking plaster from the ceiling. Husim had stopped responding, but at least was allowing himself to be mindlessly led by his sister. 'Not long now,' she lied.

Something crashed down the stairs, clattering into the buckets and trays.

'Just keep going,' she said, barrelling into a narrow corridor that led out to the street, unsure if she was encouraging herself or Husim. 'A few more steps, that's all.'

They reached the door. They were going to get out. Shifting

Husim's weight, she reached forward, pulling on the handle. It didn't move. She panicked, her heart thudding in her chest. Why wasn't it moving? Then the realisation dawned. Push to open. She laughed at the ridiculousness of the situation, and shoved at the metal door. It swung open easily; too easily. Alundra and her brother tumbled forward, Husim's legs giving way, dragging her down. The two of them splayed on the floor, Husim crying out. It was the last sound she'd ever hear him make.

Alundra groaned, her wounds, shallow though they were, burning like a furnace in her side. She looked up, realising that she was staring at melanoid boots that crunched on the dirt as they turned. She cast her eyes skywards, squinting in the sun, not one but two unmistakable silhouettes above her.

'No,' Alundra cried out, trying to throw herself over Husim as armoured fingers pulled her roughly back to her feet.

'Superficial wounds,' rumbled a red-helmed Death Spectre, yanking her arm up to examine the dark stain across her tunic. 'Scan her, Quintus.'

'At once, Sergeant Vilda.'

Alundra tried to wriggle free but the sergeant just stood as immovable as a statue, its brother sweeping a handheld augury up and down the length of her body. The device buzzed and chirped as the results scrolled on a screen.

'She is surprisingly well-nourished, sir. No known maladies or infections,' the Death Spectre called Quintus reported, looking up from the augury. 'Safely within selection parameters.'

Her captor nodded. 'Excellent. She will be taken with the others.'

Alundra fought against Vilda's grip. 'What about my brother? You need to help him.'

The Death Spectre released her, and she tumbled back into the dirt, instinctively reaching out to touch Husim. He was so still.

Quintus didn't even check his scanner.

'Subject rejected,' he intoned. 'Injuries fatal.'

'No,' Alundra yelled, springing back to her feet and pounding her fists against the Space Marine's chest, no longer caring if such actions were tantamount to a death sentence. 'You've got to do something. He can't die.'

The red-helmeted sergeant grabbed her arm once again, but this time the fingers bit deeper, bruising muscle, making her cry out.

'And spirited too,' he commented, sounding what, amused? She wanted to kill both of them.

From the passage behind them a voice rumbled out, agreeing with the sentiment. Alundra twisted to see her saviour marching down the restricted space of the corridor, his pauldrons scraping against the narrow walls. As he stepped out into the sun, Alundra couldn't help but stare. The Space Marine had lost his helm in the battle, revealing a stark visage, almost completely devoid of pigment. The skin was corpse white, with closely cropped hair the colour of snow and eyes as red as the blood that flowed freely from a fresh wound across his pale cheek.

'She took on a Flayed One single-handed,' he reported, almost sounding proud. 'Strength of will as well as body. Unusual for a human.'

'Then we have chosen well, Karnos,' Vilda replied, shoving Alundra towards the albino. 'Prime stock. Take her to the transport.'

'Wait,' Alundra pleaded, as Karnos clutched her arms tightly. 'I'll go with you, as long as you take my brother too.'

Vilda reached forwards, grabbing her cheeks between thumb and forefinger.

'Listen to me, girl,' the Death Spectre snarled. 'If it were up to me you would all burn. Too many of my brothers have been lost rescuing you from these unholy aberrations.'

'Sergeant Vilda,' Quintus warned, glancing up the road. 'Another wave of necrons is approaching...'

But Vilda didn't acknowledge his battle-brother. 'The Megir has ordered we select the best specimens from your settlement, those strong and healthy enough to bear future generations who might join the ranks of the Death Spectres.'

Prime stock. Vilda's early comment replayed in her mind, filling her with a deeper horror than the Flayers had ever induced.

'Suitable colonies are few and far between this far from the heart of the Imperium. An Exterminatus order has been issued and you will be taken to a suitable breeding world near Occludus. A glorious future awaits, girl. You will serve your Emperor well.'

Behind her, Karnos released one of her arms to fire into the approaching Flayers. It was the chance Alundra had been waiting for, a distraction she could use to escape, but the fight had gone, stripped as easily as the ghouls could have flensed her skin.

'Sir,' Quintus prompted, 'we should make for the extraction point.'

'Agreed,' Vilda acknowledged, pushing Alundra's face away sharply. Her head cracked painfully against Karnos' chestplate. 'Bring her.'

Alundra didn't struggle as Karnos plucked her from her feet. Instead she stared into the glazing eyes of her brother as he lay in the rampaging necrons' path, bleeding out in the baking sun.

A MEMORY OF THARSIS

JOSH REYNOLDS

The black mills of Quir never slept.

Volcanic furnaces constantly vomited clouds of grey ash up through sky-scraping chimneys. The thunder of mining equipment echoed forever up from abyssal quarries. Everywhere was the cacophony of industry run wild. It echoed even unto the uppermost reaches of the stratosphere, and the half-finished orbital docking ring that girdled Quir like a halo of metal. But it wasn't merely that hellish clamour which caused Fabius Bile to wince in discomfort as he descended the ramp to the landing platform.

Rather, it was the sound of raw voices, raised in song. The atonal din caused the thin air to reverberate, and made Bile's remaining teeth itch down to their cancerous roots. His fingers clenched about the skull of brass that topped the sceptre he leaned on. It glowed faintly with an unnatural sheen. Power thrummed through it, menacing and covetous. There was an intelligence there, if rudimentary, and it desired to be put to use. The sceptre was an amplifier, and its slightest touch could elicit a raging torrent of agony in even the strongest subject. He'd named it Torment, in a fit of whimsy.

Bile had no doubt that a similar compulsion had motivated this unwelcome display. Hunched, malformed shapes clad in the ragged remnants of ancestral hazard suits stood on the rust-riddled landing platform before him. No two of the factory workers were alike. Some were mostly human, save for an unsightly deformity, while others were barely bipedal. A few sported feathers or scales. Many had coiling, cephalopod-like tentacles rather than hands. One lumbering brute bore a rack of antlers that would have put a Fenrisian elk to shame. They were arrayed in two rows to either side of the disembarkation ramp, like soldiers awaiting the arrival of a visiting dignitary.

The mutants swayed in time to the orchestral piece echoing down from the gargoyle-shaped vox-casters mounted high above the landing platform. The bursts of music drew forth a crude hymn from the ravaged throats of the gathered workers. Cybernetic cherubs swooped overhead, brass-and-steel wings hissing. The tiny creatures shrilled at one another in corrupted binary as they swept incense-spewing censers back and forth above the gathering, further adding to the baroque ridiculousness of it all.

Bile stood for a moment, taking it all in. Hololithic readouts shimmered into view before his eyes as his power armour's sensors scanned his immediate surroundings. Familiar genetic patterns sprawled lazily across the data, each one marked with the telltale spiral of his signature. His lips stretched in a thin smile.

These creatures were his children, in all the ways that mattered. He had grown their ancestors in vats, pulled them screaming from the darkness and delivered them up to their destiny. To see their descendants now evoked in him a rare flicker of pity, if only for the squandered potential. And yet, they thrived. They were strong, in their way. Durable. Adaptable, if lacking in the ability to carry a tune. Fit for purpose. That was all the Lady Spohr, Magos-Queen of Quir, asked of them.

Spohr was a strange one, even by the standards of renegade Mechanicus adepts. Like all queens, she demanded fitting tribute from her supplicants. If she was displeased with her gift, things could get out of hand very quickly. The rotting remains of those who'd disappointed her hung from the chimneys of her factories. No one lived to repeat such foolishness.

Each time he came to Quir looking for repairs to his ancient and dilapidated medicae equipment, he had to bring something new and utterly unique. Things that no other supplicant could offer her. It was almost a game. He had crafted her workers, woven a fleshweave, even cloned her original organic form, for purposes she had not divulged. But she had been growing bored with his arts even then. Still, he would persevere. He had a responsibility.

That was his work. To improve upon the flawed designs of those who had come before, and seed the stars with a New Man – one adapted to the grim darkness of the current millennium. The weight of such a destiny threatened to crush him, at times. But he would press on, whatever the cost. The task must be completed.

He sighed and started down the ramp. The ancient servos in his armour whined in protest, and the stretched faces of his skin-coat moaned softly. Securing Spohr's services was imperative. And for that, he needed to keep her engaged. Once she had her tribute, she would inevitably lose interest.

During their previous interactions, it was only by holding her attention, by engaging her organic half, that he had been able to ensure that he got what he needed, afterwards. Like the queens of old, Spohr had little interest in fair bargains.

An honour guard of cybernetic soldiers waited at the foot of the ramp. They were clad in shell-like ceramite beneath thick coats and cowls, and clutched antique radium carbines. Strange sigils had been carved into the ceramite, and their coats, like his own, were made from a patchwork of stolen flesh. Some wore grotesque masks beneath their cowls, while others had exposed faces that were more metal than meat. They watched his approach warily, targeting lenses whirring as they took stock of him. His own targeting systems returned the favour, intercepting and meshing with the foreign systems, albeit briefly. His armour, like many things exposed to the persistent environmental uncertainties of warp space, had developed something akin to a rudimentary sentience. Its curiosity, like his own, was insatiable.

For an instant, he saw himself through the artificial optics of the cybernetic warriors. A helmet, pockmarked by impact craters, its colouring scraped away to reveal bare grey ceramite in places. Metallic arachnid limbs, topped by blades, saws and glistening syringes, rose over his bent frame, twitching in time to some faint, internal modulation. Like his armour and Torment, the chirurgeon had a mind of its own. Bile smiled. At times, he fancied that he wasn't so much a singular being as a colony of like-minded symbiotes – each of them feeding off and being fed on in turn by the others. They were as much a part of him as the blight that gnawed at his vitals like an all-consuming fire. He grimaced. Thinking of it made the pain worse. The blight was eating him hollow. Soon, he would be gone entirely.

The chirurgeon hissed, and a syringe jabbed his neck. A cool flush filled his system, burying the pain beneath a chemical balm. There were more important matters to attend to than his own inevitable slide into dissolution. Only his work mattered. Work that would stutter to a halt unless he secured the services of his hostess.

An enclosed mechanised palanquin wheezed its way across the loading platform on six pneumatic limbs. It was an ornate monstrosity, dripping with unnecessary gilt and machine-carved grotesquery. Its curtains were made from a chromatic fleshweave of his own design, which shifted hues with every step of its heavy, clawed feet. It was one of his more recent gifts to the mistress of this world, and one he took no little pride in. Though he often preferred to err on the side of function over form, it was nonetheless a rare pleasure in these fraught times to indulge his creativity.

More of the cybernetic soldiers followed the palanquin at a disciplined lope, their radium carbines held at the ready. These were more heavily armoured than the others, less meat and more machine, sealed in crustacean-like shells of almost organic-looking metal. They wore masks that had been wrought in the shape of daemonic faces, and their coats were branded with the runes of the four Ruinous Powers. They steamed with unnatural heat in the open air, as if whatever passed for their blood was on the cusp of boiling over.

Bile could feel a familiar quiver in the air that had nothing to do with the off-key singing of the assembled workers. The warriors were conversing with one another, and with their mistress, through a neural node-link. He smiled politely, awaiting her arrival. The palanquin slowed as it approached, and its limbs bent with a querulous groan. It lowered itself to the ground. The curtains curled aside with a somnolent murmur as the Magos-Queen of Quir rose and stepped down onto the platform.

The Lady Spohr was a work of art destined never to be completed. She was tall and heavy, built for war rather than idle contemplation. Thick robes, intricately woven with scenes from Martian legend, hid her lower half, and her upper was encased in a heavy golden cuirass bulging with bundles of cables, pumps, hoses and sensory nodes. Smoke issued from vents on her armour, filling the air around her with a cloying miasma.

Thin sensor-filaments extended outwards from her chest and shoulders, their tips pulsing in time to a silent rhythm. Her arms were folded before her, loose sleeves dangling. Her cowl was thrown back, revealing a skull of gold, etched in binary, and a profusion of isolated power cables, which spilled across her shoulders like the mane of some veldt-born felinoid. She wore a loose belt of silver-plated skulls about the swell where her hips might once have been. Each of the silver skulls was marked with a different cogwheel rune.

Her eyes clicked, focusing on him. She moved forwards smoothly, with artificial grace. Bile bowed as low as he was able, and said, 'You are truly a most welcome sight for this weary traveller, my lady. A beacon in the eternal night of our exile.'

Spohr paused. 'Flattery. A sure sign you have come to bargain, Fabius.' Her voice was not the rasp one might expect. Instead, her words clicked like well-oiled gears. 'I hope you have brought a suitable tribute.' She glanced up at the gunship. 'A sensor sweep of your vessel revealed nothing of interest.' There was a warning note in her voice. 'I considered destroying you as you descended, as a warning to others. It is not wise to come here empty-handed.'

It was Bile's turn to hesitate. This was always the most dangerous part of the negotiations. She might decide to kill him out of hand, if he didn't prick her curiosity. He made a show of glancing around, and gestured to the singing workers with Torment.

'Was this gathering your idea?'

'They sing your praises. A hymn to Pater Mutatis, Changemaster of the Sixfold Helix. Your creations love you, even when they belong to another.' Her tone told him nothing of how she might feel about that. Nor, in truth, did he particularly care. That his creations were designed to venerate him seemed only sensible. A tool that could turn on its creator was of little use, and love was a stronger chain than fear.

But these were not his creations, only their descendants. Like the fleshweave curtains of her palanquin, the ancestors of her workers had been a gift. They had been designed to her specifications, and grown in his few remaining flesh-vats, in the aftermath of his expulsion from Canticle City and the destruction of his facilities there. An expenditure of dwindling resources, in those days. That they had survived at all was impressive. That they had bred true was nothing short of a miracle. Bile looked at Spohr.

'A fine gift, their ancestors. Don't you agree?'

Spohr turned. 'Come.'

Her manner was as terse as ever. He took no offence. Spohr's mind was a vast web, stretched between every node and cogitator on the forge world. Her attentions were split between a thousand different tasks. The sheer amount of raw data would drive a lesser mind insane. Bile had often thought that his own work would be easier if he could approach it from multiple angles simultaneously. Perhaps one day such a thing might be possible. Until then, he would have to settle for his own two hands, and the aid of his chirurgeon.

He walked with her across the platform, followed at a discreet distance by her maniple of guards. An itch at the nape of his neck told him that there were others he couldn't see, watching him through targeting scopes. It was to be expected. Anything less, and he might have been insulted.

'It has been seventy-five point eight rotations of the seasonal cycle since your last visit. On average, your visits occur every one hundred rotations. You are early.' She paused, listening to something only she could hear. Her attentions snapped back into focus a moment later. 'Explain.'

'Perhaps I missed you.'

Spohr looked at him. 'Your attempts at humour have not improved in the intervening rotations.' Cylindrical gibbet cages hung here and there from the uppermost reaches of the facility, to dangle over the platform. Inside several of them, mutants crouched, groaning. As Spohr led him past several cages, one of the prisoners reached through the bars towards Bile, slurring a plea for mercy.

He batted its groping claw aside and laughed as the cage spun in a lazy circle. 'It has never been a strength of mine, I admit.'

'Prevarication. Why are you early?'

'Necessity.' Bile coughed. He felt the chirurgeon tense, pulling tight against his spine, and internal readouts flashed across the inside of his helmet. He dismissed them. 'My requirements are simple, but urgent. I am at a... delicate stage in my work. I cannot afford any delay.'

They left the cages behind and continued on to the edge of the platform. A heavy rail, decorated with machine-precise carvings of an obscene nature, separated them from the smog-choked skies. Bile looked out over the horizon, bracing himself against the high winds that tore at the edges of the platform. Below, a massive ore-hauler, its hull dotted with tumorous malformations, surfaced from the smog-bank with a rumble of engines and rose towards the ring of atmospheric processing centres. It was accompanied in its flight by a flock of smaller bat-like shapes, which shrieked and spun almost playfully through the air. The strange flock dispersed and swept back down into the smog as the ore-hauler gained altitude.

The processed and refined ore it carried would be transported out of the upper atmosphere and to the ever-growing circumference of the orbital docking ring. Quir, like its mistress, was a work in progress.

That urge to tinker was a familiar one. He felt it himself, whenever he considered his own physiology. Unlike Spohr, however, his efforts yielded precious few improvements. At best, they held things in stasis. For now, that would have to do. His obsolescence could not be avoided, but his work would live on. That was all that mattered.

'Your heart rate has elevated by a percentile of point nine nine nine. Are you ill?'

Bile coughed into his fist. Blood speckled his gauntlet. He could feel his hearts straining in their traces, and the weight of something cancerous growing in his abdomen. 'No more so than usual,' he said. He peered at her. 'Do you ever wonder what might have been?'

'I endeavour to weigh all potentialities microsecond to microsecond.' She paused, head cocked. He felt an itch in his cortex, and knew she was initiating a neural congress with a node somewhere on the planet below. A hiss of binary slipped from behind the golden rictus, pattering across his ears like the whisper of rain. The moment passed as swiftly as it had come. 'That which cannot be calculated is irrelevant. That which cannot aid in calculation is also irrelevant.'

'And are those the same calculations that led you to abandon Mars all those long centuries ago?' A careful question, designed to prick her curiosity. He turned, watching something that might have been a shadow stagger-dance across the platform. More of the shadow-things whirled and twitched in the corners or among the gathered mutants. He'd seen such things before, in transit through the warp. Echoes of the dead, flickering across the perceptions of the living. The flotsam and jetsam of the great Sea of Souls.

Spohr glanced at him as his words registered. An inadvertent, almost human, gesture. She hesitated. It was a small thing. A twitch of lenses, a brief series of clicks, but Bile saw it and congratulated himself. She was intrigued.

'I do not remember Mars,' she said, finally. 'Memories serve no useful purpose. They are–'

'Irrelevant, yes,' he said, pretending to watch the shadows creep and dance. 'You know, from orbit, the landmass your facilities inhabit quite resembles those on the slopes of Tharsis Tholus. I thought you'd chosen it knowingly.'

Another hesitation. So brief as to be unnoticed save by one alert for it. 'The resemblance is irrelevant. I chose it because it best serves my needs.'

Bile turned away from the shadows. Below, a flock of the flapping, bat-like things took flight from beneath the platform. They spiralled up into the air, shrieking a strange, sad song. He watched them for a moment, before replying.

'I noted signs of ongoing terraforming efforts as I entered orbit. Almost as if someone were attempting to incite the formation and eruption of volcanic activity. Tharsis Tholus was built into a volcano, was it not?'

'It is for thermal harvesting purposes. I grow weary of this discussion. Where is my tribute?' The question was delivered sharply. Her optic lenses clicked in irritation. He had her. Anger was one of the few emotions left to her.

Bile smiled and pressed his advantage. 'Still, it was beautiful, in its way.'

'Beauty is irrelevant. Irrelevancies are purged from the dataflow. Mars – Tharsis – was – is – irrelevant to current operating parameters. Quir is my home, now.' There was a certain finality to that statement. An irrevocable implication. Nonetheless, he continued.

'Irrelevance is a matter of perception, I suppose. What is a person but the sum of their experiences, good and bad? All things contribute to the whole, even the most insignificant of occurrences. Weigh them, pare them away, and soon you will be left with nothing.'

'Not nothing. Something better.'

Bile shrugged. 'There are too many fools in Eyespace who seek to divest themselves of past failures. They yearn to rewrite history, as if by doing so they might erase the sins of history. What is done is done. One must build on a foundation of regrets, mistakes and frustrations if one is to ascend properly. One must always look forward, not backward.'

'Nothing of value can be built on weakness.'

'Weakness is the soil in which the seeds of future strength are sown.' He gestured to himself. 'Weakness of flesh, of body and mind, compels me to heights undreamt of by my former peers. I have remade demigods in my image, and drawn from the wellspring of life itself. If I were certain in my strength, pure of function, I would not have achieved half of those deeds which see my signature writ in the blood and marrow of innumerable peoples.'

Spohr studied him. 'By my estimates, your biological functions will cease in–'

Bile gestured sharply. 'Spare me, I beg you. I have my own hourglass, and enough sand to fill it.'

'Elevated pulse. You are frightened. Have you forgotten my tribute, Fabius? Is that why we are discussing irrelevant things?'

'Annoyed, not frightened,' he corrected, ignoring her question. 'Death comes for all things, in one way or another. Ships rust, planetary cores collapse, suns go cold and even demigods die. My only fear is that I will pass on unfulfilled, and my work uncompleted.' He looked at her. 'Hence, I come to you. I am in need of some equipment.'

Spohr waited, in silence. Bile gestured airily. 'Specialised equipment. I have designs. I lack the ability to make those designs a reality.'

'Admittance of weakness. Unexpected.'

'There inevitably comes a point when aid is required, regardless of one's wishes,' Bile said, leaning on Torment. 'I am no enginseer. Machinery is as alien to me as the inner workings of the limbic system are to you.'

'I am well aware of the purpose of that biological network.'

'Of course, forgive me.' Bile smiled thinly. 'I should have guessed that one who has shed so much of it would understand its intricacies.'

For a moment, the only sound was the whirr-click of Spohr's internal augurs. Then, 'Condescension. You are being tedious, Fabius.'

He laughed. 'Yes. Again, my apologies. One does grow used to being the most adept mind in the room.' He bowed, slightly. 'But your cognitive processes were legend among the servants of the Omnissiah, even before it all went wrong.'

She looked at him. 'It did not go wrong. The plan was flawed from conception.'

'Then why follow it – follow us – into damnation? Why abandon Tharsis for this smog-laced hell, at the behest of the Warmaster?'

Spohr was silent. He could hear the machinery within her chugging along, like a cogitator long past its prime. Calculating.

'The reason is irrelevant,' she said. 'It was done. That is all that matters.'

Bile looked away. 'As you say. Only one question remains – will you do as I ask?'

'Others have enquired much the same, of late,' Spohr said. The wind whipped at her robes, momentarily revealing the anarchic configuration beneath. Neither legs nor serpentine coils, but some juddering mixture of both. 'They say to me – do this thing, and we shall repay you tenfold. Do this thing, and our lord will be grateful.'

Bile frowned, suddenly wary. 'And what thing was this, that they wished of you, dear lady?' he asked, carefully.

Spohr laughed. An artificial, staccato sound, the approximation of humour by one who had forgotten what it means. 'They wish me to cage you, Fabius. To seal you in iron, until such time as they require your services. You are a tool which has exceeded its function, and that cannot be borne.'

'The same might be said of you.' An unexpected – and unwelcome – development. This was no longer the old, familiar game. He had many enemies. He wondered which of them were responsible for this, out of those who considered him to be too useful to dispose of. Lorgar's sons had tried more than once to bind him, as if he were one of their wretched daemons. Even his own Legion had sought to enslave him, in a way.

'No,' Spohr said. 'I perform my function. I mine ore. I smelt metal. I construct engines of war. As has always been my task.'

'But no longer in the service of the Red Planet. No longer for the glory of Tharsis Tholus, with its great dome of ochre and crimson.' He glanced around. Was this nothing more than a distraction? He ground his teeth, frustrated. He was close to a breakthrough. He needed the equipment Spohr could provide. He had no time for this.

'Irrelevant. I perform my function. I do not exceed it. All is in balance.' She turned, power cables rustling like agitated serpents. 'You are not. You exceed your parameters. You distort your purpose. You must be stripped from the mechanism, so that it runs smoothly.'

'So it has been said.' Bile stepped back. His augurs were being jammed. Hololithic overlays showed only static. It might simply be atmospheric interference, but he doubted it. This was a trap. And he had walked right into it, blindly. He bared rotten teeth in a grimace. It wasn't the first time, and it certainly wouldn't be the last. It was becoming clear to him that someone wanted to stop him. To stop his work, to prevent him from achieving his destiny. This was simply the latest in a string of attempts.

'That has always been the difference between us, my lady,' he said. 'I have chosen my function, and it is to ensure my obsolescence, while you – and those you speak of – seek only to preserve your antiquated purpose in the crumbling husk of the universal machine.' He shook his head. 'Strip me out? There is no need. I have removed myself.'

'And yet your function impedes the whole.' The accusation was delivered with mild force. Her mind was elsewhere again, racing along strands of caged lightning. He was unimportant, in the greater scheme of things. An item to be crossed off a list of duties. He admired her efficiency. 'You must cease.'

'On whose authority?' Bile looked around. 'I see no familiar faces here, save your own. My enemies leave the burden to you. Why is that, I wonder?'

Spohr gestured.

There was a blurt of static, as if in response. The proximity augurs of Bile's armour spat a warning and he turned, eyes narrowing in consternation. A telltale flicker alerted him a half-second before the blow landed. Combat stimulants automatically flooded his system. He ducked aside, avoiding a blow that would have flattened him, if not snapped his spine. His hand dropped to the Xyclos needler holstered on his hip. He drew it smoothly and fired. Even the smallest scratch from one of the needler's thin darts could induce madness or death.

Providing that the target was organic, of course.

This one, unfortunately, was not.

Colours ran like condensation, revealing the hulking form of what had once been a Kastelan robot. The machine was almost three times his size. Its oil-black carapace was draped in a shroud of writhing fleshweave, which had camouflaged the machine. Bile frowned, annoyed at himself. Spohr had reverse-engineered his gift, making it over into something more useful.

'Ingenious,' he muttered, lowering his needler. It would do him no good against a foe such as this. Between the omnipresent din and the fleshweave, he'd been blind to its presence.

Nerve-like tendril webs had spread and become bloated, bursting through the armour plating like roots through stone. Steaming runes marked its chassis, and clusters of

tiny, inhuman faces sprouted like barnacles from the seals
of its joints. The ancient war machine panted like a hungry
beast as it paced towards him, powerful claws flexing. Its
dome-like cranium was twisted, the metal reshaped into an
approximation of a bestial leer. The steaming barrel of the
combustor weapon mounted on its carapace swung towards
him, the air wavering from the heat.

He stepped back, and the weapon tracked him. He glanced
towards her. 'They have offered you nothing for your efforts,
my lady.'

'As you offer me nothing. Where is my tribute, Fabius? You
come empty-handed to my world, and try to bargain with me?
Insult. Condescension. Arrogance.' The power cables about
her golden skull sparked with sudden life, and the lenses of
her eyes flashed. 'They are right. You must be chained. This
is my world, and I will not be insulted.'

Bile twisted aside as the Kastelan's claw sprang towards
him. It clanked shut, shearing off a piece of his coat. Bile
swung Torment towards the back of its knee, hoping to slow
it down. The sceptre screamed in frustration as it struck the
unfeeling metal. There were no nerves to enflame. The robot's
arm swept backwards, nearly taking Bile's head off.

A glancing blow caught the machine on one of the root-like
tendril webs. It retreated with a growl of static. Bile smiled.
It did have nerves of a sort, after all. That was promising. He
backed away, drawing it after him. The combuster mounted
on its shoulder spat molten death, and he ducked away. The
heat of it blackened the skin of his cheek, but there was no
pain. Not yet. Later, if he survived.

A half-step took him inside its reach, and he slammed Torment against the largest fibrous bundle of quasi-flesh. The
Kastelan reacted with alacrity, emitting a screech of binary.

It swung wildly and its combustor vomited heat. The stimulants in Bile's system carried him swiftly around the frenzied machine. He leapt for its back, hooking his fingers into a buckled plate. He nearly lost his grip as the robot turned, still shrieking an inarticulate stream of zeroes and ones, but managed to haul himself up. His power armour's ancient servos groaned from the strain as he perched on the war machine's shoulder and smashed the combuster from its housing.

The robot groped blindly for him, its claws snapping at his legs. He rose to a crouch and lifted Torment over his head, the skull-top facing down. He drove it downwards with piston-like force, crumpling the black metal and releasing a storm of sparks. The Kastelan staggered and its shrieks sputtered into silence. A second blow sent it to one knee. A third obliterated the bestial leer. Smoke spewed upwards, enveloping Bile as the robot toppled forwards. He slid off the robot's chassis a moment before impact, and crouched on one knee, hearts thundering.

Beneath the balm of stimulants, he could feel his overtaxed systems attempting to compensate for his efforts. He coughed, and blood speckled his chin. Spohr's cybernetic guards paced towards him out of the smoke, radium carbines at the ready. Balancing himself with Torment, he drew his needler.

'For shame, my lady.' He tracked the stalking shapes as targeting overlays filled his vision. They would be more vulnerable to his concoctions than the robot, but not by much. 'What offence have I given, that warrants such treatment? Will you turn a friend over to his enemies without a second thought?'

'You have no friends. You demand, without giving.' Spohr raised her claw. 'You bring no tribute. Therefore, I will make one of you.'

'No tribute? I never said that.' He laughed. 'Indeed, had you given me the chance, I would have offered it up to you.'

Spohr studied him for a moment. Calculating. He felt a tremor in the air, and her warriors lowered their weapons. They sank to their haunches, weapons braced across their knees, and fixed him with a communal watchfulness.

'What can you offer me that is more precious than the satisfaction of your imprisonment?' she asked.

A hidden slot opened on his gauntlet, revealing an innocuous data-spike. He extracted it and extended it to her. 'Judge for yourself.'

Spohr took the spike and examined it. 'Explain.'

'It is a data-spike. Rather self-explanatory, don't you agree?'

'I have data-spikes.'

Bile peered at her. 'Humour?'

'An observation. What is on it?'

Bile's thin features split in a wide smile. 'Why, a memory, my lady.'

Spohr hesitated. 'A memory?'

'A single moment in time, dredged from the consciousness of an unfortunate archmagos and preserved in electronic amber.'

'What time? What memory?'

Bile gestured. 'See for yourself.'

Still, the hesitation. She was wary. Ready for treachery, though he had never dealt any less than fairly with her. Spohr had not become queen by being trusting of strange men bearing gifts. She inserted the data-spike into a port on her cuirass. The lenses of her eyes clicked. A soft hum filled the air as it shimmered and turned red. Hololithic images hazed into being, springing from in-built emitters.

'Oh,' Spohr said, softly.

Bile rose to his feet, his coat rippling in the memory of a

Martian wind. Th
the setting s
with loos
immense v
plains below
Tholus. The me
acrid Martian air,
even if he did say s

'Mars. As it was bef

Spohr stood silent and
better days.

Bile continued. 'A weakness. A
of calculation.'

Spohr reached up, towards the red sun,
the dome of the volcano. 'I forgot the wa
the thermal resonators,' she said. 'And the syro-
clastic sifters, as the temperatures dropped fell.
She looked at him.

'Irrelevant,' Bile said again.

'Humour,' she said.

He smiled. 'An observation. Is it acceptabl

Spohr turned away. 'Yes. I will consider yo
paused. 'And I will tell you the name
you wish. Your tribute is worth th

Bile considered her offer, b on
a hand. 'No. Their identiti

His enemies were le
crowded with pyrom
ashes. Bile had no
its celebrants. O
From its ashes w

One created by him.

LEFT FOR DEAD

STEVE LYONS

The war on Parius Monumentus was over.

Hive Opus had been pried from the claws of depravity, thank the Emperor! Blessed order was finally restored.

The Astra Militarum could claim the victory. The local militia, chronically undermanned, had misjudged the spread of corruption; it had overtaken and overwhelmed them, forcing them to transmit an astropathic distress call.

A Death Korps of Krieg regiment had arrived to take control, and for a full month, day and night, the sky had flashed and thundered to the relentless beat of their siege guns. The city's walls had shuddered and inexorably crumbled. Its decadent captors had been put to flight – and then, most of them, to the sword.

The Korpsmen had departed, with other wars on other worlds to fight. Silence had settled in their wake – only long enough for the Emperor's loyal subjects to breathe a collective prayer of relief. Then the real work had begun.

The sky now resounded with the roars of construction vehicles. The shattered debris of habs and factorums groaned beneath the weight of caterpillar tracks. The gilt-edged finery of the city's cathedrals, reduced to fragments, was shovelled away by claw blades. Exposed guts of great mining machines spat and hissed and touched off fires.

Jarvan was a corporal in the Parius Interior Guard.

He was new to the rank since his predecessor had been captured and butchered by the enemy, and was eager to prove himself. He had charge of a labour gang, one of thousands: just under a hundred weary and traumatised civilians charged with sifting through the wreckage, recovering what they could. Whip-wielding servitors stood over them, encouraging them in these duties.

Thus it was that Corporal Jarvan encountered the stranger.

His labour gang was dragging bodies from a fallen hab-block. They had found a number of survivors yesterday; not quite so many today. Tomorrow, they would be reassigned to a higher priority area. Power was yet to be restored to this hive sector. Freestanding lumen units coughed and sputtered out sprays of pale white light, between which lurked brooding shadows.

Jarvan turned his head at just the moment to see a shape flitting through those shadows. One with no right to be there. He snapped up his rifle with its flashlight attachment, pinpointing the figure of a man.

His skin was pale, as with any lower-level hive-dweller deprived of direct sunlight. He was young and wiry, with a military buzz cut. Jarvan's eyes were immediately drawn to the lasgun in his hand, though the stranger wasn't aiming it.

'Drop the weapon! *Drop it!* Down on your knees. Lace your

hands behind your head.' The stranger complied with each instruction in turn.

'Identify yourself,' the corporal demanded.

The stranger didn't answer. He knelt, staring at Jarvan with dull eyes, unblinking. Jarvan thought he might be a soldier. He had the build and bearing of one, but no uniform. He wore a set of shapeless grey coveralls, singed, tattered and soiled.

'Identify yourself,' repeated Jarvan. 'Name and rank?'

'Don't remember,' said the stranger, the words catching in his throat.

Drawing closer, Jarvan saw that the stranger's head was cut. Blood had crusted around the wound and striped his cheek. He was probably concussed. The corporal motioned to the nearest of his labourers; he hadn't bothered to remember their names or faces. He sent three of them to strip the stranger and search him.

He didn't resist.

One labourer brought the stranger's weapon to Jarvan. At a glance, he could see that it wasn't Parius issue. He had seen enough like it in recent weeks, however. The lasgun was modified to fire a more powerful shot, but at a cost. Extra sink rings had been fitted around its barrel to bleed off excess heat. It bore the stamp of the Imperial forges on Lucius, which made it Krieg property.

'Where did you get this?'

The stranger didn't answer him. His eyes remained fixed upon Jarvan as the labourers ran calloused hands over him, searching for tattoos or mutations. They reported that the stranger was clean – and one of them had found his ident papers. At the corporal's impatient urging, he read out the details haltingly.

'His name is, uh, Arvo, sir. Registered to… this sector. He's a menial, third-grade.'

Jarvan was almost disappointed. So much fuss, he thought, for a maintenance drudge. He must have taken the lasgun from a fallen trooper. Likely had no idea how to use it. Jarvan was inclined to shoot him on the spot and save a medicae's time and effort.

He lowered his rifle instead, crouching to inspect the stranger's eyes. Clear enough, he judged. He straightened up, beckoning to his labourers again. 'Take him to the medicae and be swift about it. Back in twenty minutes or I'll have you both flogged.' More than enough time had been wasted on distractions. He had no intention of missing his end-of-shift quotas.

The stranger was hauled out of Corporal Jarvan's sight and, almost as quickly, faded from his thoughts.

The medicae facility was no quieter than anywhere else. The air buzzed with urgent shouts, rushing footsteps and the howls and screams and dying gurgles of the untended wounded.

In fact, the word 'facility' over-dignified this place: a makeshift camp strewn between the cranes and hoists of a broken-down factorum. A hundred drudges scrubbed the walls, only gradually eroding centuries of ingrained soot. Their mops swirled fresher vomit and blood around the floor. Haggard medics stumbled between them, red-eyed and dishevelled, urgent pleas pulling them in all directions.

The man known as Arvo was dumped on a creaking gurney. He lay on his back and let the clamour wash over him. It merged with the ringing in his head to deny him the sleep he sorely needed. He breathed in the stench of infected and diseased bodies. Occasionally, he slipped into a fitful doze, to be woken by a gunshot. For many of his fellow patients, it appeared, a bullet to the brain was the most efficient treatment.

For hours, only two people showed Arvo any attention. The first was an Administratum clerk who checked his papers, tapped his details into a data-slate, clicked his tongue to himself and moved away. The second was a middle-aged woman, dripping piously with religious symbols, who searched him as the labourers at the hab-block had searched him, for signs of Chaos corruption.

In between these interruptions, his mind fled to the recent past.

Hive Opus had been split open, its cannons silenced. The Death Korps had risen from their trenches and surged forwards. They were strafed with small-arms fire, to no avail. For every skull-masked figure cut down, two more appeared to replace him. Their advance continued, unstoppable. A tidal wave of screaming madness.

Their enemies were worshippers of excess, wanton revellers in carnal pleasure. They possessed not a fraction of the Korpsmen's iron discipline. In the face of the Emperor's holy vengeance, they broke. Holes gaped open within the cultists' masses, into which the Korpsmen poured and widened them with guns, combat knives and the strength of their own sinews.

Arvo's head rang to each beat of the battle. His ears had been deadened, his eyes flash-blinded by a bursting grenade. The stink of blood and fire, cordite and death assailed his nostrils. He lay on his stomach in the dirt, pinned down. Blood crawled, hot and sticky, down his right cheek.

His vision was beginning to clear, though it was still blurred. Shapes shifted around him, through a thickening smoke haze.

He must have briefly lost consciousness as the battlefront had passed over him. Death Korpsmen surrounded him, encased in flak armour and heavy greatcoats. Their boots pulverised the debris beside his head.

How inhuman they looked, he thought, with their faces concealed behind rebreather masks so that even their eyes were hidden. From this lowly vantage point, he couldn't tell one from another.

They must have seen him, in turn, but no one came to help him. Why would they? He was nothing but a stranger to them too – and each Korpsman was looking for a clear shot at the enemy, through the crush of his comrades before him, following an imperative drilled into him from birth. Pushing forward, ever forward.

Then, minutes, hours or days had passed, and they were gone.

Arvo barely remembered dragging himself to his feet, throwing off the hunks of masonry that had piled up on his back. He found himself, for the very first time in his life, alone. He had clung to his lasgun throughout his ordeal, so hard the fingers of his right hand had seized up around its trigger guard.

His mask had been knocked askew. The rebreather unit on his chest was dented and inoperative. He shucked off his coat and discarded his broken equipment. The air was unpleasant, but at least it wasn't toxic, not like the air of his birth world. Not like Krieg.

The man who would be known as Arvo held his mask in his gloved hands. He stared at the reflection of a face he didn't recognise in its blank, skull-eye sockets and an unfamiliar thought, an unworthy thought, occurred to him.

He was free.

* * *

Arvo was yanked back to the present, and to his makeshift sickbed.

A medicae squinted at him through an augmetic eyepiece. He clicked his fingers at a servitor, which trundled over. It brought up a heavy hypodermic arm, inside which serum-filled tubes cycled until one locked into place. The servitor thrust a huge needle into Arvo's stomach and a chemical bolt dulled his pain and tiredness, sharpening his mind.

'Discharged,' the medicae grunted, turning away from him.

Arvo called after him, 'No, wait. Where do I go?'

'No further treatment necessary. Discharged.' The medicae hovered over another patient, presenting his back to Arvo. 'Full recovery impossible. Termination advised,' he pronounced in this case, and moved on.

Arvo climbed off the gurney. The moment his feet touched the floor, a pair of drudges deposited an unconscious woman in his place. Their downcast eyes avoided his and he chose not to question them. He was wary of asking too many questions. He took his papers – rather, *Arvo's* papers – from his pocket. He found an address on them. A hab? It wasn't clear. He had never known such a thing.

Other discharged patients were joining a line. It stretched from a desk at which a middle-aged man worked unhurriedly. Arvo followed the line out of the building, halfway around a city block. He eavesdropped as someone else asked what the line was for and was told 'habitation and labour assignments.'

He took his place at the back of the line and waited.

He spoke only once, when someone behind him grumbled that his sprained ankle hadn't been bandaged. 'The Emperor gives us all we need,' snapped Arvo, 'and resources must be managed.' He regretted abandoning his depleted medi-kit along with his uniform. He could have sterilised his head wound.

'Name and ident number?' asked the desk clerk, three hours later.

He thumbed a data-slate, nodding occasionally to himself. Arvo waited, half-expecting the clerk to uncover his deception as soon as he looked up and saw his face.

'Your hab-sector has been condemned, I see. I'm assigning you to a shelter and a labour gang.' The clerk took the stub of a pencil to Arvo's papers, made and initialled some amendments, and slid them back across the desk. He didn't glance at Arvo at all. Checking his wrist chrono, he said, 'Your first work shift begins at twenty-six-hundred hours. The time now is twenty-four-eighteen. Next!'

Public vehicles were leaving the medicae camp all the time, dispersing ex-patients across the sprawling, multi-layered city. Now Arvo knew what was expected of him, he acted accordingly. Among the bleary-eyed crowd, he located six others bound for his sector and an Interior Guard groundcar and driver to take them there.

Arvo rode on the fender as they snaked their way through burning industrial blocks and around impassable thoroughfares. He drank in the sounds, sights and smells of a world unlike any he had seen before, a world that few of his kind would ever see: a broken world, for sure, but a world – for the moment – at peace. Arvo's new world.

The girl watched Arvo for four days before she dared approach him.

Her labour gang, now his gang too, was excavating a collapsed grain store. Their Interior Guard overseer had impressed upon them the import of this task. Emergency supplies had been requested from the closest agri world, but thousands could starve waiting for them.

Arvo had one of the larger tools: a pickaxe. He was shattering the biggest, most intractable hunks of debris so that others could scoop them up with shovels. The girl had a shovel and had worked her way closer to him.

As soon as she was allowed, she took a beaker of water to him.

'Hello,' she said. 'My name is Zanne.'

He responded with a disinterested grunt. He swung his axe, shattered stone, hefted the axe again. He didn't take the water from her. She had rarely seen Arvo talking to anyone else. This had been by choice to begin with. Having been rebuffed, however, his fellow labourers now tended to shun him.

'Your name is Arvo,' Zanne persisted. 'I heard the overseer say so.'

'Yes,' he allowed. 'My name is Arvo.'

'And you're from Hab-Sector Kappa-Two-Phi. I used to live there.'

Arvo swung his axe, shattered stone, hefted the axe again.

'How did you get so strong?'

This question fazed him, just a little, interrupting his rhythm.

'I think you're the strongest in our gang,' Zanne told him. He was, in fact, easily the best and most tireless worker among them. She didn't think the servitors had ever had to whip him. The others often talked about him in resentful tones because he made them look idle, more deserving of the lash in comparison.

'The work is good,' Arvo grunted.

Zanne was surprised. 'You enjoy it?'

'It is good to build, to improve things rather than destroy them.'

She considered that statement, chewing on her lower lip. 'Yes,' she agreed at length, 'I suppose it is.'

A servitor wheeled its ponderous frame their way. Quickly, Zanne dropped to her knees and began to shovel again. She set Arvo's beaker down beside him. 'You should drink it,' she insisted. 'You don't know when there'll be more. This is good water too, hardly any slime in it. Some days, there is none at all.'

Arvo looked at her for the first time. 'How old are you?'

'Eleven,' said Zanne proudly. 'Ten and three-quarters, really, but I've been looking after myself since I was six.'

'What happened to your...?' He struggled to find the right word.

'My parents? I don't remember my dad. He died when I was a little girl. They said it was a monster that got loose in the mines. Then Mum was ill and I had to look after her. I had to work to earn food for us to eat. But she died too.'

'The illness took her?'

Zanne shook her head.

'The cultists, then?'

'She was in our hab-block when it collapsed. The blasphemers were hiding in there, you see, so the soldiers had to–'

Arvo's eyes narrowed. A muscle in his cheek twitched. 'The soldiers killed her?'

'They had no choice. They had to stop the blasphemers. For the Emperor.' Zanne spoke in a perfectly matter-of-fact tone, as if relating something she had read in a book. Her life, she had always been taught, was what it was and there was no point being sad about that. Self-pity, in fact, was the very worst kind of ingratitude.

She was almost grateful for the hard work too. It kept her mind busy.

Arvo pushed his untouched beaker towards her. 'Here,' he said. 'You drink it.'

He didn't have to offer twice. Zanne downed the quenching water in one gulp. The servitor, it transpired, was still watching her; she felt its lash across her shoulders for taking more than her share, but it was worth it. What was one more stripe to add to all the others? She wiped her lips on her filthy, ragged sleeve.

'I did not mean to get you in trouble,' Arvo mumbled, once the servitor's attention was safely elsewhere again.

'It wasn't your fault,' Zanne assured him.

'We have our orders,' said Arvo stiffly, 'and we must follow them.'

Between work shifts, they ate, slept and did little else, alongside a thousand others in a designated refugee shelter.

The building had been a chapel, but was desecrated beyond hope of salvation. Wooden pews had been hacked to pieces, stained-glass windows shattered. Blood and faeces had been scrubbed from the walls but had left a lingering pungent scent – while the outlines of spray-painted blasphemies endured.

Arvo collected his ration of gruel that night and, as always, consumed it sitting cross-legged on his blanket. Tonight, for the first time, someone joined him. He didn't object to Zanne's presence, though again it was left to her to break the silence.

'Do you have any family?' she asked him.

Arvo shook his head.

'What, never? But you must have. There must have been someone. Everyone has a mum and a dad, even if they never–'

Arvo interrupted her angrily. 'I had no one. Nothing. Just a…' He checked himself, as if regretting his candour. He sighed. 'I do not belong here.'

Zanne longed to ask what he meant by that. She had had her first glimpse behind the stranger's façade, however, and feared what else she might unleash. She summoned her courage anyway. She had never met anyone unlike herself before; she wanted to know everything about him. But as she opened her mouth, her moment was stolen.

A howl of rage and panicked yelling emerged from one of the transepts.

Arvo was on his feet before Zanne had seen him move. His bowl clattered to the tiled floor, spilling its contents. Zanne, too, was brushed aside. While others gaped and cowered, too weary and afraid to act, Arvo waded through them. Zanne began to follow him but stopped, suddenly afraid.

A man burst from the transept: gangly, half-dressed and dirty, wild-eyed with a straggly, lice-infested beard. He screamed in a way that Zanne had seen few times before, like a man possessed, scattering those around him with the force of his insanity.

A few braver souls tried to catch him, struggling for a grip on his sinewy arms and legs, tearing his once-white shift. They and many others shouted warnings, prayers or just shouted mindlessly, afraid. Their voices crashed into each other so that only their fear was communicated, spreading like wildfire.

Arvo stepped confidently into the madman's path. His hand lashed out like a python. There was a crack of bone and the madman was abruptly silenced. He collapsed to the floor, his eyes rolling back into his head – and the fear subsided, though the crash of voices did not.

Overseers in the chapel were only beginning to react to the

disturbance, pushing through a newly energised crowd. The madman, though certainly dead, was punched and kicked and spat on.

Everyone was keen to offer their version of events. Zanne made out some of the details therein: '–shirking his duties–', '–more than his share of water–', '–muttered something that sounded like–', '–only mouthing the words of the prayer–', '–hiding something on his shoulder, like a tattoo or–'

Arvo shrank from the centre of attention, reappearing at Zanne's side. No one appeared to notice him, for all he had just done for them. His part had been played in the blink of an eye and he retreated back into anonymity.

The overseers swiftly concluded their investigations. They didn't bother to inspect the madman's body, but picked out two labourers at random and instructed them to dispose of it. Funeral pyres had been burning across the city for weeks. This was just a little more fuel for the closest of them.

'How did you know?' Zanne asked Arvo. 'How did you know what to do?'

'Decisive action was required,' he stated flatly.

'Yes, but *how did you know* – that what they were saying about that man was true? Did you hear or see something or…?' Zanne turned to her newfound friend and saw the truth in his dull, grey eyes. Her voice tailed off.

'Decisive action was required,' he said.

'I understand,' Zanne told him.

It was half an hour later and most of the lumen units had been shut off. Tired refugees hunkered down on the cold tiles, wrapped in their threadbare blankets. Some of them, exhausted by the day's travails and needing to replenish their strength for tomorrow's, were already snoring.

'I've been thinking about it,' said Zanne, keeping her voice low in deference to the slumbering mounds around her, 'and I really do. I understand.'

Arvo grunted. He had poured his water ration into his bowl and was bathing his head wound with it. Once he was done, he put the bowl to his lips and drained it.

'You saw how everyone was starting to panic and you had to do something to stop it. If you hadn't, things could've been much worse. People could have been trampled and... that man probably did something to deserve it, anyway.'

One life for many more; it seemed a reasonable equation, at least to those who knew how capricious death – and the will of the Emperor – could be.

'They're saying that a group of cultists hid in the shelter in Sector Eta-Two-something,' Zanne whispered. 'During the night they took out their knives and they went around slitting the throats of–'

Arvo placed a hand on Zanne's. 'Fetch your blanket,' he said gruffly. Crowded though the chapel was, there was some space around him. No one wanted to get too close.

The girl's face lit up. She hurried off to do as she was told. By the time she returned, Arvo was asleep.

In his dream he was on the ground; paralysed, helpless, as soldiers in skull masks were being blasted to pieces around him. He knew he shouldn't care. For every one that died two more appeared to replace him, there was no stopping them – yet somehow, in the garbled world of the dream, every skull-masked soldier was him.

The dream disturbed him, yet oddly it brought him comfort too. When the waking bells wrenched him back to consciousness and he remembered where he was, a knot tightened in the pit of his stomach.

The dream, at least, had been of a familiar world. He had known his place there, known his duty and there had been others, many millions of others, like him. In the waking world, this world at peace, Arvo found himself lost.

Overseers were on the move, encouraging the slow-to-rouse. Arvo located Zanne and nudged her with his toe, sparing her the lash. 'Stay close to me today,' he whispered. He could already hear the clatters of ladles, depositing grey slop in tin bowls. He couldn't tarry if he wished to eat. There was rarely enough for everyone.

Artificial hive light streamed through the broken windows, catching shards of coloured glass and diffusing into rainbows. Another day stretched out ahead of Arvo. Another long, hard workday. It wasn't the work that made him feel weary, however.

Arvo was wearied by the effort of pretending to be an ordinary Imperial citizen – when he hardly knew what that meant.

'Attention, all citizens.'

The voice blared out from vox speakers across the sector. Everyone was expected to heed its words without pausing in their labours.

It occurred to Zanne that, after all the devastation, the speakers had been the first things restored, which was only right of course. Communication was vital and the morning bulletins delivered good news to lift the spirits. Today, for example, there had been a great victory on Orath, as the Emperor's Angels descended from the skies to cleanse that world of pestilence.

There was also a warning about diehard cultist cells in hiding across Hive Opus. *'A spy was uncovered in a refuge only last night, scheming to sabotage our reconstruction efforts. It was by the Emperor's grace and through the vigilance of ordinary citizens such as yourselves that his vile plot was foiled.'*

Zanne had no shovel today, having been late in line for tools. She had to dig with her hands, which was no excuse for slacking. Private Renne was overseeing. He was a little more mindful of Zanne's young age than most. He let her take water to the other labourers, so they could drink without leaving their posts.

She found Arvo kneeling, cradling something in his lap. He had laid down his axe. Zanne crouched beside him, concerned that he might be hurt, and saw what he was holding. It was a mask; a gas mask with a hole for a rebreather tube. One of its round eyepieces had been shattered and the cloth was stiff with dried blood.

Arvo had half uncovered a fallen man. Zanne had noticed the body, but paid it no heed – it was just one of many, very many. It seemed to have affected her friend, however.

The dead man's right eye was a mess. Zanne recognised a bullet wound by now, and knew it would have been instantly fatal. Arvo must have peeled the gas mask from the corpse. What was it about this one in particular that had made his eyes glaze over?

'Did you know him?' she asked.

Arvo hesitated. 'In a way,' he confessed.

'He isn't wearing anything.'

'The quartermasters must have reached him before he was buried.'

She frowned at the unfamiliar word. 'Quartermasters?'

'They salvaged his weapon, his armour, his equipment.' Arvo turned the mask over in his hands. 'They only left this behind because it is broken beyond repair. It served its purpose and is useless to them now. Just like its owner.'

'Who was he?' asked Zanne.

'One of our liberators.'

'The Astra Militarum?' Zanne had thought she'd never seen an Imperial Guardsman before. She now realised that she had seen plenty in recent days. She had just never seen one alive. Much had been rumoured about the implacable, faceless soldiers of the Death Korps of Krieg. Bereft of their fearsome armour they looked like anyone else, any casualty of war.

Why did Orath merit Angels when Parius had to make do with ordinary men?

'Praise the Emperor for their sacrifice,' she said, mimicking the morning bulletins.

'They are bred to fight and to die for Him,' Arvo murmured. 'They believe their lives are worth less than other lives. This man had nothing but his duty. He was glad to take a bullet in the eye, so that we could... We could...'

'We could be free,' said Zanne.

'Yes,' said Arvo dully. 'So we could be free.'

They had rested too long. A whip servitor sprang up behind them, the muscles in its overdeveloped shoulders cording. The lash that replaced its right arm struck at Arvo's back, crackling with a mild electric charge for good measure.

Arvo accepted his punishment with hardly a wince. He dropped the blood-encrusted mask and retook his pickaxe. Only Zanne heard the bitter words he muttered to himself as he resumed his toil with redoubled efforts: 'So we could be free.'

They achieved a breakthrough later that afternoon.

The labourers cleared a way into a storage cellar. Private Renne shone a luminator down there and announced that it appeared intact. He sent a dozen labourers down into the darkness at once. Zanne would gladly have been one of them and was small enough to fit. Arvo held her back with a shake of his head.

For the next few hours, bulging grain sacks were hauled up from the cellar, passed along a line of workers, loaded into waiting trucks. One boy was whipped insensate when a sack tore in his arms, disgorging its load. Zanne was among those who had to kneel and claw back what they could from the dirt.

They worked an extra hour, so flushed was Renne with their success.

By the end of it, the cellar was almost picked clean. Then, a woman in the entranceway lost her footing with a full sack in her hands. Her flailing hand snatched at a creaking, groaning rafter for support – and the whole world shifted.

A terrible roar pierced Zanne's ears. She thought they might be bleeding. She found herself hugging the ground, choking on black dust, blinded by tears. She came to realise only gradually that the shaking had stopped. As her eardrums cleared, she heard coughs and splutters, wails of pain and cracked, feeble cries for help.

Zanne's first thought was to get back to work before a servitor saw her. She made it to her knees before doubling over, hacking up dust and bile. There were bodies strewn about her. Some were twitching, some ominously still. Others struggled to escape from beneath fresh mounds of wreckage.

'It's all right.' She heard a familiar voice in her ear. A strong arm encircled her shoulders. 'It's over. You're safe.' Arvo had produced a beaker of water from somewhere – probably his own ration. She accepted it gratefully.

'All those p-people,' Zanne stammered, trembling with shock.

Arvo shook his head. 'We can do nothing for them.'

'You stopped me going down there. You knew the cellar was unsafe. You could have... Why didn't you say something?'

'The overseers saw what I saw,' Arvo assured her. 'They knew what I knew. It is not for us to question their decisions.'

The weary trudge back to the shelter that night was made under a heavier pall of silence than usual. As the workers filed through the chapel doors, Private Renne joined a small group of his comrades outside. He boasted to them about his successful day, about the amount of food he had recovered.

Inside the chapel, there was no sign of extra food, just fewer mouths to eat it. What little gruel remained was lukewarm, starting to congeal. Zanne was too tired to feel hungry anyway. She went straight to bed. Despite her gang's extended shift today, work would resume exactly on schedule tomorrow.

'I heard something today,' said Zanne. 'From someone at the refuge. His labour gang found another soldier, a Death Korps of Krieg-er. Alive.'

Arvo shook his head. 'No.'

'Why not?' protested Zanne, although she had in fact been lying.

'The quartermasters count every Korpsman back into the dropships.'

'But what if–?'

'Only the dead are left behind – or the missing, presumed dead.'

'Yes, but what if one of the–?'

'A survivor would make himself known to the planetary authorities and arrange return to his company as soon as possible, else be a deserter.'

They were tramping through the streets of the hive. Their gang was being herded to its new assignment, which was further away than the old one. This gave them half an hour's respite each morning before the real work started. Zanne liked that the over-seers tolerated some talking, as long as their charges walked.

'What would happen, then?' she asked. 'To a deserter?'

He didn't answer. Zanne studied his face for a clue to what he was thinking, but found none. 'You said,' she prompted him, 'that the Krieg-ers were *bred*. To be soldiers?'

'For a Korpsman to disobey orders,' Arvo murmured, so she had to strain to hear him, 'it is unknown, inconceiva-ble. His conditioning... Unless...'

'Unless what?'

'Unless the Korpsman himself was... deficient. Or touched by Chaos.'

At the sound of the word, Zanne made the protective sign of the aquila across her chest. 'They must be frightened, sometimes, even soldiers.'

'We are taught not to question. We are taught that the Emperor has all the answers, even when we are blind to them. We are taught that to think forbidden thoughts is a sign of insanity, but how... How can we know for sure?'

'If I had to be shot at and blown up every day and had to face all kinds of monsters, I think I'd be frightened.'

'Not frightened,' Arvo muttered. 'Never frightened.'

He wouldn't be drawn further on the subject.

He didn't speak again until later that afternoon. They were clearing the site of a demolished hab-block, to allow a new one to be erected. They had overfilled a waste disposal cart, which Arvo had to wheel to the incinerators. Zanne went along, a volunteer, to steady his load and to shovel up the debris that sloughed from it.

'What will you do?' Arvo asked her unexpectedly.

She frowned. 'When? What do you mean?'

'Once the reconstruction is complete. What did you do before?'

Zanne laughed at him. 'There was no "before."' Seeing Arvo's brow furrow, she tried to explain. 'There is always rebuilding to do. We build, the traitors and the monsters come along and knock everything down, and we have to build again.'

'Then this, the labour gangs, this is all there is?'

They were standing at the furnace mouth. Its breath seared the side of Zanne's face and cast her friend in a fiery orange glow. 'We serve the Emperor if we build faster than our enemies destroy.' She was reciting old words again, words she had learned in her schola. 'When we build more than we need on Parius, we can send metal and chemicals to the Emperor's forges and men to fight for Him.'

'Then what...?' Arvo thought better of the question and stifled it.

He turned away, applying himself to the emptying of the cart. Zanne had to prompt him twice before he looked at her again.

'What are those men fighting for?' he asked in a deathly whisper.

His eyes demanded an answer, but she had none to give. Instead, to fill the uncomfortable silence, Zanne blurted out, 'I knew him. He was our neighbour, back in the old hab-block. He used to come around and fix our lumoglobes when they... I thought I should tell you, that's all.'

Arvo didn't move, didn't speak. Zanne wondered if she had made a terrible mistake. There was no taking back the words, however. Not now she had finally released them. She couldn't bottle her secret up again.

'I knew the real Arvo,' she confessed.

* * *

Arvo returned to the shelter that night to find Zanne's blanket gone.

She had moved it as far away from him as she could. She avoided him at work too, though he kept an eye on her as much as possible. Only three days later did he find – and take – a chance to speak to her again.

Zanne looked tired. She had been lashed three times already. She was beginning to sag again, and whip servitors were circling. Arvo took water over to her. Zanne smiled weakly through the sheen of dirt that covered her round face. She was shivering. He felt her forehead. It was hot and his hand came away damp.

She let him help her dig, until the servitors turned their gazes elsewhere.

'He was dead when I found him,' he muttered to her. 'I did not kill him.'

Zanne gaped at him. 'Of course not. I never thought–'

He knew now why she alone had talked to him, why she had been so curious. He owed her an explanation. For three days, he had striven to formulate one.

'I woke and I was alone,' he began, interrupting her. 'I found his body, Arvo's body, and I... It may have been the blow to my head, but... I wondered why his life, your lives, were worth more than our lives. I wondered what you had that was so precious, worth the sacrifice of so many of my brothers.'

'You thought too many questions.'

Arvo nodded. 'Yes. I did. I wanted to understand.'

'I...' began Zanne. She swallowed, averting her eyes from him. 'I have questions sometimes, too. Just in my mind, but...'

'Go on,' he said.

'Sometimes, in the block, I'd hear people saying, "why can't we have more food and longer rest hours?" I should have reported them as traitors, but I didn't. I knew they had alcohol. They were making it on the thirty-fourth floor. Then there was graffiti in the stairwells and the next thing anyone knew–'

'Everything fell apart,' muttered Arvo.

'So, do you?' asked Zanne with disarming directness. 'Do you understand?'

Arvo's brow creased. He took a breath.

A sudden eruption of noise forestalled him. Familiar noise, the soundtrack of his old life. At first he thought it was in his head, another memory. Gunfire and voices raised in anger, fear and pain – and explosions. He could see from Zanne's face that she heard it too. In the distance, but rapidly approaching: the sound of war.

Arvo reached by reflex for a gun that wasn't there. He clung to the haft of his pickaxe instead, rising from his crouch.

Most of the overseers had also drawn weapons and were headed towards the disturbance. Their leader, Corporal Maxtell, remained. 'Ignore it,' he barked at his nervous labourers, spraying spittle. 'Whatever is happening is no business of yours and no excuse for shirking. This gang will meet its end-of-shift quotas or I'll take the difference out of your hides!'

'Sir, I can help,' Arvo spoke up. 'I–'

He felt Zanne's elbow in his ribs and bit his tongue. She was right. It would be unwise to reveal his secret. A glowering servitor was pushing its way towards him. He did as he was told and returned to work – though not for long.

The war, with all its noise and fury, crashed into them.

It began with a single running figure, spitting profanities

over his shoulder. A black-and-purple cultist's cloak was slung over his grey labourer's coveralls. Maxtell fired. He missed, but a lasgun beam from behind blew out the traitor's knee. He fell in a spray of bone fragments and blood to lie in gasping, twitching agony.

The corporal bowed to the inevitable, yelling to his gang to retreat but keep hold of their tools. Arvo kept a tight grip on his axe. More cultists burst onto the scene, and he stepped to greet them. Not expecting resistance from a simple labourer, they ran into his bludgeoning attack.

They were everywhere, suddenly, stinking shadows emerging from the half-light, seeking human shields to hide behind. One made a grab for Zanne and earned Arvo's pick through his skull.

Muzzles flashed. Arvo saw Maxtell cut down as he dived for cover. He pulled Zanne down behind a half-demolished wall. One of the gang's lumen units was shot out, followed swiftly by the other.

Parius Interior Guard troops, including some of Arvo's overseers, were hard on the cultists' heels. Their lasgun and luminator beams criss-crossed in the darkness. Voices yelled to the labourers to flatten themselves on their stomachs, but many were held captive or just too panicked to comply. The soldiers, having given fair warning, were not reticent about shooting any shadow that moved.

Zanne had curled into a trembling ball.

'There are only a few of them,' Arvo whispered to her reassuringly. 'A dozen, at most. This is not a planned attack. They have been smoked out of some bolthole and are on the defensive.'

They're doing as much damage as they can, he could have added but chose not to, *one last howl of rage before they die.*

He recalled what Zanne had said: *We build, the traitors and the monsters come along and knock everything down, and we have to build again.*

'Stay down.'

Arvo knew his surroundings. By instinct, he had committed every detail of them to memory. He also knew where each cultist had been when the lights went out. He edged out from behind the half-wall, keeping low to reduce the risk of friendly fire. Some of the cultists could be pinpointed by their gibbering and shrieking. They were sending entreaties to their vile deity. Arvo strained to block out the actual words. Words could be dangerous.

He came up behind a likely shadow. He slipped his axe haft around its throat and strangled him with it. The cultist had no time to squeal. The fight left his limbs and he dropped. Arvo was already seeking out his next target.

A knot of figures crouched behind a barricade of promethium barrels – empty, thank the Emperor. They had two guns between them. Their wielder's faces, twisted by insanity, lit up with each shot taken. In those flashes, Arvo identified two other figures as cultists, four more as cringing hostages.

Stealing up to the group, he interposed himself among them. Only one cultist saw him, shooting him a suspicious glare. Arvo dropped his gaze as if cowed; just one more hostage. The cultist, he saw, was not quite as unarmed as he had appeared to be. He was wearing a belt hung with grey metal eggs, at least four of them. Krak grenades.

The cultist was muttering to himself, as if building his resolve. *One last howl of rage before they die.* In these urban surroundings, with so many innocents, he would cause devastation. Arvo had no choice. He lunged at the bomber, driving a fist into his stomach. It took two more punches to

extinguish the fervour in his eyes. By then, his fellow deca-
dents were alert to the enemy among them.

Arvo snatched a grenade and rounded on them. They
weren't quite ready to die yet, after all. They shrank from
him, for a second, long enough for him to tackle the closest of them. He wrenched the cultist around into another's
sights as he fired. The cultist stiffened in Arvo's arms and he
threw the body into the others, at the same time wrenching
the lasgun from its deathly grip.

The gun was local issue, lighter than Arvo was accustomed
to. It felt good to hold it, all the same; like an extension of
his self. His hands had felt empty for too long. He gunned
down the remaining two cultists, unskilled combatants, with
ease. Another ran up behind him, betraying his approach
with a fanatical roar, and he spun – not fast enough to bring
his gun to bear, but in time to snap his attacker's jaw with
its butt, driving bone through muscle.

A wave of concussive force blew him over. Arvo heard the
explosion a fraction of a second later. He stayed down as
flaming debris rained upon him. *Another bomber!* The blast
had come from – he couldn't get his bearings – his right.
Where he had left Zanne.

He rolled to put out any flames before they took hold.
Smoke was smothering his oxygen, making him miss his
gas mask, blinding him further – but concealing him too.
A cultist, with his back to Arvo, strafed the shadows with a
lasgun indiscriminately. Arvo, in contrast, squeezed his trigger only once, punching through his target's head.

Sensing movement to his left, he snapped his gun around.
An Interior Guard trooper had him in his sights. *Nice work*,
thought Arvo. He lowered his weapon and gestured to show
he was an ally. The soldier held his fire. He motioned to Arvo

to get down on the ground anyway. Arvo complied. 'Thank you for your service, citizen,' the soldier grunted as he took the lasgun from beside him. 'We'll take it from here.'

Arvo waited, but seethed impatiently.

There couldn't have been many cultists standing. He had downed at least half of them himself, while the bombing had surely taken out more. Still, long minutes passed – interspersed with brief but violent outbreaks of shouting, scuffling and gunshots – before calm was restored. Then a lumen unit had to be found and kicked into sputtering action. Interior Guard troopers swept the area, prodding at every prostrate body, alive or dead, in search of enemies in hiding.

At last, the survivors, the innocent labourers in Arvo's gang, were given leave to stand. Doubtless next would come the order to return to work, as soon as Maxtell's replacement was established. In the meantime, they had a precious moment to process what had happened, deal with their shock and count their dead.

Some attacked their tormentors' bodies, hacking them with blunt tools or tearing them apart with bare hands. It was a pointless kind of revenge, other than to vent their misery and frustration. Nobody tried to stop them. Arvo made straight for the wall behind which he had left Zanne.

The wall had been sundered in the explosion.

Zanne's pale hand protruded from the debris as if she had fought her fate. As if she had tried to claw her way to freedom before the breath was crushed out of her. He took the hand between his own. It was cold. He had seen so many deaths in his short life, he told himself, so very many. Why did this one feel different?

Why was her life worth more than other lives?

So, do you? He recalled the very last thing Zanne had said to him. *Do you understand?* Her last question. Arvo answered her aloud, as if there was a chance she might hear him. 'Yes,' he whispered. 'I understand now.'

The sky was split by the shrieks of Imperial engines.

Sergeant Jarvan looked up, shielding his eyes, as the first ships hit Parius' atmosphere, blazing gloriously. He shifted his gaze to the vast, straight lines of humanity stretched across the newly cleared assembly terrace on Hive Opus' upper tier, and his chest swelled with pride.

He almost wished he was travelling to the stars with them. Almost.

Of course, their departure would leave the labour gangs shorthanded, but this couldn't be helped. Parius Monumentus' tithe to the Imperium was due and no allowance could be made for recent losses. The labourers who remained would just have to work harder, until their population was replenished.

Jarvan hadn't witnessed the tithing ceremony before. He had just been promoted – for the second time in less than four months – after his predecessor was killed in a bombing attack. He strode along the endless ranks of young men, pausing to question some. He asked their names and how they felt about being chosen to fight for the Emperor, to which all but one professed to being suitably honoured.

That one gave his name as Arvo. The name, along with his pale, dull-eyed face, almost sparked a flicker of recognition in Jarvan. 'Begging your pardon, sergeant,' said the new recruit, 'but I was chosen to fight a long time ago.'

Jarvan checked Arvo's name on his data-slate. 'So I see. The last draft overlooked you, so this time you volunteered for service. You achieved the highest scores of your intake in your selection tests – the best scores I have ever seen, in fact.'

'I know my life's purpose now,' said Arvo.

Jarvan raised an eyebrow. 'Pray tell?'

'I was bred to fight and to die for Him.'

'An admirable attitude.'

'I shall face the Emperor's enemies, therefore, without fear or doubt. I shall exchange this life He has granted me for the greatest possible advantage to Him. If I can only advance His cause in the slightest, then I shall consider my brief existence worthwhile. I shall do my duty – for what else is there, after all?'

'What indeed?' Jarvan smiled approvingly. He clasped his hands behind his back and moved on.

The first of the dropships was coming in to land, to gather up its complement of soon-to-be-martyrs. Jarvan had forgotten most of their names already, but he would remember one name for a time, at least – along with the question he had posed. The sergeant repeated it to himself in a thoughtful mutter.

'Yes. What else is there, indeed?'

UNEARTHED

ROB SANDERS

Taking his magnoculars, Kiefer took in a 360-degree sweep of the surrounding area. The once-lush fields that stretched for kilometres across the surface of Grendl's World were now but dust and sand. Slender twisters made their way across migrating dunes, while swarms of off-world vermin jumped and flew alongside the Inquisitorial column in great buzzing clouds. With nothing left to eat, the alien scourge that the Alpha Legion, led by the Traitor Sisyphon Vail, had introduced to this planet had resorted to feasting on each other, turning Grendl's World into an infested dustball, trapped in a grotesque cycle of rampant reproduction and cannibalism. Kiefer pulled his headscarf across his mouth as the Salamander laboured up a dune and through a cloud of chittering insects.

'I have a return, interrogator,' Ipluvian~461 told Kiefer, his modulated voice rising above the Salamander's gunning engine. The calculus logi was interfaced with the vehicle's multi-spectral surveyor station, which dominated one side of the command bay. 'Long-range augurs show a large structure, four degrees south-south-east.'

'Confessor,' Kiefer said into his vox-bead. 'Can you confirm?'

'*Stand by,*' the priest returned, his voice a warping crackle over the channel. High above the column, Kiefer had given orders for the *Internecia* to hold station and provide support with the cruiser's instrumentation. '*Shipmaster Fairuza tells me orbital pict captures confirm the structure as a freighter.*'

The interrogator leant across the twin-linked heavy bolters of the Salamander's turret and banged his fist on the top of the driver's compartment. Hatches popped and Kiefer found himself looking down at the Salamander's driver and gunner. Sitting in the nest of levers was a goggled Guardsman, Khoga – one of Captain Sartak's Attilans. Next to him, his shoulder nestled against the stock of the forward heavy bolter, was Kiefer's servant, Fenk.

'Four degrees south-south-east,' Kiefer called above the Salamander's roaring power plant. He gestured with a flattened palm. As Khoga hauled at the levers, the vehicle's tracks churned in the sand. The Salamander turned on the top of a dune, before bouncing down the slope. Within moments, Captain Sartak's barked orders had his Rough Riders and the Molidor Ogryn Auxilia changing direction to follow the command vehicle.

As the Salamander chewed its way through the wasteland, Kiefer peered through his magnoculars. Before long, blinking through the haze of dust and swarms of alien vermin, Kiefer saw the half-buried outline of a vessel.

'All stop,' the interrogator said, banging on top of the driver's compartment once more. As the Salamander jerked to a stop, the Attilans formed a column of horsemen behind.

The ogryns, barely breaking a sweat, ran up beside them – the abhuman warriors were taller than the Rough Riders on their steeds.

'Can you identify it?' Kiefer asked Ipluvian~461. 'What do the auspex scans say?'

Interfaced with the surveyor station, the construct didn't immediately respond as it concentrated on processing the incoming data.

'Come on, hurry it up,' said the interrogator.

'A small system ship,' the calculus logi said finally. 'A pocket freighter.'

'Crashed?'

'Landed,' Ipluvian~461 reported. 'No doubt abandoned after the infestation took. It appears to be nothing more than a derelict.'

'Entrances?' Kiefer asked.

'The ship has been mostly buried in the migrating dunes. The main cargo hold, however, is open to the elements. Might I suggest that to be the easiest way in?'

Kiefer bit at his lip in thought. They were hunting for the Alpha Legion. His old master, Godefroy Pyramus, had been drawn into an ambush and killed, and the darkness of the open hold screamed trap at the interrogator.

'Easy isn't always easy,' he told the construct.

'Indeed, my lord,' Ipluvian~461 said. Kiefer didn't have to explain his caution to the construct.

'I need two riders,' Kiefer called across to Captain Sartak, who drew up on his steed. 'For a circle of the structure.'

Sartak gestured in mock confusion at the interrogator. The captain could understand Imperial Gothic perfectly well, but liked to make a show for his men. Similarly, the Guardsmen also pretended not to speak any language other their own.

The Attilans' pride in their culture ran deep. Kiefer made several circular gestures with his arm then stabbed a finger towards the downed freighter. Ipluvian~461 translated the order into the Attilan dialect.

As two of Sartak's best riders trotted off, creating separate dust trails, Kiefer launched Xerxes into the air. The interrogator had had Ipluvian~461 attach a vid-caster and a small auspex array to the bird's body. Kiefer needed eyes on the top of the half-buried crashed freighter. As the Rough Riders circled the derelict ship in opposite directions, the psyber-eagle soared overhead. Kiefer listened for the bird's call – any indication of movement or a living presence among the crumbling architecture of the ship. He heard nothing, however.

'Heat signatures?' Kiefer asked. 'Vox-transmissions? Electromagnetic spectra?'

'Nothing,' Ipluvian~461 confirmed.

As Sartak's riders rode back to the column, Xerxes swooped in overhead. With a beat of its wings the psyber-eagle hovered and then landed on Kiefer's outstretched arm. The Attilan riders exchanged brief words with their captain, which Sartak translated.

'No signs of life or habitation.'

'We must search the derelict,' Kiefer announced finally to the Salamander crew and the Attilans.

Kiefer banged on the Salamander's hatch again, and the driver gunned the engine. With the horsemen and ogryns forming a column behind, the command vehicle chewed up the deserted wasteland between the dunes and the derelict. Rounding the superstructure of the sand-covered freighter, the Salamander made for the open hold. As it did, Kiefer deposited Xerxes on the rail and took position before the turret. Resting his shoulder against the stock of the twin-linked heavy bolters, he aimed the barrels at the darkness within. Captain Sartak and his Rough Riders took position in two lines either side, while the ogryns milled around uncertainly, looking inside suspiciously.

'Stay sharp,' Kiefer said into his vox-bead, as the lamps on the Salamander cut through the dusty darkness of the hold interior. The interrogator found it difficult to relax. Every buried agri-complex and silo they searched felt like an Alpha Legion ambush waiting to happen. The sloping floor was made up of sand that had poured in through the open hold, but the Salamander, horses and hulking abhumans managed to negotiate the incline. The chug of the command vehicle's engine and the heavy rattle of its tracks echoed about the chamber. Activating lamps on their saddles, a contingent of the Rough Riders urged their steeds carefully into the expanse of the hold. Other Attilans dismounted, leaving their hunting lances in their saddle sheaths. Clutching laspistols and lamps, they made their way across the large hold. Talking quietly to one another, they checked the corroded bulkheads and hatches.

The ogryns were blunt instruments, ill-suited for reconnaissance work. Hating enclosed spaces, they stared about the interior of the hold with brutish suspicion. On board the *Internecia*, the abhumans had been housed with the Attilan steeds on the livery deck. They stood in their squad, muttering, under the watchful eye of Captain Sartak, who coordinated the search of the hold interior from his saddle.

'Logi,' Kiefer said as the Attilans managed to fully crank open a bulkhead leading off the main hold. Ipluvian~461 stepped off the back of the Salamander and released several servo-skulls into the air. Hovering for a moment, the constructs shot off silently through the air, disappearing through the bulkhead.

'Servo units away,' the calculus logi said, retaking his position at the surveyor station. 'Augurs and motion detectors engaged.'

'Begin a scan of the structure,' Kiefer ordered. 'Any evidence of recent habitation or activity.'

As he stepped down, an Attilan replaced him on the turret heavy bolters. Nearby, Kiefer could see commotion, and approached. Several Rough Riders had climbed a large mound in the centre of the hold and called their captain across. It took Captain Sartak and Kiefer some to time to clamber up to reach them. The hill was made of hundreds of cargo containers, all piled in the middle of the floor, as if by a rough landing. Now in a pile of battered angularity on the floor of the hold, they had been all but buried in sand.

'What have you found?' Kiefer demanded.

The Attilans were gathered about an open container that had evidently once been pressurised. Kiefer leant in and immediately wished he hadn't. The stench was unbearable. Within was crammed full of chitinous remains, the rancid corpses of vermin – the same swarming creatures that had laid waste to the agri world's precious crops. In several more open containers they found the same pungent putrescence. Thousands – perhaps millions – of voracious creatures had multiplied before expiring.

'A nest?' Kiefer put to the Rough Riders. Captain Sartak shrugged with unsmiling disinterest. The two Attilans who had discovered the mound spoke quickly at their captain, however, and then at the interrogator. They were pointing out a container that appeared to still be intact. Kiefer nodded slowly. He began to understand what the Attilans were indicating.

'Help me,' he said and the three of them levered it open. Within was the same rotting mess as the others. Kiefer grunted.

He could believe that the swarming insects might nest in the
sheltered confines of the hold and the boxes. What he couldn't
understand was how they came to be sealed within pressurised containers.

'Confessor,' Kiefer said into his vox bead as he made his
way down the mound of crates.

'Yes, interrogator,' Creech returned from the bridge of the
Internecia.

'I believe we have found the original source of the agri
world plague. The pocket freighter appears to have been
abandoned here intentionally. It was carrying the swarm in
its cargo hold, to be released. The infestation was intentional.
The Alpha Legion were here – and still might be.'

'*May the God-Emperor guide you,*' the confessor said. '*Be careful, my lord.*'

Within moments Fenk was with him, the servant carrying
a plasma gun from the *Internecia*'s armoury.

'Anything?' Kiefer put to Ipluvian~461 as he marched past
the stationary Salamander.

'No, interrogator,' the calculus logi said. 'The servo-skulls
are conducting their sweep. Motion sensors have picked up
nothing. No heat signatures registering. No evidence of recent
activity on the vid-casters.'

'Stay with the command vehicle and maintain the search,'
Kiefer ordered.

'Very good, interrogator.'

'Secure the horses. Leave the auxilia here,' Kiefer ordered
Sartak and his Rough Riders. The labyrinthine interior of
the freighter was no place for horses, and the ogryns hated
cramped spaces. 'I want this derelict searched for any sign
of a recent enemy presence. Anything the servo-skulls might
have missed.'

The Attilans didn't like to leave their horses, but obeyed the interrogator's orders. Taking pommel lamps and readying their laspistols, the Rough Riders began to organise themselves in squads for the search. Sartak strode to the open bulkhead and directed lines of Attilans. Kiefer turned around to see that the captain had left Sergeant Urgamal in charge of the horses and Molidor ogryns.

Khoga stood up, peering out of his top hatch after the interrogator. Ipluvian~461 and the Attilan gunner did likewise. Xerxes let loose a twin screech that reverberated about the hold. With the last of the Rough Riders through the bulkhead opening, Kiefer slipped his bolt pistol from its holster and joined Fenk and Captain Sartak in bringing up the rear.

The freighter was as silent as the grave. Sand and dust had found its way in from the hold, swirling through the ghost ship with the wind, choking the deck corridors and accumulating in the chambers. Kiefer found himself negotiating indoor slopes, wading through sand-swamped openings and stalking through piles of debris with his bolt pistol gripped tight in his gloved hand and his eyes darting between every shadow-choked bulkhead and opening. Every corridor, corner and stairwell had the potential to be an Alpha Legion ambush. Despite the danger, Kiefer and the Attilans pushed on deeper into the downed freighter.

The light of the Guardsmen's lamps cut through the murk, throwing unnatural shadows across the wrecked interior of the ship. The search was not a natural mission for the Rough Riders, who preferred to carry out their duties in the open, in the saddle. As Sartak directed his troops down the corridors and ladderwells, they jabbed their laspistols into the darkness. Fenk stuck to the interrogator like a bad smell, clutching the weight of his plasma gun to his chest. All the while, Ipluvian~461's servo-skulls zoomed through the structure about them, scanning for heat signatures and movement.

'They must be here,' Kiefer growled as they entered the freighter's gloomy engineering section. He felt the pressure not just of his efforts to locate the leader of the Alpha Legion, Sisyphon Vail, and his renegades, but also to finish everything Godefroy Pyramus had tried to accomplish. Between them they had picked through the detritus of this backwater subsector piece by piece and found only disappointment and death. No less than Sartak's sullen Attilans, the interrogator wanted this over. It was cold here in the bowels of the abandoned vessel.

Shouldering his plasma gun on its strap, Fenk pulled out the flask of amasec he used to carry for his inquisitor master. He offered it to Kiefer, who stared at the servant with hollow eyes before murmuring his thanks and taking the bottle. As Rough Riders returned from searching the upper decks of the engineering section, muttering, Captain Sartak turned to Kiefer. The Attilan officer played with his greasy moustache, waiting in expectation for the order to withdraw. They had found no sign of the Alpha Legion. It was time to continue the search elsewhere.

'Alright,' Kiefer said. As he went to holster his bolt pistol, the Attilans drew to a halt. The search was over. It was time to move on. 'Prepare to–'

'*Interrogator,*' Ipluvian~461 called across the vox-bead. '*I have readings. I have signals.*'

'What signals?' Kiefer said, his heart beginning to race.

'*Auspex returns from the servo units,*' the calculus logi said. '*Heat signatures and coded vox-streams.*'

'Where?'

'*The engineering sub-levels,*' Ipluvian~461 reported. '*Just ahead of your present position.*'

'We have them,' Kiefer growled, bringing up his pistol. 'They're here.'

'*Interrogator,*' the calculus logi said. '*I feel obligated to remind you that this could indicate the presence of pirates, as we discovered on Mimbosa Prime, or perhaps a small group of agri world survivors, sheltering in the derelict and living off the freighter's supplies. My calculations indicate a chance that we might have accidentally activated a dormant system during our search.*'

'And what do your calculations tell you about the chances of encountering the Alpha Legion here?' the interrogator asked, slowly pushing his way up the corridor and through the Attilans.

The calculus logi hesistated. '*I calculate a fifty-two point four-six-seven chance that the enemy are located here.*'

'Thank you,' Kiefer snarled, surging towards the returns the servo-units had recorded. He snatched a lamp out of the hands of a nearby Attilan and pushed on through the benighted freighter. The interrogator could feel his sworn enemy in the darkness. Monstrous renegades, hiding in the shadow. Retreating into their lair. Leading with his bolt pistol, Kiefer held his lamp high. He would find the heretics, avenge his master and rid the Imperium of a hated enemy.

Slinking along corridor walls, Kiefer aimed his pistol around corners and threw the light of his lamp into modules and antechambers. With Fenk close behind, and Sartak and his Attilans moving in squads searching side compartments along the way, the interrogator moved ever down into the sub-levels of the engineering section. Kiefer's boots clunked along one of the many metal companionways suspended above an engineering control chamber. As he saw lights in the darkness, the interrogator halted and aimed both his pistol and the light of his lamp down into the chamber below. The Attilans followed his example as they moved up alongside him.

'I have you now...' Kiefer said, but the illumination revealed only a single rune bank, blinking with dull lights and glyphs. Cables running to the console showed how it had been jury-rigged, while one of Ipluvian~461's servo-skulls hovered above it taking readings. The snarl on the interrogator's face faded. He thought that he had finally tracked down Sisyphon Vail, but there was still no sign of him or his warband.

The servo-skull suddenly whipped around.

'*Signatures,*' Ipluvian~461 reported across the vox. '*Heat and motion.*'

Kiefer and the Attilans aimed their weapons about the gloom of the large chamber. He could hear the hum of power packs booting from dormancy and the hiss of servos and powered hydraulics.

In the darkness below Kiefer thought he saw movement. Light glinted off the curvature of pauldrons and helms. He could make out ten, perhaps twenty figures in powered plate. Cloaks of flayed flesh clung to the armoured Traitors. Even in the gloom, Kiefer could make out the serpentine swirl of patterns etched into the dirty blue-green plate. Optics burned with expectation. Helmet grilles drizzled breath that misted on the air. The decorative muzzles of boltguns were presented like the gaping mouths of serpents up at the catwalk above.

'Enemy in sight...' Kiefer roared, yanking back upon the trigger of his bolt pistol.

Before the blast had left the muzzle of the weapon, however, the grille flooring turned into a cacophonous storm of bolterfire and shrapnel. Stuttering streams of gunfire tore up through the mesh, punching holes through the floor-ing straight into the Rough Riders crowding the walkway, blowing off limbs and turning the line of Guardsmen into a blood-mulched mess.

Captain Sartak yelled orders at his men and the barbarians moved swiftly, running across the catwalk and racing down a spiral stair that connected to the floor. Dancing through the carnage, they pushed on into the chamber, picking their way lightly through the exploding mesh and merciless bolt blasts. The few Attilans who tried to hold their ground on the catwalk died, blasted apart by enemy fire from below.

The Attilans fought hard. Bolts of energy flashed off rene-gade plate, leaving glowing craters, but nothing could stop the Traitors.

As Kiefer blasted his own bolt rounds down at them, he cursed the Alpha Legion and their nefarious ways: their traps, their scheming and their dark strategies. They had powered down their suits and lain in wait, as still as serpents, ready to strike. With the Inquisition forces committed, the Alpha Legion had initiated their plan. They had powered up, moved into position, watched Kiefer and the Attilans enter their trap, then unleashed the fury of their weapons.

The interrogator's bolt rounds crashed down into Traitor Space Marines below. He heard the grunt of an Alpha Legion-naire as a blast from Kiefer's pistol hammered through his plate.

The catwalk was shuddering beneath their boots. The Alpha Legion were directing some of their firepower towards the joists and walkway supports, and the structure was now on the verge of collapse. He felt Fenk grab hold of him.

The chamber reverberated with the excruciating sound of tortured metal as the catwalk started to give way. Kiefer lost his footing and slid over the edge, but was saved from falling by Fenk, hauling back on his master's cloak. The servant had reached a stable section of walkway and secured himself there. Attilans toppled down into the gloom of the engineering section, the light of their lamps bouncing about the chamber wildly, screaming as the fall broke bones and shattered limbs.

As Kiefer dangled he saw the Guardsmen grimace through their pain and try to right themselves. The engineering chamber flashed with the frenetic bolts of their laspistols. The Alpha Legionnaires were merciless, however. The Chaos Space Marines marched through the broken bodies littering the floor. The Attilans were fighting for their lives but little could stop the frenetic economy of the warband's advance. The renegades stamped down on the bodies of prone Rough Riders and ended the Guardsmen with their armoured boots. They aimed the muzzles of their boltguns down at the injured Attilans, blasting off their heads and turning their chests into smouldering craters.

Kiefer could not allow his men to be brutally slain like dogs. He had led them into this. It was his pain and frustration that had led them into the jaws of the serpent. As Fenk tried to help the interrogator back up onto the stable section of companionway, Kiefer deliberately wriggled out of his cloak. He fell away from the servant and the remaining walkway. Bracing himself, the interrogator dropped down to the floor, many metres below. He landed with a jarring crunch, and screamed with pain as his right leg gave way underneath him with a sickening crack. With a groan of agony, Kiefer fell into an ugly roll that saw his bolt pistol bounce away from his grip.

The interrogator blinked the torment from his eyes. Attilans were dying all around him as the Chaos Space Marines carried out their slaughter. Amid the screams, the interrogator felt the floor of the engineering chamber shake with the approach of a heavy armoured form. Looking up, Kiefer saw an Alpha Legionnaire standing over him, his ghoulish plate cloaked with the flayed flesh of his victims. A magazine clunked to the floor as the Chaos Space Marine reloaded his weapon and aimed the serpent barrel down at the interrogator.

Kiefer scrambled desperately for his gun, waiting for the horrible moment when the Alpha Legionnaire would put a stream of bolts into his back. Scooping up the heavy pistol, Kiefer twisted around and put the traitor in his sights. Yanking back on the bolt pistol's trigger, the interrogator put round after round into the Alpha Legionnaire's chest and faceplate. With half a magazine blasted into him, the Alpha Legionnaire stumbled back and tripped over an Attilan body – despite the terrible state of it, Kiefer recognised it as that of Captain Sartak. Crashing to the ground, the monstrous renegade fell still.

In the confusion of the fight, Kiefer could hear Ipluvian~461 over the vox, desperately trying to make contact with him, but there was too much noise going on for him to hear what the construct was saying.

'Send the ogryns!' Kiefer roared into the vox-bead. 'Send them in now!'

As a stream of bolt rounds cut past Kiefer's face and through a screaming Rough Rider, the interrogator turned the remaining wrath of his pistol at the dark, armoured shapes moving through the chamber. Thrusting his pistol this way and that, the interrogator blasted furiously at the traitors as they moved through the fallen Attilans.

'Come on!' Kiefer roared. 'Face me, you venomous traitors.'

The gunfire inevitably drew the attention of nearby Alpha Legionnaires, who aimed their weaponry through the gloom of the chamber. Once again, the engineering section was lit up. Holding the bulk of his plasma gun at his hip, Fenk fired from the catwalk. The weapon bucked and steamed as the servant blazed orb after sun-like orb of plasma down at the Alpha Legion. Many blinding spheres of agitated energy sizzled into the deck, creating craters of spitting brilliance. Several slammed into traitors, however. Alpha Legionnaires thrashed and roared as balls of plasma burned through their plate.

Redirecting their firepower, the Traitors turned the remaining catwalk into a precarious remnant of bolt-mangled wreckage. Fenk backed away from the storm, up the walkway. Kiefer sent the last of his bolts at the distracted Alpha Legion, managing to put one in the side of a traitor's helm, turning him into a thrashing, brain-mulched mess. The shot of a compatriot traitor, aiming through the wildly waving limbs, punched into the wall and floor next to Kiefer. The explosive impact sent shards of burning shrapnel into the interrogator's gut. The interrogator felt as if he had been cut in half. His carapace was a ragged, bloody mess and his stomach was a bottomless pit of agony. He went down, face first onto the deck, curling up in agony.

His vox-bead squawked, but he could barely hear the message. '...ogryns... ...ching your... ...ition...'

Looking up through the pain-fuelled haze, he saw more Alpha Legionnaires advancing along the walkway, up behind Fenk. The servant was swathed in steam from his plasma gun, which Fenk was pushing to its limit, splitting his furious fire between the Alpha Legion in the engineering chamber and those approaching on the walkway.

Despite the onslaught, the Alpha Legion on the walkway continued to move forward, ahead of a helmetless officer. The officer's plate and cloak had a rancid, understated extravagance compared to the other members of the warband. As Kiefer stared up, the lines of his face taut with pain, he saw the officer glance down. He had a shaven head and a dark nobility to his genetically engineered features, while one blinking eye gleamed yellow and black like a cat's, indicating some kind of xenos or daemonic corruption. Kiefer knew that he had locked gazes with his opposite. This could be no other than Sisyphon Vail himself.

Kiefer tried to bring up his weapon but couldn't lift it. Sisyphon Vail levelled his serpentine bolt pistol at the interrogator from the walkway.

Instead of the darkness of death, it was the fury of light and heat that found Raughn Kiefer. Fenk's plasma gun finally overloaded. The servant had intentionally pushed the weapon beyond its capabilities. Exploding with what hydrogen remained in the weapon's flask, the eye-scalding inferno of the detonating plasma gun wiped Fenk from existence. An expanding globe of blinding light threatened to swallow the advancing Alpha Legionnaires on the walkway. Sisyphon Vail's patchwork cloak of flayed flesh caught alight and his plate was scorched black. Kiefer buried his head in his arms as the heat of the detonation washed over him.

The blinding light and noise seemed to last an eternity. Finally bringing his head up and squinting up at the walkway, Kiefer found it all but gone – the detonation had melted the mesh catwalk to nothing. Thunder rumbled through the superstructure of the freighter. Kiefer watched as pieces of wreckage were shaken loose from the remaining walkway.

The ogryns had arrived. Like a herd of stampeding grox,

the floor of the engineering chamber. The detonations had immediately followed Sispyhon Vail's tactical withdrawal. With his heart thumping in his chest, Kiefer came to the furious realisation that Sisyphon Vail planned to bury the surviving Inquisitorial forces – and even some of his own men – alive.

Kiefer's throat was already thick with blood, and the haze of dust made it almost impossible to breathe. He gagged and coughed, trying desperately to catch his breath. The ogryns were reacting no differently. They might have been hulking brutes but they still needed to breathe – unlike the Alpha Legionnaires, protected by their armour. By the time the embattled ogryns and Traitors realised the peril they were in, it was too late. The abhumans dug furiously with their big hands but the sand was coming in faster than they could clear it.

Sand was filling the chamber, forcing Kiefer to crawl upwards just to keep himself above the surface. Clutching his throat, one of the ogryns fell and was swallowed up by the rising sands. The air was thick with dust. Towering figures stumbled through the miasma, wildly flailing their arms in fury and panic, seeking a way out.

What little light remained in the chamber came from the Attilans' abandoned lamps, and even that was fading, obscured by the swirling dust. Asphyxiation and unconsciousness threatened to claim Kiefer, and a cold fury burnt in his chest. He had found the Alpha Legion but had lost Sisyphon Vail. Who knew what calamity the leader of the Honourless would wreak upon the subsector? Kiefer could not let that happen. He had made a pledge, to Godefroy Pyramus and to himself, that he would see the threat of Sisyphon Vail and his vile warband ended.

Crawling arm over arm, the interrogator dragged himself through the sand flooding into the chamber. He grabbed an abandoned lamp and hooked it on his belt. He had spotted a melted breach in the wall, close to the floor, where several of Fenk's plasma blasts had missed advancing Alpha Legionnaires. Struggling to think clearly, Kiefer made for the hole. Perhaps he could squeeze through the opening and escape the doomed engineering chamber this way. He did not get far, however. The sand was pouring in so fast that he was unable to drag his injured body any further forward. As the sand started to cover his body, he cried out for help and started clawing at the air. In those dark, oxygen-starved moments, he imagined himself buried alive in the freighter – an Alpha Legion trap, prepared and sprung. Then he felt something huge with a vice-like grip grab his leg. His broken leg. The excruciating pain made Kiefer sit bolt-upright, despite the wound in his abdomen, and scream the dust from his lungs.

Before him, the interrogator saw the hulking shape of an ogryn, a solitary abhuman. Grabbing the interrogator by the leg, the ogryn trudged through the deepening sand, instinctively heading for shattered wall of the chamber. The pain kept Kiefer conscious and as they reached the hole he shouted at the ogryn to dig, digging with his own hands to show it what to do. The ogryn knelt down beside the interrogator. It was wearing goggles and the same kind of scarf the Attilans wore around their necks to keep the dust out of their mouths whilst riding. Between them, they had given the ogryn a fighting chance.

Using his great hands like shovels, the creature excavated the area close to the wall, clearing the blasted hole in the metal. Grabbing the broken edges, the ogryn heaved with all his monstrous might, widening the gap so that it was just wide enough for a human to fit through. The interrogator slid head first through the opening. With sand cascading about him, he heaved his torso and legs through the rent. Scrabbling around in the sand, Kiefer reached out for the abhuman. Perhaps he could help the ogryn get through also, but as more and more sand poured in, it became clear that the hulking abhuman wouldn't be able to get out. He was simply too big. Before long, his great hand – which Kiefer could still see digging back the sand – went limp. Half dragging himself, half swimming through the sand, the interrogator was forced to leave the last of his men to die. He promised himself that he would avenge them.

The crawl was exhausting. Chamber after smashed chamber. Corridor after sand-choked corridor. His shattered leg felt numb once again and his body cold as behind him the interrogator left a smear of blood from his belly. Shrapnel ground his innards with every excruciating movement. He was bleeding badly. For a little while, Kiefer used the sound of distant gunfire to guide him and give him a sense of direction in unfamiliar surroundings.

'Ipluvian,' Kiefer coughed into the vox-bead. 'Command vehicle, come in.'

The sound had been heavy bolters firing. The Salamander must have been under attack by the exiting Alpha Legion. The gunfire and the vox had long been silent. Nothing from the Salamander and nothing from the *Internecia*. As he made an ugly roll out of an open bulkhead and into the cargo hold he could see why. The Salamander was a smoking wreck. Crawling across the cargo crates, Kiefer found what was left of his driver Khoga and the Attilan gunner smouldering near the remains of the command vehicle. Sergeant Urgamal he found trapped under his bolt-blasted horse, with half of his head missing, in what must have been an execution-style killing. Ipluvian~461 was everywhere, the calculus logi literally blasted apart by bolter fire.

'*Internecia*, come in,' he croaked into the vox-bead, cycling through channels. He heaved himself painfully up against the track of the smashed Salamander. '*Internecia*, respond,' the interrogator repeated, clutching his hands to the ragged wound in his side. Fading in and out of awareness, Kiefer continued to mumble into the vox-bead until he lost consciousness.

Shuddering awake, Kiefer felt numb, cold and wet. Looking down weakly, he saw that the sand about him was sodden and red. Sitting in a puddle of his own blood, he realised that he had been out for hours, quietly bleeding his life away.

'*Internecia*...' the interrogator managed, his lips barely wrapping themselves around the words. 'This is Interrogator Kiefer. Requesting immediate... medical assistance. We found them. The Alpha Legion are here. I repeat: Sisyphon Vail is here on the planet. This is Interrogator Kiefer... Answer me, damn it.'

'*Interrogator*,' a voice returned. It was a voice he had never heard before; a voice that sounded like honeyed death. '*This is* Internecia. *We receive you. You are wrong, of course – as you always have been. For Sisyphon Vail is not on the planet surface. I am here – on board your precious ship.*'

Kiefer's heart went numb. Sisyphon Vail's voice echoed about his skull and infected his mind.

'Vail...'

'Yes,' the Alpha Legion commander said, with no little relish. 'Your ship is mine but unfortunately I cannot spare anyone to assist you. In fact, I'm readying the ship to break orbit. We have a new destination: Constantium Secundus.'

Kiefer slowly closed his eyes. Vail had named the location of a secret Inquisition base in the next sector. He now had access to the *Internecia*'s runebanks and all of the data they contained. Details of inquisitors, deployments, covert operatives and ordo installations.

'To anyone else monitoring this channel,' Kiefer said, his words like ice, 'I am changing to emergency vox channel, now.'

Cycling through the channels, the interrogator slumped down onto the sand.

'Is anyone receiving… me?' he said, his voice cracking under the strain and his grievous injuries.

'*Interrogator,*' a voice returned finally. '*This is Confessor Creech.*'

Kiefer groaned in agony and relief. 'Confessor?'

'*I am here, interrogator,*' Creech replied.

'You evaded capture?'

'*For now, interrogator,*' the confessor replied. '*Servitors alerted the high enginseer of gunfire in the launch bays.*'

'The high enginseer…?'

'*He's with me,*' Creech confirmed. '*You are wounded, my lord?*'

Kiefer nodded to himself, unconsciously moving a hand from his shattered leg to the mess of his stomach. Creech must have been listening to the vox channels.

'It was an ambush,' Kiefer told him. 'All are lost.'

'*Not you, interrogator.*'

'Yes, me too,' Kiefer said, feeling the cold, numbness moving through his body. He tried to resist it. With gritted teeth he said, 'Status report.'

'*The Alpha Legion returned in your lander,*' Creech told him.

'*They overwhelmed the ship's security forces and took the command deck – with Shipmaster Fairuza, the astropath and the Navigator.*'

'They have the broken open the runebanks,' Kiefer said.

'*Aye, they have,*' Creech agreed.

'What is your disposition?' the interrogator asked.

'*The high enginseer and I have about thirty men with us,*' the confessor admitted. '*Not enough to take back the ship.*'

'Where are you?'

'*In the engine room,*' Creech said. '*The Alpha Legion have yet to secure it.*'

Kiefer gulped. His throat was so dry.

'Confessor,' he said, trying to regain a steely edged authority. 'The Alpha Legion now have access to the information in our runebanks. With it, they could cripple the ordo's operations in this entire region and bring death to millions. That cannot be allowed to happen. Do you understand me? Sisyphon Vail and his men cannot be allowed to leave this place, or pass on that information.'

'*Yes, interrogator,*' the priest said finally. '*I understand.*'

'You haven't much time. I don't care how you do it,' Kiefer said. 'You must find a way.'

'*The God-Emperor will show us the way,*' Confessor Creech said. '*The high enginseer is working on a solution right now.*'

'Do it for Godefroy Pyramus,' Kiefer said.

'*Interrogator,*' Creech replied. '*We'll do it for you… May the Emperor be with you. Creech out.*'

The channel crackled and then went dead. Kiefer had never felt more alone. Pulling the vox-bead from his ear he tossed it away. He lay there for a moment before deciding that he would like to feel the wind on his face one last time. Rolling over, he heaved his numb, cold body arm over arm across the cargo hold and out onto the desolate sands of the agri world. When his strength finally failed him, the interrogator rolled over again and stared up into the sky. He lay there and waited for the inevitable. He felt a stagnant breeze across his cheeks. High above, he saw a bird circling. Xerxes, Inquisitor Pyramus' psyber-eagle. The bird had been driven up into the sky by the battle in the hold.

Suddenly, beyond Xerxes, Kiefer saw a flash in the sky. Something had exploded in orbit. Kiefer was certain it was the *Internecia*. Perhaps an engine column or drive, sabotaged or rigged to overload or blow at the high engineer's instigation. Kiefer watched as a flaming wreck plummeted down through the atmosphere at high speed, streaking smoke across the sky. The interrogator closed his eyes and nodded slowly to himself.

'Got you,' Kiefer mouthed. He had no more strength for words. It seemed to take an age but finally the doomed vessel hit the surface of the planet. He never heard the distant boom of the crash – the sound of the Inquisitorial cruiser taking its ordo secrets and everything else on board into fiery oblivion. By then, his wait for the inevitable was over.

THE AEGIDAN OATH

OATH

L J GOULDING

'I could count myself a king of infinite space,
Were it not that I have bad dreams.'
– from *Amulet, Prince Demark*
(attributed to the dramaturge Shakespire), circa M2

The strips of parchment darkened quickly upon the brazier coals, the heat curling their edges and setting hungry flames over the illuminated script that marked each one.

As the three Space Marines watched, the words of their primarch were erased. Forgotten. Consigned to the murk of history as surely as if they had never been written.

Indeed, there were those who would deny that they ever *had* been written. The laws of men had finally overridden the word of the demi-gods, and the universe seemed so much more hollow and uncaring for it.

Oberdeii stared into the fire.

'I am an oath-breaker,' he murmured to no one in particular. 'No matter what happens from this moment on, that truth will remain with me until the end of my days.'

* * *

The halls of the orbital platform were dark, the beacon lights spinning reluctantly to life only as the craft passed the atmospheric threshold. Tarpaulins hung from the gaunt silhouettes of several decommissioned shuttles, their frayed edges stirred for the first time in months by the downdraft of the Thunderhawk's manoeuvring thrusters, with empty storage bins and cargo crates stacked well beyond the operational grid-lines marked out on the deck. The pilot, Brother Wenlocke, eyed each obstacle through the frost-rimed armourglass of the canopy, easing the gunship into position as carefully as he could in the gloom.

One of the landing struts grazed an abandoned tool bench, sending a brace of oily engine parts clattering to the floor as the dropship touched down. The Space Marine cursed.

'This is a wretched disgrace. Could no one have cleared the landing bays for our arrival?'

Remaining where he stood behind the empty co-pilot's seat, Segas ran his tongue over his teeth and sniffed. 'No one knew we were coming,' he replied, 'and there are precious few personnel still stationed here, anyway. I doubt that cleaning up their predecessors' mess was ever high on their list of priorities.'

Cycling the engines down, Wenlocke turned. 'Forgive me, my lord Chaplain, but we travel with the authority of the Chapter Master himself in this matter. Does that not count for anything? We might at least have let them know the purpose of our visit ahead of time, and they could have prepared what we need.'

Segas shook his head.

'No, brother. We cannot reveal our purpose, save in person and only to those who *must* know of it. No physical record must remain of this enterprise, regardless of the outcome.'

The pilot grunted and rose from his seat, moving his armoured bulk sideways through the cockpit to the rear hatch. Segas slid around the unmanned navigation console to meet him, recovering his skull-faced helm from the stowage locker overhead. He ran a finger over the clean edges of the Ultima engraved upon the brow, and considered all that for which it stood.

Wenlocke made to load his bolt pistol sidearm, but the Chaplain stopped him. 'No. No weapons.'

'And yet you will take your crozius? I've seen you break our foes with it, as often as lead a sermon.'

'Aye, I will take my crozius. We will have one chance, and one chance only, to put this delicate matter right. Our primarch's eternal legacy is at stake. That was why Chapter Master Decon sent me in his stead, and why I brought only you.'

Pausing with one boot on the topmost rung of the descent ladder, Wenlocke frowned. 'What, because you can trust me to keep my mouth shut when awkward questions are inevitably asked? Or just because we're both old enough to remember what happens to Chapters that keep dirty little secrets from the High Lords of Terra?' Without waiting for an answer, he swung his weight out and began to climb down into the gunship's hold. 'I did as you said – I purged all navigation data from the system. There is no record of our journey left for anyone to find.'

As the grey-haired warrior disappeared from view, muttering to himself in irritation, Segas considered Wenlocke's question.

I brought you for all of those reasons, and more besides, he thought. *Because you and I may never return from Mount Pharos.*

The air was cold and stale, and the deck plates of the corridors felt gritty beneath the Ultramarines' armoured tread.

Segas and Wenlocke met with the skeleton crew of the Sothan orbital, all mortal serf-officers of the Chapter who were long past combat retirement age. The men and women saluted stiffly, and they walked with the stilted gait of humans who had lived all their natural life in artificial gravity. They were tired, and had evidently been forgotten by the Imperium at large.

As tired and forgotten as the orbital platform itself, perhaps?

At the Chaplain's request, they arranged transit for the two Space Marines on board an anonymous cargo lighter bound for the planet's surface. The flight was cramped and uncomfortable for warriors of their size, but the need for an unheralded arrival made it a necessity.

Some kilometres outside the ordered coastal city of Sothopolis lay the freight terminals of Odessa, and it was there that they emerged into the first rays of dawn's light ready to walk the overgrown paths to the mountain.

The mountain.

It appeared far more impressive from the ground than when Segas had first laid eyes upon it from orbit. It towered over the distant, lesser peaks of the Blackrocks, utterly dominating the skyline. Many were the myths surrounding its dark history, and only a select few within the Chapter knew them all.

No matter how deeply Segas and Wenlocke pressed into the creaking quicktree forests, the mountain was always just visible beyond. For the most part they walked in silence, feeling faint and sporadic tremors in the earth beneath their feet.

Though it was a laughable notion, it seemed that Mount Pharos might be following their progress.

Or, at the very least, listening out for their approach.

As the day's heat grew, their path began to climb into the foothills. Without warning, Wenlocke froze mid-step – Segas saw the veteran's hand flick reflexively to the empty holster at his hip, then up in a halting gesture. Something cracked in the thick undergrowth ahead of them, and Segas' own fingers closed around the grip of his crozius maul. The two warriors edged apart, scanning for the unseen threat.

A man trudged into view, walking with a rough wooden staff in one hand and a las-lock rifle slung at his back. His clothing was simple, his frame lean, his gait assured. His tanned flesh and lined features spoke of countless summers beneath the open skies, and a wholesome life working close to the land. Only when he looked up to see the two armoured giants before him – one in cobalt blue, the other in black – did he slow his pace, his expression more vexed than alarmed.

Segas and Wenlocke held their ground, saying nothing. The man leaned on his staff, and mopped his brow with a ragged sleeve.

'Good day to you, friends. Tell me, have you seen a stray quarian pass this way?'

The Chaplain kept his voice level, his gaze as piercing as he could make it. 'Quarian?'

'Aye,' the man replied. 'Herd beast. Crafty little boggarts. They give me the slip every chance they get, up and down the hillsides.'

Brother Wenlocke looked to Segas. They both knew that the mountain was forbidden. The paths were supposed to remain untrodden by the people of Sothopolis, and yet here was a simple herdsman wandering wheresoever his animals took him. But he had a straightforward manner about him, and he held the Chaplain's eye without fear. He clearly believed that he had every right to be there. Was this, then, the famed pride of the Sothan people?

It mattered not. They did not have time to dwell upon

the trespasses of the locals, and Segas waved Wenlocke back. 'We have not seen your beast, citizen. We cannot help you.'

The man grinned, scratching his chin. 'Citizen, he says? Heh. You've never been to Sotha before, that's for sure.' Still showing no hint of being intimidated, he sidled up to Segas and reached out to paw at his battleplate, appraising him. 'The Chapter, then? You're a tall one, like the Scouts and their training sergeants. More than twenty hands from toe to tooth, I'll bet...'

Segas remained guarded. The herdsman rapped his staff on the packed, loamy earth.

'Do you know anything of this world, my tall friends? When I was young, the Chapter sent many Scouts. They were taught their craft on Sotha, and took what they learned to the stars, yes? They arrived as boys, but left as gelding-warriors, taller than any man from the plains or the cities. Not as tall as you two though, I think!' He screwed his face up, thoughtfully. 'And not as tall as the old man.'

At that, Segas leaned in sharply. 'The old man? Another Chapter warrior, like us?'

The herdsman grinned again. 'Aye, a gelding-lord like you, but without any pretty war-plate or badge of rank. *The old man on the mountain*, we always called him. Even before the Scouts stopped coming, he was the only one allowed up to the top of Mount Pharos. The braver lads from the herds used to help him clear the pathways, and he would tell us such tales about the horses and whatnot from his home world. But you'd never cross him. He has a fearsome manner, when he's riled.'

Wenlocke stepped in behind the man, and placed his gauntlets firmly upon his thin, mortal shoulders, enveloping them completely.

'This old man on the mountain,' he whispered, 'you know where we might find him?'

The herdsman frowned, looking from one gauntlet to the other and then back up at Segas.

'I dare say, my tall friends, that he'll be up at the old castellum. The ruins are hard for you to see from the air, I'll bet. If you'd be so kind as to unhand me, I'll take you there.'

The Aegida Castellum, Segas recalled from the Chapter's archives on Macragge, had been constructed during the Great Heresy as a base of legionary co-operation on Sotha. Ravaged by traitor assault and never fully rebuilt in all the centuries since, it stood now only in name upon the lower slopes, with tumbles of mossy ferrocrete strewn down the mountainside beneath it. What a casual glance might have mistaken for a rocky outcropping, Segas now saw was the overgrown remnant of a blocky, armoured keep, shot through with pale quicktree trunks and choked by vines.

Over the afternoon chorus of insects and birdcalls, there came the rhythmic threshing of a blade, and the mumbled refrain of what sounded like a work song.

Segas looked often to their guide, who seemed at times as surefooted as any quarian might be upon the uneven surfaces of the steep forest floor. Where previously he had been happy to engage the two Space Marines in inane chatter about the changing seasons and the preposterous price of a sack of grain at market, he fell to a respectful silence as they climbed the outer curtain wall of the ruins. Now that they could hear the old man's gruff voice, the herdsman had become visibly uneasy.

'I shall leave this to you, my lord Chaplain,' said Wenlocke with a bow of his head. 'As you said before, this could be *delicate*.'

Handing off his skull helm to the other warrior, Segas

approached the final gate. Wenlocke followed at a distance, with the herdsman trudging warily after him. Through the fallen arch lay what had once been a courtyard or mustering ground, the flagstones now cracked with grasses and weeds.

At the far end, in the shadow of the ruined keep, the old man on the mountain toiled.

His transhuman physique had been little dulled by the centuries. Age had not wearied him as it might a mortal, yet he remained largely free of the battle scars or augmetics that one would expect upon such a venerable warrior of the Adeptus Astartes. His bare limbs were clean, his torso rippled with corded muscle, and only the neural interface ports of his black carapace broke the skin of his back. His wild, white hair was tied back, slick with the greasy sweat that covered his body and darkened his tattered breeches.

He hefted an immense agricultural scythe, oversized for his grip, with which he cut back the vegetation. The rhythm of the sweeping, repetitive motion was a counterpoint to the song on his lips.

'*In avis, in novas, farsoni...*' he murmured as he worked. '*Invere, vesu ves ni vox...*'

Segas cleared his throat, and called out.

'Brother-Captain Oberdeii, Warden of the Pharos and commander of the Ultramarines Aegida Company?'

The warrior let his scythe fall still. He straightened slowly, and turned to face the Chaplain. There, in his cold stare and not upon his physical form, were borne all the hardships of his life.

Segas came to attention, saluting him with the sign of the aquila over his breastplate. Behind him, he heard Wenlocke do the same, and waited for a response.

Oberdeii stared at them for a long while, the butt of his

scythe resting upon the ground. He showed no sign of recognition at their livery, nor even the Ultima adorning it. Segas began to wonder if they had made a mistake in coming unannounced after all, and whether or not they would live to take word of it back to Macragge.

Reaching up slowly to smooth his long whiskers, the aged captain's gaze moved to the mortal cowering in the archway. 'You,' he barked. 'I remember you. You are called Benvis. You brought me milk when my bovid was taken by the rot.'

The herdsman let out a gasp of relief. 'Yes! Many years ago, I think you mean, when I was a boy.' He patted the strap of the las-lock on his back. 'You taught me the best way to hold a rifle, as thanks, and–'

'Shut your mouth,' Oberdeii growled. Benvis did not need to be told twice.

Segas looked to the captain's chest, and the twin-scythe emblem tattooed in faded golden ink across it. He saw the afternoon sun glinting from the curve of the actual blade at Oberdeii's shoulder, and recalled the provenance of that simple icon – the noble Sothan martyrs that it represented, the soldiers who had been farmers, and who had always intended to be so once again.

Oberdeii glowered at him in return.

'Who are you? A Chaplain?'

'Yes, my lord. I am Brother-Chaplain Segas of Second Company. My companion here is Veteran-Brother Wenlocke.'

'Hnh. What do you want? As you can see, I have work to do.'

This was it, Segas realised. This was the moment. He steeled his nerve, feeling the weight of a thousand years of Ultramarian glory resting firmly upon his shoulders.

'Brother-captain,' he declared, 'by the authority of the Lord

Macragge, ruler of Ultramar, we are here to relieve you of your command here on Sotha.'

The wooden snath of Oberdeii's scythe creaked as he tightened his grip on it. 'No you aren't,' he spat. 'Your Lord Macragge *has* no authority in this. Only one individual could release me from my oath, and he's dead.'

Caution. Segas had advised caution from the start. He cleared his throat again.

'My lord Oberdeii, I understand that this must come as–'

Oberdeii let out a wordless roar, and snapped the wooden haft of the scythe between his immense hands. In spite of himself, Segas flinched even as he heard the whimpering Benvis fleeing back down the forest path and away to what he probably considered safety.

'Do not speak to me,' Oberdeii bellowed. 'You understand nothing. I am the last Lightkeeper...' He began to trail off, frowning. 'Though... no light comes from Sotha anymore...'

A curious turn of phrase, under the circumstances, Segas thought. Nonetheless, he stiffened into a deferential bow.

'You have upheld your oath, brother-captain – none could ask for a more worthy guardian. But this world no longer requires the protection of the Aegida Company.'

Oberdeii's jaw worked silently for a moment. 'If you want my command,' he mumbled, 'then you'll have to take it from me. I won't yield without a fight. You can't deny me that.'

It was an honourable enough request, Segas had to admit. A ritual duel, against a living legend of the Great Heresy, no less. He turned to Wenlocke for approval, though the veteran was eyeing the broken scythe that remained in Oberdeii's hand, and the edge of the wickedly sharp blade that still glinted in the sunlight.

Nevertheless, the Chaplain nodded. 'Very well then, my

lord. I shall stand as Chapter Master Decon's proxy in this, and let the matter be decided between us in combat. Brother Wenlocke will– '

The blow was devastating. It lifted Segas from his feet and sent him sprawling to the broken flagstones in a clatter of plate, ears ringing, his vision hazed red.

Oberdeii stood over him.

'Get up.'

Gaping and blinking, Segas tried to shake the dullness from between his temples. He hadn't even seen the old warrior move. Wenlocke stepped forwards to help him to his feet, but Oberdeii shot the veteran a look that would have reduced a mortal to panicked tears.

'What do you think you're doing, *boy*? This is what he agreed to.'

Without breaking his gaze, he drew back one bare foot and kicked the Chaplain squarely in the face, snapping his head around. Blood splattered onto dusty stone, and Segas let out a pained gasp. 'S-Stay back, brother...' he managed, between coppery gulps that caught in his throat.

Wenlocke shook his head, backing away slowly. 'This is lunacy.'

Segas rolled onto his hands and knees, with Oberdeii pacing around him. The captain twitched and murmured to himself, twisting the scythe blade free of the broken haft and holding it like a falx. 'This is *my* duty, *my* honour...' he hissed. 'And my worthiness is not for the likes of you to judge...'

As Segas brought one unsteady foot underneath himself, he reached for the crozius arcanum at his belt once more. Oberdeii froze, his improvised blade ready.

'Better make it count, Chaplain. You'll get one chance. One chance only.'

It was true. Segas knew now that Oberdeii would kill him –
and Wenlocke immediately after – if he could. To him, this
was no merely symbolic duel for the sake of saving face.

This was the only honour that the old captain had left. For
that, Segas found that he pitied him.

The Chaplain rose painfully, activating the maul's power
field and holding it in a guard position. His words came
at first in a slur. 'Forgive me, my lord. I was given this task,
though in truth I feel blessed to journey here and meet you
in person.' He took one last, steadying breath. 'Long have I
made study of the Chapter's hidden records – I know who
you are, and what you have done for the Imperium.'

Oberdeii hesitated only a moment before he lunged, the
blade moving in a masterful feint intended to bring him
inside Segas' guard and strike for his vulnerable neck-seal.

But this time, the Chaplain was ready.

He stepped the same way as Oberdeii and jabbed at the
base of his opponent's skull with the head of the crozius.
There was a bright flash and a crack of percussive energy
discharge that threw them apart. Had Segas dialled the weapon's power field for anything more than minimal output,
it would likely have blown the captain's head from his
shoulders.

As it was, Oberdeii stumbled forwards, failing to regain
his footing before crashing down onto his side, stunned and
wracked by fading neural tremors. Spittle foamed at the corner of his mouth, and his right eye was bloodshot as it rolled
in its socket. Wenlocke reluctantly moved to aid the stricken
officer, kicking the scythe blade out of reach.

From a distance, Segas ran two fingers of his gauntlet
across the back of his head where the captain's wild slash
had caught him. They came away traced with cinnabar-red,

his genhanced physiology already clotting the ugly gash in his scalp.

He looked down at Oberdeii, and saluted him with the crozius.

'As I said, my lord – please forgive me, but you are relieved of your command.'

When the captain had taken water and regained his senses, the three of them climbed the mountain together. Wenlocke, usually quick to voice any discontent or to join in someone else's conversation, remained quiet. He listened intently as Segas put various questions to Oberdeii, and the embittered captain gave such replies as he saw fit.

At times, those replies bordered on the nonsensical, and neither Segas nor Wenlocke believed this was entirely the result of a powered blow to the head. Yet it was clear that even the most curious eccentricities of 'the old man on the mountain' carried the weight of years and experience in them.

'I have learned much in my time,' Segas mused as they neared the summit, 'from the writings of such luminaries as Lamiad, Corvo and Prayto. But here I am, walking with another great hero of our Chapter – one who stood at their side, in their finest hour, and spoke with them as easily as we speak now, and yet lives still among us.'

'I am no hero,' Oberdeii grunted.

'Come now, brother-captain. You–'

'No hero,' he repeated, firmly. 'I did what was asked of me, without question, knowing that to do so would deny me any future glory. No warrior of the Legion was ever a hero simply for doing what was expected of him...' His attention began to wander again, as it had several times already during their ascent. 'They say, "Only in death does duty end". But my name will never appear on any roll of honour, no monument to the Legion *or* Chapter.'

Segas nodded. 'Such was the solemnity of your duty, and the secrecy of your appointment to it. Even so, there is a great deal written of you, in the grand Library of Ptolemy on Macragge.'

Oberdeii shrugged. 'Never heard of it. Never been to the capital world.'

'It is a wondrous sight, brother-captain – the greatest of archives, save for those of the Imperial Palace itself on holy Terra. It was named for the first presiding master of the old legionary Librarius, and has been much expanded in the centuries since. Though my calling has ever been to the Reclusiam and the righteous soul of our Chapter, I am often drawn to the halls of the great library in the course of my duties. It represents the sum total of all Ultramar's knowledge, culture and philosophies. And its histories, both remembered and… *otherwise*.'

Unease welled up in Segas' gut. He was not used to discussing such things openly, though he knew that, in all likelihood, Oberdeii was privy to far more dangerous secrets than he. The Chaplain glanced sidelong at Wenlocke, who glanced at them both in turn before mouthing a silent prayer and touching his fingertips to the golden crux upon his breastplate.

'I feel that we need not be coy, you and I,' Segas went on, putting his concern aside. 'There is a place within the Library of Ptolemy wherein lie the two halves of our primarch's legacy. The first is the great Codex, the foundation of the Adeptus Astartes penned by his own noble hand. Such an important work can never be lost or allowed to fall into the hands of our enemies, and so it is watched over night and day by tireless guardians. Guardians much like yourself, in fact.'

Oberdeii did not visibly respond. He continued to place one callused foot in front of the other, loose stones skittering from his tread and away down the mountainside.

'The other half is similarly guarded, though for very different reasons. There has been much debate in recent years, between Chapter Master Tigris Decon and his inner circle, as to whether we should purge it from the library altogether. Some urge him to do so, to rid ourselves and our successors of the only remaining proof of Lord Guilliman's failure and folly during the Great Heresy. Others would seek to remind Master Decon that to destroy our past would blind us to the lessons we might come to learn from it.'

'And you, Chaplain? What do you say?'

Oberdeii's question caught Segas off guard. He considered his response carefully.

'My lord, I believe that such an unadulterated truth can present nothing other than a serious liability to the honour of our Chapter. The Imperium loves and cherishes the Ultramarines, and the memory of Roboute Guilliman, wisest of all the Emperor's sons. We are beyond reproach.' He raised a finger. 'But only as long as all knowledge of Imperium Secundus is kept from the rest of the galaxy. The archive record contains every surviving document and source relating to those confusing times, and it could shatter the reputation of our primarch and the credibility of everything he has done for the Imperium since. Can you imagine if even the hallowed *Codex Astartes* were to be branded as the work of a heretic, one only revealed centuries after his demise?'

'You would destroy it, then?' Oberdeii looked to him expectantly for an answer.

'No,' Segas replied, holding the captain's gaze. 'At this stage, what would be the point?'

The sunset kissed the peak of Mount Pharos as they emerged onto a jutting promontory. As below at the castellum, the remains of a fortress clung to the rock above, nonetheless seeming almost to graze the heavens with its crumbling ramparts. A fortified gate, cracked and weather-beaten, led inside the mountain itself.

'The Emperor's Watch,' said Oberdeii. 'You will know its name from the archives, Chaplain.'

Indeed, he did.

With the world spread out before them, Wenlocke and Segas paused to take it all in, and were rendered speechless by the legendary beauty of Sotha. Beyond the forests and the Blackrock range, they could see all the way past Odessa to the hills of the Chrepan region, and the tiny lights of some secondary township growing far from Sothopolis. To the east, night was falling for true over the ocean, and the first stars were already visible in the sky.

Oberdeii sat upon the bare ground, disinterested. Next to that breathtaking vista, he appeared smaller. Older, even.

'I did not ask for this,' he muttered. 'I did not ask to linger on, long after everyone I have ever known has fallen to the reaper's blade. No glory for Oberdeii, no foes to face – can you imagine that? The misery of a former legionary who cannot die as he was meant to, on the end of a sword or to a well-aimed bullet. We are made too well. A life without war makes us immortal. Our bodies endure, though our spirits may wither...'

He looked up, his expression suddenly haunted.

'I don't want to live forever. I see too much.'

Something in the captain's tone made Wenlocke turn. Segas marked it well. He stepped closer.

'Brother-captain, do you speak of the xenos device?'

Oberdeii rolled his eyes, and shifted his weight. 'It is nothing. I don't hear their voices anymore.' He looked up into the darkening sky overhead. 'You would not understand. You young warriors of the Chapter are of a different time. I don't like to think what the primarch would make of his own sons, now. The songs of Ultramar have fallen flat without him to lead us.'

He got to his feet slowly, as though such dour thoughts alone could age him. He looked at Wenlocke, and let his stare slide into the empty space beyond, his eyes dimming with memory.

'He stood there, where you stand now. Roboute Guilliman, the Avenging Son, stood in that exact spot over nine centuries ago, and addressed me and my battle-brothers. When I learned of his death, I stood in the same spot again and mourned his passing with a few quiet words. If you had ever known him, ever heard his voice, then you would not question his legacy. Master Decon would not consider himself the lord of Macragge. Not one of us who remains is worthy to question the eternal will of our primarch. Not one.'

The evening breeze brought with it a new chill. Oberdeii closed his eyes and breathed deeply.

'I'm not mad,' he muttered. 'I know what I am to you, to the Chapter. I am a living, breathing reminder of what you consider, in your vanity, to be Lord Guilliman's mistakes. You could not erase them from the pages of history while I remained here on Sotha, oathed to the final duty that he gave me. Not even if you burned every library on every world.'

Segas said nothing. He was relieved that, one way or another, the captain had arrived at this realisation for himself.

Oberdeii shook his head. 'But what was my oath, Chaplain? Do you even know? Is *that* recorded in the archive?'

'It is. You are the captain and last surviving member of the Aegida, a division of the Ultramarines Chapter whose origins can be traced back to the days of the Thirteenth Legion, whose very existence contravenes our primarch's own law. For reasons known only to a select few, Lord Guilliman saw fit to maintain a phantom *eleventh* company on Sotha even as he forced every other Chapter to conform to the Codex model of ten. Quite aside from the secret shame of Imperium Secundus, the existence of the Aegida Company could be seen as proof of his wilful and deliberate flouting of Imperial decree – a decree that he and his surviving loyal brothers agreed upon only after much conflict. The Second Founding of the Adeptus Astartes was all that kept the dream of a unified Imperium alive, after the Great Heresy.'

Grimly, Segas drew his crozius once more, and held it before him.

'To say that a revelation of this sort would be a scandal for our Chapter does not even begin to cover it. We and all our Successors would be cast out, the defenders of mankind would be divided and the Imperium would tear itself apart all over again. You are not simply the reminder of a mistake, my lord – you are the embodiment of it, and the last scrap of living proof. The time has come for the Aegida itself to be purged.'

Regarding the Chaplain's winged sceptre of office, Oberdeii shook his head. 'Why now? What has changed? What has rattled Tigris Decon?'

Rather than Segas, it was Wenlocke who replied. 'It must be now, my lord, because the Ultramarines will soon fall under the scrutiny of the High Lords once more. There is to be a Third Founding.'

Oberdeii snorted, though there was no trace of humour

in it. 'A *third*? That is impossible.' He made the sign of the aquila with trembling hands. 'Who dares to suggest such a thing? Now that our Lord Guilliman is gone and cannot protest it, who has led the Imperium to consider this… this… shallow heresy?'

Wenlocke and Segas shared a hesitant glance. Oberdeii sagged.

'Dorn,' he whispered, the realisation breaking him. 'It could only be Dorn. Such a pale imitation of our primarch's greatest achievement.'

Segas nodded. 'Lord Dorn, brother to our departed father, brought this before the High Lords more than forty years ago. The preparations have already begun. Petitions have been filed, Chapter assets marked and divided. The Adeptus Mechanicus has pledged a thousand new–'

'We are too few,' Oberdeii interrupted him. 'The Ultramarines, the Fists, the Angels – we are each only a thousand strong at best. From nine loyal Legions were the Chapters born, and our father did not even live to see the Successors reach full strength in a hundred years.' He gestured to the Sothan horizon, from east to west, and then to the stars above. 'I have seen it, brothers. I know how long it takes to turn raw neophytes into seasoned battle-brothers, and no one better. You speak of the Aegida dividing the defenders of mankind? This "Third Founding" will leave the first nine Chapters of the Adeptus Astartes without teeth, mired in petty mortal bureaucracy for another century or more.'

Segas raised his hands placatingly. 'Brother-captain – I should tell you that Rogal Dorn has urged the High Lords to grant writs of succession to the Second Founding Chapters as well. Any, in fact, that have the veterans, gene-seed reserves and materiel to support them. Over a hundred have already been approved, with the same number again currently being assayed.'

Oberdeii was rendered almost speechless. 'Shallow heresy...' he said again, his voice barely a whisper.

'Regardless of how you may feel about this matter, my lord, this is the moment that Chapter Master Decon has chosen for us to act. We will dissolve the Aegida Company, quietly, under the cover of this new founding. You are to be released from your oath to the primarch.'

The venerable captain whirled around, his hands balled into fists.

'Never!' he spat. 'You do not have the authority! Not even Dorn can command this! Take the Aegida. Take it and pretend it never happened. Paint over the dark stain on our spotless history, and return to your "Lord Macragge" and tell him you did as you were told. But I will not abandon my duty. I will not leave Sotha unguarded. Her people have earned that much, at least.'

Segas sighed. It would come to the final choice, then.

He reached to his belt and produced a gilded scroll, sealed with the haloed Ultima of Macragge, and unfurled the freshly scribed vellum within.

'This is a writ of succession for the Ultramarines Chapter, one of nine already approved by Terra. You will notice that the minutiae have been left incomplete.' He offered the scroll to Oberdeii, but the captain did not take it. Segas shrugged. 'Two courses of action remain open to you, my lord. As a mark of respect, for all that you have given and sacrificed for Macragge, Master Decon is willing to approve your immediate transfer to the Fifth Company. You would be assigned to new combat operations focused on the fringes of Old Ultramar, with an exceptionally high probability of glorious martyrdom. Your days will end, on the battlefield, as an Ultramarine. Only in death does duty end.

'The alternative is that you abandon your old oath, here and now, and sign your name instead upon this scroll. You will become the founding Master of the Aegida Chapter, noble Successors of the Ultramarines. I will join you, along with Brother Wenlocke and seventy-two other appointed veterans of the Orlan Conquest. We will take Sotha as our home world, and defend Mount Pharos from all threats, from now until the end of all things.'

Oberdeii stared at the vellum scroll. He did not seem to be considering the offer so much as attempting to disbelieve it.

'You don't understand,' he muttered. 'The Aegidan oath I swore to the primarch was not to protect Mount Pharos from the enemies of the Imperium.'

Segas faltered. His mind leapt back to the archives, the many affidavits, records and testimonials that he had curated in his years of study, every second spent in contemplation of this very moment. What had he–

Gesturing to the fortified gateway in the bluff beneath the Emperor's Watch, Oberdeii answered the question before the Chaplain could ask it.

'My oath was to protect Sotha from the Pharos itself.'

With those words, the yawning maw of the gate seemed wider and darker than before.

The vaults began as smooth stone, crafted and embellished in the blunt Imperial style. Lumen orbs hung in delicate brass cradles, illuminating the chambers and votive spaces that opened up on either side. This, Segas supposed, had been the work of the Imperial Fists after Sotha was retaken from traitor forces – austere and functional, but artisan-crafted with the strength of rock and steel upon which the VII Legion had built their unyielding legacy.

Soon, this strength gave way to the rough framework of a template in construction. The ancient scaffold and incompletely hewn masonry ended with a graceless step down to the glassy, obsidian surfaces of the mountain's interior.

At Guilliman's command, Rogal Dorn's sons had been building their new fortress within a far older labyrinth of unknown design.

Why had they ceased their labour so abruptly?

The deeper the three of them trudged into the darkness, their way lit now only by Segas' and Wenlocke's suit lamps, Oberdeii became visibly more agitated. He glanced up and down the tunnel every few moments, muttering to himself.

'He thinks me mad? It is enough that I know... and that I uphold it above all else...' He bent to examine cracks in the smooth, black curve of the rock, then called out with a forced levity. 'Would you believe, eh, these walls used to heal themselves? I saw it with my own eyes, many times. But not anymore. Not after the primarch tore out the mountain's heart.'

A barely perceptible tremor, nothing more than a low vibration, shuddered through the ground beneath their feet. Oberdeii's eyes widened in the gloom.

'And yet, the heart still tries to beat...'

Segas removed his gauntlet, placing one hand upon the tunnel wall. The rock was icily cold.

'Do not concern yourself with the local superstitions, my lord – the mountain and even the distant Blackrocks have long suffered from geological instability. Tectonic shifts are to be expected.'

Oberdeii shook his head, pushing past the Chaplain and

leading them onwards. 'When he returned to Ultramar after the war was lost and won, Lord Guilliman ordered the Pharos destroyed. The Mechanicum priests carved up the quantum pulse engines like a feast-day fowl, and carted thousands of tonnes of xenos machinery out into the light of day, spiriting it all away to their secret vaults across the galaxy for further study. There was so much of it. Too much to even think about taking it all, not with the short time we had. No one knew how it could just keep on coming, and coming.'

He tapped himself on the chest, where the twin-scythe tattoo was just visible beneath his jerkin. The hurt pride in his voice was mixed with a note of trepidation.

'I could have told them. I've seen further than most.'

The angle of the tunnel grew steeper, and they had to steady themselves against the slope of the floor. Oberdeii moved with many lifetimes' familiarity, helping Wenlocke to find the best footholds. Still, he seemed distracted.

'The locals used to have their superstitions – my brothers and I used to sit with the herdsmen in the outer halls, as they tried to sing the mountain to sleep. But it was never the same as it had once been.' He fixed Segas with that same wide stare as the ground trembled again. 'So don't tell me that those vibrations are natural tectonic activity. That doesn't explain why they are always the exact same frequency, and the same duration. The mountain doesn't sleep... and nor do I...'

Segas took Oberdeii by the arm. 'What do you mean?'

'I don't sleep. I never sleep. You wouldn't either.'

Even Wenlocke halted at that. 'You haven't slept since you swore your oath to the primarch?'

'Give or take. Catalepsean slumber, but never true sleep. I always like to keep one eye on the mountain.' The captain smiled for the first time since they had ventured beneath the surface. 'And besides, I don't like the things I see in my dreams.'

Segas saw the incredulous look in Wenlocke's eye. An explanation was in order.

'Brother, the venerable captain was known to experience visions, precipitated by his connection and proximity to Mount Pharos – this was verified by many, including the primarch himself. Both times the young Oberdeii's most vivid dreams went unheeded, and both times he was proven correct. He foresaw the arrival of the Blood Angels Legion at Ultramar, and he also foresaw the invasion of Sotha by traitor forces.'

Oberdeii twitched. 'I was just a neophyte. But even now, nearly a thousand years later, those visions remain. Has my whole life been a dream? And if so, whose dream is it...? They saw our light... in the dark between the stars...'

Segas felt his hearts sinking. This old warrior was not fit to lead a Chapter of the Emperor's finest. His centuries away from the Chapter, denied a life of battle and instead given the thankless task of clearing undergrowth with his bare hands, had clearly taken their toll. These frequent babbling rants were proof enough of that.

What had Segas agreed to?

They continued down the incline in silence, until Oberdeii pointed out a smear of dark grey against the blackness of the tunnel. 'There,' he sighed. 'Shoddy work, and inelegant compared to what was built on the surface. But time was short and Lord Guilliman's patience was at an end.'

The way ahead levelled out into a much broader space – not in the natural curve of the passageway, but with a rising blockage that edged all the way up to the ceiling. Their armoured boots struck the uneven surface with dull thuds as they stepped out onto it.

'Ferrocrete,' Wenlocke murmured. 'Poured down here? Why?'

'To seal the mountain,' Oberdeii replied, inspecting the edges of the tunnel where the join was most noticeable. 'To keep everything down there... *down there*. The serf labourers poured millions of tonnes of 'crete into the main tributary tunnels. That was the primarch's last word on the matter of the Pharos, and it is one for which I am thankful.'

'Aye!' Wenlocke snorted. 'If anything yet lives down there, in the depths, then it must squirm and writhe in dark places that no man or primarch has ever-'

Oberdeii turned slowly to face him. His glare was cold and fierce.

'Do not speak of such things. Not here. Not in this place.'

Aside from the low, broad arch of the chamber's sloping vault, the only other feature was a plain stone bier, set with a brazier on the ferrocrete floor before it. Oberdeii approached it reverently, striking a flame into the bowl with a simple flint and rasp.

As the oiled tinder took, the flickering light revealed what lay upon the bier's top.

An iron mask, worked into the semblance of a skull.

The metal was pitted with age, but had been kept polished and oiled through the centuries. Unaccountably, the sight of it sent a chill into Segas' hearts. There was something there, something in the emptiness of the eye sockets, in the stylised line of the jaw that was neither a grin nor a grimace.

'The mask of Barabas Dantioch, first Warden of the Pharos,' Oberdeii murmured. 'A loyal hero of the Great Heresy, by Guilliman's own decree. I live in the shadow he has cast upon this place, in more ways than one, though I can never hope to be so worthy of the title of Warden.'

Beneath the mask were three strips of decrepit parchment, fixed to the bier with wax that had become little more than a discoloured crimson bruise upon the stone. The imprint of the Ultima of Macragge was barely visible in the seal.

'You knelt here?' Segas asked, his voice feeling weak with awe. 'You took the knee before our primarch and made your oath, at the threshold of the Pharos itself?'

Oberdeii nodded. He ran his fingertips over the fine calligraphic script that adorned each of the oath papers. 'Aye. The primarch drew his blade, the Gladius Incandor, and I swore the Aegidan oath upon it. By the flames of this brazier was the seal made, by his own hand.'

Brother Wenlocke sank to one knee, his head bowed before the bier and the artefacts laid upon it. The captain regarded him curiously, but continued.

'And now young Master Decon urges me to make a simple choice – a choice between surrendering my rank and my life, or continuing to watch over this place as something I am not. You tell me that I cannot remain an Ultramarine and still act as Warden of the Pharos, as the noble primarch appointed me.'

Segas considered his words. 'I had not thought to put it so, captain. But yes, that is the essence of it.'

By the glow of the brazier, Oberdeii appeared differently, like some haunted phantasm of the abyss. 'No good will come of this, Chaplain Segas,' he said grimly. 'Mark my words – I am as certain of this as anything I have ever known. This lie that you craft will be the death of all that Guilliman strove to accomplish.'

He reached out and plucked the oath papers from the seal, the wax yielding easily, and what little of the Ultima that remained visible was broken.

'Pray that our primarch never awakens from his deathly slumber, or we shall know his wrath.'

Segas stoked the brazier, the ashes of the oath papers crumbling as they were ground between the smouldering coals. He saw the grief in Oberdeii's eyes.

'Think of it not as the breaking of an oath, but a renewal of the same. When you swore upon the primarch's blade and your own, the galaxy was a very different place.' He rose, and placed a hand upon the captain's shoulder. 'But I am glad you have chosen this path. The Imperium is changing, and we shall change with it. The past will soon be forgotten, and the future is not what it used to be.'

Oberdeii did not respond. Brother Wenlocke reached for the iron mask upon the bier, and presented it to his new Chapter Master. 'Hail to you, my lord – Warden of the Pharos in perpetuity, and Master of the Aegida Chapter!'

The proclamation hung in the silence of the sealed chamber for a moment. The trace of a frown crossed Oberdeii's brow.

'No. That name is gone also. Gone with my fallen brothers, and my primarch.'

Segas handed him the writ of succession, and a matrix-quill. 'It is to you, then, Master Oberdeii. By what name shall we bring death to the foes of mankind?'

Absently, the Chapter Master raised a hand to the tattoo over his heart. His jaw was set, his voice low.

'The Aegida was the shield, but no more. Sotha shall not be defended, but shall strike at the darkness before it can grow, and reap a bitter harvest. Put out the call to the proud men and women of this world – they have earned the right to fight and bleed and die alongside any warrior of this

Chapter, and their sons shall be our brethren. Let them turn their ploughshares into swords, and stand with us as equals.'

A fire was kindled in Segas' hearts by Oberdeii's words, and the Chaplain watched as he put his mark upon the vellum.

'If I am to be damned then it shall be on my own terms, and red with the blood of my foes. We stand no longer as the Emperor's shield, brothers, but as his noble Scythes.'

HIDDEN TREASURES

CAVAN SCOTT

Elias didn't know what he hated more: this dark stinking hole or his brother for making him come down here. He wished they'd never discovered the place.

They'd been hiding from the Kerlons. They were always hiding from the Kerlons, the bloodiest gang in Manos City. It had been his brother's fault, as always. Marco had crossed a line, stealing from a Kerlon-protected store. He hadn't even needed the food. He did it to get a reaction, to prove what a big man he was.

He hadn't looked so big cringing in the dark, snot running over a bloodied lip.

Then they had seen it, glinting in what little light filtered through the hole in the ceiling.

The first treasure.

Elias swore as his elbow scraped against the stone wall. This was the last time, he promised himself. The last time he'd let Marco bully him into coming down here with the vermin and the shadows and Throne knew what.

He didn't care what he'd find or how much money it would bring. Nothing was worth this. Nothing.

Something scuttled over his hand as he squeezed through the gap in the wall of the back room. He snatched it back sharply. The building was a shell, too derelict for even vagrants to make shelter. But that wasn't the worst of it.

The walls felt wrong. He couldn't explain it. They were cold, covered in muck and mould, but there was something else. Something deeper. They felt rotten. Diseased. The air itself felt sick.

His feet dangling into the void of the cellar below, Elias eased himself through and hung for a minute, half tempted to pull himself back up and run; away from Marco, away from everything.

Who was he kidding? Marco would kill him, brother or not.

He closed his eyes and let himself fall.

The sound of his boots hitting the slabs below echoed around the musty space. Something small ran out of earshot, clawed feet scrabbling against the stone. Elias fumbled for his luminator, dropped it and cursed. He fell to his knees in the darkness, groping around the floor, flinching as his hands splashed through ice-cold water.

Finally, his fingers found the cold metal. Thank the Emperor. He gripped the luminator in shaking hands, but froze, unable to hit the activation rune. What if something else was in the dark with him?

'Idiot,' Elias hissed. 'There's no one down here. There's never anyone down here.'

No one else was that stupid.

He forced himself to hit the rune. The beam of light was weak and yellow, but calmed his nerves. A little.

Elias swept the light over the wreck of an ancient staircase, collapsed long ago, the trapdoor above boarded safely shut.

To keep people out or trap something in?

Nothing had changed. The same mouldering crates shoved into the corner. The same dusty webs draped from the rafters. The same stench stinging his nostrils, making his stomach flip.

He scanned the floor. Nothing on the cracked rockcrete slabs save the droppings of vermin. As he'd expected. The treasures were always in the other room.

Elias swallowed hard as he flashed the light over the doorway that led into the next chamber, summoning the courage to approach the threshold.

Run away, screamed the voice in his head. *You shouldn't be here. No one should.*

But the memory of Marco's fists won the battle. Elias took a step forwards, his breath fogging in front of him.

They found a knife on that first day, lying in the next room, discarded on the floor, like nothing they'd ever seen before. A vicious serrated blade with a curved metal handle, scarlet trimmed with gold, runes set along the edge. Runes encrusted with blood.

Elias tried to pull Marco back, but his brother didn't listen. He snatched the weapon up, greed glinting in his eyes.

'Look, Elias,' he grinned, forgetting all about the Kerlons. About his fear. 'Must be worth a fortune.'

They came back the next day with a luminator and found a sword; long, heavy and strangely warm to the touch.

But that wasn't all. As Marco examined his find, there was a flash, and movement in the corners of their eyes. Something clattered across the floor as if thrown. They spun around, but the luminator's glow found only an old wall, full of cracks and creeping damp.

A helmet rolled to a stop by Elias' feet.

'Pick it up,' Marco barked.

'You pick it up!'

Marco brandished the huge sword with two hands, his arms shaking with the effort. For a second Elias thought his brother was about to run him through, plunge the blade deep into his chest.

'Pick. It. Up.'

The helmet's faceplate was crushed as if by a hammer blow. Elias didn't want to touch it. He knew what it was. And he knew who had worn it.

'For Terra's sake,' Marco spat, letting the sword drop and marching towards Elias, who threw up a hand.

'No. Marco, don't, it's–'

Too late. Marco was holding it in front of him now, like a trophy.

'Yeah,' he said. 'I know. An Angel of Death.'

Elias pleaded with him. This belonged to a Space Marine. How it was here, he didn't know, but it didn't bode well. They should leave it alone, climb out of here and never return.

He didn't see the blow coming. Marco smashed the helmet into Elias's face, the sharp metal and ceramite slashing across his cheek. He fell to the floor, spitting out teeth and blood.

His brother just stalked from the room, leaving him alone in the dark.

And that was it. They came back every day. Sometimes the cellar was empty, but sometimes there were new treasures on the floor. Weapons. Scraps of armour.

Marco was right: they were worth a fortune. He found

collectors. Gang members. Those rumoured to be members
of illicit cults. Anyone willing to pay for their scavenged
booty.

Marco never asked where they came from. Never wor-
ried where they were going. Why should he care what his
customers did with their purchases? It wasn't his problem.
And when Elias dared ask the question, he just answered
with his fists.

Marco had always been a brawler, but never like this. It
was as though he'd discovered more than a helmet in that
cellar. He'd discovered a bloodlust, an anger.

After a while, no one stood up to him. Not Elias. Not even
the Kerlons.

Marco stopped going down into the cellar himself. He
didn't have to, not when he had Elias to descend into hell
and return a prize.

The torchlight played across the floor of the second room.
Elias sighed in relief. There was nothing there. Yes, Marco
would beat him, maybe break a rib, but at least Elias wouldn't
have to touch any more of the accursed stuff. Not today.

Then he saw something in the corner of the room, not far
from the door. Something metal – something that didn't
belong. Fear gripped him. He could lie, go home empty
handed. Leave it for another day. But Marco would know.
He always knew.

Elias hurried over and bent down. Nothing much. A few
links of a barbed chain that hadn't been there yesterday.

There was no point in putting off the inevitable. He reached
forwards and carefully picked the chain from the floor, spikes
scraping against the flagstones. It was heavier than it looked.
Should raise a few credits, at least.

Swinging his leather pouch from his shoulder, Elias started dropping the chain into the bag, praying that the barbs didn't slice through the hide. They clanked together, the noise filling the small room. Too loud. Not that anyone would hear, or come to see what was happening.

He turned to leave – and the world *changed*.

At first there was a noise like thunder, but not from the permanently grey skies above the derelict hab.

It came from behind the walls. From behind *that* wall. From the cracks.

Elias should have run, but he was fixed where he stood, staring wide-eyed into the gloom, listening to the approaching storm. No. Not a storm. There was nothing natural in the sound. It wasn't thunder, it was weapons-fire. Battle cries.

Then he appeared. The Angel of Death. There was a flash and a grey-armoured Space Marine was tumbling back into the room, his back slamming into the floor, weapon still firing into the wall itself.

Elias jumped, crashing into the corner, the shock sending his luminator spinning from his hand. It clattered onto the floor, the sound lost beneath the din of the Angel's weapon. The light stayed on, illuminating the scene as shells disappeared into the wall. There should have been chips of brickwork spraying around the room, but the round just vanished, as if spirited away.

Until they met something else.

A second figure pushed through the wall, a massive axe held high, bigger even than the Space Marine that lay sprawled on his back. It roared as explosive bolts pounded into it. Its red chest-plate was lined with gold. Like the knife. Like the helmet.

'Die!' it screamed, spittle spraying from thin lips. The axe came down hard, missing the Space Marine, who rolled clear at the last moment. The whirring chain-toothed weapon buried itself where the Space Marine's exposed head had been, sending shards of rockcrete flying.

The Space Marine swung his body around and kicked out. Armour met armour as the axe-wielder's feet were taken from beneath him. It fell back, throwing up an arm that passed cleanly through the wall as if it wasn't there.

It crashed to the floor, reaching for its axe, but the Space Marine was already on his feet, his weapon's muzzle thrust into the fallen warrior's face. The Space Marine didn't hesitate. The gun barked, discharging its payload straight into his opponent's head. There was no armour to protect the enemy now, only flesh and bone. Elias clasped his hands over his ears, trying to block out the gun's clamour. But it was hopeless. Nothing could silence its terrible report. He would hear it for as long as he lived.

The red-armoured warrior's body convulsed as his head was reduced to mush. Finally, after what seemed like a lifetime, the weapon fell quiet, a wisp of smoke curling from its barrel. The Space Marine stood frozen, gun still in place, as if he expected his foe to leap from the ground again and continue the fight.

But the corpse remained still.

Elias couldn't move. He couldn't even breathe. He watched, convinced he would be next as the Space Marine dropped his weapon and looked up from his kill. The Angel of Death cocked his shaven head as he studied the wall. He raised a gauntleted hand and cautiously reached forward. His fingers slipped through the bricks and he pulled them back sharply. There he stood gazing at the impossible portal like a statue, the profile of a white skull embossed on one large, grey pauldron.

Then his head turned slowly to glare at Elias.

Elias tried to push himself through the corner of the room, but the walls that trapped him remained steadfastly solid.

The Space Marine stomped forwards – covering the small space in two strides – and towered over Elias. He glared down with one piercing blue eye that seemed to shine in the half-darkness of the room. But Elias was staring at the hole where the other eye should have been, an empty socket beneath a heavy brow.

'I'm sorry,' Elias whimpered, not knowing why he was apologising.

'The bag,' the Space Marine snarled, showing a mouth full of silver teeth. 'Open the bag.'

When Elias didn't move the bolter swung up to cover him. The Space Marine didn't need to ask again. Elias almost threw the pouch from his shoulder as he wrenched it open, the chain tumbling between his legs.

The Space Marine's solitary eye followed it down, before flicking back up to Elias. It narrowed for a split second before he reached down and retrieved the chain. He slung it over his shoulder and turned back to tramp towards the fallen warrior.

Elias watched, expecting the Space Marine to spin and tear his body apart with a volley of hot metal, but instead the giant reached for his belt and unclipped a device. There was a series of beeps followed by a heavy clunk as he dropped it down on the corpse's chest.

'Get out,' he growled over his shoulder. 'And remember.'

Elias didn't wait to be told twice. He scrambled to his feet and made for the door, glancing back as the dark figure marched forwards to the wall. There was another flash of light as the Space Marine disappeared from sight, and Elias didn't look back again. He was through the door and scrabbling up the wall towards the hole before he realised he'd left his luminator on the cellar floor.

He didn't need it. He knew the way, and he would never go back down into that pit again. Marco could kill him. He didn't care anymore.

He squeezed through the hole, panicking slightly as he got stuck half way, imagining the dead fingers of the red-clad warrior closing around his flailing ankles. Then he was free, rolling up onto the floor above, stumbling to his feet and running – running fast. He tore out of the back room, over to the window with the loose shutter. He flung it aside.

He had only swung one leg over the sill before the blast hit him. It was like a wall of sound and fury, blossoming beneath him, throwing him out into the street. He didn't feel himself hit the road outside, didn't feel his collarbone crack as he rolled clear, burning rubble crashing all around him.

He couldn't even feel his skin bubble where it had been exposed to the flame.

He didn't care. The cellar was gone, consumed in fire, with its impossible walls and hidden treasures. Marco could do what he wanted now. He was free.

Chuckling weakly to himself, Elias let his eyes close, his face pressed against the cold, hard street.

The laugh caught in his throat. In his mind he could see the Space Marine looming over him with his empty socket and metallic sneer.

Remember.

Elias's eyes snapped open, wider than ever. If he closed them again, the Angel of Death would be waiting. Forever, in the dark.

THE REAPING TIME

TIME

ROBBIE MACNIVEN

+ Sub-file 8762-443 +

+ Jurisdiction: Ethika Subsector +

+ Timestamp: 3551670.M41 +

+ Subject header: Tithe Non-Payment Response Protocol 33/8 +

+ Clerk Attendant: 4872-Amilia +

For the attention of the Adeptus Administratum, Sub-Division Theta 16, Ethika Subsector. Contact has been lost with Tithe-Ship 531, designate *Praetorian*. Last known astropathic message relay confirmed successful warp jump into the Zartak System [file ref. 228-16a]. Contact is now two weeks overdue, Terran Standard. Recommending dispatch of Imperial Navy Mars-class Cruiser *Andromidax* [see attachment DX1-9] to investigate.

+ Sub-file 8762-443 record-logged for review +

+ Added to review queue +

+ Estimated processing time: 6 years, Terran Standard +
+ Thought of the Day: The faithful suffer in silence +

The guildmasters were terrified. Their postures were stiff, their eyes darting, sweat slicking their pale, wrinkled flesh. One old man, stooped beneath the weight of his own sagging fat, was twitching uncontrollably. The motion juddered grotesquely through his heavy jowls, growing more pronounced the more he tried to hide it. Another balding, rheumy-eyed figure's skeletal hands were clenching and unclenching on the grip of his silver pick-cane. A third was clutching her ermine ruff so hard her scrawny, velvet-draped limbs were shaking.

The entire assembly, packed onto the walkway of an observation gantry, cringed at the presence of the giants towering over them.

They were monsters, primordial terrors clad from head to foot in battleplate the colour of ash. They reeked of weapons unguents and a cloying, alien scent that turned the humans' stomachs. None had moved since stepping onto the gantry. Their motionless state spoke of a razor-edged, predatory patience.

Eventually, one of the ashen giants spoke.

'These are all of them? All the young?'

None of the guildmasters answered. For a moment, nothing happened. There was a click. Then, abruptly, one of the giants lunged.

For something so large, it moved with terrifying speed. Its bone staff shattered the skull of the fat, twitching guilder. Those around recoiled from the splattering of brains and blood. Without hesitation, the other giants lashed out.

The screaming started. It didn't last long.

The figure at the heart of the coral chamber woke with a start. He bit back a cry, fists clenched and shaking around his force staff.

It had been no dream. His kind were incapable of something so human, so innocent. No, this was the third time he had seen the exact same scene – the exact same slaughter – play out since the ship had broken in-system. It was a warning. It could be nothing else.

The figure shifted his cross-legged stance fractionally, the incisor-charms hanging from the leather bands around his wrists rattling. Without his etched blue battleplate and psychic hood, the true horror of his ancient form was revealed. The simple black shift did little to hide the ivory whiteness of his flesh, or the ugly grey denticle-scabs that blotched his elbow joints and neck. It was an affliction, the result of his unique and degraded genetic inheritance. Even more startling were the figure's eyes. They were utterly black, without iris or sclera, as pitiless and unfathomable as the void that was his home.

The figure drew in a long, slow breath. Should he inform Company Master Akia? Not doing so would be a dereliction of duty. But telling him ran complex risks. They could not afford the dangers of a self-fulfilling prophecy. Nothing could be allowed to interfere with the Tithe.

After a while the vox bead in his ear clicked. The figure known to his brethren as Te Kahurangi – the Pale Nomad – listened for a moment, then uncrossed his legs and stood.

The time for contemplation was over. The reaping time had arrived.

The sub-guild quota hall was in an uproar. Every guildmaster and guildmistress present was speaking at once. It took Thornvyl slamming his augmetic left fist – the result of a mining accident almost a century before – against the flank of the hall's lexmechanic podium to bring some semblance of order.

'Panic achieves nothing,' he snapped. 'There may be another explanation.'

'Another explanation for an Adeptus Astartes ship arriving unannounced in our system?' Elinara of the Freehold Prospector Guild demanded. 'A more probable explanation than the Imperium finally coming to investigate the disappearance of the *Praetorian*?'

The arched vault of the quota hall descended once more into wild chatter. The guildmasters, leaders of the mining colony of Zartak, had come together for an emergency session after the augur masts had detected an unidentified vessel breaking in-system. When the logisticators had identified it as a Space Marine warship, the meeting had descended into chaos.

'They are the Emperor's servants,' Thornvyl, Guildmaster of Chronotech Inc., snapped. 'As are we. And we shall greet them as such.'

'Are you insane?' demanded Maron of Broken Hill Industrials.

'Unless you wish to call out the Guard, the local defence force and the mine-militia?' Thornvyl responded. 'Tell me, which course of action sounds more insane?'

The other guildmasters quietened, realising the truth of Thornvyl's words. He pressed on.

'There has been a misunderstanding. We will resolve it, quickly and quietly. Trust me, Guild Brethren, these god-warriors will be gone by tomorrow.'

It was raining hard when the Space Marines arrived. The downpour made the surrounding jungle canopy hiss, and seethed off the rockcrete surface of sink shaft 1's primary landing plate, sited just beyond the edge of the great burrow-mine habitat.

A behemoth descended from the near-black skies, water cascading from its broad flanks, the white oceanic predator emblazoned on its grey hull glistening. The assembled guildmasters huddled closer together as the mighty gunship screamed overhead, shivering in their drenched finery. The flier's afterburning turbofans whipped at the embroidered hems of their robes and sent one matriarch's shawl twisting away through the rain. The engine's painful howl finally dropped to an idling snarl as the transport settled itself atop the plate. The dark muzzles of its many weapons systems gleamed in the rain.

For a moment, nothing stirred. The guilders looked on, fretting. Eventually there was a thump, loud enough to make them jump. The gunship's prow hatch began to lower, venting gouts of hydraulic steam. Through it, their armoured footfalls ringing rhythmically off the plasteel plates, came seven primeval giants.

Each one towered head and shoulders above the tallest guilder, and all were clad in grey battleplate of different shades. Their eye lenses were black, glittering in the harsh light of the landing zone's jury-rigged lumen strips. Around their wrists and gorgets were bands hung with vicious fangs, claws and incisors, while many parts of their armour were inscribed with flowing line-markings that formed stylised maws or darting fins. They carried weapons in their gauntlets, mighty boltguns and chainaxes, their rotors thankfully inactive.

The seven stepped out onto the landing plate two abreast, forming a line in front of the guildmasters. With a crash of ceramite they came to a halt, the rain pattering from their armour.

For a moment they remained still and silent. Then one, his armour a whiter shade and embossed with numerous brass molecular bonding studs, took one step forward. The guilders cringed.

'Who rules this world in the Void Father's name?' the white-plated giant demanded, his voice crackling up through the arched grille of his helm's vocaliser as though from some great depth. The words were delivered in High Gothic, stilted and unnaturally formal. The guilders didn't respond. The giant said nothing more. Eventually, unable to stand it any more, Fargo Tork of BorerCorp Mining summoned up the few words of High Gothic he recalled from his scholam days.

'We rule as a collective council, sire. We have no one leader, bar Him on Earth.'

For a moment the giant did not respond. The guilders detected a series of low clicking noises. Some recognised it as the sound of an internal vox conversation, held in private over the Space Marines' helm comms. Eventually, the giant spoke again.

'Well met. I am Master Akia, of the Third Battle Company. We are the Carcharodons Astra, and we have come for you.'

The viewscreen monitor flickered and died. The sub-guild quota hall descended once more into furious recriminations, until Thornvyl snapped for quiet. After a moment's pregnant silence the viewscreen blinked back into being again, the grainy image of Vasil Krane's body double reappearing.

'Repeat yourself,' Thornvyl ordered. 'We lost you.'

'They are demanding to see our records,' the Krane double said, pausing to glance back over his shoulder. He was muttering into a handheld vidcam, squeezed into the entrance tunnel of one of the tiny ratholes that wormed its way through the mineworks of Lower Six-Sixteen.

'Records?'

'Imperial data. Reports on psyker levels, Guard recruitment rates, xenos and heretic activity.'

'And tithes?'

'Yes, tithes. Their leader, Akia, claims to be here specifically for the tithe.'

'It's as we feared,' Ghorst of New Western Mining hissed. 'They know about the *Praetorian*!'

'Silence,' Thornvyl barked before the room descended once more into mayhem. He turned back to the viewscreen.

'Where are they now?'

'Waiting in upper ore hall west,' Krane's double said, again glancing back, as though he expected to see one of the giants loom suddenly from the half-darkness behind him. 'Their latest request was to inspect the most junior Guard battalions.'

'The most junior?'

'The cadets, the new foundlings of the 10th Regiment.'

'Why is that their first priority–' began Elinara. Thornvyl cut her off.

'It doesn't matter why. It presents us with an opportunity.'

'They're here for the tithe, you heard it yourself,' Tork said, jowls wobbling as he sought to contain his terror. 'When they discover what happened they'll kill us all!'

'They won't,' Thornvyl said firmly. 'Not if we keep our heads. Their ship is still in orbit, yes?'

'So the augur beacon says,' Maron said. 'Holding anchor directly above sink shaft 1. Its ident-tag and keel scans are still coming up blank, but it's definitely of ancient design.'

'Their main strength will still be onboard,' Thornvyl said. 'But their leaders are down here, with us. That presents an opportunity.'

'I do hope you have a plan, Thornvyl,' Elinara said, her eyes narrowing. 'Remember that not all of us supported the last one you had. This is where it has led us. We won't all be held accountable should you fail.'

The rest of the guilders muttered their agreement.

'But you'll expect to reap the rewards once it's successful,' Thornvyl said, smiling despite the steel in his voice. 'Trust me one more time, Guild Brethren. Tell the holding blocks to prepare to enact Order 19. And pass word for Inspector DeValin. I want the 10th paraded in full combat kit in drill cavern 11 within the hour.'

'We should just slaughter them,' Akia said over the inter-squad vox. Te Kahurangi didn't deign to reply. The Company Master was speaking in jest, venting his frustration. The Pale Nomad couldn't begrudge him that.

According to the chrono digits ticking over in the corner of the Chief Librarian's visor display, First Squad had been standing at parade rest, waiting in what appeared to be called the drill-head chamber for upper ore hall west, for almost forty minutes. Akia had delivered the company's demands to the gaggle of flunkies who claimed dominion over Zartak, and they'd been ushered into a quota collection analysis chamber, the cogitators and tithing boards currently abandoned. The flunkies had then fled. A wide-eyed attendant had offered them some sort of fungus-like local refreshment, the tray clattering in his shaking hands. The Carcharodons hadn't so much as moved, and the human had left with haste. Since then they'd seen no one.

'They dishonour us,' said the Company Champion, Toa.

'The concept of individual honour is a dead thing,' Te Kahurangi replied, quoting from *Beyond the Veil of Stars*. 'It is a lie invented by arrogant men to excuse their own foolhardiness.'

'They dishonour the Chapter,' Toa corrected. 'And through it, *Rangu*.'

'You think the Void Father cares if we wait an hour or two?' Strike Veteran Dorthor rumbled. 'We must follow protocol. The Edicts of Exile were not issued by the Forgotten One in vain.'

Throughout the exchange, Te Kahurangi could sense Akia brooding. The Company Master had lately reached his full maturity as leader of the Third through the august title of Reaper Prime, but with experience had come a bloodthirsty edge that left the Chief Librarian in no doubt as to his particular genetic heritage. The suggestion that they simply slaughter the Zartakian mine-leaders had not been spoken entirely in jest.

'Movement,' Signifier Karra said, a moment before Te Kahurangi's auto-senses detected approaching footsteps. A moment later the same terrified attendant reappeared, this time without his tray of fungus. Te Kahurangi suspected he was one of the few Zartakians fluent in High Gothic. The little man bowed hastily.

'Lords, the cadets of the 10th Regiment of the Zartakian Astra Militarum have been assembled, as per your request. The guildmasters await you on the primary observation point of drill cavern 11.'

'They do not understand, do they?' Akia asked privately over the vox.

'Perhaps it is best that they do not,' Te Kahurangi replied. He switched to his external vocaliser, speaking in Low Gothic.

'Lead on.'

The attendant took the Carcharodons along a series of long, low earthen tunnels, propped up with plasteel beams. He was forced to scurry at an unnatural pace in an effort to match the stride of the towering transhumans. They took a grav-lift deeper into the mine workings, the mechanism rattling as it descended into Zartak's depths. Dorthor spoke to First Squad as the lift slowed to a halt, its mesh doorway juddering open.

'We've lost contact with *White Maw*.'

Te Kahurangi realised the brutally scarred Strike Veteran was right – the sigil representing the strike cruiser's vox uplink was gone. Even the powerful communications of the ancient capital ship could not reach the company's Command Squad now.

They stepped from the grav-lift and out into another tunnel. This one was more sturdily constructed, its flanks plated with hazard-striped flakboard, the lumen strips wired overhead bright and unblinking. At its end the attendant scraped into a low bow and, wordlessly, ushered the Carcharodons through the auto-doors.

Te Kahurangi was the last to duck through. He found himself on an observation deck, a mesh gantry built into the flank of a great, dark cavern whose walls displayed the bit-mark scars of megaborer drilling. A sheet of plexglas separated the gantry from the rest of the artificially carved chamber. Most of the space was occupied by the same terrified guildmasters that had greeted them on the landing plate. Beyond, in the cavern below, were hundreds of ranked figures. They were clad in flakplate and black fatigues, and carried Munitorum-stamped lascarbines, but even a glance told the Chief Librarian that the pallid, thin-faced figures were mere youths. They were the boys who would become men in the ranks of the Astra Militarum. There were not, however, enough of them, their ranks were shoddy, and their uniforms ill-fitting. They reeked of fear.

His attention was only on the badly paraded cadets for a split second. His focus turned almost immediately back to the guilders standing between the Carcharodons and the plexglas. He had seen this before. He had seen it all, in every last, exacting detail.

'These are all of them?' Akia asked. 'All the young?'

For a second, there was only silence. Te Kahurangi knew exactly what came next.

'It's a trap,' he said over the internal vox. 'Kill them.'

He lunged with his force staff, crushing the skull of the nearest guilder. As the fat man crumpled, Akia and the rest of First Squad responded without hesitation. The helpless humans wailed as the Carcharodons slaughtered them.

Te Kahurangi kicked another guilder out of his way and slammed himself into the plexglas separating the gantry from the cavern below. The sheet gave way with a crash, and the Pale Nomad found himself in freefall. Armour streaked red, the rest of the Carcharodons followed him out, beating aside the guilders blocking their path. They were still falling when the mining charges taped to the underside of the gantry detonated.

The shockwave flung Te Kahurangi across the chamber. His servos absorbed the impact, but the landing still kicked up a hail of grit and left the bare rock floor scarred. He found his feet swiftly, auto-senses piercing the haze left by the blast, his gen-hanced body unfazed by the sudden and violent dislocation.

He'd landed less than two dozen paces from the front ranks of the Guard cadets, who themselves had been pitched from their feet by the blast. His void brothers were around him, rising. The markers representing each member of the Command Squad still blinked green and unharmed on the visor display.

The cadets opened fire. The first las-bolt – well-aimed or fortunate – struck Te Kahurangi's helm, cracking off and snapping his head to one side. Another shot scored off his right pauldron, while a third and fourth slashed past to his left and right, their snap-crack reports joining the echo of the mining charge blast still bouncing back from the cavern's scarred ceiling. He snarled. More shots darted wide. Some of the so-called cadets simply scattered.

Toa raised his bolt pistol, steadied against the rim of the Coral Shield.

'Hold, brother,' Te Kahurangi snapped, a sliver of his psychic potency stilling Toa's finger on the trigger. 'Remember why we are here.' Toa grunted unhappily and lowered the weapon as more bolts cracked off the Carcharodons.

'Whatever the damned reason is, we can't stay,' Strike Veteran Dorthor growled. The weight of fire was intensifying as more cadets recovered their weapons and took snap-shots through the dust. Whether it was deliberate treachery, or just a panicked reaction to the blast, Te Kahurangi didn't know. But Dorthor was right.

'The grav-lift,' Akia said, motioning to the mesh doors that stood below the sagging remains of the gantry behind them.

'Whoever has done this may well be able to override the controls,' Te Kahurangi said.

'We'll take it anyway,' Akia responded. 'Unless you wish me to butcher every boy in this chamber on my way to the stairs on the other side.'

Another las-bolt hit Te Kahurangi, earthing against his breastplate and leaving the blue ceramite scarred. There was no more time for dispute. With Akia at his side, he led First Squad towards the waiting lift, punching the doors open. Las-bolts pursued them, snapping at their heels or sizzling overhead.

'Take us to the surface,' Akia ordered as they forced their way into the lift plate. 'We must re-establish contact with *White Maw*. Then we'll discover the extent of this treachery.'

'Company Master, I cannot,' complained Signifier Karra as he tried to enter commands into the lift's rune panel. 'The mechanism isn't responding.'

Before Akia could reply, the lift lurched beneath them. Akia and Te Kahurangi's helm lenses met.

'Mag-locks,' Te Kahurangi voxed. A split second after the thudding sounds of mag-boots engaging, the floor fell away.

Te Kahurangi had been right – whoever had wired the gantry for destruction also possessed the master key for the grav-lifts. The one they stood upon had been sent into plummeting freefall, plunging at an ever-increasing speed towards what could only be total annihilation at the bottom of the shaft.

The Pale Nomad reached out with his mind as they fell, bending the lift's mechanisms to his will. He slammed vices of psychic force around the rotors and grav-shafts, triggering the disabled emergency breaks. Feet locked to the lift's floor, he slammed his force staff down, its rune-carved, psy-reactive bone channelling his powers and making the green shard at its tip glow.

Almost imperceptibly, they began to slow. The tortured shriek of the lift mechanism eased. The plummeting sense of dislocation passed. Te Kahurangi said nothing, his stance firm and braced, the servos in his armour locked and his sharp teeth clenched as he focused every ounce of mental strength into arresting the plunging descent. Blue witchlights snapped and crackled around the carved ceramite of his psychic hood, and burned behind his helm's black lenses.

Finally, the grav-lift clattered to a complete stop. Te Kahurangi managed to utter a single word.

'Out.'

With a series of thuds the Carcharodons unlocked their mag-boots. Akia tore back the mesh door, revealing a red-lit corridor beyond. The entrance was misaligned with the door to the lift, so that the Space Marines had to duck down into the tunnel, scraping their power-armoured bodies through the gap.

Te Kahurangi was the last to go. After a moment more of shuddering concentration he threw himself at the gap, rolling through. The instant his psychic will was gone the lift fell again, like a drop pod plunging through a planet's atmosphere. Its descent was lit by a hail of sparks and heralded by the shriek of burning brakes, until both were lost in the utter darkness of the shaft's depths. Eventually, a distant crash boomed up from the deeps.

'You have our thanks,' said Akia, offering Te Kahurangi his gauntlet. The Librarian took it, struggling to find his breath. Every enhanced muscle in his transhuman body ached, and his temples throbbed with pressure-pain. He could feel blood running from his nose, swiftly clotting.

He took a moment to gather himself, assessing their location. The tunnel they were in was more of a natural fissure, the only evidence of human engineering a narrow metal walkway that ran above the slow-moving lava flow constituting the tunnel's floor. It was largely scabbed over with a dark, cooling crust, but the Carcharodons' auto-senses still read the temperature in the corridor of blackened rock as infernally hot.

'We have no schematic traces,' Akia said. 'No idea where we are. And no connection to *White Maw*.'

'If we do not make contact soon, Strike Leader Oruka will enact protocol and begin an assault on our last known location,' Te Kahurangi said.

'Which is an expenditure of resources I would rather avoid,' Akia replied. 'Our objective is to re-establish contact and end this foolishness with all expediency.'

Te Kahurangi knew that 'expediency' likely involved Akia's two-handed chainaxe, Reaper, and the leaders of the treacherous Zartakians. He gestured up the bending tunnel.

'At least our course is clear enough. There is no other way.'

'That much is true,' Akia said. 'Brother Dorthor, take point.'

The Space Marines advanced along the walkway, feet clanging sonorously against the metal. Unprotected humans would not have been able to survive the tunnel's infernal heat, but the scavenged, mismatching power armour worn by the Carcharodons was capable of withstanding far more inimical conditions. Provided the walkway held, Zartak's depths were no danger to them.

'How did you sense what would happen in the cavern?' Akia asked Te Kahurangi. 'Was it a vision?'

'It was,' the Chief Librarian admitted.

'But you didn't deign to warn us beforehand? You knew we were walking into a trap, yet you said nothing?'

'The future is not a straight path, Company Master,' Te Kahurangi responded. 'It is a murky, bottomless depth. I could not be certain that by speaking of my vision, I would not guarantee that it came to pass.'

'Yet it did, all the same.'

'This time, yes. How a vision will play out is never certain.'

'Contact,' Dorthor interrupted. Te Kahurangi looked past the Strike Veteran to see that they'd turned a corner. Ahead was a heavy-looking door, and a man in a bulky grey thermoweave suit. As he caught sight of the Space Marines he went for the door's wheel lock, trying to slam it shut.

'Terminate,' Akia ordered. A second later the boom of

Dothor's bolter thundered through the tunnel. The man's head burst apart and he slumped against the half-open door.

The Carcharodons moved up to the end of the tunnel and passed through, bolters raised. Te Kahurangi let the tendrils of his consciousness reach out, seeking what lay ahead. He found thoughts, lonely and desperate, edged with fear.

They were in a holding block. The bare rock walls had been bolted with prison cages, the mesh wires electrified. Figures huddled on rocky ledges within, clad like their captors in heavy thermoweave. There were dozens of cages ranking down the long, dark chamber. Their occupants stared at the Space Marines as they entered.

There were guards too. They went for their heat-wrapped autoguns. One tripped an alarm, its wail filling the subterranean space. The Carcharodons put them down quickly, a rapid staccato of bolter shells bursting the gaolers apart, their remains steaming in the hot air.

'There is a stairwell at the far end of the chamber,' Dothor voxed as his auto-senses probed the half-dark.

'Make for it,' Akia ordered.

'Wait,' shouted a voice over the wail of the alarms. One of the prisoners had risen, a stooped, elderly figure. Wordlessly, the Carcharodons turned towards her.

'We're not common criminals,' she said, words muffled by her thermoweave suit. 'We're loyal to the God-Emperor and the true Guild Houses. We can help you.'

'What does she want?' Akia demanded of Te Kahurangi over the vox, anger colouring his voice. 'She wishes to be freed?'

'These prisoners are not just criminals,' Te Kahurangi said. 'I have touched upon their thoughts. They are victims of the rebellion here. Loyalists.'

'Then they will be released once we have purged the traitors responsible for this,' Akia responded.

'They likely possess local knowledge. Our chances of reaching the rebellion's leaders would be improved with their guidance.'

'They will slow us down. We do not have time to shepherd them all.'

'Not all,' Te Kahurangi said. He slammed his staff into the rune lock of the elderly prisoner's cell. The electricity shorted and died, and he tore the door mesh aside with one fist. The woman and the cell's other occupant, a boy, cowered back, eyes wide behind the grimy vision strips of their thermos.

'Who do you serve?' Te Kahurangi demanded in Low Gothic. The woman responded first.

'Groundworks Corporation Guild, and the God-Emperor.'

'What are your names?'

'I am Eustice Maudlin, former guildmistress,' the woman said, putting a hand on the boy's shoulder. 'And this is my grandson, Caderik.' The boy stared up at Te Kahurangi.

'Do you know the route to the surface from here?'

'I do,' the boy, Caderik, said before Maudlin could reply.

'What about the location of the ringleaders of this rebellion?'

'The sub-guild quota hall,' Caderik said. 'That is where all their announcements are routed from.'

'Show us,' Te Kahurangi replied, taking the boy by the scruff of his suit and dragging him from the cell.

'Not without grandma,' the boy shrieked, reaching back. After a moment, Te Kahurangi relented.

'We will not slow for you,' he told Maudlin as the matriarch stepped out on uncertain legs.

'You're going to kill those treacherous bastards?' she demanded.

'We are.'

'Then I'll be right beside you,' she said. Te Kahurangi fancied she was smiling behind her suit's respirator. He ushered them out.

'Caderik,' Maudlin said. 'Lead on,'

'What about all the others?' the boy asked. The dozens of prisoners held in the adjacent cells had begun to shout and clamour, getting as close to their electrified bonds as they dared.

'They're loyal, like us,' Maudlin said to Te Kahurangi. 'Anyone who didn't agree with Thornvyl and his plot was thrown in here.'

'There's no time–' Te Kahurangi began. Before he could go on there was a series of cracking sounds, and the alarm suddenly shut off.

The silence lasted only a second. With a crash of collapsing bedrock, part of the chamber wall caved in. Lava burst through the fissure, a blazing, molten jet that hit the bare floor and quickly began to spread.

'The escape failsafe,' Maudlin said. 'Someone's triggered it.'

'We go, now,' Akia said over the squad vox. There was no more time for persuasion. Te Kahurangi threw the protesting guilder woman over one arm and snatched the boy in the other. The rest of the Command Squad were already making for the stairwell. The other prisoners began to wail and scream as they realised they were being abandoned. The Carcharodons paid them no heed.

The lava was spreading rapidly, more of the rock walls either side collapsing to admit a blazing rush of heat and magma. The screaming of the prisoners reached new heights as the lava reached them, and even the resistant thermosuits began to burst into flames.

Te Kahurangi saw none of it. He reached the stairs, and began to climb.

* * *

The sub-guild quota hall was once again in an uproar. Thorn-vyl drew his gilt-edged laspistol and raised it in the air. The ornate weapon wasn't loaded, but the sight of it was finally enough to bring silence.

'Your petty arguing is achieving nothing,' he snarled at his fellow guilders. 'We need to work together, now more than ever.'

'Where has working with you got us?' Xeron of Carbon-wing Ventures snapped. 'You assured us you had this entire situation under control!' The other guilders shouted their agreement, until Thornvyl waved his sidearm again.

'It is under control,' he snapped, gesturing at the views-creen banks. The split images showed vid feeds from across sink shaft I. The assembled guilders had watched as the Space Marines had evaded the explosives set for them in drill cav-ern II and, through some sort of damned witchcraft, escaped the trap of the plummeting grav-lift. Now they had not only survived Thornvyl's initiation of Order 19 – the directive to execute the loyalist prisoners seized when the rebel guilders had taken control – they had even absconded with two, the old matriarch of Groundworks Corp and her grandson.

'The Sub-Western mineworks,' Ghorst said. 'My assets. The tunnel workings there are incomplete. We'll lose track of them.'

'But they have to reappear somewhere within the main works of the sink shaft if they want to reach the surface,' Thornvyl said.

'Or if they want to reach us,' Krane added darkly.

'We should evacuate,' said Maron shrilly.

'No,' Thornvyl replied. 'If we flee we guarantee that they'll make for the surface, and once they have re-established con-tact with their ship more will come. If they can be convinced to come to us directly, we'll have them. And once they're dead we can seal the mines. The rest in orbit will have to pay in blood for every tunnel and rathole they take. It would take them years.'

'Have you seen what we're dealing with?' Maron demanded. 'Have you seen *what* they are?'

'Did you see what they did to my man?' Tork added, still in shock after having witnessed one of the ashen giants smash the skull of his body double on the drill cavern's viewing gantry.

'Enough,' Elinara said, rising. 'You've led us from bad to worse these last six years, Thornvyl. We've trusted you for too long. I am going to secure my own assets, personally.'

The mistress of the Freehold Prospector Guild drew her ceremonial shawl about her shoulders and made for the quota hall's doors. The click and hum of a charged power pack stopped her.

'Nobody is leaving this room,' Thornvyl said, raising his now-loaded laspistol. 'Not until this situation is resolved.'

'You can't stop all of us,' Elinara said defiantly.

'No,' Thornvyl said, smiling coldly. 'But the drill walkers outside can.'

'You've requisitioned my walkers?' Maron demanded.

'Only as a precaution. A last line of defence, should our unwelcome guests make it this far.'

'You wouldn't dare turn them against us,' Ghorst said. Thornvyl's smile didn't waver.

'I'm surprised you haven't realised how far men will go for wealth and position. After all, that's why we're here, is it not? Now sit down, all of you, and relax. Everything will be fine.'

Caderik led the Carcharodons into the darkness. Te Kahurangi worked a sliver of calm into the boy's mind, taking the edge off the terror he felt in the presence of the gigantic warriors. He spoke to the Pale Nomad, his words halting as he took them up narrow stair shafts and along increasingly low, tight work tunnels and loco-rail haulage lines.

Caderik and his family had been imprisoned for almost six years. That was when a faction of the guildmasters that ruled Zartak's disparate mining companies had first launched their coup. Apparently driven by the belief that the Imperium's adamantium tithes were extortionate, a ringleader named Thornvyl had ordered the destruction of an Administratum tribute ship, the *Praetorian*, in high orbit above Zartak. The rebel guilders had used their influence to gain complete control over the colony. The Imperium hadn't responded, until now.

Te Kahurangi let the boy talk. The Librarian needed him – his grandmother less so. The Space Marine didn't waste any of his psychic power in easing her own fear or mistrust. She wheezed along behind Te Kahurangi, seemingly forgotten.

Caderik spoke of how his parents had died in the holding block, years earlier. The boy claimed he barely remembered it, but when he described their passing Te Kahurangi sensed his anger spike. The Librarian stoked the emotion, using it to give fresh vigour to the flagging boy. They were rising steadily, the dimly lit mineworks they passed through seemingly abandoned.

Until the blast charges in the tunnel they were passing through detonated, pulverising Caderik and Maudlin and pounding the Carcharodons with tonnes of earth.

Te Kahurangi had a split second to respond to the sudden vision. He snatched Caderik and Maudlin and turned to his left, shielding them both. In the same moment the charges, concealed in a rathole on the far side of the right-hand tunnel wall, detonated. A concussive wave of dirt and rock slammed into the seven Carcharodons, hammering them into the opposite wall, smashing plate and spraining muscle. Only Te Kahurangi, his servos locked, withstood the blast.

He didn't have time to check whether Caderik and Maudlin had survived. He didn't have time to do anything but rise. From the wall of smoke and debris, men in respirators and bagged grey work overalls charged them.

The first of them shot Te Kahurangi at point-blank range. The las-bolt, set to its highest megathule range, seared deep into the Chief Librarian's breastplate, nicking at his black carapace. The second and third speared the cracked rock ceiling above, for the Librarian's force staff shot out to intercept his attacker, cracking the weapon from his hands. Before the man could respond an uppercut from the staff snapped his head back, tearing his respirator seal. He crumpled.

Around him his fellow ambushers waded in. Clad in their masks and mining overalls, they came at the Space Marines with manic desperation, eyes wide behind the filmy lenses of their respirators, wielding lascutters, lasguns and simple half-picks.

Any normal enemy would have been left maimed and dying by the blasting charges. But the Space Marines, though battered, were not even remotely stunned. The veterans of First Squad responded with immediate, brute force. The shrill war cries of the miners were drowned by a bestial, throbbing howl as half a dozen chainaxes roared to life, their volume a deafening counterpoint to the chill silence observed by the Carcharodons. Without a word Dorthor and Karra, Tama, Raggen and Toa set about their assailants with hard butcher's strokes.

Most brutal of all was Akia himself. The initial blast had

split his helm, shattering one black lens and cracking the faceplate. Even as Te Kahurangi fought he could sense the Company Master's monstrous fury, the rage he was battling to keep in check. The Blindness was beckoning to him, that precipice poised above a black sea of hatred and needless slaughter-sacrifice.

Blood was in the air, and Akia had its scent.

The Company Master's great chainaxe, Reaper, roared through flesh and bone. Akia wielded it with short, furious strokes, confined by the narrowness of the tunnel. The constraints only seemed to drive him to greater butchery – his pale armour was soon dripping and red. Nothing faced him and lived.

Te Kahurangi marshalled his own strength, the thrust and lunge of his force staff breaking bones and shattering skulls. One attacker managed to strike him with the beam of his lascutter while the Librarian smashed down his comrade, the powerful tool searing through his right vambrace. Warning markers blinked across his visor as pain registered from the burn wound, swiftly suppressed. He lashed out with an invisible wave of psychic force, focusing the crushing weight of an entire ocean upon a single point of the man's forehead. The attacker's skull burst beneath the pressure and he crumpled.

It was over as abruptly as it had begun. Suddenly the damaged tunnel was empty. One by one the Carcharodons deactivated their chainaxes, thick strings of gore pattering slowly from their armour, their breathing raspy over the vox system.

Te Kahurangi flexed his fingers on the grip of his staff, feeling his secondary heart decelerating. Caderik and Maudlin still lived. His foresight and reflexes had saved them. Their thermoweave suits were ragged and torn, but a quick scan revealed that they were unharmed. Besides the shock. It grew worse when Akia removed his cracked helmet.

'Next time, warn us,' the Company Master said to Te Kahurangi.

'If time permits,' the Chief Librarian allowed. He could see Caderik and Maudlin staring at Akia's exposed head. The Carcharodon's pale, grey features had been revealed, the exile tattoos that swirled about his throat and jaw giving way to eyes as black and bottomless as the lenses of his helm. His words revealed razor-sharp teeth in a hard, square jaw, their whiteness matching the shock of hair that ran in a strip from the Reaper Prime's brow to the back of his head. Such a nightmare visage was the last thing most humans expected to see when they gazed upon the face of one of Rangu's killer angels. Te Kahurangi suspected Akia hadn't even realised the affect he was having on the two mortals. The Librarian pressed his mind into theirs, mentally quelling the terror and shock that had paralysed them.

'Damage assessment,' Akia demanded. Te Kahurangi checked his visor display. His backpack had taken a beating from the mining blast, and he had las wounds on his chest, right forearm and left thigh. Beyond that, however, he was unharmed. The rest of the squad were similarly battered but unbowed.

'We carry on,' Akia said. 'Before they can marshal their strength. Darkness there and nothing more.'

The miners were not done with them. As Caderik took them back into sink shaft 1's primary tunnels there were more ambushes. The journey through the works became a blur of blood and combat stimms. Overall-clad miners and turncoat Guard, local defence and guild militia came at them in waves of desperate fear, blades and pick tools glinting in the flickering tunnel lights, their screaming hoarse.

Only Te Kahurangi's presence averted disaster. The psyker's premonitions twice warded them away from cave-in traps.

On other occasions the Carcharodons would use the opportunity to take different routes at the last minute, cutting all but their most vital servos and auto-senses. They melded with the shadows, black-eyed, statuesque revenants looming silently in the darkness of access-ways and ore chutes while their erstwhile hunters passed by.

Two levels below their objective, they encountered the first free Zartakians that weren't trying to kill them. Caderik's shrill warning stopped Toa, in the vanguard, a second before the void sword cut down one of the men who'd started from the shadows of a sub loco-rail haulage line.

'We know him,' Maudlin said as the man cringed back. He was wearing the respirator, ochre smelt-suit and rudimentary black flakplate of a guilder mine-militiaman.

'Master Caderik?' he said and then, when he caught sight of Maudlin, offered a hasty bow. 'Guildmistress! It does me well to see you after all these years.'

'Guildmarshal Calent,' Maudlin said. 'I didn't think you still lived.'

'By the Emperor's grace,' the militiaman said. Te Kahurangi sensed more men further back down the haulage line. 'We've been waiting for this day for six years. As soon as news reached us of fighting in the Sub-Western works we took up arms again. For Groundworks Corp.'

'We do not have time to waste,' Akia said. Calent cringed visibly as the huge, bloody warrior spoke.

'These men will be of use to us,' Maudlin said. 'They are armed and loyal.'

'We are sufficient,' Akia replied.

'We can follow in your wake,' Calent said. 'We won't slow you.'

'I hope for your sake that you do not,' Akia said.

They went higher, the loyalist militia falling in behind the Adeptus Astartes. The tunnels seemed empty again, as though the rebels had withdrawn, even as the Space Marines pressed towards their command centre. The reason became apparent as they secured the loading bay ambulatory outside the quota hall described by Caderik.

Only a dozen rebels stood between them and the hall's barred doors. These ones, however, were well equipped. Each one was piloting a mining drill walker, a heavy gauge engine that stood on two stubby, thick-set legs. Their torsos were covered with heavy sheets of plasteel plating, reinforced with adamantium rods, designed to withstand cave-ins while the machines continued to work. A shielded cluster of optic nodes and stab-lumens constituted their heads, set into their thick shoulder supports, while multiple mechanical limbs ended in diamond-hard drill borers and rocksaws.

The mechanised miners didn't approach with military coordination, but each one at their own wary pace, mechanisms wheezing and clanking, like pugilists sizing up a fight. Akia triggered Reaper, its hungry roar followed by the chainaxes of his void brothers. This time, however, there was an answer. The heavy drill heads and rocksaw rotors filled the air with spinning metal.

'Get back,' Te Kahurangi said to the human loyalists.

'There's another way into the hall,' Caderik shouted above the din. 'The ratholes above lead straight into the maintenance vent shafts.'

'They will be too small,' Te Kahurangi replied.

'Not for us.'

'Then go,' the Chief Librarian said. There was no more time for words. The walkers were lumbering into close combat. Shots from First Squad's bolters cracked harmlessly from their reinforced frontal armour. Te Kahurangi began to draw and bind together strands of psychic energy, muttering focus litanies as he channelled power into his force staff. His Lyman's ear blocked out the first sounds of chainblades striking steel as he crafted annihilation. His genhanced muscles clenched, and his keen senses were suddenly full of a greasy, pervasive stench. The throbbing in his temple built. His vision flickered. With a final, short word, he unleashed the beast.

The floor beneath two of the advancing walkers buckled. Stone deformed and shattered, pulled apart and reshaped by his will. The bedrock of Zartak churned upwards, forming great jaws of jagged stone that slammed shut around the twin walkers with a splitting crash.

Few engines besides the walkers could have withstood such an impact. Their thick armour meant nothing, however, when the earth beneath them had disappeared. The great jaw of debris fell away into the sink hole its rise had created, dragging the two machines down. Te Kahurangi released his psychic grip, skull throbbing.

Around him, his void brothers were not faring as well. The chainaxes made little impression on the thick plate of the drill walkers, scarring and chewing but failing to penetrate. And, though lumbering, the things were powerful. One snagged Karra's arm in a vice-claw before swinging down its rocksaw. Sparks flew as the vicious blade sheared first through ceramite and plasteel and then pale, tattooed flesh. Even as his arm was lopped off, the Carcharodon Signifier made no sound, swinging his chainblade down to amputate the machine's own saw-limb. Blood and fyceline splattered together onto the floor as the two combatants remained locked.

Toa did better. He plunged the void sword straight through

the torso of one of the walkers, the obsidian-like relic blade parting the machine's armour with ease. Its drill chewed against the Champion's Coral Shield but found no purchase, not even scarring the rugged surface. As Toa slide his blade free the walker slumped, its green optic clusters fading.

Another walker was coming at Te Kahurangi, negotiating the rubble unearthed by the Librarian. He clutched at the strands of power dissipating from his rending maw and swung his staff in an arc, binding the eddying psychic energies into a bow wave. Even as the walker reached for him, its drills screeching, he sent the invisible fury of the warp crashing into its torso. The frontal plate buckled as though hit by some great fist, and its forward movement juddered to a halt, the pilot within crushed.

Beside the Librarian, Dorthor went down wordlessly, a rocksaw scything deep into his thigh plate. Only the narrowness of the ambulatory corridor, stopping the walkers from surrounding them, was keeping the Carcharodons alive. Te Kahurangi moved to help Dorthor, force staff raised, but another of the lumbering mine engines slammed into him with a crack of unyielding plasteel, its sheer bulk forcing him to the ground. Before he could rise, the walker placed one splayed metal hoof on his breastplate, pinning him in place. His auto-senses chimed a warning as the pressure threatened to burst organs and crush his fused ribcage.

That was when Akia struck. The Company Master was lost to his death-frenzy, the Blindness exerting almost total mastery. Reaper howled like a primordial beast as it took the walker at full swing, striking its cranial block like a hammer meeting an anvil. Optics shattered. Metal buckled. Reaper tore on, powered as much by Akia's terrifying genhanced strength as its own revving motor. Armour plating sheared off, hundreds of shards of razor metal spinning away in all directions as the chainaxe's wicked teeth bit and bit.

Eventually, they locked. Finally, the blow lost momentum. Then Akia ripped the weapon free and struck again.

The walker went back, its grip on Te Kahurangi lost, bending before the Carcharodon's fury. Finally, its armour split. Finally, Reaper tasted flesh. The machine crumpled, blood pouring from its shattered metalwork. Akia's voice grated out a single order over the vox.

'Kill.'

Te Kahurangi found his feet. Just in time to meet the next machine.

The sounds of battle from beyond the quota-hall doors were making the guilders moan with fear. Thornvyl glared at them, unable to hide his own tension any more, hand on the butt of his laspistol.

A grating noise disturbed the sounds of bloodshed from outside. The guilders around Thornvyl jumped, searching for the source of the noise. Only when a vent covering clanged against the floor did any of them look up.

A figure followed the covering into the room. It rolled as Thornvyl raised his laspistol and fired, the shot punching into the floor beside it. Before he could correct his aim another assailant had followed the first, and then another. The hall's buzzing lumen strips gleamed from the autogun barrels levelled at Thornvyl.

'Drop it,' ordered the mine-militiaman with the rifle. The ornate laspistol clattered to the floor.

'Keep up your aim,' the last figure to come down through the vent ordered. He was little more than a boy, but he was a boy Thornvyl recognised.

'I remember the day you came for my family,' Caderik said. Thornvyl said nothing. Caderik turned to the militia, and Guildmarshal Calent.

'Unbar those doors and bring them in.'

In the hall ambulatory, the drill walkers were winning. Although less than half still functioned, they had driven the Carcharodons back against the stone walls, leaving them savaged and bloody. The crack of Thornvyl's laspistol, seized by Caderik, made them pause, rotor weapons still spinning.

'It's over!' the boy shouted as the mine-militia hauled the captured guilders out at gunpoint. 'Stop resisting.'

The walkers turned awkwardly, optic clusters scanning the new arrivals. A guild soldier was keeping Thornvyl, head bowed in defeat, on his knees before Caderik. The boy waved his pistol.

'You may kill these god-warriors,' he said. 'But more will come. They will slaughter you. If you stop now, I promise to have you spared. All of you. Our colony has seen enough bloodshed.'

Still the walkers remained immobile. More loyalist guild soldiers appeared at the far end of the ambulatory, led by Maudlin, her face grim.

'This is your last chance,' Caderik said.

One by one, the walkers deactivated their drilling tools. One by one, the torso plating juddered open on damaged servos, and the sweat-streaked, half-naked pilots within clambered out, hair tousled, eyes blinking, expressions caught between exhaustion, fear and defiance.

The Carcharodons had stopped fighting the moment the walkers had ceased their own attacks. As soon as the last pilot left his machine, they formed a tight phalanx that strode towards Caderik and the guildmaster prisoners. They were a terrible sight – their armour had been beaten and rent by lasrifles and autoguns, bayonets, mining tools and blast charges, and then the brutal implements of the drill walkers. They were all wounded, several grievously – one had lost an arm, another had the white gleam of bone showing amidst the torn ruin of his thigh. All were covered almost head to foot in blood, their own and their enemy's. And yet, since making planetfall, not one had fallen. Few had even uttered a sound.

'This is the leader of the rebellion?' the one with the horrific, bared head demanded, looming over Caderik and Thornvyl. The boy nodded, suddenly lost for words. Without hesitation or ceremony, the giant snatched Thornvyl and snapped his neck.

'No,' Maudlin cried out. 'You can't! We need due process. We need to display them publicly to the rest of the colony.'

'You can still display them,' the giant said, stepping over Thornvyl's twitching corpse.

'I-I said they could live,' Caderik stammered, cringing back from the Space Marine.

'I came to this world to reap, not to judge,' the Carcharodon said. 'And that is what I will do.'

The gore-streaked monster hefted his chainaxe. The executions did not take long.

The rebellion was over. The population of sink shaft 1 gathered on the walkways and gantries that lined the inside of their great burrow hole. Maudlin, flanked by Caderik, Calent and the guild guard, spoke to them from the minehead, the address spur jutting from the sink shaft's pinnacle.

'We have done the God-Emperor's will here today,' she said,

her stern voice reverberating through the shaft via vox hailers, gargoyle-headed claxon maws and shift change announcers. 'After six long years of treachery and misrule, the corrupt men and women who betrayed our colony have finally tasted justice.'

The crowd's gaze turned to the horrific, dripping remains hanging from one of the heavy haulage cranes that jutted like industrial teeth from the sink shaft's upper sides.

'And what justice it is,' Maudlin went on, voice hoarse. 'Administered by our glorious Emperor's holy angels.'

The crowd gasped as Akia, Te Kahurangi and the rest of First Squad emerged onto the spur behind Maudlin. They looked more like monsters than angels, the few parts of their armour that weren't coated with drying viscera gleaming a scarred, pitted silver. Maudlin gestured once again to the silent giants towering behind her.

'These are our protectors! Salvation sent to purge away our sins! We owe them our thanks, and our devotion. As part of our great debt, they will take the tithe that is now so long overdue.'

None of the Carcharodons moved, though a clicking sound betrayed their internal communications. Moments later, a rising shriek filled the sink shaft. Leaden shapes plummeted from the skies, heavy grey gunships that lowered into landing plates ringing the jungle surface around the great burrow. From the darkness of their open holds came more giant warriors, their ashen armour unblemished by battle. They began to move down into the mine habitat, corralling and manhandling the colonists along the walkways. Maudlin turned to Akia.

'What is happening?' she demanded over the rising noise filling the sink shaft. 'You have come for our missing tithe? We are ready to pay it in full, and much more besides.'

'We know nothing of this,' Te Kahurangi said. 'Your debts do not concern us. We have come to take a tithe of our own. The Red Tithe.'

'I don't understand,' Maudlin said. 'Guildmarshal–'

Guildmarshal Calent went for his pistol. He never laid a hand on it. A black blade cut his head from his shoulders.

As the sink shaft descended into screaming chaos, Te Kahurangi watched Caderik. The boy alone didn't react as those around him were snatched and subdued by the silent giants. He didn't react as his shrieking grandmother was picked up, as easily as a parent might lift a child, and taken towards the waiting fliers. He didn't react as the skies filled with the fat-bellied shuttle sows that would take the population of Zartak to the *White Maw*'s slave bays. He watched it all with dull, dead eyes. Te Kahurangi touched upon his mind, and knew that the boy had already begun his first steps towards Initiation. If he survived he would bear an honour-name, a rarity among the Carcharodon Astra.

The Chief Librarian unclamped his helm and mag-locked it to his belt. Then he knelt before the boy so that their eyes met, Caderik's light blue gaze a contrast to the bottomless void-black of the ancient Adeptus Astartes. The Librarian smiled, the razor-toothed expression without warmth or comfort. Caderik would need neither from now on.

'Bail Sharr,' the Carcharodon said, uttering the name-honorific for the first time. 'Welcome to the Outer Dark.'

+ Sub-file 6675-112 +

+ Jurisdiction: Ethika Subsector +

+ Timestamp: 21151676.M41+

+ Subject header: Imperial Navy Mars-Class Cruiser *Andromidax* In-System Report #3+

+ Clerk Attendant: 3772-Wilhelm +

Naval Report Summary: Zartak mining colony [ref. 228-16b] has been entirely depopulated. There are no traces of life remaining whatsoever. Ordo representatives have been contacted. Pending Inquisitorial quarantine, Subsector Auto-Clerk 21811-Veissmann has recommended redesignation of Zartak as a penal colony. Calculations show this will ensure minimum disruption of the planet's adamantium tithe quota. The suggestion has been filed for consideration.

+ Thought of the Day: Oblivion awaits us all +

THE GREATER EVIL

PETER FEHERVARI

'Evil grows from within, not without. It is a dis-harmony of the self, not the shadow of some elusive, predatory other.'

– The Yasu'caor

– THE FIRST CIRCLE –
OUTSIDE

No matter how often Voyle relives it, the end always begins the same way. A deep clang reverberates through the airlock as the Sable Star's *boarding umbilical latches on to the derelict ship. Voyle checks the air tank strapped to the back of the trooper beside him, then turns so his comrade can return the gesture. The routine is mirrored by every member of the squad with practised swiftness. They have run through it twice already, yet nobody hesitates. Nobody complains. A Void Breacher's life hangs by the integrity of his tank as much as his weapons.*

'Squad Indigo is bloodtight,' Voyle reports into his helmet vox when the ritual is complete. 'Repeat, bloodtight.'

'Bloodtight confirmed, Indigo,' Lieutenant Joliffe acknowledges from the bridge, unable to hide the tension in his voice. Captain Bester took his own life fourteen days ago. Nobody knows

why, but they all sense Joliffe isn't ready to lead the company – not on this warp-cursed patrol. Voyle has considered seizing command. No one would stand in his way, least of all Joliffe, but then the burden of choice would be his to carry. No, it is better to live or die with clean hands.

'Commence breach,' *Joliffe orders.* 'Emperor walk with you, Indigo.'

With a hydraulic hiss the external hatch slides into its recess, revealing the metal tube of the umbilical. Most of the strip lumens running its length have failed and those that still work flicker fitfully. The company's five-month tour of the Damocles perimeter has taken a heavy toll on both supplies and men, including both its engineseers. The Sable Star *was just three days out from Kliest when it found the intruder, silent and powerless, yet perfectly intact. Its markings designate it as the* Halvorsen, *but though the massive derelict is evidently Imperial in origin, they can find no record of it. That is not unusual, for numberless ships ply the vast tracts of the Imperium and countless more have been lost over the millennia. Factoring in the contortions of the warp, the derelict might be decades or even centuries old. It is a cumbersome hulk devoid of guns or advanced sensor arrays – probably a civilian cargo freighter and certainly no match for a warship like the* Sable Star, *but that is little reassurance for the men tasked with boarding it. With derelicts it is what lies within that matters, for the void crawls with phantoms seeking the solace of metal or flesh.*

Let it rot, *Voyle wants to say.* Better yet, blast it back into the warp!

But instead he says what he always says: 'Acknowledged, crossing commences.' *And enters the umbilical. He is a Void Breacher. This is what the Astra Militarum has trained him for.*

They lied to us! *Voyle yells at his former self, but it is a silent cry, for if the ghosts of the past are without eyes, so those of the future are without voice.*

The Void Breachers' magnetised boots clatter on the corrugated decking as they advance along the narrow tunnel one by one, their helmet lights slicing back and forth. The concertinaed tube creaks and shudders around them as it strains to keep the ships conjoined, the living to the dead. Despite their sealed carapace armour and therma-padding, the cold is gnawing at them within seconds and their movements grow sluggish before they are half-way across. The rasping exhalations from their helmets are like steam in the frigid air, forcing them to wipe their visors clean after each respiration, lest breath becomes blinding frost.

Voyle halts as his light finds the derelict's access hatch. The metal is dark and pitted, contrasting starkly with the gleaming umbilical clamps that encircle it. One glance tells him the locking mechanism is hopelessly corroded.

'Cut us a door, Hoenig,' he orders, moving aside as the squad's specialist steps forward. He watches as the trooper engraves a glowing oval around the hatch with a las-cutter. The tool's power pack whines and Voyle wills it to fail, knowing it won't. It never does. The nightmare won't allow it.

'Done, breach sergeant,' Hoenig says, then shoves the hatch. With a screech of harrowed metal it crashes into the darkness beyond. As the reverberations subside, Voyle levels his meltagun and steps through.

His own shriek wrenched him back from the brink.

But I've already fallen, Voyle thought wildly as he surged to his feet. *There's no coming back…*

The nightmare fractured and fell away in sluggish fragments, revealing a large windowless chamber. Its walls were tessellated with hexagonal panels that glowed softly, washing the space in subdued blue light. Voyle stood at its centre, his bare feet tangled in a silvery blanket. He tore himself free and spun around, trying to make sense of things.

Where–

He froze as he caught sight of something watching him from one of the walls.

Black eyes gleaming with a hunger colder than the void…

The sound that rose in his throat was somewhere between a scream, a snarl and a sigh, born of fear and loathing and… *longing?* Voyle stifled it as the predator dissolved into a human form. A woman. She was crouched in a recess in the opposite wall where a hexagonal panel had retracted, her eyes glinting in the gloom as she appraised him. Her face was tattooed with concentric rings, the first shearing through her forehead, cheeks and chin, the second encircling her eyes and mouth and the third set directly between her eyes. Voyle knew she bore a fourth and final ring, but its lines were invisible, for it embraced the mind.

'Unity,' Voyle breathed, naming the symbol… and remembering. The woman's tattoos mirrored those on his own face. With that recollection the rest flooded back and he scanned the chamber quickly, but the other serenity cells were still sealed. Only the woman, who always slept with hers open, had been roused by his nightmare and she wouldn't say anything to the others.

'Forgive me, sister,' Voyle said. 'I was walking old roads.'

Her expression gave nothing away. Sometimes she seemed as inscrutable as their liberators. Though they had been comrades since Voyle's emancipation from the Imperium almost five ago, they had exchanged few words. Other than her name – Erzul – he knew little about her save her loyalty to the cause and her talents as a pathfinder. But that was fine by Voyle. He wasn't much inclined to talk about his own past either. Remembering was bad enough. Dreaming even worse…

Why now? he wondered, reluctantly considering the old nightmare. It hadn't troubled him in years – not since he'd mastered the mantras of self-sublimation during his induction. He'd almost convinced himself it was a false memory, as his instructors had encouraged.

Almost.

Voyle rubbed the old scar under his chin. It was itching furiously, as if inflamed by the sting of the past. He wasn't going to sleep again this cycle. Maybe the sour-sweet tranquillity wafers the liberators issued their auxiliaries were losing their potency.

I should report it, Voyle brooded, knowing he wouldn't. He trusted the liberators of course, but his weakness shamed him. Void dammit, he should have taken a cell. At least that way he'd have kept his nightmares to himself. He was a big man, broad-shouldered and a head taller than anyone else in his squad, let alone the liberators, but that wasn't why he shunned the serenity cells. If his commander had demanded it, he would have squeezed into one of the hexagonal coffins, but the Stormlight had not pressed the issue. That wasn't his way.

'It is your shadow to burn,' the xenos had said, identifying his subordinate's dread with an acuity that would have confounded the Imperial officers Voyle had served under. 'You alone can light the fire.'

But the ship was already five days into its voyage and that fire remained unlit. Every sleep cycle Voyle had bedded down at the centre of the chamber, ignoring the questioning looks of his squad as they clambered into their cells.

It doesn't matter, he thought as he pulled his boots on. His loathing of tight spaces was only a whisper of the shadow that stalked him.

'I'll be in the Fire Grounds,' he told Erzul as he stepped towards a wall. It split open at his approach, revealing a brightly lit corridor. Nothing could hide in that crisp, sane light.

Void black eyes.

Why now? Voyle asked again. A new life and purpose hadn't dispelled the shadow. It had simply lain dormant. Waiting for him to wake up.

The Seeker faced the maelstrom of swirling, prismatic mist with his back straight and his staff extended horizontally before him at eye level. Its lifeless metal was untarnished by the farrago of colours assaulting him so he kept his gaze locked upon it, using its truth to filter out the lies. He had diffused his breathing to a low susurration, each exhalation extending across several minutes, yet encompassing no more than eleven heartbeats. His master had attained seven beats in the ritual of the *arhat'karra*, but Aun'el Kyuhai knew he would never match such serenity. Nor would he ever ascend beyond his current station in the Ethereal caste's hierarchy. That knowledge brought neither resentment nor sadness, for he had cast aside all desire save service to the Tau'va. All else was as illusory as the storm that raged around him.

And behind illusions prowled beasts...

They came for him together, springing from the mist in perfect synchronicity, one from behind, the other from his left, which they had identified as his weaker side. Traditionally their kind attacked in a cacophony of squawks and hoots, yet this pair came in silence, denying their prey any warning.

They are learning, Kyuhai approved. He spun to his left, thrusting his staff towards the dark shape flanking him, but it sprang away into the fog like a gangling acrobat. He felt a rush of air at his back as the other assailant's blade hacked through the space he had occupied a moment earlier. The ferocity of the swing committed the attacker for a second too long, chaining it to the impotent arc as Kyuhai whirled his staff over his shoulder. It was a blind strike, but the displaced air had told him all he needed to know. When he entered the *arhat'karra,* every moment stretched into many and every whisper shouted.

'*Ka'vash!*' he pronounced as his staff brushed his opponent's throat. Had the weapon's blades been extended it would have been a killing blow. Before his foe could offer the ritual response, the second beast lunged from the fog, its cranial quills erect with rage. Beady, deep-set eyes glared at him from either side of a prognathous, serrated beak. The creature was naked save for a leather tabard and its sinewy form was riddled with tribal tattoos and piercings. This time it didn't attack in silence.

Rukh expects defeat, Kyuhai recognised as he swept his staff around to meet the avian warrior's scimitar. *When Zeljukh falls, Rukh always falls with her.*

The creature struck in a whirlwind frenzy that would have overwhelmed a lesser foe, yet none of its blows passed the gliding, almost languid parries of Kyuhai's staff. To the Seeker the onslaught was akin to an infant's tantrum, but he allowed it to run its course. Perhaps it would be instructive.

Once again anger blinds Rukh, Kyuhai gauged as he blocked. He was disappointed, but unsurprised, for they had played out this scene many times before.

It was Zeljukh who ended the hopeless duel, bringing her

bonded mate to heel with a derisory tirade of hoots and clicks. With a squawk of frustration, Rukh threw his scimitar aside and proffered his neck.

'Ka'vash,' Kyuhai said, gently tapping the creature's throat. 'End simulation.'

The swirling fog vanished instantly, revealing the ochre coloured expanse of the Fire Grounds. The *Whispering Hand*'s training bay was divided into six sectors, some housing demi-sentient sparring machines, others devoted to low-tech challenges like climbing frames or ropes. Kyuhai and his opponents stood in the simulation arena, where a large saucer-like machine hovered overhead, its underside bristling with sensors and projectors that tracked their movements. This late in the ship's sleep cycle the bay was almost empty, yet Kyuhai and his companions were not quite alone. A human was training on the far side of the bay – the big man who led the expedition's second gue'vesa support team. Their paths had crossed here before while their fellow travellers slept, but they had never spoken.

'Reflect upon this defeat,' Kyuhai told the avian warriors. 'Leave me.'

The pair inscribed the symbol of Unity with their claws then loped towards the climbing arena, where they would continue training until he summoned them. Once they would have berated each other for their defeat, but they were past such foolishness. He had brought them that far at least.

'*Your honour guard is formidable, exalted one,*' the expedition's ranking Fire Warrior had observed when Kyuhai had come aboard the ship. '*The kroot are fierce allies.*'

'*I am a Seeker, Shas'el Akuryo. I have no honour guard,*' Kyuhai had replied. '*Rukh and Zeljukh are simply companions on my path.*'

Many of Kyuhai's fellow t'au were repelled by the avian auxiliaries, but he had detected only respect in the Fire Warrior's voice. Though Akuryo and he were of the same rank within their respective castes, the Ethereals were elevated above all others, creating a gulf of authority between them. Had the Seeker commanded it, Akuryo would have taken his own life without hesitation. Such blind faith had troubled Kyuhai when he had first stepped onto his path, but he had soon learnt that it was not blind at all, for his caste was the living embodiment of the Tau'va.

'We rule to serve,' he said, echoing the words of his former master.

The sounds of combat drew him from his reflection. While his mind had wandered, his body had followed its own path, carrying him to the arena where the big gue'la was duelling with a pair of drones. The saucer-like machines buzzed around the man, harassing him with low intensity lasers as he whirled about, blocking their beams with the mirror shields strapped to his wrists. His only method of retaliation was to reflect the lasers back at their source, but only a direct hit on an emitter would disable a drone, while three strikes to his torso would end the bout. Judging by their tenacity the machines had been set to maximum aggression – a challenge even for seasoned Fire Warriors. Though the man moved with a speed that belied his bulk, it was apparent that his ambition exceeded his ability.

Like Rukh, he fights in the expectation of defeat, Kyuhai judged.

He anticipated the gue'la would meet failure with a curse, but when it came he simply said, 'Start over.'

'Hold,' Kyuhai interjected and the drones froze.

The gue'la turned, surprised, then bowed his head. 'I didn't mean to intrude...' He faltered, evidently unsure of the correct form of address. 'Lord,' he ventured. He spoke in a hoarse growl, as if his throat was damaged.

'Seeker,' Kyuhai corrected. His sharp eyes scanned the identity disc on the man's tunic. 'And the intrusion is mine, Gue'vesa'ui Voyle.'

'I am honoured, Seeker.'

Even by the standards of his species, with their jutting snouts and curled ears, Voyle was ugly. Like all the expedition's gue'vesa, he was shaven-headed and his skin was stained blue to mirror his liberators' complexion, but such contrivances couldn't soften the brutish cast of his features. His eyes were set deep in a craggy, scar-crossed wasteland that terminated in a slab-like jaw. It was a strange canvass to bear the concentric rings of Unity, yet also an eloquent one, for if such a damaged being could be redeemed then surely there was hope for the rest of its species. To the Seeker's mind the gue'la were infinitely more dangerous than honest savages like the kroot, but equally their *potential* was far greater.

'They are an ancient race, crooked with the malignancies of age,' Kyuhai's master had taught, *'and yet the aeons have not diminished their passion. In time they will either become our most ardent allies or our most dire foes.'*

'You fought with skill, but chose your battle without wisdom,' Kyuhai said. 'To overextend oneself is to welcome defeat.'

'I stand corrected, Seeker. My thoughts were clouded.'

'Sleep evades you?'

'I don't like what it brings. Or where it takes me.' The man rubbed at his neck and Kyuhai spotted a pale scar under his jaw. It was circular, almost like another ring of Unity. 'There are things... things I thought I was done with.'

'Are you having doubts, gue'vesa'ui?'

'Doubts?' Voyle looked up sharply, evidently surprised. 'No, no doubts… I want to see the Imperium burn, Seeker.'

'That may not serve the Greater Good. Our mission here in the Damocles Gulf is peaceful. We may yet find common cause with the people of your Imperium.'

'It's not *my* Imperium, Seeker,' Voyle said, his expression hardening. 'It never was.'

There it is, Kyuhai saw, *the potential for terrible light and darkness.*

'That is why awakened minds like yours must strive to reclaim it for the Greater Good,' he said.

Voyle didn't answer, but the denial in his eyes was apparent.

He is correct, Kyuhai reflected. *His species yearns for strife. There will be no accord with their Imperium. And yet we must attempt it, even if it only delays the inevitable. This is an inopportune time for war. When it comes it must be of our choosing, not the enemy's.*

A melodious sequence of chimes reverberated through the bay, announcing the dawn cycle.

'We will talk again, Gue'vesa'ui Voyle,' Kyuhai said, studying the man's face. 'Think upon my words.'

As the Seeker turned and strode towards the door he felt the man's shadow-wracked eyes following him.

'Review transmission Fai'sahl-359,' Por'el Adibh commanded.

The data drone embedded in the glassy table before her burbled and its dome erupted with a corona of pixels, illuminating the dimly lit conclave chamber where the embassy's leaders had gathered at her request. The iridescent particles flickered then resolved into a diminutive figure floating above the drone in a rigid lotus position. The hololithic avatar's fine features and high-collared robes identified him as a member of the t'au Water caste, like Adibh herself.

'*I bear greetings in the name of the Greater Good,*' the avatar announced in a mellifluous baritone. '*I am Por'vre Dalyth Fai'sahl, first emissary of the eighth branch of the Whispertide Concordance, entrusted with the enlightenment of the nineteenth parallel of the Damocles Gulf, designated the Yuxa system.*

'*Please forgive the excessive interval since my last communication, but my expedition has been beset by grievous travails and many of my associates have passed into the Deep Silence. Yuxa is a troubled region where the dominion of the gue'la Imperium has grown profoundly frayed. Such disorder is fertile soil for anarchy and violence, yet also for opportunity, for as the storm spawns ruin, so ruination foreshadows fresh hope. And in hope there is Unity.*'

You were never one for succinctness, Fai'sahl, Adibh reflected. Her colleague had always leaned towards the flamboyant, and not only in his rhetoric. It was why she had rejected his many proposals for a pairing, despite his comeliness – and also, she suspected, why she had advanced beyond him in their caste's hierarchy. Yet despite Fai'sahl's limitations his disappearance had saddened her. How like him to confound her assumptions and reappear, seemingly alive and well.

'*Know that our sacrifice has not been without purpose,*' Fai'sahl's image was saying, his nasal slits dilated with pride. '*Under my auspices, Yuxa's dominant gue'la faction, the Illumismatic Order of the Ever-Turning Cog, has embraced the Greater Good with formidable conviction! Though I have dedicated my life to the dissemination of the Tau'va among the ignorant, I have never witnessed an ideological metamorphosis to rival the one that blossoms here. Indeed, I believe the key to the spiritual redemption of this vexatious species – perhaps even the unravelling of its barbaric Imperium – may lie here in the Yuxa system!*

'*Regrettably, however, this efflorescence of reason is imperilled by recidivist elements and technological impediments beyond my capacity to salve. My gue'la associates have prepared a report of our predicament that I have appended to this transmission for your elucidation. Esteemed colleagues, I urge you to despatch a relief mission to Yuxa without delay. It would be a betrayal of our exalted commission if this promising light were extinguished in its infancy.*

'*Spatial coordinates and supporting specifications follow.*'

The hololith flickered out and the lights rose, revealing the others seated around the conclave table. Adibh and Fio'vre Daukh, the expedition's senior engineer, had already seen the recording, but for the pair of Fire Warriors it was the first time. The older one's weathered face wore its customary disapproval for all non-military matters. Even by the standards of her caste, Shas'vre Bhoral was a dour creature, but doubtless she hadn't been chosen for her intellect. She was a tightly focused weapon, nothing more. It was the officer sitting beside her who mattered to Adibh.

'The recording is genuine?' Shas'el Akuryo asked.

'It was encoded with gue'la equipment, but the identity ciphers are correct,' Adibh replied. 'Moreover, Por'vre Fai'sahl and I are former colleagues. It is certainly him.'

'His manner is… singular.' Akuryo's brow furrowed slightly to indicate *the-irony-that-anticipates-derision*. For a Fire Warrior he was unusually expressive, Adibh thought, even handsome in a coarse way. More importantly he was perceptive. His gue'vesa troops, to whom he was nothing less than a hero, had named him Stormlight for his stalwart guidance in both war and peace.

'How long has this emissary been missing?' Akuryo asked.

'Prior to this transmission our last contact with Fai'sahl's embassy was almost three spatial years ago,' Adibh said. 'They were presumed lost and the Yuxa system was designated non-viable.'

'The matter was not investigated?'

'As you are aware, the Whispertide Concordance is only an exploratory venture into the Damocles Gulf – a bridgehead to the gue'la. Our resources are limited.'

'His sudden reappearance troubles me,' Akuryo said, cutting to the crux of the matter.

'Naturally. That is why you are here, shas'el.'

'Then why have I been allowed only Bhoral and two gue'vesa support teams to protect you, por'el?'

'It was the High Ambassador's decree.' Adibh extended her hands, palms upward. 'We walk the path of the Open Hand. An excessive military presence might be misconstrued and opportunities of the kind Fai'sahl describes cannot be squandered.'

'Then you believe his story?'

'That is for our revered Seeker to determine,' Adibh said. 'My purpose is to facilitate a fruitful discourse.'

'As yours is to watch over us, Stormlight,' a quiet voice said behind her. 'I have no doubt you will both perform your duties admirably.'

Adibh turned and saw the Seeker standing in the entrance of the conclave chamber, his arms crossed in a posture of tranquil authority. He was attired in plain grey robes cinched at the waist by a black sash. As always, a deep cowl pooled his features in shadow, obscuring his eyes. His honour staff was clipped to a simple harness on his back.

How long has he been there? Adibh wondered as a thrill of devotion surged through her. It was rumoured that Seekers could pass unseen among the other castes and Kyuhai had done nothing to dispel that notion. Formally known as *yasu'aun* – 'the-finders-of-the-truth-that-hides' – Seekers were solitary mystics who wandered the T'au Empire, following paths only the Ethereal caste could comprehend. Sometimes they would attach themselves to an expedition, appearing unexpectedly, but always welcome, for their presence was a great honour. Though Adibh was officially still the mission's leader the *reality* of that had changed the moment Kyuhai had joined them, yet she felt no acrimony towards him. In her most introspective moments that equanimity sometimes troubled her, but the unease would never crystallise.

'We shall not fail you, Seeker,' Akuryo vowed, clearly as awed by the mystic as Adibh.

'Nor I you, Stormlight,' Kyuhai replied. He turned to Adibh. 'Por'el, when we reach Yuxa you will conduct our negotiations.'

'Under your auspices of course, Seeker.'

'You misunderstand, por'el. You will lead the embassy alone. I will observe, unobserved. The unseen eye sees further.'

'Then you suspect a trap, Seeker?' Akuryo asked intently.

'That is my path.'

When the next sleep cycle came round Voyle climbed into a serenity cell. The last thing he saw as the hatch slid shut was Erzul watching him from the cubicle in the opposite wall. Fighting down his nausea, Voyle extinguished the light.

'It's nothing,' he whispered.

But it didn't *feel* like nothing. Not at all. His heart was pounding as the memories surged up with almost physical force. Darkness and the stench of stale promethium…

Then he is inside the other *coffin again – the empty fuel silo he has crawled into and welded shut with Hoenig's las-cutter. His ear is pressed against the slick metal, listening for the abominations that have slaughtered the boarding party. Hoenig is slumped against him in the tight space, his breath coming in ragged, bubbling gasps as he bleeds out. The specialist trooper's left arm has*

been torn off at the shoulder, along with most of his face, yet
oblivion eludes him. His surviving eye roves about, as if seeking
answers to questions he can't understand, let alone ask. Voyle
knows he should give his comrade mercy, but then he will be the
last of them and he isn't ready for that yet.

'I can't,' he says.

Hoenig's questing eye fixes upon him, mutely condemning, then
darkens to black.

'Face your fear or it will consume you.'

Voyle recoils and slips further into the nightmare, back to the
moment when it truly begins.

'Proceed,' Kyuhai commanded.

'Subject: Voyle, Ulver. Species: Gue'la, male,' the data drone
answered in its sexless, perfectly modulated voice. 'Age: thirty-
six biological years. Height…'

'Omit somatic data,' Kyuhai interrupted. 'Proceed to
biographic.'

'Yes, Seeker,' the drone replied. 'Former Astra Militarum
trooper, Eleventh Exordio Void Breachers…'

Alone in the conclave chamber, Kyuhai listened as the
drone related Voyle's history. He didn't know what he was
looking for, but he was certain he would *recognise* it when
he found it. In time that recognition would blossom into
understanding, but it was an ambiguous process, driven by
intuition rather than intellect. A Seeker perceived connections
and anomalous elements – be they events, objects or individuals – as an artist of the Water caste perceived the rhythm of
colours, words or melodies. Like that artist, Kyuhai's calling
was to create harmony, but his canvass was spiritual rather
than aesthetic.

'Subject Voyle was subsequently promoted to the rank

of breach sergeant and assigned to patrol duties along the perimeter of the Damocles Gulf,' the data drone was saying. 'His first tour...'

His eyes closed and arms folded, Kyuhai let the story wash over him. Thus far nothing in Voyle's service record had struck the discordant note he was waiting for. The man's career was competent, but unexceptional. Grey. Yet *something* had drawn him to Voyle, just as it had drawn him to this mission when so many others had vied for his attention.

Who are you, Ulver Voyle? Kyuhai mused. *Why do you matter?*

Though Voyle has fallen only minutes further into his nightmare's past it is enough to resurrect his comrades and the delusion of order. The squad has travelled far in search of the dead ship's bridge, for if there are any answers to be found they will surely be there. Unexpectedly the derelict is still pressurised, though its atmosphere is stale and none of the troopers have opened their visors. They don't trust this place enough to taste its air.

'How much further, Hoenig?' Voyle hears himself ask.

Whole again, the specialist trooper consults his scanner. The glowing map on its readout is only an approximation of the hulk's layout derived from similar vessels, but Hoenig has a talent for navigating on the fly.

'Another deck up, breach sergeant,' he replies. 'Should be an access ladder three or four junctions ahead.'

But Voyle, both past and present, isn't listening anymore. Did something move in the intersecting corridor he just passed? He steps back and illuminates the passageway. Its length is choked with a snarl of pipes and corroded machinery that spin strange shadows from his light. That constricted abattoir of junk isn't somewhere he wants to go, but he has to be certain, so he steps into its maw.

'Don't!' *Voyle present yells silently into his past.*

With a wet hiss a pile of debris uncoils before him, extending long arms that end in hook-like talons. A moment later a second pair unfurls beneath the first, but these taper into long-fingered hands that look almost delicate. The creature's gangling form is sheathed in chitinous blue plates that bulge into a carapace of bones over its chest and shoulders. Though its posture is hunched its bestial head is level with Voyle's own – so close he can see its mauve flesh pulsating.

It was waiting for me, *he understands.*

Voyle's meltagun is trained on the thing's ribcage, but his trigger finger has turned to stone, along with his legs and throat, all held rigid by its gaze. Its eyes are a lustreless black, yet the hunger in them is unmistakable. Unassailable... even *beautiful in its purity...*

Now one of Voyle's hands moves, rising to the seal of his visor. He gasps as the derelict's freezing air hits him, but it is not enough to snap him free of those mesmerising eyes.

'Breach sergeant?' someone calls behind him as the creature's jaws distend and a rigid tongue extrudes, dripping viscous ichor. The organ is thorn-tipped and pregnant with promise.

'Burn it!' *Voyle bellows at himself as he raises his head and offers his throat.*

Perhaps his warning rends time, space and logic to stir his former self to action. Perhaps it is nothing more than a shock reflex. Either way, when the beast's tongue pierces his flesh he squeezes the trigger. As cold corruption courses into his bloodstream a blast of purifying heat incinerates the thing's torso. Its tongue is wrenched free as it falls, but Voyle feels no pain through the numbness in his neck. He snaps his visor shut as gunfire erupts in the corridor behind him.

'Xenos!' somebody shouts.

In the pandemonium that follows the first attack Voyle can't tell how many of the abominations there are, but within seconds his squad is fighting for its life as the things assail it from all sides. Soon three troopers are lost and the fight has become flight. Reaching the sanctuary of the Sable Star *is their only hope, but the rout has transformed the corridors into a maze and Hoenig's scanner has been lost along with the arm that carried it. Voyle wields his heavy gun one-handed as he supports the wounded man. They are both drenched in the blood pumping from the raw stump of Hoenig's shoulder, yet the specialist is still conscious – still their best chance of finding a way out.*

The seven survivors become six then five then only four as claws yank troopers into dark recesses or the pipes above.

'Sable Star!' *Voyle shouts into his helmet vox, but the only reply is a hiss of static. The squad left a string of comms relays in its wake to maintain contact with the ship, but the rout has carried them far from that path.*

'Take… right,' *Hoenig gasps as they reach another junction.*

Abruptly the vox crackles into life: '–status, Squad Indigo? I repeat…'

'Lieutenant!' *Voyle interrupts.* 'We're under attack. Taking heavy casualties.'

'Confirmed,' *the acting commander replies.* 'What are you up against, breach sergeant?'

'Unknown xenos… Don't know how many. We need a support team now!'

There is a long pause: 'I am disengaging the umbilical.'

'Wait…'

'I can't allow the Sable Star to be compromised.' *Lieutenant Joliffe's voice is walking a knife-edge of panic now.*

'Listen to me, we're…'

'Emperor protect you, breach sergeant.' *The vox goes dead.*

Voyle curses him as the trooper ahead is pulled through the floor by something unseen. He sends an incinerating blast into the torn ground as he steps past, virtually dragging Hoenig now. Moments later a plangent metallic scraping echoes through the corridor. Every Void Breacher knows that sound.

'That was the umbilical!' Thorsten yells from somewhere behind.

We were almost there, *Voyle realises bitterly.* 'Keep moving,' *he orders as he staggers on, going nowhere now, but too angry to stop.*

Soon Thorsten is also gone and only Voyle and the wounded specialist remain. Hoenig has passed out, but he's still breathing and Voyle won't leave him behind even if it makes no difference anymore. As he wanders the labyrinth he senses the black-eyed xenos watching him from the shadows, inexplicably reticent now his comrades are dead. Are they toying with him? No… Voyle is strangely certain that cruelty isn't in their nature. Stranger still, he can't bring himself to hate them. Whatever else they are, the creatures are honest *in their desires. The beauty he glimpsed in his first encounter wasn't entirely false. Besides, he has no hatred left to spare for them.*

'We were so close,' he rasps, thinking of Joliffe. Dimly he recalls Breacher protocol – even recognises that the lieutenant was right *– but rage drowns such reasonable nonsense. 'So… damn… close.'*

The corridors reverberate with a deep, distant pounding and Voyle realises the Sable Star *has opened fire on the dead ship. He doubts its depleted weapons can destroy the colossal vessel, but the outer sections will certainly be depressurised. Even if the ship survives he might not.*

'I'm dead anyway,' Voyle hisses. But his body denies it. And suddenly – fiercely – he realises he wants to keep it that way. His fury demands it. That and something colder.

Shortly afterwards he finds the fuel silos.

* * *

'Five spatial years ago subject Voyle was recovered from an abandoned vessel found in the ninth Damocles parallel,' the data drone said. 'The report specifies he had been adrift for three months following an encounter with hostile life forms of an unknown nature. No trace of these aggressors was found, however evidence...'

Kyuhai was listening intently now. According to the report Voyle had displayed remarkable resilience, both physical and mental, in the face of his ordeal.

'On site examination concluded that...'

'Hold,' Kyuhai said sharply. 'Repeat previous segment.'

Voyle clawed his way out of the nightmare like a panicked corpse from its grave, but the taste of rotten flesh in his mouth wasn't his own. He had finally remembered the last, worst part of the horror – the part his liberators had supressed during his induction. Only they weren't liberators at all. Not for him. How could they be when he was knee-deep in damnation?

Gut-deep.

'It was evident that the subject had sustained himself by cannibalising a dead comrade,' the drone repeated.

Cannibalism? Kyuhai thought. The practice was not unknown among some species – indeed it was revered by the kroot – but among the gue'la it was regarded as extremely deviant behaviour.

'The matter was not noted as a cause for concern?' he asked.

'The presiding Ethereal, Aun'vre Kto'kovo, deemed it within acceptable parameters of gue'la degeneracy.'

'Proceed,' Kyuhai said, supressing a rare flicker of irritation. Even among his own caste there were too many who dismissed the gue'la as primitives.

'Following screening and remedial therapy, the subject was inducted into the Kir'qath auxiliary academy on Sa'cea sept, where he demonstrated exceptional aptitude aligned with a robust commitment to the Tau'va. His initial posting...'

Five years of faultless service to the Greater Good followed, with Voyle fighting on various battlegrounds at the fringes of the empire. The Seeker listened to it all, though he was certain he had already found the key to Voyle's anomaly. Now he had to make sense of it – and decide whether Ulver Voyle was an asset or a liability.

'No,' Voyle rasped, over and over, but no matter how often he repeated it, the truth would not be denied. As the days of his confinement had stretched into untold weeks, his soul had narrowed towards nothingness. Starved of hope for retribution, even his rage had dimmed, yet his body had fought on. Somewhere blood deep – much deeper than he could see – it had been unwilling to die. When his suit's rations were exhausted he'd scavenged from the corpse beside him in the silo, and then when its supplies were also gone...

Voyle retched and slammed a fist against his sleeping cell.

'What am I?' he snarled into the darkness within.

And for the first time the darkness answered, but its voice came from without.

– THE SECOND CIRCLE –
THRESHOLD

The Yuxa system had eleven planets, but only two harboured life – Phaedra, a fungus infested water world, and Scitalyss, a bloated gas giant whose outer layers swarmed with phantasmal aeriform vermin. It was to the second of these that the *Whispering Hand* was bound, though its destination was not the planet itself, but the lesser leviathan suspended in its anaemic exosphere.

From a distance the structure appeared to be a dark blemish against Scitalyss' ochre and russet swirl, but as the vessel drew closer the mote grew spiny and misshapen, like a tumour in metastasis. Closer still it resolved into a sprawl of interconnected metal modules of varying size and shape. A monolithic spindle rose from the centre of the tangle, towering over the other structures and trailing titanic extraction pipes into the world below. The spindle's cog-like tiers shimmered with lights as they revolved, but further from the centre the expanse grew dark and the domes of its component modules were cracked open to the void, as though they had been wracked by some terrible violence.

Though the sprawl was artificial it was still a cancer, for its growth had long ago become rampant and perverse, twisted out of any semblance of order by the countless masters who had presided over it. Most had begun their stewardship in sobriety, but few had ended that way, for despite the intent of its architects, discord ran deep in this place. Whether it was the influence of the baleful giant it leeched upon or the consequence of some intrinsic flaw, the skyhive was *tainted*, its history saturated in strife. And yet it had endured across millennia, grudgingly paying its tithes to the Imperium and never quite embracing a heresy that would have invited retaliation. There were myriad such cancers growing in the cracks of the Imperium, but few as furtive.

The place had acquired many names, some truer than others. Its formal designation was Scitalyss-Altus, and its current masters had ennobled it as the Unfolding Nexus, however to the millions who eked out a living in its corroded avenues it was simply the Rat's Cradle.

I do not like it, Por'el Adibh decided, *not at all.*

The skyhive rotated slowly above the conclave table, its tangled lineaments reproduced in perfect holographic fidelity. Its presence felt like a taint upon the room. Upon *her*…

Taint? Adibh dismissed the notion. Such irrationality had corroded the collective psyche of the gue'la. It had no place in the thinking of a t'au.

'Your thoughts, shas'el?' she asked.

'It is dangerous,' Akuryo replied. He stood on the opposite side of the table, his form distorted by the hologram.

'I concur,' Adibh said, 'yet we must proceed with the mission.'

They were alone in the conclave chamber. Her first impressions of the Fire Warrior had proved correct and over the passing days she had come to value his counsel, even to regard him as a friend. After the artifice of the Whispertide Congress his directness was bracing.

'Why?' Akuryo asked. 'Why are we taking this risk, por'el? *The true reason.*'

'Because the High Ambassador has decreed it,' she replied. 'The Yuxa system interests him.' She raised a hand to stem his next question. 'I do not know why. Por'o Seishin keeps his own counsel, but we must trust his judgement.'

'He is young,' Akuryo said flatly.

'He is *gifted*,' Adibh corrected, thinking of her idealistic, driven superior. 'Exceptionally so… The empire recognises and rewards talent.'

Akuryo was silent for a moment, brooding. 'It is fortunate that a Seeker walks beside us on this path,' he said finally. 'We are due to dock in nine hours. I must go, por'el.'

'Why Bhoral?' Adibh asked as he turned to go.

'I do not understand?'

'Why did you choose Shas'vre Bhoral as your aide?' The question had nagged at her for some time. At first she had assumed the warriors were old comrades, perhaps even Ta'lissera bonded, but she had seen no warmth between them. Indeed, Akuryo seemed closer to his gue'vesa than to his fellow Fire Warrior.

'I did *not* choose her,' he said stiffly. 'She was assigned to me for the mission.'

Do you trust her? Adibh wanted to ask, but that was absurd. 'Thank you, shas'el,' she said instead. 'See to your troops.'

When he was gone she returned her attention to the hologram. She wasn't sure why she had asked the question or why Akuryo's answer troubled her. In fact, the closer they drew to their objective the less certain she was of anything.

Alone in the darkness of his serenity cell, Ulver Voyle listened to the Voice. It had grown stronger over the past few days, swelling from a subliminal murmur to an evanescent whispering, yet its *words* still eluded him.

'What are you trying to tell me?' he hissed.

– THE THIRD CIRCLE –
INSIDE

Por'el Adibh's nostril slits dilated with disgust as she stepped onto the ship's disembarkation ramp and the acid stench of the skyhive hit her. She imagined a broken machine leaking the black sludge that powered so much of the Imperium's technology. Quelling her nausea, she studied the immense expanse of the hanger bay as she descended, her data drone hovering above her head like a domed halo. The walls of the cavernous chamber were corroded and slick with filth, its floor knotted with trailing pipes and discarded tools. Dozens of sub-human labourers toiled among the labyrinth of machinery, their bodies crudely fused to metal limbs, their eyes as vacant as their minds. It had always puzzled Adibh that the Imperium embraced such atrocities while condemning the elegant drones of the T'au Empire.

So much of their suffering is self-inflicted, she mused.

'Noteworthy,' Fio'vre Daukh declared beside her. Adibh didn't know whether the stocky engineer was referring to the odour or some obscure detail only he could see, but she had learnt not enquire after such remarks; Daukh's concept of *noteworthy* rarely converged with anyone else's. He had found much of note during their approach to the hive, while Adibh had seen only decrepitude. Why had Fai'sahl led them to this floating sewer city?

Akuryo and another armoured figure were waiting for her at the foot of the ramp. They had donned their helmets so their faces were hidden behind flat, sensor-studded visors that gave them an impassive machine-like aspect. Akuryo's mottled crimson armour bore a five-armed sunburst on its breastplate – personal colours and heraldry granted to him when he'd earned his rank. In contrast, his companion's uniform was the stark, unadorned white of the Whispertide Concordance.

'Your gue'vesa understand there is to be no violence, shas'el?' Adibh asked, indicating the human soldiers lined up on either side of the ramp. Both the support teams were present, the troops' rifles slung over their shoulders as they crouched in the stance of watchful-repose. They wore lighter variants of the Fire Warriors' armour, retaining the breastplates and shoulder pads, but lacking the contoured plates that sheathed their superiors' limbs. Their helmets were fitted with tinted lenses that covered their eyes, but left their faces bare.

'The Stormlit know their duty,' Akuryo replied, referring to his troops as an extension of himself. It was a great honour and several of the gue'vesa puffed out their chests at his words.

'I have faith in *your* faith,' Adibh acknowledged, then appraised the warrior beside Akuryo. The deception was flawless. Despite the armour and helmet, she had expected to *feel* something, but all she sensed was what her eyes told her: this was just another Fire Warrior. It was as if the Seeker had somehow constricted his spirit when he had donned the armour.

He has become what he seems to be, she thought.

There was a pneumatic hiss as the hanger's hatch split down the centre and retracted to either side, spilling bright light into the chamber.

'And so we begin,' Adibh murmured as a robed figure entered.

His vision enhanced by the sensors of his borrowed helmet, Kyuhai studied the newcomer as it approached. Though it was swathed in a hooded purple mantle there were subtle qualities of posture and gait that spoke volumes to his refined sensibilities.

'Por'vre Fai'sahl,' Adibh declared when the stranger stopped before them.

She saw it too, Kyuhai realised, impressed. Few outside the Ethereal caste were so perceptive.

'You know me too well, old friend,' the newcomer said, pushing back its hood to reveal the familiar face of the missing emissary. He smiled and stretched out his arms to encompass the others. 'On behalf of the Order of the Ever-Turning Cog, I offer you welcome to the Unfolding Nexus, a new born engine of reason among the benighted gue'la!'

Kyuhai was perplexed. On the hololith Fai'sahl had appeared pompous – superficial even – but in person he was almost *electric*, as though an avid vitality burned within him.

'It has been too many years since we last conversed, Por'vre Adibh,' the emissary continued warmly, turning back to Adibh.

'Por'*el*,' she corrected. 'I was elevated shortly after your disappearance.'

'My apologies, *por'el*.' Fai'sahl bowed his head. 'It pleases me that your talents have been recognised.' Smoothly, he reached out and grasped her hands. It was a brazen gesture that breached all etiquette and Adibh stiffened visibly.

'I have so much to share with you,' Fai'sahl said, his eyes bright. 'This gue'la relic harbours many wonders that may advance the Greater Good.'

'You came alone, emissary?' Akuryo asked bluntly.

Fai'sahl turned to the Fire Warrior, his smile unwavering. 'No, but we thought it best that you were greeted by one who is known to you.'

'But I do *not* know you.' Akuryo indicated the iron talisman hanging from the emissary's neck – a four-toothed cog embossed with the double-loop of infinity. 'Nor do I recognise the sept you now speak for.'

'I bear the Cog Eternal as a mark of *respect*,' Fai'sahl said. His smile remained, but the warmth had slipped from his eyes.

'Your message indicated urgency, por'vre,' Adibh interjected, extricating her hands. 'I would like to meet these remarkable gue'la you have uncovered.'

'Of course, por'el...' Fai'sahl's gaze swept over the party. 'Your embassy was not accompanied by an exalted one?'

'Unfortunately they are few and the needs of the empire many,' Adibh replied.

Kyuhai studied Fai'sahl's face, expecting relief or disappointment, but there was nothing.

I cannot read him, he realised. *How can that be?*

On impulse he glanced at the gue'vesa troops, searching for Voyle. The big man stood at the front of his team, his expression distant, as if his attention was elsewhere. Though they had talked occasionally during the remainder of the voyage Kyuhai was no closer to deciphering the man's significance. And yet he did not doubt it.

'Chance is a myth perpetuated by those who only see what seems to be,' Kyuhai's master had taught. *'A Seeker looks beneath the lies and finds the lines that bind. And where they have become twisted or frayed, he follows, for his path is to mend when he can or excise when he cannot.'*

It was the first axiom of the *Yasu'caor*, the philosophy by which a Seeker served the Greater Good.

My path has led me true, Kyuhai judged, returning his attention to Fai'sahl's smiling, empty face. *Nothing is what it seems here.*

'Support Team One, the ship is under your watch. Be vigilant!' Akuryo commanded as he strode towards the hanger doors. 'Team Two, with me!'

Voyle shook his head, trying to break free of the Voice that haunted – *or hunted?* – him.

'Gue'vesa'ui?' someone said behind him. He turned and stared at the expectant faces of... *Who were they?*

'Voyle, the shas'el calls us!' a hatchet-faced woman snapped.

Erzul, he remembered and the rest followed.

'Move out,' he ordered. 'Go!'

Am I losing my mind? Voyle wondered as he followed his squad. Somehow the prospect troubled him less than any of the alternatives he could imagine.

Three vehicles waited outside the spaceport. Two were open-topped trucks, the third a massive armoured car emblazoned with the sigil of the Ever-Turning Cog. A group of robed figures watched over them, their long-barrelled rifles levelled at the surrounding buildings. More were stationed along the segmented wall that encircled the spaceport like a metal serpent. Floodlights illuminated the perimeter, but beyond their reach everything was swathed in gloom. Voyle looked up and counted less than a dozen lights in the iron sky of the dome. He knew each was a vast, burning globe, but it would take *hundreds* to illuminate a city-sized territory like this one.

This whole region is dying, he guessed, remembering the many dark modules he'd seen from space.

As the party approached the vehicles Voyle saw the guards' purple robes were embroidered with the concentric rings of Unity, but the bronze masks they wore under their hoods were less reassuring, for they were fashioned to resemble something more insect than man, with jutting compound jaws and bulbous, multi-faceted lenses.

'Watchmen of the Second Rotation,' the t'au emissary explained. 'They are here for your protection.'

'Protection from what?' the Stormlight demanded.

'Regrettably the Order's enlightenment is not entirely unopposed. A few dissident factions remain active in the outer districts, but they are as inchoate as they are ignorant,'

Fai'sahl said dismissively. 'The spaceport is under the Order's jurisdiction, but to reach the Alpha Axis we must traverse a… troubled… region.'

'I advise against proceeding, por'el,' the Stormlight warned Adibh. 'Let their leaders meet us here.'

With a whir of gyros one of the guards marched towards them, its footsteps reverberating under its weight. It was taller and more powerfully built than its fellows, its chest encased in a slab-like breastplate. In place of a hood it wore a back-swept helmet with a vertically slit visor that pulsed with blue light. An augmetic arm extended from its right shoulder, dwarfing the limb below and terminating in a three-fingered claw. Alongside that monstrous appendage the watchman's ornate rifle looked almost delicate.

'My designation is Aiode-Alpha, Warden Prime,' the warrior said in a pristine, but lifeless female voice. 'Your security is my primary directive. Please board the transports.' It rapped a gauntlet against its breastplate. 'For the Greatest Good.'

'There is no cause for concern,' Fai'sahl urged. 'The Warden is the Order's preeminent guardian.'

'Be advised that I have made provisions for our safety,' Adibh warned him. 'My ship expects to receive a coded data-burst from my drone every hour. Any breach of this will be construed as a hostile act.'

'I am familiar with first contact protocol,' Fai'sahl said gently, 'but this is *not* a first contact. I assure you, the Order's offer of friendship is sincere.'

'As is the Empire's,' Adibh parried, 'but the Open Hand must be firm of grip. You will respect my precautions, por'vre.'

'Naturally, por'el.' Fai'sahl bowed.

Adibh turned to Akuryo. 'We will proceed.'

The gue'vesa climbed into the back of a truck while Fai'sahl ushered the t'au into the armoured car. The watchmen boarded the second truck, lining up along its sides in regimented ranks with the Warden at their centre. Voyle gripped the guardrail as his vehicle surged forward and took its place at the rear of the convoy, with the other truck leading and the car shielded between them. Once they were underway his troops began to talk, eager to weigh up their strange hosts, but he silenced them.

'Stay sharp,' he ordered, unslinging his pulse rifle. 'Trust nothing.'

'How far?' Akuryo asked. He hadn't removed his helmet and its sensors glowed in the dingy cabin of the armoured car. Adibh suspected he would have preferred to travel with his troops, but was unwilling to leave her side.

'The Axis is five zones distant. A journey of many hours,' Fai'sahl answered from the seat opposite them. 'Regrettably our only functioning port is on the hive's outskirts. That is one of the limitations we hope to rectify with your aid.'

'Fio'vre Daukh will make a full assessment of your requirements,' Adibh said, keeping her tone neutral.

'My team stands ready to assist you,' Daukh concurred earnestly, though his eyes didn't leave the car's window slit. Doubtless he saw much of note outside. 'I predict there is considerable work ahead of us.'

'The Order's resources will be placed at your disposal, honoured fio'vre,' Fai'sahl promised. 'Together we shall achieve great things.'

'Assuming we reach an accord,' Adibh cautioned, sounding querulous even to herself. In the cramped cabin Fai'sahl's presence was almost overpowering.

'We shall, por'el. When we reach the Axis you will understand everything.' Fai'sahl smiled and Adibh felt a rush of unwelcome affection for him. No, it was simpler than that – more primal.

How he has changed, she mused. *He looks younger than he–*

Bright light flashed into her face, breaking the fascination. Abruptly Fai'sahl was gone and a hollowed out, predatory *thing* sat in his place, appraising her with hungry eyes.

'Forgive me, por'el,' the Seeker said from the seat beside the apparition. He extinguished his helmet light – and with it the horror. 'I fear my helm has developed an error.'

'See that you correct it, Fire Warrior,' Adibh replied, surprised that her terror hadn't reached her voice. Perhaps it was because *shame* eclipsed the fear. The Seeker had seen her desire...

No! The desire was not mine, she thought angrily, willing Kyuhai to see *that.*

'Are you well, my friend?' Fai'sahl asked, his face furrowing with concern.

'Perfectly well,' Adibh said. It was the most profound lie she had ever told.

The twilight district passed in a blur of crooked tenements, their growth stunted by the confines of the iron sky. Some had been reduced to scorched husks, while others had collapsed into rubble. Citizens haunted the squalor like flesh-bound ghosts, either alone or in small groups, often huddled around open fires. All were emaciated and grey, their bodies as wasted as their world. Most ignored the convoy, but a few watched it pass with empty eyes. Sometimes squads of purple robed watchmen moved among them, their weapons swivelling about as they patrolled. Once the vehicles swerved around a towering bipedal automaton with a warrior sitting astride it. The machine stomped through the streets, rocking back-and-forth to its own graceless rhythm as its searchlight scoured the hovels.

This is a warzone, Voyle judged, *or the tail end of one. Occupied territory.*

They had been travelling for almost an hour when the road narrowed and carried them into a stretch of gutted manufactories. The vehicles slowed to a halt and Voyle heard a clamour from somewhere up ahead – presumably the watchmen disembarking.

'Erzul, take a look,' he ordered. The pathfinder nodded and clambered onto the truck's cabin.

'Something on the road ahead,' she said. 'Looks like another truck, but–' She threw herself flat as a barrage of gunfire erupted from the ruins to their right. One of the gue'vesa snapped backwards and fell as a bullet punched into his face. Another ricocheted off Voyle's helmet.

'Stay low and return fire!' Voyle shouted, ducking as bullets battered the vehicle's sides. There was a chorus of electronic chimes as his troops activated their pulse rifles, followed by the sibilant whine of plasma bolts when they opened fire.

Voyle raised his head and scanned the ruins through his rifle's scope, weaving about until he locked onto a figure lurking behind a broken window. His weapon pinged as he increased the magnification and drew his target into sharper focus. It was a man in ragged grey fatigues, his head protected by a rusty iron helmet painted with a stylized 'M'. An archaic rebreather mask covered his mouth, its tubes snaking over his shoulders into a bulky backpack. Above the mask his eyes were bloodshot wounds in a pallid face riddled with scars and sores. He appeared to be in the terminal stages of some flesh-eating pestilence, yet he stood straight, unbowed by his bulky stubber gun.

This lot look worse than ours, Voyle decided sourly, lining up on the attacker's face.

Before he could fire there was a voltaic crackle and a streak of light flayed his mark like an electric whip. The man convulsed as current played about him, igniting his clothes and charring his flesh. Voyle turned and saw the Warden marching across the building's rubble-strewn courtyard with her watchmen following in a wide arc. Venting an electronic ululation, she seized a chunk of debris with her claw and hurled it at a crouching enemy. Simultaneously her rifle's glassy barrel glowed blue and spat another jagged bolt into the ruins. Without slowing their stride, her troops fired a volley of explosive rounds in perfect synchronicity, every bullet finding a different foe.

'They're fighting as one,' Voyle murmured, studying their lethal combat symmetry. He felt calm now, as if the skirmish had elevated him above his private damnation. The Voice was still there, oozing around the battlefield like an auricular spirit of war, but it almost made sense now.

Can they hear it too? Voyle wondered hazily as he slipped into harmony with the Order's enforcers, becoming another cog in a precision killing machine, aiming and firing and executing the raiders without hesitation.

Bullets exploded around the advancing watchmen, frequently tearing through their robes and ricocheting off the armour beneath. The Warden appeared impervious, but occasionally one of her cohorts would jerk or stumble as a bullet penetrated its armour. One fell to its knees with a shattered leg, but continued to fire as its comrades marched on. Another took a round in the throat and toppled over.

'They don't lack courage!' one of the gue'vesa yelled.

Maybe, Voyle thought, stirring from his combat reverie. *Or maybe they just don't know any better.*

'No heroics,' he cautioned. 'This isn't our fight.'

And they don't need us anyway, he gauged. The ambush was already faltering under the Warden's counterattack. Whoever the raiders – or rebels? – were, they were woefully outclassed by the Order's troops, but they were fighting to the bitter end.

This wasn't a chance attack. The poor bastards threw everything they had at it. Why?

As the Warden reached the building a raider threw a grenade from the window above. She seared him with lightning and lashed out with her claw, snatching the grenade from the air and hurling it back, but it detonated a few metres above her. She staggered under the concussion, her augmetic arm whipping about as she fought for balance.

What…?

Voyle's rifle pinged repeatedly as he zoomed in on her whirling limb. The explosion had torn away a patch of its armour, revealing not raw machinery but what looked like more plating, though it was rounded and dark blue in colour. Almost organic…

Like insect chitin.

Voyle froze, staring down his scope as the Warden recovered and stomped into the building, leaving him zoomed in on nothing but memories.

Void black eyes, holding him transfixed as the predator uncoils to embrace him…

'Status report, Two?' his helmet's communicator hissed. The Stormlight.

'One gue'vesa dead, one lightly wounded,' Voyle answered automatically. 'Situation under control, shas'el.'

'Acknowledged, Two. Hold your position.'

As the last of the watchmen entered the building Voyle made up his mind.

'Cover me,' he ordered his squad and vaulted from the truck. Keeping his eyes on the injured watchman who'd been left behind, he sprinted to its fallen comrade. The warrior lay flat on its face, motionless.

What do you expect to find? Voyle asked himself as he knelt by the body.

A cold and thirsty poison awakening in his blood and watching the world through his eyes...

He heaved the warrior onto its back and a *third* arm slid free from its robes. Like the Warden's 'augmetic', it was encased in segmented iron plates, but it ended in a scythe-like blade that was unmistakably *bone*.

'Mutants,' Voyle spat, feeling his gorge rise.

He appraised the gaping wound in the warrior's throat. A large calibre round had torn right through it, almost decapitating the creature. Nothing human could have survived such trauma, but did that mean anything here? As he reached for its mask the subterranean swirl of the Voice surged into sudden clarity: '*No...*'

Voyle froze. That denial was the first meaningful word it had said to him – perhaps even the first time it had been truly *aware* of him.

'You were never talking to me, were you?' Voyle whispered, following a tenebrous intuition. 'I was only ever listening in.'

'*No.*' The prohibition was more forceful now, yet it held no sway over him.

'What don't you want me to see?' Voyle challenged. 'Why–'

A bullet drilled into the ground by his feet. He turned and saw the kneeling watchman had levelled its rifle at him.

'They're yours, aren't they?' Voyle said to the Voice. 'All of them.'

'*Go... now...*' it breathed. Now it had the key to his head it was learning fast. Did that mean it would start pulling *his* strings soon?

'No,' Voyle snarled back and activated his helmet's transmitter. 'Erzul, wounded watchman to my right. Take it out.'

A bright bolt lanced across the courtyard and erased the warrior's head in a burst of plasma.

She didn't hesitate, Voyle thought with grim satisfaction. *I might be losing my mind, but my squad still trusts me.*

Ignoring the Voice, he pulled the dead watchman's mask aside. And froze.

Watching and waiting for the moment when he can claim another to feed the hunger that can never be sated...

Voyle switched his transmitter to the squad-wide channel. 'Seize the vehicles,' he ordered. 'The watchmen are hostile. Take them down.'

He looked up and saw the Warden emerging from the building, doubtless summoned by her unseen master. Her helmet swung about, its visor slit pulsing with blue light as she scanned the battleground.

What's under there? Voyle wondered, glancing back at the corpse. Its face was a travesty of humanity, with deeply recessed eyes and rubbery, mauve-hued skin. A chitinous ridge ran from its forehead to the bridge of its nose, beneath which its face erupted into a nest of pink tendrils. Many of them were still twitching, as if animated by a life of their own.

The Voice was gnawing at Voyle's mind now, but he shut it out, sensing that every word it spoke would sink another root into his soul, like one of the corpse's undying tendrils.

'I'm not yours,' he rasped as the gue'vesa opened fire on the watchmen.

* * *

'*Seize the vehicles,*' Voyle's voice hissed inside Kyuhai's helmet.

The Seeker acted without conscious thought, moving before the command had even concluded. The tone of Voyle's *first word* was enough to tell him that the wheel of possibilities had turned, carrying them from diplomacy into conflict. The cause and consequences could be assessed later. For now only action mattered.

'Do not be alarmed,' Fai'sahl was saying beside him, responding to the muffled sounds of battle. 'The watchmen will–'

Kyuhai's armoured elbow slammed into the side of his head. As the emissary slumped over, the Seeker leapt up and surged towards the driver. The man turned and Kyuhai's fist hammered between his eyes, throwing him against the wheel with stunning force. Fai'sahl had called the pale, hairless creature a timekeeper of the Fourth Rotation. Had he been one of the armoured warriors Kyuhai wouldn't have risked holding back, but for now killing was best avoided.

'*The watchmen are hostile,*' Voyle's warning continued as Kyuhai hauled the unconscious driver from his seat and took his place. '*Take them down.*'

'What is happening, Seeker?' Adibh asked, shocked by the sudden violence.

'We are betrayed,' Akuryo answered flatly, activating his pulse rifle. He had also heard the message, but his reaction had inevitably trailed behind Kyuhai's.

'See to your men, Stormlight,' the Seeker commanded, assessing the controls. The car appeared to be standard gue'la technology – rudimentary, but robust. 'We must return to the ship immediately.'

'Understood.' Akuryo opened the hatch and leapt out, slamming it closed behind him.

'How may I serve?' Adibh asked. Once again Kyuhai was impressed with her. She had adjusted quickly.

'Search the emissary for weapons then alert the ship, por'el,' he said. 'The status code is *mal'caor*. Fio'vre, see to the driver.'

'Yes, aun'el,' they chorused.

What have you done, Voyle? Kyuhai wondered as he gunned the engine into life.

Voyle raced for the vehicles, weaving between piles of rubble as plasma bolts swept overhead and solid rounds exploded around him. Sometimes a whiplash of electricity crackled past, but he sensed that the Warden was only trying to slow him.

'You want me alive,' Voyle muttered between breaths, addressing the Voice. 'You want to know... how I work... or why I don't.'

Up ahead both the armoured car and the rearmost truck had begun to reverse along the road. Erzul and two other gue'vesa crouched in the truck's back, exchanging fire with the watchmen. Unlike the raiders' antiquated guns their pulse rifles punched through the mutants' armour with ease, forcing them to stay in cover or die. Even the tank-like Warden had retreated behind a wall. Suddenly Voyle felt a ferocious pride in his xenos liberators. In a galaxy drowning in corruption they were surely the best – perhaps the only – hope.

'*Gue'vesa'ui, be swift!*' the Stormlight transmitted.

Voyle saw Akuryo leading the rest of his team against the lead truck. The Warden had left a pair of watchmen behind and they had taken cover behind the driver's cabin, one on either side, where they held his comrades back with alternating volleys. Two gue'vesa were already down and Voyle cursed as another was blasted from her feet as she tried to flank the mutants.

'Unity!' he growled and swerved towards them, sighting down his rifle as he charged. It was a precision weapon, ill-suited to such assaults, but he knew its rhythms better than his own mind and his third shot brushed the nearest watchman's hood, setting it alight. The fourth bored a molten crater into its chest as it turned, throwing it backwards. An obscene hissing bubbled from behind its flame-wreathed mask as it tried to level its rifle at him. With a roar of loathing, Voyle barrelled into it, sending it crashing into its comrade. The impact threw him to the ground, but he kept firing, riddling the entangled watchmen with plasma bolts. He didn't stop, not even when they fell – then fell still. His hatred was too deep. Too hungry...

And the hunger gazes back at him from the void it has carved out in his soul. And then it speaks, for it has a Voice: 'Voyle...'

'Voyle!' someone shouted, hauling him up. He stifled a snarl as he recognised the Stormlight.

'We must go!' his commander snapped.

'The truck...'

'No time! More enemies come.' The Fire Warrior jabbed his rifle at the road ahead. A bipedal walker was striding through the wreckage of the vehicle that had blocked the convoy's path. It was similar to the one Voyle had spotted earlier, but its saddle was fitted with a massive cannon. The gun's spinning barrel was still smoking from the destruction it had just wreaked on the obstruction.

'Move, Voyle!'

They sprinted after the retreating vehicles, following the surviving soldier who had accompanied Akuryo. Both the captured vehicles had picked up speed now, but they were still hobbled by their inability to turn on the narrow road. As the fleeing trio drew level with the car a bolt of electricity struck the gue'vesa, throwing him against the vehicle. Voyle leapt over the charred corpse that rebounded into his path and glanced over his shoulder. The Warden was marching across the rubble in pursuit, flanked by her surviving watchmen. Worse still, the strider was bearing down on the car with frightening speed, its cannon spinning up to fire. Moments later a storm of high-velocity rounds rained down on its prey.

We're done, Voyle realised, ducking as ricochets whistled past him.

Suddenly the car thrust forward, its engine roaring as it accelerated towards its hunter. The strider lurched off the road, but the vehicle veered after it, its iron-shod tires clattering over the debris. There was a thunderous crash as it rammed the automaton. The strider's legs buckled and its saddle plunged forward, sliding along the car's roof and ploughing a deep fissure in its wake. Voyle and Akuryo dived aside as the wreckage hurtled past them, still bearing its stiff-backed rider and cannon. The gun detonated when it hit the road, vomiting a fireball into the dark sky.

'Sacred Throne,' Voyle growled, dredging up the old Imperial curse as the car whirled out of control and overturned. It spun about on its roof, shedding armour as it screeched along the ground. Caught in its path, the Warden was swept up and ground down, along with the watchmen flanking her. Finally the car's momentum gave out, leaving it wedged halfway up a mound of rubble.

'*The Seeker!*' Akuryo yelled over the transmitter. He was already on his feet and racing towards the wreckage.

'Rouse yourself, por'el,' the Seeker commanded, his calm voice cutting through the cacophony that lingered in Adibh's ears. Ignoring the protests of her battered body, she uncurled from the foetal huddle she'd adopted and rolled to her knees. Kyuhai's sensor-studded faceplate loomed into view, appraising her.

'You are fortunate,' the Seeker pronounced. 'Did you send the signal?'

'I... yes...' Adibh said, struggling for focus. 'Just before... before...'

'Then come, we cannot linger here.' Kyuhai turned away, ducking under the seats that hung from the inverted roof like stalactites. Through the smoke-filled gloom Adibh saw that the others had been much less fortunate. Fai'sahl lay beside her, a spar of metal jutting from his chest. Daukh was on the cabin's far side, slumped against the hatch, the top of his head mashed into a ragged crown of blood and bone. The timekeeper was sprawled brokenly across the drive panel, his robes smouldering.

'Tread carefully,' Kyuhai cautioned as he stepped over the gaping fissure running through the floor. Choking on the smoke, Adibh moved to follow. As she climbed over Fai'sahl's body his eyes opened.

'Adibh... what...?' His words splintered into a blood-flecked cough and he clutched at her. She took his hand instinctively, gripping it as spasms rippled through his body. The predator she'd glimpsed earlier was gone, along with its baleful magnetism.

In death he is only himself, she sensed.

'The emissary still lives!' she shouted to Kyuhai.

'His injury is mortal,' the Seeker replied. 'You cannot help him.' Reaching the hatch, he heaved Daukh aside and tugged at the opening lever, but it wouldn't budge.

As the emissary's convulsions subsided Adibh leaned in

close. 'The Cog Eternal,' she urged. 'What is it? The truth, Fai'sahl.'

'Told you… truth,' he wheezed as his eyes clouded. 'Greatest… good…' His head fell back, revealing a circular scar under his chin.

'That is a lie,' Adibh said sadly. 'But I don't believe it is yours, old friend.'

She released Fai'sahl's hand and crawled towards the Seeker. As she approached the fissure an electronic burbling sounded from somewhere below. *Her drone.* She leant over the rift's lip and reached down, expecting to touch the ground, but there was nothing. The car must have come to rest above a cavity. She stretched further and her fingers brushed smooth metal.

'Seeker, I–'

A cold blue light flared into life below, dazzling her. She jerked away, but something seized her wrist in a vicelike grip.

'Do not be alarmed,' a sterile voice boomed. 'Your security is my primary directive.'

Adibh shrieked as the Warden yanked her through the fissure.

'Watchmen. Heading this way, shas'el,' Voyle warned as a group of robed figures appeared on the road ahead.

'You must delay them,' Akuryo ordered.

'Yes, shas'el.' What else was there to say? They could not abandon an Ethereal. After the crash they'd climbed to the stranded car, where the Fire Warrior was wrestling with the hatch while Voyle covered the road. It hadn't taken long for more of the Order's troops to arrive, but as they drew closer he saw there was something new among them – something much larger. He sighted down his scope and grimaced. The hulking figure was swathed in the customary purple robes, but it was almost twice the height of its fellows. A bulbous helmet encased its head and shoulders, locked into place by heavy chains that criss-crossed its chest. Its visor was carved into the likeness of a cog, with a single lens at the centre and smoking censers affixed to each tooth. The giant's right arm split at the elbow, spawning a pair of armoured tentacles that were wrapped around the haft of a massive industrial hammer. Its right arm was a weapon in its own right, bulging into a serrated claw that dragged along the ground behind it.

They've given up on hiding their secrets, Voyle thought, targeting the cog-faced hulk. As his plasma bolts seared its helmet the giant swung its hammer up to protect its lens, almost as if it had read his mind. Moving like clockwork, the watchmen raised their rifles and retaliated with a volley of bullets, then stepped aside, opening a path for their champion.

I can't put that thing down, Voyle realised as the behemoth broke into a lumbering charge. *This is where I die.*

'Then lower your weapon… and live,' the Voice suggested, slithering into his thoughts like a shameful secret. It spoke fluently now, its words redolent with sombre authority. Voyle couldn't remember why he had ever questioned it.

'Because you were lost, child.'

There was a metallic creak behind him. Voyle turned unsteadily and saw Kyuhai emerge from the vehicle.

'I will assist the others, Seeker,' Akuryo said, his voice seeming to come from some distant, meaningless place.

'They are gone,' Kyuhai said.

'Por'el Adibh…'

'All of them, Stormlight.'

The Ethereal turned to Voyle, as if to speak. Instead he *moved*, whipping a metal tube from his belt and whirling it towards the dazed man. It elongated from both ends as it swept through the air, its telescoped segments snapping free with a staccato burst of clicks. In the heartbeat it took to complete its arc it had become a staff. It struck Voyle's helmet and threw him off balance. As he fell against the vehicle he saw the Seeker twirl the weapon back then thrust it forward – into the visor of the giant that had climbed up behind Voyle while the Voice held sway. The blunt tip shattered the mutant's cyclopean lens and drove through to whatever lay below.

'Mont'ka!' the Seeker shouted and the behemoth shuddered as the staff's blades sprang free inside its skull. Kyuhai twisted the weapon then wrenched it free, tearing away the creature's visor, along with most of its face. As the giant toppled backwards Voyle glimpsed a protean morass of tendrils and broken bones inside its helm. Kyuhai leapt back into cover as the watchmen answered their champion's death with a salvo of bullets.

'Your actions have invited great danger, gue'vesa'ui,' he said to Voyle.

'Yes, Seeker,' Voyle answered, lowering his head. 'I–'

'Later.' Kyuhai whirled his staff and it contracted back into a tube. 'We must go.'

'Support team, your status?' Akuryo transmitted as they retreated down the mound with Voyle bringing up the rear.

The truck is clear,' Erzul replied. *'Do you need us, shas'el?'*

'Negative. We are en route to you now.'

The Voice almost had me, Voyle thought as he followed the two xenos.

'Child, you must–'

'No!' Voyle hissed, biting his lip until he drew blood. 'Get out… of my head.' But now that it had tasted his soul he knew it never would.

* * *

– THE INVISIBLE CIRCLE –
UNITY

Shas'vre Bhoral triggered the jetpack of her Crisis battlesuit and launched herself into the air, arcing high above the spaceport. Ensconced within the control cocoon of the hulking machine, protected by multiple layers of angular nanocrystal armour, she felt invulnerable. It had been many years since her duties had called upon her to wear the battlesuit in combat, but the old discipline had returned the instant she'd activated the machine and its sensors had interfaced with her nervous system, transforming her into a towering bipedal tank.

It has been too long, she thought fiercely.

As she neared the city's dome she cut her thrusters and plunged back towards the spaceport, confident in her armour's durability. She came down hard, pulverising an enemy warrior under her massive piston-like legs and sending tremors through the ground. Triggering the flamethrower attached to her suit's right arm she spun at the waist, washing the dead guard's comrades in a whooshing arc of fire. Their robes were scorched away in seconds, revealing the misshapen forms beneath.

These are not common gue'la, Bhoral judged as one of the burning figures flailed at her with a scythe-like claw. *A mutant strain perhaps?*

She stomped over their charred corpses and fired a fusillade of plasma bolts with her secondary weapon, targeting the guards on the far side of the roof. A squadron of gun drones swept by overhead, their path guided by her battlesuit's tactical system. The ship had carried eighty of the saucer-like machines and Bhoral had activated them all when she had received the Seeker's signal.

Mal'caor.

The word meant 'spider', but the *code* signified 'a-great-peril-awakened'. The protocol for the situation was clear: ensure the ship's safety at all costs. Accordingly Bhoral had launched a surprise attack on the port's guards immediately, but they had reacted with uncanny swiftness and a total lack of fear.

'They fight like machines,' Bhoral observed as a pair of three-armed deviants broke cover and charged towards her. One sported a muscular tentacle, the other a chitinous appendage that ended in a snapping pincer. They were bigger and better armoured than the others she had encountered, their heads protected by sealed helmets bearing ribbed crests.

'For… Greatest… Good!' they hissed, their words slurring as if their mouths weren't shaped for speech.

Before Bhoral could fire, a lanky avian figure sprang past her and raced to meet the mutants with a hooting cry. The Fire Warrior clicked her tongue with irritation as she recognised the kroot carnivore, though she had no idea *which* of the two it was. She had fought alongside the pair in service to the exalted Kyuhai for many years, yet she still couldn't tell them apart.

'The Yasu'caor forges strange bonds,' the Seeker had instructed when she had joined his circle, *'but it is their very strangeness that makes them strong.'*

Bhoral's suit chimed a warning as something landed on its blocky shoulders. A moment later the second kroot vaulted from its perch to join the fray. The carnivores whirled about the mutants in a feral dance – hacking, stabbing and feinting with their broad-bladed machetes then leaping away, always one step ahead of the ungainly mutants. Bhoral did not doubt the outcome of the contest, but her allies' *frivolity* irked her.

'The Seeker has taught you well,' she observed, 'but you remain beasts.'

She felt a twinge of pain as an explosive slug dented her battlesuit's left arm. It was a sympathetic sensation generated by the suit's cocoon, sharp enough to bind her to the machine, but not enough to distract her. Her sensors pinpointed the aggressor in moments – a sniper crouched in a tower to her left. An evaluation of the enemy's capabilities flashed across her awareness, relayed by her battlesuit's tactical system. The threat was minimal so she dispatched a pair of drones to eradicate it and continued her advance, leaving the frenzied kroot to their game.

The last of the guards had taken cover behind a cluster of machinery. Drones buzzed about them, kept at bay by the defenders' disciplined volleys. Bhoral strode towards their position, pinning them down with a hail of plasma bolts as she approached. When she was in range she scoured their shelter with fire.

'Disharmony portends dissolution,' she decreed, quoting the *Yasu'caor* as her enemies burned. She rotated her battlesuit, scanning the rooftop. The fighting was over. Even the kroot had finished their foes, though they were still hacking away at the corpses, jabbering at one-another as they tried to make sense of their outlandish victims. The Seeker had forbidden them from eating the dead, but their fascination could not be completely curtailed.

'Forward perimeter is secure, shas'vre,' a voice reported on her transmission link – Hurrell, the leader of the first gue'vesa support team. Something was playing havoc with their communications systems and the signal was badly distorted.

'Confirmed, gue'vesa'ui,' Bhoral replied.

'I have three dead and three more wounded, shas'vre. Permission to evacuate them to the ship.'

'Denied. Remain at your post.'

'Baumann is in bad shape…'

'I will despatch a salvation team to your position.' Bhoral cut the link. The casualties were significant, but she didn't share the Stormlight's sentimentality towards the human auxiliaries. She was more concerned by the number of drones she'd lost; her strategic display recorded thirty-nine damaged or destroyed. When enemy reinforcements arrived the situation would rapidly become untenable.

She switched her transmitter to long range.

'Seeker?' Predictably she was met by the howling electronic whine that had flooded the channel shortly after the fighting commenced. Coming to a decision, Bhoral stomped back to the kroot. They looked up from their butchery as she loomed over them.

'Bad meat,' one of them grunted, holding up a glistening tentacle.

'*Eee-veel*,' its companion added sagely.

'Enter the city,' Bhoral commanded, speaking slowly. 'Find our master.'

The carnivores exchanged a glance then sprang up and sprinted away.

It is almost as if they already know where he is, Bhoral mused. And maybe they did. She had reluctantly accepted that the savages' bond with the Seeker was tighter – or perhaps *deeper* – than her own.

Her battlesuit's strategic display bleeped as another drone's signature went dark. She frowned as the rest of its squadron followed in rapid succession. Somewhere in the spaceport the enemy was still active. Bhoral checked the squadron's last known location and hissed through her teeth. *The hanger bay…*

* * *

The truck rumbled along the dark streets, its headlights boring a tunnel through the gloom. Voyle was driving, with Erzul beside him; if anyone could retrace their outbound journey it was the squad's pathfinder. The rest of the survivors were crouched in the back, their rifles levelled over the sides. The district was deserted, its citizen-slaves presumably banished to their hovels, but an expectant watchfulness pervaded the streets. Every one of the fugitives could sense it, t'au and human alike, but none as keenly as the Seeker.

The dissonance here runs deep, Kyuhai reflected, *yet I have learnt nothing. Voyle sprang the trap too soon.*

But was that really true? The threads of ambivalent fate had woven Ulver Voyle into this tangle. There was no reasoning behind it, for the firmament of reality was blind, but there was a *rhythm* to it. It was a Seeker's path to listen and learn then tune the composition to serve the Greater Good, conducting events by intuition alone. And Kyuhai's instincts had urged him to trust this broken gue'la. Perhaps Voyle had not sprung the trap too soon, but just in time.

'Seeker, a question…' the Fire Warrior crouched beside him began hesitantly.

'Speak your mind, Stormlight,' Kyuhai urged.

'You are quite certain that Por'el Adibh was dead?'

'I could not save her,' Kyuhai said. *I could not attempt it.*

He had seen Adibh fall into the fissure – had even stepped forward to help her – then stopped when he'd heard the soulless voice booming from the rift and understood what lay beneath the wrecked car. The risk had been too great.

'Her loss will not be without purpose,' he promised.

'As you say, Seeker.' But there was no conviction in Akuryo's voice.

Kyuhai could not share the Fire Warrior's sorrow. Like love, hate and the myriad other shades of emotion that elevated or degraded his kin, sadness was a conceit he had transcended. That was what it meant to be *yasu'aun*.

'The void within stands vigil against the void without,' Kyu-hai whispered to the lost city.

'Take the right,' Erzul instructed as the truck approached another junction.

She was always the best of us, Voyle thought, obeying. *She should have been our gue'vesa'ui. Maybe the others would still be alive then.*

'**You led them to ruin,**' the Voice agreed. '**Because you are lost.**'

It hadn't let up throughout the escape, cajoling one moment then threatening the next, but mostly just wearing him down. The worst part was that he *needed* it now.

'**As I need you, Ulver. As do your kindred in the Cog Eternal.**'

'Why did you shoot the watchman?' Voyle asked Erzul, trying to shut out his blessed tormentor. 'Back at the manufactory when I ordered it – why did you obey?'

'Because you are the gue'vesa'ui,' Erzul answered without hesitation.

'You trust me?'

'Should I not?'

'**Not at all.**'

'I'll warn you when to stop,' Voyle said seriously.

'Why *did* you order it?' Erzul asked.

'Because they're monsters.'

'**The Imperium damns everything but itself as a monster,**' the Voice observed.

'Sometimes that's true.'

'I don't understand,' Erzul said.

'Sometimes the monsters are real.'

'Then you are a monster too, Ulver Voyle.'

'I know it.' He spat, remembering the taste of rotten flesh. 'What are you?' He sensed he shouldn't encourage the entity, but he had to know.

'A traveller who became a god in service to a greater god. My children revere me as the Animus-Alpha.'

'Why can I hear you?'

'We share the same divine, star-spawned seed, though you are not of my blood. That is why you were invisible to me for so long.'

'Voyle,' Erzul said, eyeing him warily, 'you're not making any sense.'

'What do you want with me?' he pressed, ignoring her.

'I offer you freedom, Ulver. Your masters have deceived you.'

'That's a lie.'

'They are not liberators, but oppressors.'

'They... saved me.'

'They gelded you, body and soul. Have you felt any desire save obedience since they took you?'

'It's for the Greater Good,' Voyle muttered, remembering the endless mantras of self-sublimation and the contentment the tranquillity wafers had brought. 'Unity.'

'Slavery!' the Animus-Alpha corrected. And as Voyle recognised its truth, the invisible god slipped past his guard.

'Turn left!' Erzul snapped.

He turned right.

'Voyle! What are–' His left hand thrust out and grabbed her hair. Her instincts had always been razor sharp and she reacted quickly, snatching her combat knife free and swinging it towards him in the same motion. If he'd hesitated even a moment it might have been enough. But he didn't hesitate. Before the blade could connect he rammed her face into the dashboard.

No! Voyle tried to scream, but he no longer had a mouth. It belonged to the Voice now.

Bhoral's burst cannon vented smoke as it spewed plasma bolts at the four-armed abominations infesting the hanger bay. The creatures zigzagged between banks of machinery as they circled her, their sinuous forms hunched into an insect-like scuttle. Their bodies were sheathed in blue chitin that flared into spines at their joints and along the ridge of their bulbous skulls. In place of jaws their faces trailed thorn-tipped tentacles that whipped about as the creatures moved.

Drones skimmed around the beasts, chattering electronically as they harried them with bursts of plasma, but the machines were falling faster than their prey, their rigid minds confounded by their enemies' erratic movements. Bhoral hissed as another of the flying discs was yanked from the air and shredded. The beasts' claws were improbably strong. Even her battlesuit's armour wouldn't last long against a prolonged attack.

There are too many, Bhoral judged, immolating an abomination with a spurt of fire as it veered towards her. Her flamethrower's ammunition gauge chimed a warning. The weapon had already been running low when she'd entered the hanger and engaged the infiltrators. There had been seven when she'd arrived, but more had crawled from the ducts lining the walls, arriving faster than she could cull them. She had summoned all her forces, but they had turned up sporadically, never giving her the numbers to mount a concerted counterattack. Hurrell's gue'vesa team had been overwhelmed within seconds of their arrival. The drones had fared better because of their mobility, but less than twenty remained now and the chitinous onslaught hadn't faltered. The battle couldn't be won.

'Kor'vre Ubor'ka,' Bhoral transmitted to the ship's flight deck. 'Withdraw the *Whispering Hand* immediately. The Concordance must be alerted to this treachery.'

'*I cannot abandon the exalted one,*' the pilot protested.

'We must assume he is lost.' Bhoral abhorred the words, but Kyuhai had made her duty clear. 'The ship will be overrun if you delay. Authorisation cypher follows.' She sent the code as her cannon finally overheated and fell silent.

'*I understand, Shas'vre. Signal me when you are on board.*'

'That is not an option. Go!'

Bhoral kept the beasts at bay with brief bursts from her flamethrower as the docking clamps disengaged and released the slumbering ship. Before their echoes had faded the vessel's engines rumbled into life, sending tremors through the chamber.

'Come then,' Bhoral whispered as her flamethrower ran dry. The tentacled abominations surged forward, vaulting over one-another in their eagerness to reach her. She clubbed the first one aside with a clumsy swing of her cannon and rammed her flamethrower into the face of the next, shattering its skull. Then they were upon her, hissing as they raked at her armour. Within seconds her battlesuit's damage indicator was flashing red in countless places. She ignored it, knowing there was nothing more to be done. Chanting a mantra of certitude, she stood motionless. Waiting.

The hanger's massive external doors slid open behind her, unleashing a shriek of void-wracked air. A heartbeat later Bhoral was wrenched into the emptiness beyond, trailing a string of chitinous horrors. As she whirled about in the vacuum she glimpsed the departing glow of the *Whispering Hand*'s engines.

'The circle closes,' she said and overloaded her battlesuit's power core. For a brief moment she burned brighter than the engines.

I didn't warn Erzul, Voyle thought bitterly, remembering his promise to the pathfinder. He sat stiffly in his chair, his hands steering the truck of their own accord. He couldn't even turn his head to check if the woman slumped beside him was still breathing. His comrades hadn't seen the violence that had transpired in the cabin, nor could they know the treachery playing out now.

I've betrayed them all.

'No, you have saved them, Ulver. Along with yourself.' The voice was his, but the words were not.

You lied to me, Voyle accused, struggling to break free. *Where are you taking us?*

'You shall all be enlightened, but the Ethereal among you is of singular importance.'

The Seeker… How…?

'What you know, I now know, child.'

Shame washed over Voyle in a corrosive wave, scouring him of all the hopes and hates that had bedevilled him since his long fall began. Finally all that remained was a bleak yearning for nothingness.

'*It is your shadow to burn*,' the Stormlight had advised. '*Only you can light the fire.*'

Hesitantly at first, then with growing conviction, Voyle began to recite the nineteenth mantra of self-sublimation. *The-Winter-That-Rises-Within* focused on attaining a state of perfect stillness, conditioning its aspirants to slow their breathing and lock their muscles rigid as they purged their minds of desire. Voyle had always been drawn to its oblique words and the ephemeral oblivion they offered.

Emptiness unwound blinds the light that binds unseen.

He repeated the spiralling phrase over-and-over, speaking with his mind until his body listened… and *remembered*. Like creeping frost his grip on the wheel tightened then froze, locking the truck to its current path. From somewhere far away he heard his own voice calling to him, wheedling then reasoning then railing, becoming ever more strident as the road ahead curved yet the vehicle didn't follow.

None of it mattered. None of it was real.

But the deceiver was blind to such truths, and in its turmoil its control frayed. The lapse was brief, but it was enough for Voyle to stamp down on the accelerator.

Emptiness unwound…

With a roar the truck leapt forward, its frame rattling as its wheels left the road.

…blinds the light…

The usurper fled his mind as the building ahead rushed towards the windscreen.

…that binds unseen.

'Bloodtight,' Voyle sighed, closing his eyes.

Kyuhai hit the ground hard, but his armour absorbed the worst of the impact. He rolled with the fall and swept to his feet. For a moment he stood motionless, gazing inward to assess his body. There was some damage, but nothing significant. As in the recent crash, his armour and training had served him well, though he would not welcome a *third* such incident any time soon. He scanned the surrounding buildings but saw nobody. Up ahead the wrecked truck was still blazing, its death throes casting a red haze over the street.

'Your truth dies with you, Ulver Voyle,' Kyuhai said, then turned his attention to the living. Akuryo knelt nearby, wrestling with his helmet. Its dome was cracked and sparks flickered behind its shattered lenses. One of the gue'vesa lay further along the road, his neck twisted at a strange angle. None of the others had jumped from the speeding vehicle in time.

'How will we reach the ship?' Akuryo asked, finally tearing his helmet free.

'We cannot,' the Ethereal replied. 'It is too late. Either the ship is gone or it is in the enemy's hands now.'

'Then only vengeance remains to us,' the Fire Warrior said bitterly, throwing his ruined helmet aside.

'Vengeance is immaterial. No, we shall keep to the shadows and learn our enemy's truth.'

'To what purpose, Seeker?' Akuryo rose to his feet unsteadily. His scalp was scorched and bleeding.

'To destroy it.' Kyuhai sliced the air with his right hand, indicating *an-outcome-already-proven*. 'It must be done. Of this I am certain.'

'With respect... we are but two.'

'We will find others. I suspect this broken world harbours many secrets, shas'el.' Kyuhai allowed himself the ghost of a smile, though it passed unseen beneath his helm. 'And we are four.'

Akuryo swung round as a rangy avian figure dropped down beside him, landing in a feral crouch. A moment later a second one leapt from the roof behind to join it.

'For Greater Good!' the kroot carnivores growled together.

* * *

– THE SPIRAL –
OBLIVION

Por'el Adibh opened her eyes as the door of her chamber opened. A t'au stood in the doorway – a female of the Water caste like herself, but much younger and clad in the purple robes Adibh had come to loathe.

'So Fai'sahl was not the last of his embassy,' Adibh observed, rising from her chair.

'Eleven of us remain,' the newcomer replied. She shared the malignant vigour that Fai'sahl had projected, though her aura was less pronounced. 'I am Por'ui Beyaal. Por'vre Fai'sahl was my bonded mate.'

'His death was difficult,' Adibh said flatly.

'His death served the Greatest Good,' Beyaal said without a trace of sorrow. 'I trust your injuries have been attended to, por'el?'

'You know they have, traitor.' Several days had passed since the Order's minions had recovered her from the wrecked vehicle, along with the monstrous warrior that had seized her. Since then she had been confined to this room and her questions had gone unanswered. 'You are aware that your attack on my embassy will be construed as an act of war,' she challenged.

'*You* attacked *us*,' Beyaal demurred serenely. 'Without provocation.'

'I do not accept that, but I advise you to release me without delay.' Adibh softened her tone. 'Perhaps an accord may yet be reached.'

'That is our aspiration.' Beyaal extended her hands, palms upward. 'The Cog Eternal has embraced the Greatest Good. It has always sought an *alliance* with the T'au Empire.'

'Then release me.'

'As you wish.' Beyaal bowed her head. 'Please follow me, por'el.'

Adibh didn't move. 'You agree?' she asked doubtfully.

'The Animus-Alpha will address all your concerns,' Beyaal assured her.

'Who?'

'He is the First Architect of the Cog Eternal, but many of us have come to see him as a father. I believe you shall too.'

Adibh's eyes narrowed as she spotted something lurking in the passageway behind Beyaal.

'Your pardon, por'el,' Beyaal said, catching her glance. 'I wanted to introduce my son, Geb'rah.' She called over her shoulder. 'Enter, child! There is nothing to fear.'

A squat figure shambled in, its heavyset form swaddled in robes. Lovingly Beyaal pulled its hood back and smiled at her prisoner.

Adibh stared, aghast, struggling to make sense of the infant's face.

'He is but three *tau'cyr*,' Beyaal crooned, 'but children grow swiftly here.'

As the hybrid thing grinned at her through a veil of tendrils Adibh's composure finally unravelled and a dark thought flashed through her mind: *Perhaps the xenophobia of the gue'la is not a sickness, but a strength.*

THE PATH UNCLEAR

MIKE BROOKS

The dig had once been the site of a tenement block but was now a chewed-up mess of red dirt. Occasional broken-off stumps of pale pillars flecked with pearlescence had been revealed. Alyss thought they looked like giant ribs covered in drying blood.

'Xenos,' Aberfell Duscaris said, kicking one.

'Yes,' Alyss agreed.

Fell raised a greying eyebrow at her. 'And how would you know that, scholam girl?'

'I've been studying the inquisitor's texts,' Alyss told him archly. 'How do *you* know it's xenos?'

Fell snorted. 'I blew up something similar when campaigning with the Eighty-First Tarradis. Also, if it wasn't xenos, Jonas wouldn't have half-killed an astropath to contact us.' He jumped down into the main dig site, his bionic arm steadying the combi-bolter slung over his shoulder.

'Who is this Jonas, anyway?' Alyss asked, following him.

It galled her to ask the bluff ex-Guardsman so many questions, but she didn't want to pester the inquisitor, and the rest of her new companions had their own idiosyncrasies.

'Harral Jonas, archaeologist,' Fell replied. 'One of the boss' contacts. If he finds something interesting or concerning, then he brings it to her attention. Given how hard we pushed to get here, I'd say she thought he was on to something.'

Alyss followed Fell across the mud. People and servitors were working around the edges and directly in front of her was a large case apparently made of plasteel-bound crystal, across which two people were talking. The man on the left had to be Harral Jonas: unshaven, pale-skinned and sporting a battered hat of dark felt. Alyss had come to know the other well already.

Inquisitor Zaretta Ngiri was tall, graceful and ageless, her dark skin smooth and her hair an almost-pure white cut into a blunt fringe at the front. She favoured sober, dark suits and a high-collared jacket in a vaguely military cut. At her shoulder lurked the imposing, armoured presence of Davis of Rawl, the Crusader sworn to her unto death.

Jonas stopped in mid-sentence and turned towards them, then relaxed when he saw Fell. Ngiri beckoned them closer.

'Jonas, I'm sure you remember Fell. This is Alyssana Nero, whom I recently recruited from the schola progenium.'

'Mamzel,' Jonas greeted her, then turned back to Ngiri and gestured at the case. 'This is why I asked you to come.'

Ngiri nodded. 'Fell, Nero. Your first impressions, please?'

Fell looked down. 'It's an old sword. Not military, probably not mass produced at all, actually. Blade just under a metre, hand-and-a-half grip. Looks perfectly normal. I can't see a power source anywhere, or any manner of crystals for a witch to use it.' He glanced sideways at Alyss. 'No offence.'

'None taken,' she assured him.

Jonas blinked and looked at her again.

'Another psyker, inquisitor? Has something happened to Carmine?'

'No,' Ngiri replied with a faint smile. 'Carmine's excellent at employing brute psychic force, but Nero has a more... intuitive gift.'

'Would you like me to read the sword, milady?' Alyss asked.

'No,' Ngiri said firmly. 'Just your eyes for the moment.'

Alyss studied the sword, trying to look knowledgeable. In truth she could see nothing more than Fell had, but she didn't want to let the inquisitor down in front of her associate so she kept looking... and suddenly, there it was. Not the sword itself, but its surroundings.

'This is a stasis cabinet,' she said, looking up, and knew from Ngiri's nod that she'd got it right. 'I imagine you have it for fragile relics, but the sword doesn't look particularly fragile. Why is it in there?'

'An excellent question,' Ngiri said. 'Jonas?'

'As soon as we found it, the locals started claiming it was the Blade of Saint Aruba,' Jonas said, wiping his brow with his hat. 'She led the resistance against xenos slavers here in the thirty-third millennium. Sacrificed herself to kill their warchief, apparently. There might even be something to it, because then the dreams started coming.'

'Dreams?' Ngiri asked. 'What manner of dreams?'

'Can't say – never had one,' Jonas replied, 'but several of the crew did. They couldn't describe them properly but I couldn't get decent work out of them after that – they always seemed distracted, off staring at something. Unrest has increased massively since the sword was found. The governor threw a public holiday in the saint's honour to quell things, but it's not done much. Half the population appears to have been overcome by some sort of fervour. You've got factory workers downing tools and demanding to sign up for the Astra Militarum then getting ugly when they're told no. There's been mysterious deaths. Everyone seems to want to fight for the Emperor, and that's all well and good, but the timing of it made me nervous.'

'So you put the blade into stasis?' Ngiri asked.

'Yes, milady,' Jonas nodded. 'Things have quietened down somewhat since, although not to where they were. I can examine an artefact and try to work out which xenos race might have made it, and even hazard a guess as to why, but saintly relics are outside my field of expertise. I don't want to stand in the way of something holy, but I wanted to bring in someone with more knowledge.'

'And did you touch it yourself?'

Jonas barked a laugh. 'Throne, no! Everything gets lifted from the ground by servitors. You can't be too careful in xenos ruins.'

They'd just finished the dust-caked trudge back to the inquisitor's gun-cutter when Jekri approached from the other side of the small craft and threw something at Fell without a word of warning. Fell snatched it out of the air and glowered at the skitarii ranger.

'What's this?' he demanded, examining it. Alyss peered at it and saw a small box of delicately carved wood.

'A local juvenile presented this to me with the request that it be passed to you,' Jekri said. 'Specifically, "the big Guardsman with the metal arm". They said they had been paid by a tall, thin man to deliver it.'

Fell's eyes widened in alarm. 'And you just threw it at me?'

'Enginseer Lentzen has determined it is not dangerous,' Jekri said, with the momentary sideways tilt of its head that Alyss had come to associate with a shrug.

'Regardless, be more careful,' Ngiri cut in. She turned to look at Fell. 'Well?'

Fell flipped the box open and frowned, then emptied something small and shiny out onto his palm and dropped the box. Alyss caught sight of a thin chain and two rectangles of metal before Fell closed his fist, his jaw working in apparent anger.

'Ident-tags?' Alyss asked.

'These were Katzeed's,' Fell said, his voice low and dangerous. 'One of my squad from Abram's World. When the... when we killed the Manchewer.'

'*You* were part of that squad?' Alyss exclaimed. She'd heard of the heroism of the Astra Militarum kill team that assassinated the monstrous ork warboss who had devastated half a dozen Imperial worlds. She'd also heard that only one of them had survived. 'You never told me you were part of that!'

'The Emperor guided my arm,' Fell muttered. He shifted his bionic, possibly unconsciously. 'One of them, anyway. Besides, I had help.'

Ngiri pursed her lips thoughtfully. 'For these to resurface here and now... Are we being taunted?'

'There's something else,' Alyss said, picking the box up from where Fell had let it fall. She pulled out a scrap of paper and passed it to Ngiri. 'Milady? This looks to be a signature.'

Ngiri took the paper and nodded, turning it over in her hands. 'Indeed. There's nothing else on here. I wonder why it was included.'

'Someone wants us to go running around on a wild grox chase,' Fell growled.

'Then let us oblige them,' Ngiri said decisively.

Surprised, Alyss looked up at her mistress. 'Ma'am?'

'I know that look in your eye, Fell,' Ngiri said. 'You want to get to the root of this, and I can't say I blame you. However, I need to study the blade Jonas found and speak to Governor Steban. Take Alyss, Jekri and Hurzley and hunt this down. Just make sure to do it with your eyes open.'

Fell rolled his neck, producing an ugly cracking sound. 'Eyes open and guns loaded, as always.'

Alyss looked from one to the other. 'If whoever sent this means us harm then won't we be walking into a trap? Surely they'll be prepared for our response?'

'They may *predict* it,' Fell countered. 'They won't be *prepared* for it.'

The sun had set, but the eastern sky still held a rich glow. The tenement blocks of Verbaden City's central slums were stark silhouettes in the distance, and in sharp contrast to Alyss' surroundings. Grand Triumph Way was a wide boulevard lined with ancient trees, gene-spliced to always be in flower. The manses here belonged to Verbaden's wealthy, each one set back from the street and surrounded by gardens. To Alyss, still adjusting to her new life outside the austerity of the schola progenium, it seemed ridiculously extravagant.

'You can almost taste the money,' drawled Alfrett Hurzley, dropping down from the flatbed at the rear of their ground-car. He gave a short whistle and his cyber-mastiff Razorfang joined him with a whirr of servos. The Adeptus Arbites officer had been with Ngiri since she'd recruited him in the aftermath of a xenos incursion on a mining planet some three years previously.

'You're sure this is the right place?' Fell demanded of Sef

Lentzen, who was acting as driver. The diminutive enginseer muttered a binaric swear word.

'Owner is listed as Phinius Speltmann of the local Merchant's Guild,' Lentzen said. One of his mechadendrites reached out of the cab window, proffering a data-slate displaying a hololith of a narrow-cheeked, pale-skinned man. 'Handwriting analysis confirms ninety-four-point-five per cent probability that is the name signed on the paper, which is of the specific type used locally for important documents such as large trade deals. Furthermore, examination of public records shows Speltmann's name is linked with the consortium that funded the dig, albeit somewhat indirectly. That is, however, in accordance with his reputation as a wealthy recluse–'

'A "yes" would have done,' Fell grunted, slotting a magazine into his combi-bolter. It was a brutal weapon with a flamer attachment, and only his bionic arm allowed him to fire it without dislocating his shoulder.

'"Yes" would have been inaccurate–'

'Jekri, are you in position?' Fell voxed, cutting Lentzen off.

'*Affirmative.*'

'Then we're moving in.'

The manse's gates were a black lattice of plasteel three times the height of a human and secured by a heavy, automated bolt. Fell clamped a melta-charge to the main lock and stood back.

'One question occurs,' Alyss said to him.

'Which is?'

'Why would a merchant guilder tear up a trade deal document just to provide their own signature?'

'Very good, Nero,' Fell replied with a slight smile. 'Let's find out, shall we?'

The melta-charge fired with a *whoomph*, instantly reducing

the centre of the gate to slag. Lentzen sent their sturdy groundcar forwards, striking the gates and throwing them wide open, then revved the engines and withdrew again. Fell sprang through the gap and sprinted up the gravel drive past beds of turquoise rock-roses and under the trailing tendrils of the local trees, which looked to Alyss like giant cephalopods. Hurzley followed, shotgun clamped under his arm and Razorfang loping at his side, while Alyss brought up the rear with her finger hovering near the trigger of her laspistol.

They were barely halfway to the manse when Alyss stumbled, momentarily overcome by a flash behind her eyes and a familiar surge of nausea.

'Gun!' she yelled, a moment before an alarm began trilling and an automated cannon rose up out of the undergrowth ahead of them. Alyss recognised it as a heavy stubber variant just as its automated targeting sensors focused on the closest threat and opened fire.

Her warning had potentially saved all their lives. Fell dived sideways into an evasive roll while Hurzley's sharp whistle sent the cyber-mastiff bounding forwards. The security gun's barrel locked onto Razorfang, its shots kicking up gravel as it tried to track the fast-moving patrol dog. The moment of distraction was all Fell needed: his combi-bolter roared once and the explosive shell slammed into the ammunition hopper. The resulting explosion blew the stubber apart and sent pieces of metal spattering into the surrounding foliage with a noise like a short but extremely violent rain shower.

'Nice shot,' Hurzley commented.

'Nice spot,' Fell said, acknowledging Alyss. He was already back on his feet and pressing on towards the manse, weapon held at the ready. Alyss hurried after him and after a few more seconds, they were standing in front of the imposing, three-storey home of Phinius Speltmann. It was clad in the dark, local stone with a front door that looked to be made of wood.

'Door?' Fell asked Hurzley.

'Two blisters in the archway,' Hurzley replied, checking his auspex. 'Probably anti-personnel mines.'

'Windows?'

'Look clear.'

Fell shrugged. 'Window it is.'

The bolt shell smashed the crystalflex into razor-edged splinters. Fell used his metal hand to punch more of it inwards, then vaulted through with Hurzley and Alyss on his heels.

They were in a dining room containing a long oval table surrounded by richly upholstered chairs. The ponderous tread coming from the hallway, however, did not sound like a dinner guest. The door slammed open to reveal a heavyset humanoid figure, a large-bore shotgun clutched in one hand and the other replaced by a whirling chainblade.

'Imperial Inquisition!' Fell snapped at the combat servitor.

For answer, the servitor raised its weapon and fired.

It was too slow – Fell hadn't assumed his words would hold it and had already brought his weapon up. His snap shot pulped the construct's right shoulder instead of its head, but the impact caused the shotgun shell to blow a large chunk out of the ceiling rather than his chest.

'Down!' Hurzley yelled. Fell hit the floor and Razorfang pounced, latching metal jaws onto the servitor's forearm and yanking it aside, causing the next shot to discharge into the floor. The servitor raised its chainblade but Hurzley's own shotgun shell shattered the weapon, scattering rending teeth everywhere.

'There's another!' Alyss shouted as a second appeared. She threw herself down behind the table and a blast thundered into the wall where she'd just been standing, blowing a hole as wide around as her waist and showering her with plaster. She saw the servitor's feet change position as it turned towards Fell and Hurzley so she sprang back up, levelled her laspistol and pulled the trigger.

The combat servitor had fired first, its shot booming out and catching Hurzley in the chest, blowing the ex-Arbites backwards off his feet. A moment later Alyss' shot burned its way clean through the construct's skull and it staggered sideways, but to her horror it remained standing and turned to target her again.

Fell's return shot obliterated its head. Even a combat servitor's heavily altered processes still required some form of working brain to function, and the construct toppled to the floor in an abruptly motionless heap. Alyss shifted her aim towards the first threat only to see the cyber-mastiff finish ripping its shotgun arm off in a spray of blood and coolant before Hurzley, firing from his prone position on the floor, blew a hole right through its chest. The servitor crashed backwards through a sideboard and didn't move again.

'You alright?' Fell asked, looking back at Hurzley.

'Winded,' the other man grunted, peering down at the now-dented armaplas of his chest-plate. 'Alyss?'

'Fine,' she answered, calming her breathing again. She eyed Fell's combi-bolter with some envy. Unsubtle though the weapon undoubtedly was, there was something to be said for its sheer brute force.

'Jekri, any rats bolting?' Fell voxed, stepping over the bodies and easing out into the hallway, weapon at the ready.

'*Negative,*' the skitarii ranger replied. They were covering the rear of the property, and had Alyss been a betting woman, she would have wagered that Jekri's arc rifle would end any attempted flight. Fell jerked his head to give the all-clear and Alyss followed him out of the dining room.

'"Wealthy recluse",' Fell quoted grimly. 'Let's see what he's got to hide.'

The manse seemed deserted, right up to the second floor. Alyss opened doors onto a study, a personal gymnasium and a sitting room with shelves of ancient-looking books of real paper and decanters of amasec without finding anyone, alive or dead. She could, however, detect a distasteful scent.

'I smell corruption,' she said. It was faint but it was there, rank yet sickly sweet.

'Razor has something, too,' Hurzley confirmed, checking the readouts from the cyber-mastiff's olfactory sensors.

Fell grunted an acknowledgement. 'One more door on this floor. Let's see if it provides any answers.'

The door in question was the largest and most ornate yet: a monument of dark wood carved into an exquisite representation of Holy Terra and its system, down to the last moonlet and planetary ring. It was securely locked.

Fell blew it in without a pause.

The wood splintered and he burst through the remains, his combi-bolter tracking in a cover pattern. Alyss followed and found herself in a large, airy bedchamber with decorative support beams and wide windows overlooking the grounds, a bed easily large enough for four full-grown adults, and the more pressing issue of a body lying face-down on sheets soaked red. Alyss turned its head to one side and immediately recognised Phinius Speltmann from the hololith, his cheeks even more sunken in person.

'Dead,' she said, checking his pulse. She rolled the merchant onto his back and the arms flopped like the limbs of some gelatinous deep-water creature. 'No rigor mortis. Time of death would be six hours ago at most.'

'Stabbed?' Hurzley asked, pointing to the front of the man's blood-stained shirt. Alyss tore the fabric aside to reveal a small puncture wound in Speltmann's gut.

'A gut wound like that wouldn't kill him for hours, maybe days.' She peered closely at it. 'A basic medi-kit could have patched him up, there's no way a rich man in his own home should die from this.' She frowned. Hadn't Jonas mentioned mysterious killings?

'Here's the source of the signature,' Fell said from the other side of the room where he was studying a wall housing many framed pieces of paper. The glass protecting one had been smashed and the bottom of the paper torn away. 'They look to be contracts, a wall commemorating his great business successes.' Fell spat and kicked the leg of a chair. 'Why send a message to me, a message with *personal significance* to me, just to… to taunt us about the murder of a trader I don't know?'

'They moved fast,' Alyss commented, frowning. 'To get that paper to us so soon after killing this man…' She paused. Something wasn't adding up, and after a moment realisation dawned. Speltmann hadn't been dead for long enough to be the source of the corruption she and Razorfang had smelled.

Or at least, not through his death.

She tore the trader's shirt back further and grimaced. The skin around his shoulders was reddened and bore weeping pustules.

'Could be a skin condition,' Hurzley commented, although he didn't sound convinced. Alyss rolled the body back onto its front and pulled the shirt down to reveal Speltmann's back.

'Still think it's a skin condition?' she asked, swallowing back the taste of bile in her mouth. The sores here were larger and angrier-looking, and the most prominent formed a disturbing pattern across his shoulder blades.

'Emperor's grace,' Hurzley growled, making the sign of the aquila. Alyss realised that what she'd thought was a smell was at least in part the psychic spoor of Speltmann's corruption, although now she was this close to the body, the rotting flesh around his sores certainly had its own disgusting odour.

'Huh,' Fell grunted. He'd crossed the luxuriously carpeted floor to stand at Alyss' shoulder and was now looking down at Speltmann's body. 'Oh, that's not good news. That changes the game.'

'It does?' Alyss asked, looking up at him.

'I don't think we were being taunted at all,' Fell said, scanning the room again as though expecting an unpleasant surprise at any moment. 'I think we were being warned.'

'Warned of what? This wretch?' Alyss said, releasing Speltmann's shirt and wiping her hands on her fatigues.

'There's never just one, that's the problem.' Fell pointed at a small, dark tattoo of unpleasantly flowing lines at the base of Speltmann's spine. 'I'm not Karamazov, but that looks like a cult symbol to me.'

'So we've got a dead, rich cultist killed by a wound that shouldn't have been fatal, in his own bedroom that was locked from the inside and protected by security we had to destroy just to get here,' Hurzley said flatly. 'That shouldn't be possible.'

'He could have known the killer,' Fell said, 'but that wouldn't explain the locked door.' He looked thoughtfully over his shoulder at the balcony. 'The window's a potential way in and out.'

'You'd need a grapnel,' Hurzley commented. 'Or a jump pack. It wouldn't be subtle.'

'We should report in,' Alyss said, reaching for her comm-bead.

'We search the place first,' Fell corrected her, slinging his combi-bolter behind his back. 'Let's find out *what* we're reporting.'

It took half an hour before the cyber-mastiff detected a strong scent coming from what proved to be a hidden door in the wine cellar. The passage behind it sloped steeply downwards and was roughly hewn, clearly not the work of Imperial engineers.

'Nero?' Fell asked, shining his luminator into the tunnel. 'You've got almost as good a nose as the dog.'

Alyss grimaced as she got a whiff of effluent. 'I'd say it leads to the sewers.'

'And if Speltmann had a secret passage to the sewers, that suggests there's something down there we need to see.'

Fell called up a schematic of the system to his data-slate and activated his comm. 'Jekri, Sef. Speltmann's dead and a heretic. Killer unknown. Get back to the inquisitor and warn her that we've got suspected cult activity. We're following a lead and going underground.'

The stench in the sewer was overwhelming, even behind a respirator, and the only light was from their luminators. Filthy moisture dripped from the arched ceiling and oozed from walls, and the narrow service paths bordering the main channel were slippery and treacherous. All in all, it was one of the most unpleasant places Alyss had ever set foot in.

'You're sure it can't smell anything?' Fell asked Hurzley again, staring disapprovingly at his cyber-mastiff.

'It can smell *everything*, that's the problem,' Hurzley replied testily. 'This is probably the highest concentration of biological odours on the planet. There's nothing it can scan for that isn't already surrounding us.'

'Wonderful,' Fell muttered, sweeping his combi-bolter around. The luminator affixed to it revealed nothing but dark, unmarked stonework. 'Any ideas?'

'Let me try,' Alyss said. She closed her eyes and concentrated as she'd been taught. One by one she blocked out the sensations of the clothes on her skin, the faint liquid sounds of the sewer and, finally, the stench of the place. Thus centred she began to push her mind outwards, searching. Fell and Hurzley were two sparks of intellect, tangible mainly through familiarity; Razorfang was an odd, subdued glow where the remaining hunter's instincts still registered faintly. She ignored them and searched further, trying to look everywhere at once but not focus anywhere in case she missed something...

There. A whiff of corruption. *Now* she focused, trying to get a fix on it. This wasn't a physical smell creeping in through her concentration, she was sure of it. This was something different, a sense of wrongness that her mind was interpreting in a familiar way.

She raised an arm, not certain of where she was pointing but knowing it was correct. 'That way.'

Fell didn't ask her if she was sure. When she opened her eyes he was studying the schematics. 'Can you hold the connection while we move?' he asked, his voice buzzing oddly in her head.

Alyss wobbled a nod. Her head felt loose on her neck. 'I think so. It affects my other senses, though, including my balance.'

'Make sure she doesn't slip,' Fell told Hurzley. 'All right, let's see what else is down here.'

* * *

The access hatch to the purification centre didn't open when Fell slapped the activation rune. 'The hydraulic cables must have been cut from the inside,' he growled. 'Someone doesn't want anyone official getting in here.'

Hurzley peered doubtfully at the hatch. 'We could shoot through it, but we'd probably kill ourselves with the ricochets.'

Fell was already pulling another melta-charge out of his tactical webbing. 'A good thing we don't have to, then.' He clamped it to the hatch and set the timer with a practised flick of his fingers. 'Stand back.'

Alyss closed her eyes, but the actinic flash seemed to burn through her eyelids. When she opened them again there was a large hole in the middle of the hatch, the edges now glowing cherry-red, and dim light spilling out from beyond.

Razorfang bounded through first, spurred on by Hurzley's whistle. Fell followed with a diving roll that cleared the molten edges and brought him up to his feet in a firing position. Hurzley followed more slowly, encumbered by his carapace armour but simultaneously protected by it. Lacking the cyber-mastiff's agility, Fell's battle-honed reflexes or Hurzley's armour, Alyss clambered through carefully to avoid burning herself.

They were in an artificial cavern filled with towering silos and skeletal gantries, a place that Alyss guessed acted as some sort of recycling or processing facility for the city's sewage, though what the end product could have been was anybody's guess. It was unlikely to be checked on unless something went wrong, and had enough space between the tanks and on the walkways for a sizeable crowd to assemble and even to live, for a while.

Which appeared to be exactly what had happened.

'What in the Emperor's name...?' Hurzley said in horror,

staring up at glyphs daubed on the silos. Even from this distance Alyss could make out renditions of the eight-pointed star, as well as other, less familiar and far less wholesome symbols, and she felt anger surge within her that anyone had dared make such blasphemous marks in this place. She felt the pressure of it in her head, too – a crawling tide of low-level psychic filth that buzzed, hummed and threatened to eclipse everything else.

It would have killed her had Hurzley not abruptly pulled her behind him.

'Hostiles!' the ex-Arbites snapped as a shot spanged off the aquila on his shoulderpad. Alyss saw a figure on a gantry some distance away. Hurzley thumbed a switch on his shotgun to select an Executioner round, raised his weapon and pulled the trigger. A moment later the shell's tiny robot brain had found its mark and their assailant fell backwards with a scream.

He wasn't alone, however. From out between the support struts of the nearest silo lurched a ragged band of several dozen men and women wielding autopistols and crude clubs, screaming blasphemous war cries. Alyss fired at them but her shot flew wide, distracted as she was by the buzzing in her head.

Fell simply hurled a frag grenade into their midst.

The explosion flung them to the ground, clothing torn and flesh shredded. Fell walked towards them almost casually obliterating skulls with bolter shells as the heretics writhed and mewled in pain. Alyss watched in grim satisfaction as they died, but caught Fell's arm as he was about to the execute the last.

'We should question him,' she said urgently. 'Look around. I see filth, I see graffiti, I see discarded food wrappers...'

She paused, looking at a pile of fire-blackened bones several metres away that she strongly doubted had belonged to any animal, and felt nausea surge in her gut. 'There must have been more of them. Where did they go?'

'And why are these ones still here?' Hurzley put in.

'We've faced cultists before,' Fell remarked. 'These barely put up a fight. I think we've found the dregs.' He pulled his Inquisitorial rosette out and knelt down on the injured heretic's chest. 'Do you know what this means?'

Even in the grip of debilitating pain from his grenade wounds the man's face paled and his eyes widened in terror as he saw the symbol.

'No! No, please!'

'Where are the others?' Fell demanded. 'Why did you remain?'

The heretic's eyes darted desperately from side to side, but no help came. 'Too weak... Not worthy...'

'Not worthy of what?' Fell snapped. He brought his combi-bolter up into the man's view. 'I can give you a single shot to the head or I can pulverise your limbs and leave you to bleed out. *Where are the others?*'

Hurzley's vox crackled and he cursed under his breath as he listened. 'General alert. There has been a cultist uprising in the city. Even the governor's palace is under attack from a mob. I suppose that answers your question.'

Fell shook his head. 'It's a diversion.'

'How do you know?' Alyss asked, although she harboured the same suspicion.

'I'm no witch, but you don't survive war if you don't learn to follow your gut sometimes.' He got back to his feet and aimed his combi-bolter at the heretic's left knee. 'Last chance, scum. Where are the others? What are you not worthy of?'

Alyss had seen a man's will break before, but never as sharply as this. Whether through pain, fear, insufficient faith in his false gods, or a combination of all three, the heretic began weeping and his voice rose to a desperate shriek.

'The sword! The sword, the sword, *the sword!*'

Fell looked over his shoulder at Alyss. She nodded grimly – his words had the ring of truth.

'Damn,' Fell muttered. His bolter shell ended the heretic's existence in a moment and he activated his vox. 'Inquisitor! They're coming for the blade! Do you read?'

There was no answer except the crackling of static enforced by the metres of rockcrete above them. Fell swore and turned to Hurzley. 'What about the city's local channels?'

'We're locked out,' the ex-Arbites said. 'Transmission's been restricted to the military, and I don't have time to break in.'

Fell let out a wordless snarl of frustration. 'We need to get back to the dig site, as fast as possible.' He pulled out the data-slate and scanned the schematics, then pointed towards a hatch on the far side of the chamber. 'It shouldn't be too far. That way.'

This hatch was easily openable by hand from the inside, and Fell hauled it aside to let them through. Then they were back into the foetid darkness of the sewers, making the best pace they could across uneven footing and looking for the access ladder that would allow them to regain the surface.

'We're missing something,' Alyss said suddenly, realisation dawning now she wasn't concentrating on guiding them to the purification station or surrounded by its brain-fogging aura.

'Well?' Fell demanded, splashing through a noxious puddle.

'We still don't know who killed Speltmann, or how!' Alyss said urgently. 'We still don't know who sent those ident-tags, how they got them, or why they wanted us to go to Spelt-mann's manse!'

Fell grunted in apparent frustration. 'Is this really the time, Nero?'

'Yes!' More and more, Alyss was convinced that her point was vital. 'There's a third player here! Someone is manipulating us!'

'Someone's always manipulating us!' Fell snapped, stopping and rounding on Alyss so sharply that she nearly lost her footing. Behind her, Hurzley clattered to a stop as well and she heard the skittering of Razorfang's claws on wet brickwork. 'Welcome to the real world, Nero! If you serve the Inquisition as long as I have you'll learn that there's always another layer of shadows, there's always a hundred agendas that you don't even know about! All we can do is try to serve the Emperor to the best of our abilities, and right now that means–'

'You know,' Alyss said, shocked. Fell's bluster was a front; she sensed dishonesty coming off him like waves.

'What are you–'

'You know who's behind this,' she insisted, and saw his eyes narrow above his respirator. 'You know who the third player is!'

'Fell?' Hurzley asked from behind her. 'What's she talking about?'

'Throne-damned witches,' Fell muttered.

Alyss suddenly became very aware that the luminator allowing Fell to see her was strapped to the top of his combi-bolter, and her mouth went dry.

'*Fell?*' Hurzley demanded more forcefully. Razorfang's robotic growl began to rise.

The ex-Guardsman raised one hand in a placating gesture. 'Easy, Hurzley.'

'Easy, nothing,' Hurzley said, and racked his shotgun. 'If the girl's telling the truth then you're telling lies, and that means you're a threat. Out with it.'

Fell's eyes closed for a moment, then opened again, weary and resigned. 'I don't *know* who's behind it, and that's the truth. But I have a suspicion.'

'Well?' Hurzley said.

'Eldar. They're the only ones I can think of who might have been able to steal Katzeed's tags from her body.'

Alyss felt her eyebrows shoot upwards. 'Eldar? Why? How?'

Fell glared back at her with eyes like shards of knapped flint. 'Because unless I miss my guess, without them I would be dead and the Manchewer would have razed Abram's World to the bedrock.'

Alyss frowned, confused. 'They helped you slay the warboss?'

'No, Nero,' Fell said, shaking his head. '*They* slew the warboss.'

Alyss felt as if she'd been struck in the chest with a power maul. 'But you–'

'We'd underestimated the orks' numbers and strength,' Fell said coldly. 'They were monsters, Nero. My kill team was annihilated and I'd lost my arm, I was practically passed out from pain and blood loss and about to die when suddenly...' He shrugged. 'Suddenly the greenskins were fighting some-one else. I couldn't follow what was happening, I was barely conscious, but *something* wiped out the bastard's command. I never saw how they got there, how they left, or who they were. I managed to vox that the orks were now leaderless and our counter-charge got to me in time to save my life.'

'And you took the credit for it?' Alyss asked, aghast.

'That wasn't my idea!' Fell protested. 'I told the story truly to my commander, but what were we supposed to say? The sector needed to hear that we'd saved them so that's what they got told, and the general swore the few who knew the truth to secrecy.' His lip curled. 'And now I've broken that oath, to convince you that I'm no traitor while the inquisitor's in danger.'

Alyss frowned. 'Does the inquisitor know?'

'Of course the inquisitor knows!' Fell snorted. 'You think an Ordo Xenos inquisitor would be taken in by that story? Those events were what drew me to her attention. I told *her* the truth, of course. From my vague descriptions and her own knowledge, she surmised the eldar had intervened against the orks, although if she knows why, she never shared it.'

'And now they draw us into an ambush?' Hurzley said.

'Or sought to warn us,' Fell argued, waving an arm in the direction of the surface. 'They sent us after a nest of corruption, we were just too slow. If the xenos act against us then rest assured, I'll take a piece of them.'

Alyss nodded slowly. She was ashamed she'd thought Fell a traitor, but also angry that one of the great Imperial victories she'd been taught about was a lie. Yet she could see why the lie had been created.

She shunted her warring thoughts aside. There would be time enough to confront them later. Assuming she survived.

The access ladder brought them up through a maintenance hatch and into the utter mayhem that had engulfed Verbaden City. Light poles had been destroyed but flickering flames from vandalised buildings cast shifting shadows, and robed and masked figures flitted through them, whooping with grotesque mirth.

'This way,' Alyss said, getting her bearings. She activated her comm-bead. 'Inquisitor, do you read? What is your situation?'

'We're defending the dig site,' Ngiri replied after a second, to Alyss' immense relief. The inquisitor sounded tense but

calm, despite the shouts and gunfire in the background. *'The cultists appear focused on reaching the blade.'*

'We're coming,' Alyss said as the three of them and Razorfang sprinted down a street. 'We're only about a block away.' She cast a glance over her shoulder at Hurzley, who was labouring under the weight of his armour and dropping behind.

'Go on!' the ex-Arbites puffed as his cyber-mastiff fell back to match its master's pace. 'We'll get there as soon as we can!'

'Just you and me for now, then,' Fell said grimly, and lengthened his stride. Alyss accelerated to keep up, and together they pelted past blank-faced windows and piles of refuse until they reached the gaping hole in the city that marked the location of the dig site. Alyss could see robed figures swarming into a depression in the ground a hundred metres or so away, but the earth between her and them was criss-crossed with dig trenches too wide to simply jump across.

'I thought I was done with trench fighting,' Fell grunted, unslinging his combi-bolter and dropping down into the nearest. 'Come on, Nero!'

Alyss followed him, listening to the shouts, screams and gunshots on the air and trusting that Fell's military instincts would guide them along the right path. He barely slowed when they came upon cultists, gunning them down from behind before the heretics even realised they were there, and so when he skidded to a halt in the red mud, Alyss collided with his broad back.

'By the Emperor...'

Alyss got a momentary impression of a monstrous figure filling the trench in front of them before Fell's combi-bolter spat a burning cloud of promethium. The weapon bathed the apparition in liquid fire for one, two, three seconds...

...and then it came screaming through and swatted Fell so

hard he flew backwards, the combi-bolter sailing out of his grip and clean out of the trench.

Alyss had seen an Adeptus Astartes once – this thing was bigger. She thought for a moment that it was some sort of ogryn before she caught sight of its face and realised with horror that the creature was a mutated human, swollen beyond all biological norms into a raging block of muscle. Its teeth had been replaced with triangular metal blades, so sharp Alyss could see specks of blood on its lips from where it had cut itself, and it reached for her with huge hands tipped with bone-white talons. Alyss raised her laspistol and fired on full-auto, but the barrage of shots had no appreciable effect other than eliciting a roar of rage and setting a rune flashing, warning her that her power pack was nearly expended. The mutant moved with shocking speed for something so huge, and she only just managed to duck a swipe that would have taken her head off. She back-pedalled desperately, nearly tripping over Fell's groaning form.

'Down!'

Alyss threw herself into the mud as a shotgun blast took the thing in the shoulder, drawing a gout of black ichor, and Razorfang flew at it. The cyber-mastiff struck the mutant in the chest, steel jaws snapping, as Alfrett Hurzley stormed past Alyss, still unloading shotgun shells.

The mutant grabbed the cyber-mastiff and wrenched its head clean off, then snatched Hurzley up and dashed him down back-first across one monstrous knee with a sickening cracking noise. The ex-Arbites' body flopped bonelessly as it was cast aside. Alyss raised her useless laspistol again and commended her soul to the Emperor.

Something flickered into view overhead, roughly human-sized but leaping with a thoroughly inhuman agility and grace. Its outline was oddly blurred and its appearance distracted Alyss for what would have been a fatal second, had the new arrival not landed on the mutant's back and plunged a thin tube attached to its forearm into the creature's neck.

The mutant thrashed wildly for a moment, then landed at Alyss' feet with a crash and didn't move again. Its assailant hopped nimbly off, the apparently disparate pieces of its form rushing together into a cohesive whole.

Tall. Lithe. Clad in shifting diamonds of colour, its face hidden by a distorted, grinning mask. An alien-looking pistol in one hand and the other empty save for the strange device strapped to the back of its forearm, bulbous at one end and thinning to a point where it extended out over the wrist.

An eldar.

It looked at Alyss and she met its eyes for a second, mere gleams in the shadows but still deep and unreadable. Then its mask tilted towards her in an apparent nod of acknowledgement before it turned and launched itself into the air with a keening war cry.

'After it!' Fell gasped, staggering up to his feet, bleeding from claw wounds and his flak vest shredded. Alyss cast a momentary glance at her fallen comrade, then turned away. The living needed her now.

Robed corpses littered the trench floor in ones and twos, ripped apart by the alien's exotic weapon or simply dead, although Alyss guessed that if she inspected those bodies she'd find a small puncture wound such as that in Phinius Speltmann's gut, or the back of the huge mutant's neck. Certainly, the xenos seemed no friend to the Ruinous Powers.

When they got to the main dig site, Alyss fervently wished that a few more had joined it.

There were cultists everywhere, surging forward to assault

an improvised barricade of packing crates and power load-
ers. Alyss saw the incandescent discharge of Ngiri's plasma
pistol, heard the crack of Jekri's arc-rifle, and felt the psychic
blow that swept half a dozen attackers off their feet and into
the mud wall. Carmine must have been tiring, though, as
three picked themselves back up almost immediately. Even as
she watched, howling deviants hauled Sef Lentzen out from
behind the barricade and set about clubbing him to death.
The rest would be overwhelmed in moments.

'My power pack's nearly out!' Alyss warned, dropping a
heretic with her laspistol. Fell pulled out two more frag grenades and hurled them into the mob, sending bodies flying,
but Alyss could tell it wasn't going to be enough.

'I've got one krak left!' Fell panted, weighing it in his hand.
'Can you see anyone who looks like their leader?'

Their intervention hadn't gone unnoticed. Cultists were
looking around to see where the grenades had come from,
and their gazes fixed on Alyss and Fell. It would reduce the
amount trying to breach the inquisitor's barricade all at once,
Alyss supposed. Perhaps their deaths would be of use.

Then the eldar reappeared.

It was a blurring shadow that darted, spun, whirled,
cavorted, and left death in its wake. Necks were snapped,
torsos were shredded by a lethal stream of projectiles from
its pistol and bodies fell spasming from the slightest kiss of
its bizarre forearm weapon. The cultists wavered as this new
threat cut through them, and for the first time, Alyss saw Davis
of Rawl's power sword slay a heretic trying to scale the barricade with no new attacker coming to replace them.

The horde turned in on itself, but to no avail. Autogun
shots punched through other heretics, clumsy blows smashed
a neighbour's ribcage instead of connecting with their target,

and in the middle, the eldar wove its dance of death. Alyss watched in awe as the cultists floundered, like a wheeling flock of avians blundering straight into the jaws of a predator in their midst. By the time they realised it was hopeless, it was too late. The last few scattered and tried to flee, but now Ngiri had advanced out from behind the barricade. Davis skewered one cultist, the inquisitor's own power sword claimed another, and Jekri shot down a third. One fled blindly straight towards Alyss; Fell simply punched the man in the face with his bionic arm so hard Alyss heard the cultist's neck break.

'Your assistance is appreciated,' Ngiri called to the eldar. The inquisitor had apparently had either the time or the foresight to don her customised suit of power armour and she looked largely unscathed save for a cut on her forehead.

The grinning mask turned towards her and the eldar spoke, its mellifluous voice flowing oddly around consonants. 'I tried to warn you. I tried to make you see for yourselves.'

'And we thank you,' Ngiri said, inclining her head. 'I wonder if–'

'You still lack comprehension,' the eldar said, cutting her off. 'Your stupidity is dangerous.'

It flowed across the ground between them and drove its forearm weapon at Ngiri's chest before anyone could react.

The inquisitor's power armour held, so instead of being pierced by the xenos weapon she was hurled backwards into the barricade by the force of the blow. Davis of Rawl lunged, power blade crackling, but he was plucked off his feet and hurled through the air to collide with Carmine, who had just started to raise his force rod in an attempt to bring the eldar down. Jekri's arc-rifle spat bolts of energy but the eldar flipped into the air, easily evading them. Alyss raised her laspistol but the fiend was simply too fast, too blurred to target.

At least with her eyes.

She closed them, forcing the calm to come, blocking out the shouts of alarm and pain from her comrades. Her pre-cognition, always a nebulous, unreliable ally, flickered just beyond her reach. She felt her physical body grit its teeth as she reached for it, forcing it to do her bidding.

There. The eldar's path seemed to slow, traced out through her brain in glowing lines. Nothing was certain, nothing was ever *certain*, but she could read where it was most likely to touch down next. She forced her muscles to move, felt them strain as they struggled to catch up with her racing mind.

'Fell!' she shouted, the words booming and echoing in her head. She pulled the trigger, felt the lasbolt leave the weapon, heard the buzz as the powercell died.

But her shot blew straight through the eldar's knee from behind as it landed, sending it sprawling.

Alyss opened her eyes and the world seemed to speed up again. Fell primed his krak grenade and threw it, faster and more accurately than anyone with an arm of flesh and blood. The eldar was already rising, but for once it wasn't quite quick enough. The grenade struck it and detonated, the potent explosive force concentrated in one place, and suddenly the eldar's left leg was nothing but a few ribbons of meat.

It collapsed, shrieking, but twisted around to aim its pis-tol at Fell. Then Davis of Rawl severed its hand with his power sword, raised his blade again and plunged it through the alien's spine. It spasmed and keened, yet somehow still clung to life.

'The sword!' the eldar spat desperately, its shaking mask turning towards Ngiri. 'Destroy the sword!'

'The sword?' Ngiri repeated. She wrenched a part of the

barricade aside and strode through it to where the stasis cabinet rested.

'*Destroy it!*'

'I'm not as stupid as you think,' the inquisitor snapped, giving the eldar a withering glance. 'I had doubts about this the moment I saw it.' She flicked a switch and the stasis generator powered down. Suddenly Alyss heard a song, a sickening crystal disharmony that pricked her thoughts but disappeared when she tried to concentrate on it. She shook her head, trying to clear it.

'Ma'am? The sword... That's no sacred blade.'

'Not sacred to the Emperor, anyway,' Ngiri replied, sliding the point of her power sword under the Blade of Saint Aruba and flicking it out. The blade landed in the red dirt. 'I wanted to see how events played out, however. Alyss, you're certain the xenos has the truth of it?'

The song was rising. Alyss nodded, trying not to retch. 'I am, milady.'

Ngiri raised her plasma pistol and fired repeatedly.

The ravening bolts of energy tore into the blade, melting and warping it, finally blasting it into nothing. The song was replaced with a howl that assaulted Alyss' mind, a bellow of fear and loss and thwarted rage that felt as if it would leave her brain bleeding. The dying eldar hissed in response, and as the cry faded as though it were falling into an abyss, Ngiri turned back to it.

'I've been wanting to talk to one of you ever since I learned of your intervention with the Manchewer.' She looked with distaste at the blood-slicked ground where the eldar's leg had been, at Davis' power blade that still transfixed its body, then down at the chip in her armour where she'd come so close to death. 'I fear the conversation may not now be a cordial one.'

The eldar laughed weakly. 'Death comes for me. Soon I shall be beyond your reach.'

Ngiri pursed her lips. 'I believe you. But even your corpse and possessions will have academic value.' She sheathed her power sword and gestured at Fell and Davis.

'Put it in the cabinet.'

The eldar thrashed its head, but could make no other movement as Davis and Fell dragged its limp body to the stasis cabinet, then hoisted it up and stuffed it inside. Xenos blood immediately began staining the clear sides as it continued to bleed to death from its grievous wounds. Alyss' ears could hear nothing but its laboured breathing, but she could sense the dying creature's mounting horror as a silent scream.

At least, until Fell closed the lid with a snap and Alyss was left with nothing but the stench of blood, and echoing silence in her mind.

SHADOWS OF HEAVEN

GAV THORPE

Aradryan looked at the bridge with distaste. A brutal span of partially corroded metal and pitted artificial stone substitute, erected by the humans in some distant era to cross the sluggish, oil-tainted waters of a broad river. A cold wind keened through the stanchions and spars. The vegetation around the crossing was near-dead, browned by the inclement season. In the shadows of the broken buildings that flanked both sides of the river, the remnants of night frost coated the ground.

The river snaked slowly between rolling plains, curving around steeper slopes on either side that rose from the undulating expanse. The highway the crossing served was little more than a path of broken paving that cut a darker line through the wilderness flanking the waterway. In many places it had been swallowed again by the grasses and bushes through which it had once mercilessly slashed.

It reminded Aradryan of the humans in so many ways. Transient, yet arrogant. Blindly resisting the elements rather than accommodating them. Stubborn but ultimately doomed to fade from existence and memory. Just as this latest alliance with the humans would fail in time. The galaxy had been sundered by warpcraft and battle, and there was a mutual need, greater than ever, that united the two races. That was all it was, an unspoken pact of survival, nothing more. The Imperium and the craftworlds were not friends. They would always be rivals even when they were not outright enemies. For now, he and the other Alaitocii who had travelled from the craftworld were aligned to the shared cause.

A short distance away, Diamedin sat in the pilot's cradle of a large support weapon. Like Aradryan she wore a golden-yellow helm with a short crest of deep blue. Her armour was the same azure, as was the floating anti-grav platform of the weapon she rode. The vibro-cannon itself was encased in curved plates of matching yellow, banded with tiger stripes of black. From within gleamed the energy cell's pale silver shimmer.

Aradryan and his companion were situated in the tumbled-down ruins of what might have been a toll station or perhaps a hostelry for travellers. It was impossible to tell the former function of the low building from the broken walls and scattered bricks. Twisted metal reinforcing rods jutted among the crawl of climbing plants, the bare stone-like floor patched with bright green lichen and criss-crossed with runners and tendrils from the questing vegetation.

Aspect Warriors and the larger war machines had already engaged the enemy over the preceding night, manoeuvring the foe into a killing position. The farseers had warned of a splinter force of warriors despatched by the enemy to break out over the river. They could not be allowed to cross lest the whole flank of the Alaitocii host was compromised. By standing in this place, alongside his fellow Guardians, he protected the lives of others.

So Aradryan told himself.

'They are heading your way.'

The voice of Arhathain sounded directly in Aradryan's ear. It came with a slight itch at the point between ear and jaw, caused by the microscopic messenger-wave implant that had been inserted there before the expeditionary force had left Alaitoc.

It felt strange, to hear the voice of the autarch yet sense nothing of his presence. In the slow turn of the latest arc of his life Aradryan had become reacquainted with the omnipresence of the infinity circuit aboard the craftworld. He had buried deep the memories of his wilder life as an Outcast, the remembrance of the time when he had been carefree but alone like a distant, half-heard echo. The ever-present sensation of the others on the Asuryani Path had been a backdrop of constant sound and movement in his thoughts.

So it was that he heard the words of Arhathain but caught nothing of the host commander's thoughts or feelings on the pronouncement. It was a cold fact sent to the Alaitocii contingent stationed by the dilapidated bridge, devoid of emotional substance.

Aradryan's thoughts were not totally isolated. Through the local spirit circuit of the vibro-cannon he could feel Diamedin. Though he could not see her face, Aradryan felt her reassuring smile through the interface of the weapon's spirit stone.

She glanced down at him from her perch.

'Worry not,' she said. 'No foe shall cross that bridge.'

His gaze moved to the rest of the small force that had been

positioned to contest the crossing. Two more vibro-cannons flanked him and Diamedin, the targeting web that connected them currently focused on a point at the far end of the span. Like the gunner beside him, the other crews made only the faintest impression on his awareness, conjoined by the inter-linked network of the battery, which was but a pale imitation of the infinity circuit of their home.

The half-felt distance put Aradryan in mind of the spirits of the departed when they were newly joined with the other souls of the craftworld. On the Path of Grieving he had dedicated himself to remembrance and commemoration of the dead. He was no spiritseer, but in his role as Mourner he spent much time among those who shepherded the spirits into the post-mortal existence of the infinity circuit. In that capacity he had felt the fleeting loss and uncertainty of a spirit released from its stone into the endless maze of the psychic circuit.

Outside the local circuit other support weapon batteries were arranged: two more vibro-cannons on the shallow slope of a hill to the right, and a trio of distort-cannons covered the river from the left. In the thick foliage along the river bank nestled two squads of Guardians, their exact location obscured by the concealing power of a warlock, Hanlaishin.

'If you are so concerned by danger, why did you answer the call to arms?' asked Diamedin, sensing Aradryan's unease as he scanned the horizon across the river and fidgeted with the shuriken catapult in his hands.

'I am no stranger to bloodshed,' Aradryan replied quietly. 'I am not afraid of death.'

'Then what is it that agitates you so?'

Aradryan thought not to answer. He owed her no explanation. Yet if he was to purge himself of his grief, if he was to connect with his people in a way he had not been able to do in living memory, he had to make the effort.

'Death used to frighten me. The thought of being swallowed by the infinity circuit, of losing who I was, terrified my younger self. It drove me to flee the craftworld, seeking sensation and a meaning for life, though I found myself lost in the former and discovered nothing of the latter. And death followed me still, all the way back to Alaitoc.'

He paused, stunned by his unplanned confessional. It felt good to unburden himself.

'And yet...?' prompted Diamedin.

'I took to the Path of Grieving, but even then I hid from life rather than death. I thought that perhaps battle might stir something of my old emotion.' He sighed. 'It scares me that I am *not* afraid to die...'

Any further chance to cast light upon the shadows in his soul was curtailed by a sudden heightening of tension across the Guardian force. Aradryan saw the cause at the same moment he felt it: a smudge of greyness past the ridge of a hill on the opposite side of the river.

Smoke from the exhausts of the renegade Space Marines' vehicles.

Crouched in the ruins, Aradryan watched the drifting smog with narrowed eyes and a knot in his gut. The detached thought of battle had not stirred him, but it was a different matter to see the approach of an enemy. His biology reacted even though his thoughts had not, sending a shiver of apprehension through him. It was almost welcome, to feel a tingle of dread when he had known so little that had moved him in recent times.

A small squad of jetbike-piloting windriders and a larger

Vyper speared over the hillside. Explosive projectiles tore past the rapidly approaching jetbikes from the foes they had lured towards the crossing. Jinking and weaving between the volleys, the pilots guided their craft directly towards the expanse of the river, the anti-grav engines of their vehicles negating any need for a bridge.

The enemy sped into view: a trio of lumbering troop carriers that churned the earth with broad tracks. Their top hatches were open so that the embarked warriors could fire their weapons at the evasive eldar that had drawn their wrath. The transports were blocky, dark machines that belched grey fume, engines snarling and tracks sliding as they negotiated the steep slope that led down to the remains of the roadway.

Aradryan found all human aesthetic to be crude and distasteful, but there was a deliberate brutality to the black paint and golden ornamentation of the renegades' vehicles. Barbed spears and gilded chains hung with skulls decorated the flanks of the transports. The stacks of the exhausts and muzzles of the mounted weapons were fashioned in the likenesses of bestial and daemonic faces.

Augmented by the magnifying lenses of his Guardian helm, his keen alien gaze picked out detail against the expanse of the hillside. From one of the troop carriers flew a broad, long banner of dark cloth marked by the eight-pointed star with an eye at its centre. They wore their slavery to the Dark Gods like a badge of honour, the eightfold Cross of the Lost emblazoned not only on the transports but also the shoulder pads of their powered armour. As with the vehicles, so too the occupants – armoured in black and gold, adorned with spikes and blades, chains and skull-headed rivets.

'Wait until they are committed to crossing the bridge,'

commanded Arhathain through the messenger-wave implant. *'We need those forces diverted.'*

With the jetbikes out of range, the renegade Space Marines ceased their firing. Their advance slowed as they neared the bridge. The jetbikes and Vyper circled back, swerving between the cables of the suspension bridge to unleash a long-range fusillade of shuriken cannon fire. The volley did little more than shred the paintwork of the transports, but its goading effect was near-instant. Engines roared. Fresh billows of oily smoke billowed and the transports thundered towards the bridge once more.

Aradryan swallowed. His mouth felt dry. He could feel the growing anticipation from Diamedin. A former Dire Avenger, she drew upon a war mask to shut off her thoughts, guarding herself against the lure of bloodshed and the fear of battle. It had the simultaneous effect of blanking her thoughts to the soul-circuit, leaving Aradryan feeling very much alone and impotent as he watched the three armoured behemoths clatter onto the bridge. He looked at the slab-sided war engines, and the shuriken catapult felt heavy in his grip, useless against such metal beasts. His fate was entirely entrusted to the accuracy and timing of the support weapon gunners.

While the windriders drew back, ready to spring forwards once the ambush was under way, the Vyper continued to harry the approaching vehicles. The sleek craft veered one way and then the other, like an insect darting over a pool. Its yellow-and-blue carapace glinted in the pale light of winter, reflecting the flash of bolts and the glint from the polluted waters gurgling between the steep river banks.

Nearly halfway across the span, the vehicles seemed larger than Aradryan remembered from the invasion of Alaitoc. He only dimly recalled the battles that had raged through the

domes of his craftworld, though the memory of the Emper-
or's Space Marines was far more distinct. Terrifying giants with
war engines that had killed hundreds of his fellow eldar. He
had brought that slaughter to his home and it had pushed
him onto the Path of Grieving. To consider such brutal power
married to the worship of the Dark Gods sent a fresh shiver of
anxiety coursing through his body. All instinct told him that
he should flee. Yet he refused, drawing on superior reason and
intellect to overcome his biology. He peered through a crack
in the masonry at the monstrous warriors. There was no possible way the Traitor Space Marines knew what awaited them.

His jaw itched again an instant before the voice of Hanlaishin sounded in his ear.

*'Do not engage them yet. Vibro-cannons target the rear vehi-
cle. Heavy weapons and distort-crews disable the lead transport.'*

Aradryan let go of the barrel of the shuriken catapult and
flexed his fingers, his discomfort mirrored back at him by the
tension of the other crews. The weapons were perfectly sited,
their presence masked by devices augmented by the powers
of the warlock and far more sophisticated than the technology of the renegades.

And yet the vehicles paused, a third of the way from the
near end of the bridge.

A squad of armoured brutes disembarked from the lead
transport and advanced on foot, the carriers following a score
of paces behind.

'Crone's curse!' exclaimed Hanlaishin, taken aback by the
enemy's action. *'We have no choice. Open fire, now. Destroy the
vehicles and then engage the foot troops.'*

The mobile heavy weapons of the concealed Guardian
Defenders fired first. The ruby pulse of a bright lance and
a shimmering plasma burst from a starcannon slashed into

the track guards of the closest transport. The starcannon shot burst ineffectually from the thick ceramic plates but the bright lance sliced through, splashing molten droplets. The wounded transport shed broken track links as it ground to a halt.

'Our turn,' said Diamedin, a flicker of anticipation leaking across the psychic link. Aradryan did not share her enthusiasm and swallowed hard.

The bulkier support weapons rose up from their hiding places under the guidance of their gunners. A few paces from Aradryan, Diamedin turned the vibro-cannon towards a break between two fallen walls. The ribbed muzzle of the sonic generator angled towards the black vehicles, the gleam of its powercells growing brighter.

A heartbeat later the distort-cannons burst into life.

A pair of dark vortices erupted around the front vehicle, swiftly expanding. Fronds of electrical discharge danced at the edge of the growing wounds in reality, flashing across the armoured hide of the troop carrier. The air twisted with agitated molecules, dragged into the warp rifts opened by the distort-cannons. Aradryan watched in awe while rivets popped and armoured plates distended as the rippling boundary between the material and immaterial expanded from the detonation. Track housings buckled, tearing free maintenance hatches and ripping road wheels from the flanks of the transport.

'They shall suffer Khaine's fury!' Diamedin was excited now, gripped by war-fever left over from her Aspect Warrior past.

A sudden hum from the vibro-cannons escalated into a wailing screech. Aradryan followed the burst of sonic energy from Diamedin's weapon as it tore a furrow along the ground like an invisible plough, scattering Traitor Space

Marines as they disembarked. The beam thrummed through the lead vehicle, rocking the transport on its suspension, scattering flecks of paint and a cloud of dislodged dirt.

The sonic discharges of all five vibro-cannons came together at a point somewhere inside the second vehicle. Conflicting frequencies created an explosive resonance that literally shook the vehicle apart. Weak seams shattered and contorted splinters of metal flew in all directions. Dark flame gouted in odd spirals from the ruptured engine block while the occupants were thrown about like chaff in a tornado, slammed against the stanchions of the bridge and dragged violently across the cracked roadway.

A mixture of surprise and relief erupted from Aradryan as a short laugh. Ahead, from the riverbank, the Guardian Defenders erupted from their cover. The hiss of their shuriken catapults and cannons mingled with that of the returning Vyper and windriders, nearly lost among the clatter of falling debris and the crashing tread of the charging renegades.

A hail of mono-molecular discs slashed into the power-armoured warriors, striking sparks from the ceramic plates, leaving scars across the black paint and gilded decoration. Here and there one of the augmented humans fell or reeled back, an eye-lens shattered or a weaker seal in his war-plate ruptured by the stream of projectiles. Aradryan raised his own weapon but the enemy were not yet in range.

Into the teeth of the assault came the renegades, uncaring of the danger. Their bolters spat fire-trailing rounds, stitching small detonations across the walls and rocks that had concealed the ambushers.

Aradryan saw the muzzle of a boltgun turned in his direction. Propellant flickered in the chamber within as he threw himself flat.

Explosions tore at the wall where he had been crouched, turning bricks to shards and dust, the thunder of the detonations painful even through the dampening effect of his helm. Aradryan felt a stab of pain from Diamedin half a heartbeat before he heard the bolt impact and her cry.

He looked up in horror, just in time to see her chest-plate spraying shards, the mesh beneath a fountain of glittering scales mingled with droplets of bright blood. Armour lit by the deadly blossom of yellow and white in her chest, edged with dark fragments of shattered breast-plate, Diamedin was hurled out of the gunnery couch.

As he pushed himself harder into the cover of the wall, Aradryan's gaze locked on to the unmoving remains of his companion. Among the fleshy ruin of her torso glittered a bluish gem – her waystone, now imbued with spirit energy. Its ghost-flicker entranced him, like so many other spirits whose internment into the infinity circuit he had attended. His own waystone was a cold dagger of ice in his heart. So long ago he had looked upon bodies returning from battle and the fear had been raised in him. It had driven him to flee into indulgence, and set him upon the course of terrible events that had eventually brought him here. And now Aradryan drifted alone, mesmerised by the mangled remains dappled in spirit light. Diamedin's quietus severed what little contact there had been.

Another burst of enemy fire raked the ruins of the human building. Teeth gritted, he pictured himself standing and returning fire with the shuriken catapult, but his body did not respond.

A cycle. Never-ending. Even in death there was no escape.

Through the clamour of battle – a thunder of guns, crack of shattering ceramic, the patter of brick shards on his armour and the heavy footfalls of the approaching Space Marines – Aradryan felt the buzz of the messenger-bead again. The insistent tone of Arhathain cut into his numbed thoughts.

'Hold your ground! More enemy forces are diverting to your position. Keep them back as long as you can.'

It felt as though the words were meant for him, and it took a short while for Aradryan to realise that the autarch had addressed the whole Guardian host.

He dimly noted that the wall was no longer exploding around him and slowly pushed up from his belly. Five fist-sized holes had been punched through the bricks where he had squatted and the entire top course had been turned to a cloud of dust. His blood chilled at the realisation of how close his death had been. The prison of the infinity circuit still awaited him.

The sensation spurred him into action. Self-disgust at his body's cowardice overcame natural responses.

He risked a glance through one of the holes and saw half a dozen enemy bodies strewn on the grass just a few strides away. Their armour was mangled, limbs bent awkwardly, indicating a cross-fire from the other vibro-cannons. More corpses, like black-carapaced beetles, were strewn along the line of the assault, leading back to flashes of gunfire sparkling from where the survivors still fought out of the cover of their broken vehicles.

He looked at the seat on the vibro-cannon, the morphic cushion spattered with Diamedin's blood. Swallowing hard, he edged closer, still keeping below the wall as though it were the parapet of a fortress rather than a flimsy domestic construction. He dropped down and advanced on elbows and knees, the shuriken catapult in his grasp, until he reached the breach in the building. The vibro-cannon was still three strides away, floating in place as serenely as a grav-barge in a parade.

Aradryan considered his options, and his chances. He was fast, a gift of his species, but so too were the artificially crafted reactions of the Space Marines. He would probably be able to reach the support weapon before they registered his presence, but would he be able to set a target and open fire?

He waited, the fingers of his free hand pressed against the wall, shuriken catapult still in the other, attuning himself to the rhythms of gunfire. He drew up a foot beneath him, ready to run. The snap of bolters and subsequent growl of the rounds was short, targeted close to the bridge. Most likely at the Guardian Defenders. Aradryan heard the crackle of the warlock's singing spear impacting against plates of armour.

An instant later he leapt from the cover of the wall, one hand reaching for the back of the vibro-cannon. He vaulted into the gunnery seat and slapped his weapon against a grip pad. Aradryan snapped his attention towards the bridge even as his fingers curled about the controls. The platform tilted slightly on its suspensor field as he steered right, a small screen in front of him dancing with images until it settled on the shape of a helmed head poking out from behind the broken track housing of the closest enemy vehicle.

The first Aradryan knew of the still-functioning mounted weapon on the lead vehicle was a spark of bolt detonations tearing up the sloped shell of the vibro-cannon. He flung himself sideways as the support weapon disintegrated. Tucking his head down, he rolled as he hit the ground, pieces of shrapnel slicing into the dirt around him.

A shard of broken plating pierced the back of his leg, ripping a pained yelp from his lips as he slithered back to the comparative safety of the wall. Blood leaking from the flesh wound, he continued on, pushing himself across the dry grass until his back found the angle of the other wall.

Through the pounding of his own heart and the continued fusillades from both sides, Aradryan picked out a deeper boom – the sound of larger cannons. Panicked shouts from his companions preceded the whine of falling shells and a ground-shaking eruption close at hand. Dirt showered down on Aradryan over the top of the broken wall. A blinding flash of laser light scorched not far overhead, from somewhere across the river.

The enemy reinforcements had arrived.

'Five enemy tanks have peeled away from the main attack to reinforce the flanking manoeuvre across the bridge,' reported Arhathain, as dispassionately as if he were passing on a weather report. *'Hold your ground.'*

Aradryan risked a second glance over the wall. The initial probing force had been reduced to a few Chaos Space Marines, stubbornly sniping out from among the wreckage of their transports, but the Alaitocii had not fared well in the exchange. The wreckage of several support weapons littered the buildings beside the road, the bodies of their crews draped over brick and rock. The vibro-cannon beside Aradryan was a pile of psychoplastic splinters and molten metal, his shuriken catapult somewhere in the mess that remained.

Sporadic distort-cannon fire and the continuing fusillades of the Guardian Defenders kept the Chaos Space Marines at bay for the moment, but it was only a matter of time before they crushed the remnants of the ambush force. Shells burst from across the river while harsh lascannon blasts scoured through the crumbling ruins.

The surge of confidence that had spurred him swiftly

abated, replace by grim reality. Arhathain's exhortation not-
withstanding, as far as Aradryan was concerned he had played
his part, but without a weapon and faced with a company
of tanks there was nothing more he could do.

There certainly was little point to staying where he was. Even
now, just a few moments since the first shell had exploded,
the sound of fire from surviving support weapons had less-
ened, targeted by the newly arrived enemy tanks.

His options were limited. Arhathain had picked the battle
site carefully, denying the enemy much in the way of shelter
as they approached but that also meant there was little to
retreat through. There were a few scattered patches of cover
before the land dropped down into a ravine about a hundred strides behind the outpost where he hid. If he set off
now he might just make the dip before the enemy saw him.
For a moment he was possessed by a wild thought, of sprinting *towards* the enemy to throw himself in the waters below
the bridge, and thus escape downriver. Or he could remain
where he was, hoping that whatever relief force Arhathain
would certainly dispatch arrived before the bulk of the enemy
had pushed across the bridge.

Guilt needled him at the thought of retreating. The force
had been placed to counter just this type of flanking attack.
If the bridge fell it could cost countless more Alaitocii lives.
It was almost enough to make him break from cover and
seek a weapon.

Almost.

Aradryan remained where he was, pushed up against the
protective wall like a limpet on a rock, wondering how
it was that fate had chosen to put him in this situation.
There seemed little enough worth dying for on the forsaken
human world. He was not sure of the grander scheme, but

knew it involved the primarch, the Ynnari and the greater war against the minions of the Dark Gods. Farseers, Eldrad Ulthran included, had insisted that the warriors of the Black Legion could not be allowed to expand into this star system.

The messenger waves burst into renewed activity, pulsing into Aradryan's whirling thoughts.

'The enemy are amassing for another push,' warned Hanlaishin.

'Movement into the river, armoured infantry,' reported one of the other Guardians.

'Some kind of mobile artillery taking position on the hill.'

'Concentrated fire coming fr–'

'Something else, coming through the smoke. Khaine's blood!'

A burst of acute paranoia rather than bravery pushed Aradryan to dart a look around the barrier – more than enough time to take stock of the changing situation.

Armoured walkers, each three times the height of the renegade Space Marines, stomped down the road towards the river. A multiple-rocket launcher was moving into position on a ridge overlooking the attack site, its turret-pods laden with warheads. Several squads of the Black Legionnaires had forced their way onto the bridge to bolster the infantry already there, bolt-rounds whickering across the divide to keep the eldar pinned down in their scattered clumps of cover.

Everything was building for a fresh and final assault on the gun batteries.

A dread-inspiring roar echoed across the river valley – artificially modulated, a half-mechanical bellow that emanated from the address systems of several dozen Traitor Space Marines. The war cry rolled over the bridge and river like an ocean wave, heralding devastation.

If Aradryan was to die here, what would happen next? As

Mourner he had watched spirit after spirit guided into the relative sanctuary of the infinity circuit. A resting place, of sorts, far from the gaze of the Great Enemy. A reward for adhering to the pains and structures of the Asuryani Path. But what if his spirit stone fell into the hands of the depraved followers of Chaos? Were there acolytes of She Who Thirsts among their ranks?

The snarl of engines grew louder accompanied by the pounding of feet on artificial stone as the Chaos renegades thrust across the bridge.

Not for him, that semi-slumber of bare consciousness. All would be for nothing, his spirit stone broken open by the daemons of the Perfect Prince, his soul endlessly devoured.

And for what? To deny the Black Legion an abandoned world? To protect the Imperium of the *humans*?

It was all too grand to deal with, too far above Aradryan's concerns. He understood the need for greater alliance with the humans – temporarily – but his own experience with the servants of the Emperor had shown that they were self-serving and weak. He had no doubts they would put themselves before any concern for the craftworlds. He had dedicated himself to serving Alaitoc, not the Emperor.

The enemy on the bridge burst from cover, supported by the scathing fire of their brothers-in-damnation. In just a few heartbeats they would be on the near side, falling upon the Guardians holding the riverbank.

Aradryan was just about to make a run for it when he felt something stir in his breast. It was faint, just a warmth where before there had been emptiness. It reminded him of the infinity circuit, though more diffuse. A nascent connection, growing stronger.

In its midst he heard the echoes of the thoughts of others

around him. Nothing specific, just vague notions of hope and fear, longing and dread like a refracted beam of light.

A whisper in his mind.

Invigoration pushed aside loneliness. His mind pulsed with a feeling of belonging he had not felt for a long time. He held his breath, heart like a drum in his ears. Many had died already. Who was he to judge his life worth more than theirs?

Aradryan darted to the remnants of the vibro-cannon and snatched up his shuriken catapult before leaping back to the shelter of the wall. Letting out an explosive exhalation, Aradryan stood up, ready to vault the wall. He did not fight for the humans, but for his companions.

If he was to die, it would not be alone.

Twin blasts of ruby light seared past his hiding place. Not from the Black Legionnaires, but towards them. A few heart-beats later a shadow passed over him. Aradryan looked up and saw the underside of a Wave Serpent, silhouetted against the bright sky. As it moved away, firing again towards the bridge, its colours were unfamiliar. He had thought it part of a reinforcement sent by the autarch, but instead of the blue and yellow of the Alaitoc warhost, the transport was coloured a dark grey with haphazard slashes of black and dark red across it.

Other vehicles arrived, speeding across the low hills, some in similar livery, others marked as coming from Saim-Hann, Biel-Tan and other craftworlds. And with them, warriors and vehicles not even of the craftworlds – blade-like drukhari Raiders packed with baying kabalite warriors, alongside swooping Reaver jetbikes ridden by shrieking wyches.

The Ynnari!

A Raider transport swept into view even as the Black Legion warriors burst onto the near bank. It gleamed with a white aura, emanating from the figure who stood upon the serrated prow. She was garbed in finery, like a lady of the old dominions captured in stasis, her gown and cloaks streaming in the wind of the skimmer's passage. The cold light left motes of frost on the air, a sparkling wake like glittering dew on a fresh morning.

Aradryan knew her instantly.

Yvraine, Emissary of Ynnead, Bride of the God-Dead.

He had heard many tales of the Ynnari figurehead, more than a few sinister whispers between followers of the Path of Grieving. The craftworlds and their reliance on spirit technology had always skirted on the edges of necromancy, but it was claimed that Yvraine could conjure the spirit from a waystone and leech the power of the departing.

Yet Aradryan did not feel coldness as he watched the majestic Daughter of Shades. Hope bristled in him, sharp and unfamiliar. Though she seemed cast from unfeeling ceramic the sensation that washed from her passing was uplifting.

A crimson-armoured figure stood just behind her, a shimmering blade bare in his hand. The Visarch, Sword of Ynnead, as deadly a warrior as any from the legends of old. As the Raider swept over the support battery, the Visarch leapt from the speeding transport, plunging into the midst of the Chaos Space Marines charging across the bridge. More heavily armoured aeldari followed – former incubi of Commorragh, the infamous Coiled Blade that served the Queen of the Reborn. Powered blades flashing, they slashed into the traitorous Space Marines while Yvraine led the counter-attack across to the other side of the river.

Scattering clouds of dust from their anti-grav downdraught, two more Raiders sped past. He saw the heavy weapons fire of a Falcon and two Ravagers converge on the bridge, raking across advancing squads. As missiles spat forth from the Space Marines, the swift-moving grav-tanks curved away over the river to target the heavy vehicles and Dreadnoughts approaching on the far side.

A Wave Serpent settled beyond the ruin of the vibro-cannon, its back ramp lowering as it drifted to a halt. The eldar who descended was garbed in elaborate, stark blue armour, the sigil on his white helm a variation of the Dire Avengers rune.

'Time to leave, Alaitocii!' the Aspect Warrior called out. 'Fate has favoured you this time.'

'Who are you?' Aradryan started towards the other eldar and then stopped. His gaze fell upon the mangled remains of Diamedin and he almost lost his footing. The flicker of Diamedin's infused spirit stone drew his eye. 'Wait!'

'Hurry now or we will leave you,' called the Ynnari Dire Avenger.

Aradryan plucked the sparkling soulgem from its mounting. He sprinted over to the transport, which lifted up even as he jumped for the ramp. He slipped inside as the access-way closed behind him.

Eight Dire Avengers waited in the Wave Serpent, their bright armour gleaming in the lights of the transport compartment. Aradryan felt the Wave Serpent accelerate, banking to the left, back towards the main host.

'What has happened?' he asked.

'Yvraine learned of what Alaitoc ventured here on our behalf,' replied the Dire Avenger who had ushered him aboard. 'We came to help.'

Aradryan nodded, not quite sure what to think of this. Sat among these blooded warriors he should have felt alone as he had when Diamedin had assumed her war mask, but instead their presence suffused him with a sense of belonging.

'You hear it, don't you?' said the Dire Avenger. 'The voice of Ynnead.'

'We call it the Whisper,' said another.

'I... I hear it,' admitted Aradryan. 'It is growing stronger.'

'Fuelled by the departed souls,' another of the squad told him. 'In their deaths, Ynnead draws strength, as do we all.'

The thought should have been horrific. Aradryan had never been comfortable with the thought of eternities spent in the infinity circuit. Bodiless but vaguely aware. As prone to the vicissitudes of fate as any mortal. But he felt peace.

He listened to the Whisper, a wordless but understandable swell of power.

'You have an aeldari soul,' said his new companion. 'In the time of the dominion, before the Fall, all our people were reborn into new bodies. When She Who Thirsts swallowed our people our spirits were forfeit. Now Ynnead fights for them, and in time the aeldari will emerge from Her awful shadow.'

'But if I understand your creed, we must all die to live again?'

The Dire Avenger nodded. 'In time, we all die. Ynnead gives us the chance to return. We are the Reborn. Better to die in hope than dread, yes?'

Aradryan stood a little apart from the other rescued Guardians, feeling confused.

Like many who had been swept up by the arrival of the Ynnari, he had been deposited close to the fighting, though he had not participated any further. Now, with the battle won, he was at a loss. Many around him were weeping for the slain, while healers tended to those who could benefit from their ministrations.

Alausha, one of the Guardian leaders, addressed them.

'The fighting is almost over. The Black Legionnaires are being pushed back to their landing craft. Our swiftest warriors hunt down those yet to depart. The Black Legion's attempt to seize this world has been thwarted.'

Aradryan heard the words but they carried little meaning. He did not share any sense of victory. There was only one certainty. He would live, when he had come so close to death.

He usually felt grief for the lost; that was his role as Mourner. This time he looked upon the white-shrouded dead and felt... angry. Not at those who had slain them, for they had already been punished. His anger was at the waste. What now for the departed? Their spirits would mingle with the infinity circuit, just motes of energy to power the craftworld. Was that salvation or simply delaying the inevitable?

Someone approached from behind, and he turned. The new arrival was a seer, clad in robes of purple, blue and yellow, her face hidden inside a gem-crusted ghosthelm. A dozen runes circled the farseer, playing intertwining orbits about her head and outstretched hand.

'Your powers continue to grow, Thirianna,' he said, smiling at his old friend. Her expression was hidden but warmth flowed in return.

'You stand upon the blade of a choice, Aradryan,' she told him. 'Though both options lead to death.'

'Have you been skein-stalking me again?' he asked with a quiet laugh.

'I still take an interest in your affairs,' she admitted, her tone serious. 'As when you left to become an Outcast, there is great uncertainty in your future.'

'No, you are wrong. There is only certainty for us all.'

Aradryan lifted up Diamedin's spirit stone. 'This. This is our future, until there are none left to hide us away.'

'I see. Ynnead. Now I understand the branch of fate I foresaw.' Thirianna's gaze turned towards the Ynnari, who were mustering around Yvraine on the scorched and cratered plain. Overhead, launches and other craft descended from orbit to take them back to their ships. 'You think she has the answer? To doom all of our remaining people to Ynnead's embrace?'

'To release us from the grip of the Great Enemy. To become Reborn.'

'It is self-murder.'

'It is hope.'

Thirianna said nothing for several heartbeats and then, much to his surprise, stepped forwards and embraced him. He returned the gesture, feeling the flickering heat of her runes as they circled about both of them.

'We will not part in anger,' said the farseer. She stepped back, a hand outstretched. 'I will take care of your companion's spirit stone.'

'I did not really know her,' said Aradryan. He moved to hand over Diamedin and then withdrew. 'No. No, I shall not. She will be better with me. Among the living.'

The pair remained silent, looking at each other. There seemed nothing else to say, so Aradryan turned away and started towards the Ynnari.

In his thoughts, the Whisper of Ynnead grew louder.

ABOUT THE AUTHORS

Chris Wraight is the author of the Horus Heresy novels *Scars* and *The Path of Heaven*, the Primarchs novels *Leman Russ: The Great Wolf* and *Jaghatai Khan: Warhawk of Chogoris*, the novellas *Brotherhood of the Storm* and *Wolf King*, and the audio drama *The Sigillite*. For Warhammer 40,000 he has written *The Lords of Silence*, *Vaults of Terra: The Carrion Throne*, *Vaults of Terra: The Hollow Mountain*, *Watchers of the Throne: The Emperor's Legion*, the Space Wolves novels *Blood of Asaheim* and *Stormcaller*, and many more. Additionally, he has many Warhammer novels to his name, including the Warhammer Chronicles novel *Master of Dragons*, which forms part of the War of Vengeance series. Chris lives and works in Bradford-on-Avon, in south-west England.

Ian St. Martin is the author of the Horus Heresy: Primarchs novel *Angron: Slave of Nuceria* and audio drama *Konrad Curze: A Lesson in Darkness*. He has also written the Warhammer 40,000 novels *Of Honour and Iron*, *Lucius: The Faultless Blade* and *Deathwatch: Kryptman's War*, along with the novella *Steel Daemon* and several short stories. He lives and works in Washington DC, caring for his cat and reading anything within reach.

Alec Worley is a well-known comics and science fiction and fantasy author, with numerous publications to his name. He is an avid fan of Warhammer 40,000 and has written many short stories for Black Library including 'Stormseeker', 'Whispers' and 'Repentia'. He has recently forayed into Black Library Horror with the audio drama *Perdition's Flame* and his novella *The Nothings*. He lives and works in London.

Justin D Hill is the author of the Necromunda novel *Terminal Overkill*, the Warhammer 40,000 novels *Cadia Stands* and *Cadian Honour*, the Space Marine Battles novel *Storm of Damocles* and the short stories 'Last Step Backwards', 'Lost Hope' and 'The Battle of Tyrok Fields', following the adventures of Lord Castellan Ursarkar E. Creed. He has also written 'Truth Is My Weapon', and the Warhammer tales 'Golgfag's Revenge' and 'The Battle of Whitestone'. His novels have won a number of prizes, as well as being *Washington Post* and *Sunday Times* Books of the Year. He lives ten miles uphill from York, where he is indoctrinating his four children in the 40K lore.

Robbie MacNiven is a Highlands-born History graduate from the University of Edinburgh. He has written the Warhammer Age of Sigmar novel *Scourge of Fate* and the Gotrek Gurnisson novella *The Bone Desert*, as well as the Warhammer 40,000 novels *Blood of Iax*, *The Last Hunt*, *Carcharodons: Red Tithe*, *Carcharodons: Outer Dark* and *Legacy of Russ*. His short stories include 'Redblade', 'A Song for the Lost' and 'Blood and Iron'. His hobbies include re-enacting, football and obsessing over Warhammer 40,000.

Ben Counter has two Horus Heresy novels to his name – *Galaxy in Flames* and *Battle for the Abyss*. He is the author of the Soul Drinkers series and *The Grey Knights Omnibus*. For Space Marine Battles, he has written *The World Engine* and *Malodrax*, and has turned his attention to the Space Wolves with the novella *Arjac Rockfist: Anvil of Fenris* as well as a number of short stories. He is a fanatical painter of miniatures, a pursuit that has won him his most prized possession: a prestigious Golden Demon award. He lives in Portsmouth, England.

Josh Reynolds' extensive Black Library back catalogue includes the Horus Heresy Primarchs novel *Fulgrim: The Palatine Phoenix*, and three Horus Heresy audio dramas featuring the Blackshields. His Warhammer 40,000 work includes the Space Marine Conquests novel *Apocalypse, Lukas the Trickster* and the Fabius Bile novels. He has written many stories set in the Age of Sigmar, including the novels *Shadespire: The Mirrored City, Soul Wars, Eight Lamentations: Spear of Shadows*, the Hallowed Knights novels *Plague Garden* and *Black Pyramid*, and *Nagash: The Undying King*. His Warhammer Horror story, *The Beast in the Trenches*, is featured in the portmanteau novel *The Wicked and the Damned*, and he has recently penned the Necromunda novel *Kal Jerico: Sinner's Bounty*. He lives and works in Sheffield.

Steve Lyons' work in the Warhammer 40,000 universe includes the novellas *Engines of War* and *Angron's Monolith*, the Imperial Guard novels *Ice World* and *Dead Men Walking* – now collected in the omnibus *Honour Imperialis* – and the audio dramas *Waiting Death* and *The Madness Within*. He has also written numerous short stories and is currently working on more tales from the grim darkness of the far future.

Rob Sanders is the author of the Horus Heresy novellas *Cybernetica* and *The Serpent Beneath*, the latter of which appeared in the *New York Times* bestselling anthology *The Primarchs*. His other Black Library credits include the The Beast Arises novels *Predator, Prey* and *Shadow of Ullanor*, the Warhammer 40,000 titles *Sons of the Hydra, Skitarius, Tech-Priest, Legion of the Damned, Atlas Infernal* and *Redemption Corps* and the audio drama *The Path Forsaken*. He has also written the Warhammer Archaon duology, *Everchosen* and *Lord of Chaos*, along with many short stories for the Horus Heresy and Warhammer 40,000. He lives in the city of Lincoln, UK.

L J Goulding is the author of the Horus Heresy audio drama *The Heart of the Pharos*, while for Space Marine Battles he has written the novel *Slaughter at Giant's Coffin* and the audio drama *Mortarion's Heart*. His other Warhammer fiction includes 'The Great Maw' and 'Kaldor Draigo: Knight of Titan', and he has continued to explore the dark legacy of Sotha in 'The Aegidan Oath' and *Scythes of the Emperor: Daedalus*. He lives and works in the US.

Peter Fehervari is the author of the Warhammer 40,000 novels *Requiem Infernal*, *Cult of the Spiral Dawn* and *Fire Caste*, as well as the novella *Fire and Ice* from the *Shas'o* anthology. He has also written many short stories for Black Library, including the t'au-themed 'Out Caste' and 'A Sanctuary of Wyrms', the latter of which appeared in the anthology *Deathwatch: Xenos Hunters*. He also wrote 'Nightfall', which was in the *Heroes of the Space Marines* anthology, and 'The Crown of Thorns'. He lives and works in London.

Mike Brooks is a speculative fiction author who lives in Nottingham, UK. His work for Black Library includes the Warhammer 40,000 novel *Rites of Passage*, the Necromunda novella *Wanted: Dead*, and the short stories 'The Path Unclear', 'A Common Ground' and 'Choke Point'. When not writing, he works for a homelessness charity, plays guitar and sings in a punk band, and DJs wherever anyone will tolerate him.

Cavan Scott has written the Space Marine Battles novella *Plague Harvest*, along with the Warhammer 40,000 short stories 'Doom Flight', 'Trophies', 'Sanctus Reach: Death Mask', 'Flayed' and 'Logan Grimnar: Defender of Honour'. He lives and works in Bristol.

Gav Thorpe is the author of the Horus Heresy novels *Deliverance Lost*, *Angels of Caliban* and *Corax*, as well as the novella *The Lion*, which formed part of the New York Times bestselling collection *The Primarchs*, and several audio dramas. He has written many novels for Warhammer 40,000, including *Ashes of Prospero*, *Imperator: Wrath of the Omnissiah* and the Rise of the Ynnari novels *Ghost Warrior* and *Wild Rider*. He also wrote the Path of the Eldar and Legacy of Caliban trilogies, and two volumes in The Beast Arises series. For Warhammer, Gav has penned the End Times novel *The Curse of Khaine*, the Warhammer Chronicles omnibus *The Sundering*, and recently penned the Age of Sigmar novel *The Red Feast*. In 2017, Gav won the David Gemmell Legend Award for his Age of Sigmar novel *Warbeast*. He lives and works in Nottingham.